A LEARNING EXPERIENCE

CHRISTOPHER G NUTTALL

ISBN: 1497543835
ISBN 13: 9781497543836

http://www.chrishanger.net
http://chrishanger.wordpress.com/
http://www.facebook.com/ChristopherGNuttall

All Comments Welcome!:

To Ed and Mongo.

PROLOGUE

FNFIAN HORDE WARCRUISER
SHADOW WARRIOR

EARTH ORBIT

"**Y**ou are *sure* this is the correct planet?"

Alien Savant Cn!lss barely refrained from clenching his clawed maniples in irritation at his superior's doubt. Subhorde Commander Pr!lss wasn't remotely qualified to serve as anything other than an expendable warrior, at least in Cn!lss's opinion, preferably one sent to charge over barren ground towards an enemy plasma cannon nest. It would have improved the genetic reserves of the Fnfian Horde considerably if Pr!lss got himself blown away before he had a chance to sire children. Unfortunately, the universe being what it was, Pr!lss happened to be related to the Supreme Horde Commander, a qualification that had ensured his promotion to Subhorde Commander. It wouldn't have galled Cn!lss so much if he hadn't been convinced that his superior's arrogance would get his entire crew killed one day.

He hastily bent into the posture of respect when his superior's claws started to twitch, threatening immediate violence. Cn!lss was one of the few Hordesmen to understand, on more than an abstract level, just how

v

far advanced the rest of the universe – or at least the significant part of it - was over the Horde. Indeed, one of the reasons for his commander's near-constant irritation was the simple fact that *Shadow Warrior* had been designed for creatures of a noticeably different build. The Tokomak Warcruiser had had most of its original furnishings stripped out, but most of its bulkheads and internal passageways couldn't be replaced. If the Hordesmen tried, it was unlikely they would be able to put the ship back together again.

"The data we recovered from the Varnar was precise, My Liege," Cn!lss said. "This is the origin world of their damnable cyborgs."

He allowed himself a faint smile. Years ago, the Varnar had started deploying a whole new force of cyborg warriors onto the battlefield. Their enemies had been driven from a dozen worlds before they had finally realised that the cyborgs were derived from a whole new race, rather than any of the known Galactics. And it had taken months before the Horde had been hired to track down the homeworld of the new aliens and kid-nap samples that could be turned into new cyborgs.

"This is a primitive world," the Subhorde Commander snarled. "They don't even have fusion plants, let alone a proper space program!"

Cn!lss shrugged, clicking his forelegs together. There was no law against trading technology to primitive alien races – it was how the Horde had acquired their first starships – but it was clear that the Varnar hadn't bothered to share anything with their human slaves. Indeed, it looked as though they'd never attempted to make open contact with the humans, even though they'd taken humans from their homeworld. But then, given how effective their cyborgs were, it was quite likely the Varnar wouldn't want to do anything to draw attention to the human race. If the laws against genocide hadn't been the only laws to be universally enforced, he suspected that Earth would have met with a fatal accident years ago.

"This is their homeworld," he repeated. He could have pointed out that the Horde was still primitive and yet they flew starships, but it wouldn't have impressed his commander. Like most Hordesmen, the Subhorde Commander sneered at the Galactics, rather than admitting that the Galactics were centuries ahead of the Horde. "All we have to do is capture a few samples and take them back for study."

He looked down at the torrent of information flowing into the computers. For a primitive world – and one that seemed to be caught in a socio-political trap that had prevented them from settling their solar system – there *was* an impressive amount of electronic noise flaring away from the planet. The computers could translate the signals, but the tiny fraction Cn!lss had reviewed made absolutely no sense. It seemed as though the human race was completely insane.

"This section of their homeworld is the most developed," he commented, tapping one large land mass on the display. "It will serve as a rich source of educated slaves."

His commander clicked his maniples in disgust. Education wasn't something that most Hordesmen took seriously, not when they could be drinking and fighting instead. And besides, most of them had an unspoken inferiority complex when they considered what the educated races had done. It didn't stop them taking and using educated slaves whenever they had the opportunity. Indeed, Cn!lss had to admit there was great potential on Earth, once they taught the humans who was boss. A few strikes from orbit and the humans would be forced to surrender.

But, for the moment, they had other priorities.

"Find me some humans," the Subhorde Commander ordered. "And then dispatch an assault shuttle to take them onboard."

Cn!lss bowed his head in obedience.

It honestly never occurred to him, or anyone else on the Horde starship, that the information they'd obtained had been rather more than just a *little* incomplete.

ONE

MONTANA, USA

"Absent friends," Steve Stuart said.

His friends nodded in agreement as they sipped their beer. It had been a long walk from where they'd left the van to their camping site, but Steve had to admit that it had been worth it. Instead of going to one of the state parks, they'd chosen to walk out into the wide open spaces of Montana and set up a campsite of their own. Now, they sat around the fire and watched the flames flickering as darkness fell over the land.

"Absent friends," his friends echoed back. "May they never be forgotten."

Steve sighed, feeling – once again – the pain of loss. It had been seven years since he'd quit the Marines, seven years since he'd put his uniform away for good, but the memories refused to fade, no matter what he did with his life. Death was a part of military life, for good or ill, yet there was a difference between losing a soldier to enemy action and losing a soldier because politicians had tied the military's hands. It would have been easier to take it, he suspected, if the enemy had simply killed his friends in honourable combat.

He forced the depression away and looked around the campsite. His brothers Mongo and Kevin, both taller than him, but possessing the same fair heads and facial features as himself, almost to the point where their faces could have been mistaken for triplets. Beside them, his oldest friends Charles Edwards – another former Marine – and Vincent Hastings, a retired Navy SEAL.

Military service ran in the family. The Stuarts had served the Kings of Scotland, then migrated to America and joined George Washington's army, then fought in almost every war since the United States had won its independence. Hell, there had been Stuarts fighting on both sides during the Civil War. But now…in truth, Steve wasn't sure if he could advise his sons – or his daughter – to go into the military. Defending the United States was important and there were few higher honours, yet… was it worth making such a commitment when one's political leaders were worse than the enemy?

"He's brooding again," Mongo said. "Someone poke him, please!"

Steve smiled. He could always rely on Mongo to cheer him up. "I have a gun and I'm not afraid to use it," he said, quickly. "And I am not brooding. I am merely thinking deeply contemplative thoughts."

"A likely story," Edwards said. "Don't you know contemplative thoughts are strictly forbidden in the Wolfpac?"

"Yep," Kevin put in. "We wrote a ban on them into the charter."

Steve rolled his eyes. He'd started the Wolfpac – a band of amateur rocket scientists – as something to do after his retirement, but it had grown into a hobby. Building rockets and firing them into the air was surprisingly fun, even though they had never come close to their dream of building a manned rocket. But then, even if they had, somehow he doubted the government would have allowed them to launch it. It was bad enough when federal agents came sniffing around to determine who was purchasing rocket components and why. They never quite seemed to believe that the club was completely innocent of anything other than trying to have a good time.

"Then we should have barred you," he said. Kevin was the black sheep of the family; he'd gone into combat intelligence, rather than the fighting infantry. But long experience in Afghanistan had taught him

A LEARNING EXPERIENCE

that HUMINT could be just as important as raids and roadblocks when it came to countering an insurgency. "You think too much."

Kevin made a one-fingered gesture, then poked the fire meaningfully. "You think too little," he said, as Steve passed him the marshmallows. "These days, thinking men are required to win wars and rebuild societies."

Vincent snorted, rudely. "We may be doing it in America soon enough," he said. "Did you read the email from Tony?"

Stuart nodded. Tony, like Steve and the rest of the Wolfpac, had left military service and gone back to the civilian world, but unlike them he'd opened a grocery store in Chicago. And then there'd been a riot – the food stamp system had broken down for several days – and Tony's store had been robbed. Worse, he'd been threatened with arrest for attempting to defend his property with a shotgun and a bad attitude. It wouldn't be long, Steve suspected, before Tony abandoned his store and migrated to a state with a more robust attitude towards lawlessness and self-defence.

But it was something that nagged at his mind, whenever he let it. He'd been in Iraq, Afghanistan and several countries it would have surprised American civilians to know their troops had been operating, yet his country sometimes felt more alien to him than any of the foreign nations he'd visited. The old values, the ones he'd imbued along with his mother's milk, seemed to be fading away. Duty, honour and loyalty were just words, self-reliance a joke...

"Brooding again," Mongo snapped. "Tony will be fine. He always is."

Steve shrugged. He had his doubts. Fighting the enemy had been simple, fighting the bureaucracy that was slowly strangling America to death was almost impossible. He'd once planned to open a gun store, but the paperwork had been too much for him.

"Look up in the sky instead," Kevin suggested. "I think that's the International Space Station."

Steve sighed as he watched the speck of light making its way across the darkening sky. He'd once had dreams of being an astronaut, perhaps of being the first man to set foot on Mars or Venus, but his dreams had been blown away by cold hard reality. NASA hadn't gone back to the Moon, let alone the rest of the Solar System, while the Space Program had become a political football rather than a viable project. There were no dreams any longer for humanity, no Wild West waiting to take the restless and dispossessed. Instead, there was a decaying society. And, in the distance, he could hear the howl of the approaching wolf.

"That's a satellite," Vincent said. "I think NSA is peering down at us right now."

"Probably," Steve said. "We're a bunch of males out on a camping trip. Of *course* we're a subject of interest."

He sighed. He'd had enough experience with combat surveillance systems to know that they were terrifyingly good. He would certainly have hated to be on the receiving end. Technology had its limits, he knew, but when the United States cared enough to send the best the results could be remarkable. Plenty of insurgents hadn't learned how to cover themselves before it was too late.

"Could be worse," Kevin said. "Did I tell you what we saw in Afghanistan?"

Mongo elbowed his brother. "You mean what you saw while you were sitting in a comfortable armchair, sipping cappuccino, while we were slogging over the mountains?"

Kevin ignored the jibe. "There was a bunch of Afghani men making their way towards the base, walking cross-country in pitch darkness," he said. "Then they stopped. We thought they were setting up a mortar, so we focused sensors on them and primed the guns on the base to return fire. And then there was an odd heat source on the ground."

He paused. No one spoke.

"And then there were five more, lying together," he continued, after a long moment. "There we were, all puzzled, trying to figure out just what the hell they were doing. Were they laying IEDs for us? But we didn't normally patrol that area. Or did they intend to lure us into a trap of some kind?

4

"And then we realised what they were doing," he concluded. "They were having a communal *shit*!"

Steve laughed, despite himself. "And to think I thought intelligence pukes had exciting lives," he said. "Wearing black suits, chasing and screwing women, diving out of high buildings…"

"James Bond isn't real," Kevin interrupted. "Although there was this time in Bangkok…"

"You banged your cock?" Vincent asked, innocently.

"Oh, shut up," Kevin said, as the group chuckled. "But I won't deny that intelligence can get a little hairy at times. There was this village we visited…"

"We've been to Afghani villages too," Mongo pointed out.

"Yes, but you went in full armour and had a whole squad of tough buddies beside you," Kevin countered. "I was alone, unless you count two more intelligence officers, one of whom was wearing a full veil."

"And no doubt invited to marry one of the locals," Vincent said. "Was she?"

"She talked to the local women," Kevin said. "We told them I was her husband."

"Poor girl," Steve and Mongo said together.

"Guys," Charles said, suddenly.

Steve looked over at him, feeling alarm shivering down his spine. The last time he'd heard Charles use that tone, they'd been under enemy fire seconds later.

"Look," Charles said, pointing up towards the sky. "What's that?"

Steve looked up. A glowing light was making its way across the sky, its course erratic. "A satellite?"

"Too large," Charles said.

"Maybe it's a UFO," Mongo said. He snickered. "Do you think they've learned everything they can from anal probes?"

"Always knew you were a pervert," Kevin said. He stuck out his tongue in a remarkably childish manner, then looked back up at the sky. "But it must be a plane, I think."

"A plane that's coming closer to us," Charles said, before Mongo could muster a rejoinder. "Why?"

Steve stared. The glowing light was growing larger, coming down towards the campsite at terrifying speed. Instinctively, he reached for the pistol at his belt – he never went anywhere without it, no matter what the law said – as the light started to take on shape and form. It couldn't be a helicopter or a plane, part of his mind insisted; there was no noise, not even a faint clattering sound. But he knew there were some helicopters, designed for commando operations, that were almost completely silent. And yet…

Why would such a helicopter come after us? He asked himself. His imagination could produce a few ideas, but none of them were actually likely. *What do they want?*

"It's not a helicopter," Charles said. He sounded more than a little alarmed. *"Look* at it."

Steve half-covered his eyes as a bright light seemed to shine down on them. It was hard to see the shape of the craft through the light, but it looked to be a crude spacecraft rather than the smooth UFO he'd been expecting. Indeed, it was little larger than a small executive jet, yet it hung in the air with effortless ease. The floodlight swept over the campsite, then started to fade slightly as the craft slowly lowered itself towards the ground.

It couldn't be *human*, Steve realised, feeling a sudden lump in his throat. The others were silent, lost in their own thoughts. There were VTOL fighters and tilt-rotor aircraft, but nothing as large and capable as the craft facing them. As far as he could tell, it didn't have any exhausts or anything else that might have suggested how it worked. It might as well be magic. But, as the light faded away, he realised that the hull was scorched and pitted. Cold ice ran down his spine as old instincts awoke. Alien the craft might be – and he was convinced it was far from human – but it was a warship.

"Shit," Vincent said, breaking the silence.

There was a dull crunching sound as the craft touched down. Steve shook himself, then concentrated on observing as much as possible. There were no landing struts, as far as he could see; the craft had just settled down on the soft ground. For a long moment, all was still…and then the craft's hatch opened. Bright light spilled out, illuminating strange alien creatures.

Steve caught his breath. He'd expected, he realised now, tiny grey aliens. Instead, he found himself fighting the urge to panic as the aliens came into view. They looked like eerie crosses between humans and spiders, perhaps with some crabs worked into the mixture too, as if someone had stuck a human torso and head on top of a giant spider and merged them together. Each of the aliens had six legs, greenish-red skin and dark eyes set within an armoured head, as if they had no skin covering their skulls. They'd have difficulty walking on uneven ground, Steve suspected, although as they pranced forward it became clear that they were more limber than he'd realised. It was impossible to determine their sex from their appearance. Or, for that matter, if they even had the concept of males and females.

He'd seen countless aliens on television and movies, ranging from men in bad makeup and poor suits to marvels of CGI. There was no reason, he was sure, that Hollywood couldn't produce aliens as strange and inhuman as the ones facing him. But somehow he *knew* they were real. There was something about them that utterly destroyed any disbelief he might have felt, a sudden awareness that they were very far from human. Besides, he had a feeling that even a small human couldn't have fitted into an alien-sized suit.

The sense of danger grew stronger as he realised what the aliens were carrying. Four of them were carrying silver tubes that seemed to be made for their hands, the fifth was merely holding a silver box in one clawed hand. He also had a silver band wrapped around his skull, perhaps a badge of rank. The silver tubes were weapons, Steve was sure, even though they were nothing like any human-built weapon. But there was something odd about the way the aliens were holding them, as if they'd never used them before. And yet…that was absurd, wasn't it?

Mongo leaned forward as the aliens spread out. "This is real, isn't it?"

"Sure looks that way," Charles said.

Steve nodded in agreement, his mind working frantically. What *was* this? An attempt to make First Contact without trying to fly into the secure airspace surrounding the White House and the Pentagon? Or was it something more sinister? He found it hard to believe that any alien race invading Earth would bother with a handful of campers...unless, of course, they intended to dissect Steve and his friends. Or interrogate them on the state of the planet's defences...

Kevin took a step forward. The aliens chattered suddenly – a high-pitched clattering that only added to the sense of inhumanity – and raised their weapons. Whatever they were actually *saying*, the meaning was all-too-clear. Kevin froze as the aliens aimed their weapons at his chest.

Part of Steve's mind noted, dispassionately, that the aliens might not intend to use headshots – and, given their armoured heads, that might make sense. Or, for all they knew, the alien brains were actually located in their torsos, rather than their skulls. But it didn't matter, he realised. The aliens weren't *acting* friendly. Steve had been at enough meetings in Afghanistan between Coalition troops and local villagers to understand what compromised a healthy respect for security...and what was outright paranoia. The aliens were acting more like they intended to take prisoners than talk to the humans facing them.

The unarmed alien – Steve cautioned himself not to assume the alien was *actually* unarmed – lifted the silver box to his lips. There was another burst of alien speech, followed by a dull masculine voice coming from the box – a translator, Steve realised. He felt a flicker of envy – a portable translator would have been very helpful in Afghanistan – as the alien voice grew more confident. It spoke in oddly-accented English.

"Do you understand me?"

"Yes," Steve said, when it became clear that no one else was going to speak. Perhaps the aliens would have tried French or Russian next if they couldn't make themselves understood through English. "We understand you."

There was another chattering sound from the alien. "You will board our craft," the alien said. It – he, Steve decided – pointed one clawed hand towards the hatch. "Step through the hatch and into the hold."

"Wait a minute," Vincent said, shocked. "Where are you taking us?"

"That is none of your concern," the alien informed him. He indicated the craft again, his claw flexing open and closed. "You will step through the hatch."

Vincent reached for the pistol at his belt. There was a flash of light so bright that Steve moved to cover his eyes instinctively. Vincent's body fell to the ground, a smoking hole in his chest. Steve stared in horror; he'd seen wounds from gunshots, IED strikes and even training accidents, but he'd never seen anything quite like this. The damage would have been instantly fatal, the dispassionate part of his mind realised; Vincent had been dead before his body hit the ground.

He balled his fists, then forced himself to relax. The lessons from a dozen Conduct after Capture courses rose up within his mind. There would be an opportunity to escape, he told himself firmly. He saw the same understanding in the eyes of his friends. The aliens would relax, sooner or later, and they would make mistakes. And, when they did, their human captives would be ready. The aliens might have advanced weapons, but advanced weapons didn't mean anything in close-quarter combat. No one knew that better than the soldiers who had fought terrorists and insurgents for the last twenty years.

Be a good little captive, he told himself, as the aliens motioned for them to walk forwards, into the craft. Vincent's body was simply left on the ground. Part of Steve's mind wondered if it would be discovered before it decayed. What would a autopsy show if any traces were left when it was found? He pushed the thought aside and concentrated on observing the aliens. *Bide your time and wait.*

TWO

FNFIAN HORDE WARCRUISER
SHADOW WARRIOR

EARTH ORBIT

The interior of the alien craft was oddly disappointing. Steve had been expecting something thoroughly...*alien*, but instead it looked more like the interior of a military transport aircraft, one of the planes that moved US troops from one trouble spot to another. There were no seats, no portholes...the aliens motioned for the humans to stand up against the bulkhead, then stepped backwards, keeping their weird eyes firmly fixed on their captives. Steve watched them back, feeling a cold burning hatred burning through his mind. There would be an opportunity to strike...

An odd sensation washed over him as the craft shuddered slightly, then faded away into nothingness. A faint whine echoed through the cabin – he looked towards the far bulkhead and noted the hatch there, which he assumed led to the cockpit – but there was no other sound. In some ways, it was better than any of the transport aircraft he'd endured in his long military career. But the whining sound might prove to be more irritating, in the long run, than the roar of an aircraft's engines.

"No acceleration," Mongo muttered, through clenched teeth. "Are we actually moving?"

Steve thought back to all the science-fiction books he'd read. Logically, if the craft was flying back out into space, there should be some sense of acceleration. But they weren't being pushed down to the ground by an irresistible force. It suggested the aliens had some form of internal compensation protecting the craft's passengers, which made a certain kind of sense. The interior of the craft certainly didn't look as though it was designed for spaceflight without a compensator.

"I think so," he said. Any doubts he might have had about the experience being real had faded with Vincent's death. No TV producer would kill someone just to add extra realism to a TV show. The very thought was sickening. "We must be going up to the mothership."

"Or maybe this is their starship," Kevin suggested. "For all we know, this is their version of a Hercules."

Steve shrugged, then looked back at the aliens. They looked oddly uncomfortable – he had to remind himself, again, not to read anything human into their movements – as the craft powered away from Earth. Their legs moved and twitched constantly, their eyes blinking rapidly; he couldn't help wondering if they were *used* to flying. There were strong men who whimpered when their transport aircraft hit a particularly nasty patch of turbulence, yet surely the aliens had plenty of experience with their spacecraft. Or was he misreading them completely. It wasn't as if most humans could remain still indefinitely.

The craft shuddered slightly, the gravity field – something else they had that humans lacked – growing weaker. Steve looked at the aliens, noted how they seemed more comfortable and wondered if they had evolved on a low-gravity world. Their spider-like appearance probably couldn't have evolved on Earth, where there were very real limits to the size of spiders and crabs. Or maybe the aliens were the products of genetic engineering and splicing. Someone with the right science and not enough scruples might manage to create their very own warrior race. It was the theme of a dozen SF television shows he'd watched.

A dull thump ran through the craft, then the faint whine faded away to nothingness. They had arrived at their destination, Steve realised, but where were they? A mothership? The moon? Another star system entirely? If he'd been invited to come with the aliens, he knew he would have accepted without a second thought. The chance to see another star system was not something he could have let pass. But instead they were prisoners.

The hatch opened and, for a moment, the aliens were distracted. Steve moved without thinking, all of the tension in his soul unleashing itself in one smooth moment. His brothers and Charles followed as he lunged into the aliens. One alien weapon fired, scorching the bulkhead, but the others were unable to fire before the humans were on top of them. Steve lashed out with all his strength, aiming for the thin alien necks. One by one, the aliens were overwhelmed and killed. The unarmed alien was the last to die.

"Interesting," Mongo said. "Look."

Steve followed his gaze. The silver band on the alien's head had detached itself and fallen to the deck. There was something about it that called to him; he found himself reaching for the band without being quite aware of what he was doing. It tingled when he touched it, as if it carried a faint electric charge…

"Grab their weapons," Charles snapped. His voice brought Steve back to reality, back to the fact that they were trapped in an unknown location. In hindsight, they might have picked the wrong time and place to fight back. "Come on!"

He led the way through the hatch. Steve followed, one hand still gripping the silver band. Outside, there was a large shuttlebay, crammed with a dozen craft identical to the one that had taken them from Earth. A handful of aliens milled about, staring at the humans in disbelief. Some of them started to reach for their weapons, others ran for the hatches or dived into their smaller shuttlecraft. Steve couldn't help noticing, as they fired on the armed aliens, that there was something odd about the hatches, as if they hadn't been designed for their alien enemies. They were too narrow for the aliens to move through comfortably. Coming to think of it, he realised as he opened fire, the hatches were tall enough for a creature twice as tall as the average human.

"So," Mongo said. "Where now?"

Steve laughed. "Fucked if I know," he said. There was another electric tingle from the band, which had wrapped itself around his wrist. "I..."

"So we go onwards," Charles said. He led them towards the largest hatch, weapon in hand. "We'll find a way out of here somehow."

There was a third tingle from the band. Steve stopped, staring at it, then felt an irresistible compulsion to put the band on his head. Slowly, not quite aware of what he was doing, he followed the compulsion. A stab of pain flashed through his head, then...

"Connection established," a cold voice said.

— —

"THEY BROKE FREE!"

"Yes," Cn!lss said. It never failed to amuse him just how many of his superiors felt the urge to point out the obvious. But then, most of their subordinates were so stupid it probably needed to be pointed out, time and time again. "They are currently expanding out of the shuttlebay into the lower levels of the ship."

The Subhorde Commander slammed his claws against his carapace, a gesture of fury – and maybe just a little fear. "Send two hordes to intercept and exterminate them," he ordered. "We can take other subjects from their homeworld afterwards."

Cn!lss understood the fear. The Varnar cyborgs were devilishly effective on the battlefield, striking fear into the hearts of their enemies. Everyone had assumed that the cyborgs were programmed to be so effective – primitive races were not protected against the meddling of their superiors - but what if such fighting prowess was natural to the human race? If that was the case, the Subhorde Commander was in real trouble. He'd taken a group of deadly warriors onto his starship!

And if he lost the ship, all of his family connections wouldn't save him from savage punishment.

"You'll have to send the orders," he reminded his superior. "They don't listen to me."

— —

"CONNECTION ESTABLISHED," the voice repeated. "Species 8472; designate *human*. Direct neural link activated. Awaiting orders."

"Awaiting orders?" Steve repeated. "What orders?"

Kevin turned to face him. "Steve? What's happening?"

"I can hear a voice," Steve said. He reached up to touch the headband and discovered that it seemed to have merged permanently against his skin. It felt weird, yet somehow natural to the touch. "Can't you hear it?"

Kevin shook his head. Further down the corridor, Charles took up a defensive position, backed up by Mongo, and prepared to hold their position against a charging line of enemy warriors. They didn't seem very experienced, part of Steve's mind noted; they were charging towards the humans as if they were unaware that the humans were armed with their own weapons. Even the Taliban had eventually leant the folly of mass human wave attacks. But it added yet another piece of the puzzle concerning the aliens. Steve just wished he understood what it *meant*.

"What are you?" He asked, touching the headband. "And what's happening to me?"

"This unit is a direct neural interface linked to the current starship's computer nodes," the voice said. "The interface has currently linked into your mind, providing direct access to the computer systems."

Steve blinked. "What?"

"This unit is a direct neural interface linked to the current starship's computer nodes," the voice repeated. There was no hint of patience or impatience, merely…a complete lack of emotion. "The interface has currently linked into your mind, providing direct access to the computer systems."

"I see, I think," Steve said. "Why did the link interface with me?"

"You donned the neural link," the voice said. "The link activated automatically."

"I felt *compelled* to put it on," Steve said. There was no response. For a moment, that alarmed him, then he realised he hadn't asked a question. "Why was I compelled to wear the neural link?"

"The device is designed to attract attention from cleared users," the voice informed him. It was an alarmingly vague answer – how was the attention actually *attracted*? – but he had a feeling he wouldn't be able to get much more out of the system. "You were the closest to the neural interface when it separated itself from the previous user."

"Wait a second," Steve said. "*I'm* a cleared user?"

"There is no specified list of cleared users," the voice stated. "All compatible mentalities may claim full access to the control systems, should they don the link."

Steve fought down an insane urge to giggle. All of a sudden, it made sense. "They didn't build this ship, did they?"

"Clarify," the voice ordered.

"The aliens who kidnapped us," Steve said, more carefully. "They didn't build this ship or their weapons, did they?"

"Affirmative," the voice said. "This starship was constructed by the Tokomak and passed though seven successive owners before finally being purchased by the Horde."

Steve shuddered. The *Horde*. Even the name conjured up bad impressions.

The deck shook, snapping him back to reality. He was dimly aware of the neural interface retreating into the back of his mind as he looked around and realised that the next group of aliens charging at them were proving smarter. They were hurling grenade-like objects down the corridor ahead of their charge. He lifted the alien weapon, found the firing stud and pushed it, hard. The weapon had no recoil, just flashes of deadly light. He couldn't help wondering just what operating principles it used as he fired. Plasma? Laser? Directed energy? Or something unimagined by humans?

He shook his head. There was no way to know.

Or was there? He had the neural interface.

"We're going to have to fall back," Charles shouted. An alien howled further down the corridor, then fell flat on his face. One of his fellows shot him in the back, then kept charging towards the human position. "We can't stay here!"

"No, we can't," Steve agreed. But they had nowhere to go. Once they were back in the shuttlebay, they would be trapped..."Unless..."

He accessed the interface again, watching with some alarm as the real world started to gray out around him. "What sort of access do I have?"

"Complete," the voice said.

"All right," Steve said. "Are there any measures we can take against life forms on this ship?"

There was a pause. "All direct measures will exterminate *all* life forms," the voice warned. "It would not be advisable."

Steve swore, mentally. "How can we remove the non-human life forms from this ship?"

"Teleporters can remove non-human life forms from this ship," the voice informed him. "Do you wish to use them?"

"They have teleporters?" Steve said, out loud. "Why didn't they just beam us up from Earth?"

"Unknown," the voice stated.

Steve gathered himself. Whatever he was talking to, it sounded more like a glorified user interface than a genuine AI. The wrong orders could easily get them killed along with their alien enemies. And he wasn't sure if the whole system was actually what it claimed to be too. What sort of idiot let a direct link to their computer nodes fall into enemy hands? But it wouldn't be the first time a primitive civilisation had purchased something without ever quite knowing how to use it.

"I want you to teleport all non-human life forms into open space," he ordered. He couldn't resist the next word. "Energise."

"Teleport safety protocols need to be disengaged," the voice informed him.

"Disengage them," Steve snapped.

"Teleport safety protocols disengaged," the voice said. "Teleport sequence activating...now."

Steve looked up, just in time to see the horde of charging aliens dissolve into silver light and vanish. He felt his mouth drop open as he realised just what had happened...and just how simple it had been to remove all of the aliens. And easy...

"The world just changed," Charles said. He sounded as shocked as Steve felt. "What happened?"

"One moment," Steve said. He linked back into the neural interface. "Have all of the aliens been removed?"

"Negative," the voice said. "One alien remains."

"Then point us to his position," Steve ordered.

— —

Cn!lss had had bare seconds to react when the teleporters had activated. He'd grabbed the terminal that was his badge of rank – and his curse, when the warriors were sharing lies about their glorious exploits – and activated its transmitter, praying desperately that the starship's designers had been as paranoid about safety as they usually were. The signal had disrupted the teleport lock, preventing the teleporters from snatching him off the bridge and depositing him...somewhere. None of the others on the bridge had been so lucky. The Subhorde Commander had been the first to vanish in silver light.

What a shame, part of Cn!lss's mind insisted. He'd *hated* his commander, even though he knew it could easily have been worse. But the human intruders, the humans who were clearly born warriors where the Hordesmen were brawlers, had not only managed to take control of the ship, they'd wiped out all but one of her crew. Would they be worse than the Hordesmen? Or would they see the value in keeping Cn!lss alive?

He carefully pranced away from his console and waited, in the centre of the bridge. It took longer than he'd expected for the humans to appear,

stepping through the hatch weapons in hand. Cn!lss couldn't help noticing that they held the captured weapons as if they knew how to use them,
even though they wouldn't have even *seen* them until bare hours ago. The
humans were true warriors, he realised now; they'd adapted far quicker
than any of the Horde when they'd first been confronted with advanced
technology.

They were staggeringly ugly creatures, he decided, as the humans
closed in on him. Two legs, soft pale skin, tiny little eyes...and yet they'd
managed to overwhelm seven Hordesmen in unarmed combat. Carefully,
he raised his maniples, hoping they were civilised enough to take prisoners. The Horde rarely took prisoners. It was one of the reasons they were
utterly unwelcome on most civilised worlds.

One of the humans growled at him. It was several seconds before the
translator provided a translation. "Keep your hands where we can see
them."

Cn!lss obeyed, shaking. Human hands poked at his carapace – they
were stronger than he'd realised – and carefully removed everything
from his terminal to his badge of rank, such as it was. For a moment, he
was convinced they were actually going to pull his shell apart, but they
relaxed and let it go when they realised it was actually part of his body.
The humans, it seemed, wore protective clothing at all times. But what
else would one expect from born warriors?

"If you cooperate, you will be treated decently," one of the humans
said, finally. "If you try to escape, you will be killed."

"I understand," Cn!lss said, quickly. It was better than his treatment
in the Horde. "I will cooperate."

"Good," the human said. "But for the moment, we will put you in a
small cabin and hold you there."

— —

STEVE LOOKED AROUND the bridge and knew that he'd been right,
even before the neural interface had confirmed it. The aliens hadn't

designed the ship themselves; hell, their consoles were clearly designed for a humanoid race, rather than a six-legged crab-like race from Hell. They must have found it more than a little uncomfortable, he decided, as he strode over to the central chair and looked down at it. That, at least, had been designed for the aliens. It looked absurdly like a throne suitable for a crab.

He sniffed the air, experimentally. There was a faint stench of rotting meat in the air, but nothing else. As far as he could tell, the atmosphere was breathable, although he made a mental note to check that as soon as possible. And to explore the rest of the ship...*his* ship. He found himself grinning as he realised what they'd done. They'd captured an interstellar starship and the way to the stars lay open, right in front of them.

"Well," Mongo said. "What do we do now?"

Steve sighed. There was work to be done. "We research," he said. They'd have to find several more neural interfaces, although he suspected they needed a rule that barred more than one or two people from using them at the same time. "And then we make plans."

THREE

FNFIAN HORDE WARCRUISER
SHADOW WARRIOR

EARTH ORBIT

"You know, my mother used to believe that aliens would come one day and show us a whole new way to live," Charles commented. "I never believed she was right."

Steve smiled as they made their way through one of the alien sleeping compartments. He'd been in barracks inhabited by ill-disciplined soldiers, American and foreign, but this was far worse. Great piles of meat and drink lay everywhere, creating a stench that would have to be dealt with sooner or later, while tiny creatures ran across the deck. They seemed to be crosses between crabs and cockroaches, Steve had decided, and they were as hard to kill as the latter. The entire ship would have to be fumigated before they did anything else. It was probably a breeding ground for disease.

The ship itself, according to the neural interface, was four hundred metres long and designed to serve as a Warcruiser. Reading between the lines, Steve had a suspicion that the entire ship was outdated as far as the aliens who had built it were concerned, although the neural interface was a little vague on such matters. He hadn't been able to determine if he was asking the wrong questions or if the system was designed not to provide exact answers to such questions. If he'd been designing a system for primitive aliens, he would have been careful what he programmed it to do too.

But it was clear that the aliens – the Hordesmen, the interface had called them – hadn't even had a vague idea of just what their ship could do. They reminded him of training missions to Arab countries, where no one dared admit ignorance, even if it was manifestly obvious they didn't have the slightest idea of what they were doing. Their weapons were clearly modified from weapons designed for other races, the advanced technology was partnered with a technology more primitive than any available on Earth and…and they'd kidnapped a group of humans without even bothering to secure them. Such carelessness made little sense.

They don't have any real conception of technology, he decided, as he peered into another alien cabin. It was oddly barren, in some ways; there were no books, no electronic readers, no computers…not even anything that resembled porn. The thought made him smile – did the aliens even have a concept of pornography? – but the cabins testified to an odd bleakness in their lives. Or a complete lack of concern from their superiors. He'd seen both in human societies around the globe.

He pushed the thought to one side as he accessed the neural interface again. The aliens had placed their ship in high orbit, using a masking field to hide their presence from Earth's defenders. Not that they'd had much reason to *worry* about Earth's defenders, Steve had already concluded. They could simply have thrown rocks from a safe distance until humanity rolled over and surrendered. Their point defence could have shot down every ICBM on Earth without breaking a sweat. No, the whole alien operation simply made no sense. It was almost as if they'd *wanted* the humans to capture their ship.

"We should probably talk to our new friend," Kevin said, when Steve commented on his suspicions. "Do you think he'll be open with us?"

Steve shrugged, expressively. Humans showed a wide range of behaviours when taken prisoner, from defiance to outright collaboration. The alien – his name was a series of clicks and hisses that was beyond humanity's ability to pronounce – seemed to tend towards the latter, but there was no way to be sure. All they could do was keep a sharp eye on him, then find somewhere to stick him well away from unknown technology. For all they knew, he had his own way of accessing the computer nodes even without a visible neural interface.

"You can put together a list of questions for him," he said, finally. "And we can corroborate what he says with what we pull out of the computer systems."

"Yeah," Kevin said. "About that…are you sure the connection is *safe?*"

"It saved our asses," Steve reminded him. The neural interface had insisted the process was safe, but – once again – it hadn't gone into details. "Does that mean you don't want one for yourself?"

"At least one of us shouldn't use one," Kevin said, firmly. "Mongo has enough common sense to tell us when we've pushed it too far, I think."

Steve didn't bother to disagree as they worked their way into the next set of compartments, which were crammed with all sorts of pieces of technology. Almost all of them were completely unrecognisable, save for a handful of devices that looked like the silver box the unarmed alien had carried down on Earth. Two of them might be the alien versions of laptops, he decided, others might have been weapons or sex toys. Short of asking the interface, there was no way to know. The next compartment held a line of vehicles that looked like small, almost toy-like tanks. They looked too small for the aliens to use comfortably.

"Maybe designed for another race," Steve speculated. He linked into the neural interface and asked. "Yep, built for another race and stolen."

"Scavengers," Charles said. "It might explain why they were so fucking careless."

Kevin paused, then rubbed his stomach. "Is there anywhere to get something to eat here?"

"The alien food is classed as incompatible," Steve discovered, querying the neural interface. "But the food processors can produce something suitable for human consumption."

"We'd better get back up there and find something," Kevin said. "And then I think we need to start asking more questions."

"There's a spare neural link up on the bridge," Steve said. From what little the voice had said about itself, handing two or even several hundred users at once was well within its capabilities. "You might as well put it to use."

"Just be careful what you do," Charles warned. "You don't want to accidentally beam yourself out into space."

Steve nodded. The teleporter had dropped the aliens into open space and Earth's gravity had done the rest, once the bodies were outside the craft's as-yet unexplained drive field. By now, the remains of the alien crew had burned up in Earth's atmosphere and vanished. Part of him regretted slaughtering so many without a second thought, the rest of him knew there had been no alternative. The aliens wouldn't have hesitated to kill their former captives, now they'd seen just what they could do.

If all the aliens are like them, he thought, *humanity will rule the galaxy in years.*

But he knew it wouldn't be that easy.

They made their way back to the bridge and entered the dining hall. Every time he saw it, Steve was reminded of the depictions of Norsemen partying hard after a successful campaign of looting, raping and burning. They'd cleared away most of the mess – it seemed the aliens *liked* living in squalor – but it still disgusted him. He'd checked with the neural interface, only to discover that the cleaning robots had been removed, along with several automated maintenance systems. The sellers had clearly anticipated getting rich by selling spare parts and basic maintenance to the Hordesmen.

He activated the neural link as he stopped in front of the food professor, a slot in the bulkhead that remained sealed until the food was ready. "Please produce something suitable for human consumption."

There was a long pause as the device hummed to itself. "You'd think they could produce matter directly from energy," Kevin commented. "If they have teleporters, surely they could produce food and drink..."

"Or duplicate a living person," Charles muttered. "I saw a *Star Trek* episode where someone was duplicated accidentally..."

Kevin snickered. *"You're a secret Star Trek fan?"*

"We ran out of *Doctor Who* episodes to watch," Charles confessed. "And we had a lot of fun pointing out the problems..."

"A likely story," Kevin said.

Steve ignored them, concentrating on the neural interface. Most of the technobabble it produced was way above his head – it was suddenly harder to blame the aliens for being unaware of the potentials of their technology – but it seemed to be impossible to actually duplicate a person through teleport malfunctions. Furthermore, direct energy-to-matter conversion, while quite possible, was actually extremely uneconomical. It was far simpler to reprocess biomass to produce something humans could eat safely.

"There won't be any more of you running around," he said, finally. "It doesn't seem to be possible."

"What a relief," Kevin said, dryly.

There was a *ding* from the food processor. The hatch opened, revealing a plate of steaming...*something*. It looked rather like grey porridge. Steve eyed it doubtfully, then removed it from the processor and placed it on the table. There were no knives or forks, so he had to use his hands. It tasted of nothing, as far as he could tell. Just...nothing at all.

"We will have to bring some proper food up here," Kevin said, as he tasted the glop. "And a small horde of cleaners."

Steve nodded. "I'll get you an interface," he said. "And you can start asking questions."

He finished his share of the glop, then ordered the machine to make another portion and something suitable for one of the aliens. Mongo would be growing hungry too, as would their alien captive. Steve wished that he dared trust the alien enough to ask questions, but a long interrogation session would have to wait. Maybe Kevin – a trained interrogator, among other things – would be able to get more answers out of the computer network.

Shaking his head, he walked back onto the bridge, found the second interface and took it back to Kevin. "There's a stab of pain as it configures itself, then you'll be fine," he assured his brother. "And good luck."

Kevin nodded and placed the silver band on his head. "No pain," he said, after a moment. "I guess you were the unlucky bastard who got the brunt of the reconfiguration."

"So it would seem," Steve said. He picked up the food and headed for the hatch. "Charles, keep an eye on him."

"Yes, sir," Charles said.

Mongo was, as Steve had expected, glad to be fed. "When are we going to get some more people up here?"

"Good question," Steve said. Their wives and families, naturally, but who else? And what could they do, in the long term, with such a starship? "As soon as possible, I think."

"Just teleport them up," Mongo suggested. "Mariko would love it."

"Go do it to Jayne first," Steve countered. His partner wouldn't love being taken by surprise. "I dare you."

Mongo shrugged, then conceded the point.

—◂

KEVIN WAS IN heaven.

None of his family had been dumb. They'd been homeschooled by their parents and found, when they were finally tested against children from the state-run schools, that they were far in advance of their peers. Their mother had been a stern taskmistress, watching her children like hawks while they were studying and enforcing quiet where necessary. But Kevin had always been more intellectual than his siblings, even though the very word was a swear word in the mouth of their father. He'd wanted to know and know and know...

The neural interface was *brilliant*. From what Steve had said, he'd accessed only the very basic level. Kevin was *swimming* in data. It flowed into his mind, each file opening itself in front of his eyes and entering his mind. He couldn't help comparing it to surfing the internet, only the data was far more complete than anything he'd seen online. And even a random thought was enough to activate search algorithms that assisted him in his search for raw information.

But there were very definite limits to what he could access, he discovered. The data files were brimming with information on what the starship – it was called *Shadow Warrior* – could do, but they weren't very specific on how it actually *worked*. There was an FTL drive that seemed to bend local space around it, as far as he could determine, yet the theory was completely isolated from the technology that made it work. It might as well be black boxes, he realised, as he made another mental note. The designers had sealed the technology to prevent it being duplicated.

The thought discharged another torrent of data into his mind. Steve had been right, he realised; the Hordesmen were nothing more than scavengers. They'd barely entered the Bronze Age, if that, when they'd been discovered by older, more advanced races, and introduced to the surrounding galaxy. Some of them had been taken as slaves, others had been serving as mercenaries...none of them had built a significant galactic power base of their own. As far as the Galactics were concerned, the Hordesmen weren't even a minor headache. They were just gnats to be swatted aside when they got too irritating to tolerate for a moment longer.

But what did they want from Earth?

There were no answers in the databanks, he realised slowly. The Hordesmen had never bothered to keep logs, either because they were too primitive to care or because they'd worried about the security of their systems. There was nothing to show why they'd come to Earth or why they'd adopted such an absurd strategy for abducting humans. Hell, maybe they *had* been interested in anal probing after all. Given how little data there was in the computers, it was as good a theory as any.

Not that it matters, he told himself. *If they decided they wanted to invade Earth, they could.*

Images flowed through his mind from the databanks, triggered by his thoughts. There was no Prime Directive, no law preventing advanced races from overwhelming primitive races…just as the Hordesmen themselves had been overwhelmed. Hundreds of worlds had been invaded by their more advanced neighbours, then enslaved…or merely forced to pay tax. Earth had been lucky. The handful of aliens who had visited the solar system hadn't been particularly interested in the human race or anything in their star system. But there had been other visits…

He poked the databanks, but details were scarce. Or perhaps he was simply asking the wrong questions, no matter how closely he scrutinised the data. There was no way to know.

Instead, he started to ask about the technology on the ship. The sheer size of the response sent his mind reeling in disbelief, as if the data was too much to handle. He felt a dull pain at the back of his head as he tried to process what he was being shown, then tried to distract himself by asking more questions. The Hordesmen hadn't even bothered to scratch the surface of the ship's full capabilities.

He felt a sudden burst of awe, mixed with terror. If *Shadow Warrior* was something the Galactics felt comfortable about selling to a tiny scavenger race, what did *they* have at their disposal? Was the starship, for all its wonders, merely the counterpart of an AK-47? Were the odd gaps in the datanet's explanations intended to prevent the Hordesmen from developing their own starships? Or were they merely placing some limits on exported tech to prevent it from being turned against them?

The sheer potential of the technology stunned him. It would be easy, almost as easy as breathing, to reach out and download the entire human internet into one of the starship's memory cores, even the millions of pornographic sites. The 30TB portable hard drive his friend had been so proud of producing was a laughing stock compared to the alien ship. And no security protocols could keep him out of a human system. He could download the secrets of the Pentagon, the Kremlin...every top secret base on Earth.

It terrified him. As an intelligence officer, a system like the one in front of him would be a dream come true, but it was also a nightmare. The most advanced human surveillance system in the world wasn't capable of tracking everything, no matter what the designers claimed. *This could*...and it could do more. Complete and total monitoring of millions of people, at all times, was well within its capabilities. Kevin shuddered at the thought. Privacy would become a joke.

Or worse, he thought. He'd retired from intelligence work after the field had become increasingly politicised. He had never admired Edward Snowden for defecting from the United States, but he'd understood the impossibility of blowing a whistle when the most senior men and women in the nation were involved. *I don't think we dare hand this over to the government.*

The question brought another stream of data into his mind. He welcomed it, even as he fired more questions back into the databanks. How were the aliens governed? Who were the major interstellar powers? What might they do to Earth if they discovered humanity?

They already know about us, he corrected himself. It was humbling, but unsurprising. From the point of view of the Galactics, Earth wasn't even a microstate. *They just didn't care enough to try to take us into their system, even as slaves. We had nothing to offer them.*

Something *clicked*. As an intelligence officer, he knew how to put pieces together to form a coherent picture. Now, looking at the data, he understand why some aliens had been interested in Earth...and why the Horde had followed in their wake. Humanity might be significant after all...and that thought, too, was terrifying. Frantically, half-convinced he had to be looking at a false Earth-centric picture, he fired off yet more questions. The datanet struggled to respond.

There was a sudden surge of data, followed by a stab of pain so intense he couldn't help screaming. He dimly heard Charles calling his name, felt someone shaking his body...and then he fell down into darkness.

FOUR

FNFIAN HORDE WARCRUISER
SHADOW WARRIOR

EARTH ORBIT

Steve stared down at his younger brother, helplessly. "What happened to him?"

"Subject overloaded the neural interface," the interface informed him. As always, there was no trace of emotion in its tone. "Subject's brain shut down to allow time to recover."

"I...see," Steve said. "Will there be any permanent damage?"

"Unknown," the interface said. "Place the subject in a medical tube for a more detailed analysis."

Steve listened to the instructions, then Charles and he carried Kevin's body down to the sickbay and placed it inside a transparent tube. The sickbay wasn't like anything he'd seen in real life; instead of beds, there were a dozen medical tubes, each one big enough to carry a human, but too small for a Hordesman. It might explain, he decided, why the sickbay looked far cleaner than the rest of the ship. The Horde had simply had no use for it. But if the alien medical technology was as advanced as the rest of the starship...

He shook his head as the medical tube went to work, scanning Kevin's body. "Permanent damage averted, but there are minor feedback curves from the neural interface," the system reported. Steve silently prayed the system was smart enough to realise it was operating on a human, rather than an individual from any other race. "Compensating…note; subject also has numerous genetic flaws that can be corrected, if requested."

Steve frowned. "Genetic flaws?"

He listened, in some disbelief, to the explanation. Again, most of it was well above his head, but it was clear that there would be long-term problems for Kevin – and the rest of the family, if they weren't handled. Kevin, in particular, was at risk of losing his sight in the very near future, something that bothered Steve more than he cared to admit. Death was one thing, permanent disability quite another. And then there were the whole string of suggested enhancements…

"He'll never forgive you if you don't give him a bigger cock," Mongo commented. Charles had replaced him on guard duty once they'd moved Kevin to the sickbay. "Nor will his wife."

Steve rolled his eyes. Sexual enhancements weren't the only suggested possibilities. Kevin could be given enhanced strength, coordination and longevity – even intelligence – and remain roughly human. But he could also be turned into a cyborg. The suggestions ranged from implanted weapons to actually removing his brain and inserting it into a combat unit. He accessed the interface and saw a handful of images, then shuddered. If he'd had to face something like that on the battlefield…

"I think we'd better concentrate on repairing the mental damage," he said, firmly. "Other enhancements can come later."

He watched, feeling utterly out of his depth, as the alien autodoc went to work. It seemed much more efficient than any human doctor, although the potential of the system to do great ill as well as good chilled him to the bone. Moments after it started, Kevin's body jerked and his eyes opened. Steve hastily opened the tube and welcomed him back to the world.

"Idiot," he said. "What were you thinking?"

"I was downloading a considerable amount of data," Kevin said. He paused, thoughtfully. "That's interesting; I still seem to *have* the data."

"Good," Steve said, impatiently.

"And we may be in some trouble," Kevin added. He clambered out of the tube, brushing the proffered hand aside. "The entire world may be in deep shit."

He led the way back towards the bridge, seeming to find his way effortlessly through the alien corridors. Steve watched him carefully, wondering what else the alien system had done to him. Had it turned him into a spy? Or merely overloaded his head with data because it wasn't bright enough to realise the danger?

"These guys" – he indicated the alien commander's throne with his foot – "are scavengers."

"I said that," Steve objected.

"You were right," Kevin agreed. He sat down on one of the uncomfortable chairs, then turned to face his brothers. "From what I have been able to determine, they literally know almost nothing about how their technology works; they didn't build it, they can't mend it and they certainly cannot duplicate it for themselves. They barely had fire when they were discovered by an elder race and brought into the galaxy."

He shrugged. "They weren't here to invade – at least, not yet," he continued. "I think they wanted samples of humanity for their employers."

Steve narrowed his eyes. "Why?"

"This is where the speculation begins," Kevin warned. "One race clearly took some humans from Earth years ago and turned them into slaves – no, cyborgs. *Soldier* cyborgs. These cyborgs have been hellishly effective. Our captors were employed, I suspect, to find humans who could be turned into other cyborgs."

Mongo sucked in a breath, clearly remembering all the options for enhancing Kevin. "Do you think that was the fate they had in mind for us?"

"I believe so," Kevin said. "Given enough samples of human DNA, they could simply clone as many human brains as they needed and then go on from there."

He paused. "The problem is that, sooner or later, the other Hordesmen will realise this ship hasn't reported back," he explained. "And Earth might be targeted by their employers."

"Shit," Steve said. He looked down at his hands for a long moment, then back up at Kevin. "How long do we have?"

Kevin shrugged. "Unknown," he said. "Travel time between star systems that don't have gravity points..."

He stopped. "I..."

"*Kevin*," Steve snapped. "What are you doing?"

"It's weird," Kevin said. He was hyperventilating between his words. "I didn't know that and yet I did."

He shook his head, brushing off their fears. "It might be a few months or it might be a year," he said. "But we will run out of time."

"Yeah," Steve said. "And I think we need to decide what to do with our ship."

"And our prisoner," Mongo said.

"Lock him in one of the cabins, then deactivate the computer terminal," Kevin said. "He'll be safe enough for now."

— —

ONCE THE ALIEN prisoner was securely locked away, they gathered again on the bridge.

"This is the situation," Steve said. "We have a starship, we have a surprising amount of technology...and we have a desperate need to move quickly to protect Earth. The question is simple. How do we proceed?"

"We could call the government," Charles pointed out. "They'd be needed to get behind this and push."

"Hell, no," Steve said. The sheer force of his reaction surprised even him. "Do you really want to give this ship and all of its technology to the *government?*"

Bitter memories welled up in his mind. He forced them down, savagely.

"There's no way we can trust the current government to do the right thing," he said. "The best we can hope for is that they will drop the ship into Area 51, give us all a pat on the ass and classify everything to the point where no one knows a thing about it. And then they will exploit it for petty political reasons while ignoring the looming threat from outer space."

"Except for the fact there's just four of us," Charles said. "Five if you count the alien."

"We have friends," Steve reminded him. "Men and women who can be trusted to keep a secret and join us, people who would leap at the chance to escape the morass our country is becoming."

"Or we could take over," Kevin mused. "We have the technology to do it now."

Steve shook his head. "I'm not interested in taking over the federal government," he said, bitterly. "I'm interested in getting away from it. And in protecting my homeworld."

He smiled, rapidly pulling together a plan. "We reach out to people we know and invite them to join us," he said. "In the meantime, we start work on expanding our capabilities, unlocking the secrets of the alien technology and establishing a settlement on the moon."

Kevin considered it. "We'll need money," he said. "Some of the tech would have to be sold."

He paused. "You know we have four fabricators, right?"

Steve frowned. It had been mentioned, but he hadn't had the time to follow up and work out what they actually *did*. He checked with the interface and discovered that they produced items according to saved specifications, provided enough raw materials were provided. *That* wouldn't be a problem, he decided. All they had to do was start shovelling in material from the lunar surface.

"There are some limits," Kevin said. "They cannot reproduce themselves, for example, nor can they produce certain kinds of technology. But there should be quite a few examples of tech we can sell...we'd just have to be very careful how we inserted it into Earth's economic network. Something that appeared completely out of nowhere would raise eyebrows."

"You're in charge of finding something we can use," Steve decided. "And of finding a way we can…insert our new technology without raising *too* many eyebrows."

"There are thousands of possibilities," Kevin offered. "I was going to suggest fusion power and computer technology. The former, in particular, should be very lucrative."

"But would definitely attract government attention," Charles said, softly. "Computer technology might pass under the radar for the moment."

"Work on it," Steve ordered. "What else do we need?"

"Food," Mongo said, immediately. He snorted. "Food and human tech we can use on the moon."

Steve gave Mongo a puzzled look, so he explained.

"The problem with getting into orbit is getting into orbit," he said. "Getting something the size of the space shuttle into orbit costs a shit-load of fuel. But we can bypass that problem with the shuttles we have, which will allow us to start using human technology on the moon without needing to place extra demands on our fabricators. Hell, we've had all the tech we needed to set up a lunar settlement for years. All we lacked was the ability to get there in the first place."

"Fucking politicians," Steve muttered.

"Tell me something," Charles said. "Are we seriously considering setting up our own *country*?"

"Yes," Steve said.

He wondered, briefly, if his friend – a natural conservative – thought they were moving too fast. But time was of the essence. Quite apart from the alien threat, they needed to be well-established before secrecy slipped…and he knew, from bitter experience, that *nothing* remained secret indefinitely. Missing people would be noticed, strange new technology would be noticed…all in all, eventually someone would put the pieces together and realise the truth. And, at that point, there would be trouble.

The federal government *hated* it when people tried to move outside its sphere of control, no matter the reason. It was incapable of leaving people alone, even if they weren't causing trouble or doing anything more than keeping themselves to themselves. And the technology Steve and his buddies had lucked into would reshape the world. The federal government would want it, very badly,

And they'd really hate the idea of someone setting up an independent state on the moon.

He pushed the thought aside and looked at Charles. "I want the three of us to put our heads together and work out a list of people who might be suitable recruits for our new society," he said. "Mainly military veterans, but feel free to add people who haven't served, but might still be useful. Ideally, people more than a little disenchanted with the government."

"Don't go for anyone on active service," Kevin offered, "Too much room for divided loyalties."

"Understood," Charles said. He held up a hand before Steve could say a word. "What do we do if someone turns down our offer? Because someone will, soon enough. Either because they don't want to leave their comfortable homes or because they have patriotic objections to setting up on our own."

Steve swallowed. The thought of killing someone who knew too much was sickening, yet they might not have a choice. Unless they intended to take prisoners...

He paused. "Could we wipe their minds?"

Kevin hesitated. "Perhaps," he said. "But the techniques are unreliable."

"We'll deal with it when it happens," Steve said. He knew he was pushing the problem back until they actually *had* to confront it, but he saw no alternative. "It depends on the exact situation."

Charles gave him a knowing look, but said nothing. Instead, he changed the subject.

"You do realise we'll need a constitution and everything, soon enough?"

"Soon," Steve said. "Or maybe we could just crib the one we already have."

"You'd better go chat to Mariko," Mongo said. "And I should go chat to Jayne."

Charles swore out loud. "And Vincent! What do we do about *him*?"

Steve felt a sudden spurt of hope. "Could the alien tech reanimate him?"

Kevin shook his head. "Not now his brain has been dead for too long," he said. "But we could bury him on the moon."

"Except someone would notice he was gone," Steve said. Vincent hadn't exactly been unpopular. His wife might not be expecting him back for another week, but she *was* expecting him. They'd have to tell her something, preferably the truth. "We can fake his death in an accident that wipes out all traces of anything...inhuman."

"Have to be a pretty nasty accident," Charles said.

"Vincent was always modifying those old cars of his," Mongo reminded them. "It wouldn't be too hard to rig one so it exploded, burning him to death and wiping out the evidence."

"We could probably fix up his body too, a little," Kevin added. "Or we could simply report that he disappeared on our camping trip."

"Or we could simply disappear completely ourselves," Steve mused. "Wives, children...all gone to space. Nothing left for anyone to find."

He shook his head. "I want to speak to Mariko," he said. It wasn't fair to leave his partner out of it, particularly as she shared his disdain for the federal government. "But we should work out a list of likely contacts now, while we explore more of what this ship can do."

It was nearly an hour before they had a list of forty possible names. The arguments waxed and waned over some of the more controversial additions; Kevin had wanted a handful of intelligence specialists to help go through the ship's databanks, while Charles and Mongo wanted more Marines and Rangers respectively. There was a general agreement against head-hunting any of the USAF's fighter jocks, but some heavy transport pilots – and CAS – specialists – would be very welcome. And then Charles had another brainwave.

"There's always Ed," he said. "The one with busted legs. What about him?"

Steve gave him a sharp look. Edward Romford had been badly wounded during the flare-up in Afghanistan and then, thanks to the VA's incompetence, hadn't received medical treatment in time to save his spine. He was currently permanently installed in a residence home near New York, trapped in a wheelchair that he hated. Steve liked Ed – they'd shared some fun times together – but it was hard to face him after he'd been permanently crippled. The sight of the wounded veteran was a reminder that Steve could have easily ended up just like him.

He smiled, slowly, as he realised what Charles meant. "We could save his legs, couldn't we?"

"Or make him an enhanced soldier," Kevin added. "Humanity's very first cyborg."

"Why not?" Steve asked. "You start working on a plan to get him out of the residence home without raising too many eyebrows."

Kevin smirked. "Daring commando raid?"

"I was thinking more about offering to take him into the ranch," Steve said, patiently.

"Or we could just beam him out of the residence," Mongo offered. "Maybe give one of those bitch nurses a heart attack."

"Something more subtle than that," Steve said, warningly. He stood up. "Unless anyone has any objection, I intend to beam down and collect Vincent's body, then proceed to the ranch and explain everything to Mariko."

"No objections here," Mongo said. "Just make sure you bring her up here before Jayne sees you. She'll want to know what happened to me."

Steve smirked. "I'll tell her you're several thousand light years away."

"I hate you," Mongo said, without heat. "And so will Jayne, if you don't let me tell her first."

Steve nodded and accessed the user interface. After what had happened to Kevin, he was reluctant to submerge himself in data; instead, he asked questions and listened carefully to the responses. The teleporter – he had to remind himself to stop thinking of it as a *transporter* – seemed to work along the basic *Star Trek* principles. It was just a little dodgy to use it without a proper matter buffer at one end of the teleport.

"Find a science-fiction author we can recruit," he said, after losing himself in the technobabble once again. "Someone who speaks fluent Geek. Hell, we probably need someone to come to grips with just what combat in space actually entails."

"I'll find one," Kevin promised. "Good luck, bro."

"Just don't let yourself be seen materialising," Charles warned. "One of your kids might be sharp enough to realise he wasn't seeing things."

"They probably would," Kevin agreed. "And think how much *smarter* they will be once neural interface technology enters the educational system. They'll be able to imprint information into their minds."

"Not with the teachers unions," Charles commented.

"There won't be any on the moon," Steve said. He smiled as his dream unfolded in front of him. "It will be a land of individualists, with no collective responsibility for anything."

"Really?" Charles asked. "Even defence?"

"It may take us a while to work out a political theory," Steve admitted. "I'll beam down now, folks. Have fun in my absence."

"We'll try not to crash the ship into an asteroid," Mongo called.

Steve gave him a one-fingered gesture and walked out the hatch.

FIVE

Montana, USA

The Stuart Family Ranch wasn't *that* large, not compared to some of the huge ranches in Montana. Situated between two mountain ranges, it consisted of three barns, five fields and a large pond Steve had fished in, when he was a younger child. His ancestors had made it a point of pride that their somewhat isolated ranch rarely needed to hire outside help. The family could handle it for themselves, they'd decided, although they'd had problems doing both that and fighting for their country. But it had bred a self-reliance in them that had kept the family going through thick and thin.

Steve gasped as he materialised under the trees, some distance from the ranch house. The whole sensation of being teleported felt eerie, although not as bad as he'd feared. It felt as if every atom in his body had been tickled as the world dissolved into silver light, then reformed around him. As he'd expected, no one was close enough to see his arrival. The apple trees that surrounded the family cemetery hid him from outside view.

He caught his breath, suddenly very aware of his heartbeat pounding inside his chest. The experience was profoundly *alien*, raising all sorts of questions in his mind. Had the *real* Steve died when he entered the teleporter, only to be replaced by a completely identical copy that thought it was the original? Or was the teleporter sophisticated enough to duplicate a soul as well as a physical body? Somehow, he was sure that scientists and theologians would be debating the issue for centuries to come. But did it really matter?

Shaking his head, he looked down at himself. Everything seemed to be where it belonged, so he reached up and touched the silver band around his head. He'd worried about walking outside the network interface's range, but the interface had told him that he would have to be several light-seconds away from the starship before it started to have problems maintaining the connection. Even then, it could send data packets back and forth, even if it couldn't maintain a teleport lock. Bracing himself, he walked forward until he pushed through the apple trees and headed down towards the house.

"Hey, Uncle Steve," two of Mongo's children called. "You're back early!"

Steve smirked. They didn't know the half of it.

"I'm back, yes," he said, instead. "Where's my partner?"

They pointed towards the ranch house. Steve nodded to the two boys and strode past them, up to the door. Up close, it was clear that certain members of the family were more than a little paranoid; the door was painted to look like wood, but it was actually solid metal. But then, it would be hours, at best, before the law enforcement forces got out to the ranch if the owners called for help. Taking care of themselves was practically bred into them. Tapping the door, he opened it and stepped inside. Mariko looked out from the kitchen, surprise written all over her face. She hadn't expected to see him for several days.

"Hi, honey," Steve said. "I'm home."

Mariko flowed forward and wrapped him in a hug. She'd surprised Steve when they'd first met – the city girl who'd become a doctor and then a vet, purely because she wanted to get out of the city – and continued to surprise him, every few days. They might not have married – Steve had his suspicions about modern marriage – but he considered her his wife in every way that mattered. And they'd had four children together.

"So," she said, after a brief kissing session. "What's that?"

Steve smiled as she pointed to the headband. "It's a long story, honey," he said. "You'd better be sitting down."

Mariko lifted her eyebrows, but did as she was told. She was a slight girl, in many ways, her Japanese features seeming out of place in the ranch house. And yet there was a strength around her that continued to impress him, even after twelve years of partnership. She might not have been born into the ranch culture, but she belonged there now.

"You see, we were abducted from the campsite," Steve began. "By aliens."

Mariko listened, her face clearly doubtful, as Steve ran through the entire story, from the alien craft to the moment they'd decided to set up a new nation for themselves. Steve wasn't in the habit of lying to anyone, certainly not his partner, but the entire story was more than a little unbelievable. And then she leaned forward and took a closer look at the silver headband.

"It's grown into your flesh," she said, sharply. Her fingers poked and prodded at where the headband met his skin. "I've never seen anything like it."

Steve allowed his smile to widen. "You believe me now?"

"...Maybe," Mariko said. She stood up. "Show me the starship."

"Of course," Steve said. He'd already planned where he wanted to take her first, once she was onboard the ship. He stood and took her arm. "Try to relax, honey."

He sent the command through the interface. Moments later, the entire room dissolved into silver light, only to reform as a teleport bay. Mariko staggered against him as soon as the teleport beam let go of her, clearly badly shocked. Steve felt a moment of regret – had he moved too fast? – then shook his head, mentally. He had to show her the truth before she decided he was playing a joke on her – or that he'd gone mad.

She muttered something in Japanese as he led her out of the compartment and down the stained corridor, into the observation blister. The Hordesmen hadn't seemed like tourists, but the ship's original designers had been firm believers in placing windows and portholes in their starships. Steve rather understood how they felt. He'd been in submarines twice and both of them had been rather claustrophobic. The alien ship was larger than any submarine or spacecraft humanity had ever built, but the crews might well face the same problem. They needed to look out of the craft from time to time.

Mariko clutched his arm tightly as they entered the observation blister. Ahead of them, Earth glowed in the darkness of interplanetary space. Steve shook his head in awe as Mariko stepped up to the edge of the blister and pressed her fingertips against the glass – if it was glass, Steve told himself. It might as well be transparent aluminium.

"It's beautiful," she said, her eyes shining as she turned to face him. "It's...fantastic!"

"It is," Steve agreed. It was suddenly very easy to take her in his arms and kiss her. "It's the dawn of a brave new world."

He held her for a moment longer, then sobered. "There's something – someone – I'd like you to take a look at," he added. "Although I'm not sure if you will be wearing your doctor's outfit or your vet's coat."

Mariko snickered, then stared up at him. "You captured an *alien?*"

"Yes," Steve said, simply. For a doctor, the chance to study a completely non-human life form had to be the Holy Grail. But they needed the alien techie alive. "Please don't dissect him."

"I won't," Mariko promised.

Steve led her through the maze of corridors, back up to the cabin where Mongo was on guard. "You can go speak to Jayne now," he said, to his brother. "Bring her up here after you've told her the truth."

He scowled. "And then we have to prepare Vincent's body for disposal," he added. "It can't look even remotely damaged."

Mariko looked up at him. "When are you going to tell his wife?"

Steve winced. "After this," he said. "Will you come with me?"
Mariko nodded, wordlessly.

— —

CN!LSS HAD NEVER really expected to be taken prisoner. As a rule, the
Horde rarely took prisoners, not when resources had been very limited on their homeworld. The only times they took prisoners were when
the captive could be ransomed back to their Horde or when the captive
might know something useful. In the latter case, the captive was taken
somewhere safe and brutally tortured until he gave up his secrets, then
executed as soon as he had surrendered everything. It wasn't as if his fellows would want him back.

But the humans seemed to be remarkably considerate captors. They'd
refused to give him a terminal or anything else he could use to *work*,
but they had given him food, water and a certain amount of privacy.
Compared to what he'd had to endure under the Subhorde Commander,
it was almost paradise. Those who actually tried to understand alien technology got no respect from their fellow Hordesmen.

He looked up as the hatch opened, revealing two humans. It was hard
to tell the scrawny bipeds apart, but one of them wore a neural interface,
suggesting that he'd been one of the original captives. The thought made
him clack his feet against the deck in frustration. It was clear, now, that
the Varnar *hadn't* engineered fighting abilities into their cyborgs. They
were natural fighters, even when taken by surprise and transported into
an utterly unfamiliar environment.

The second human took a step backwards as Cn!lss came into view. It
was hard – again – to be sure, but the protrusions on the human's chest
suggested a female...unless the humans were radically different from the
other biped races. Not that that meant the female would be subordinate, he reminded himself sharply. There were races where one sex was
clearly superior and races where both sexes were equals...and races where

swapping sex was as natural as breathing. For all he knew, he was looking at the Queen of Earth.

"I greet you," he said, dropping into the Posture of Respect. Whatever she was, he had a feeling that rudeness to her would not go unpunished. "I am Cn!lss."

There was a long pause as the translator worked through his words. "Hi," the human female said, in return. "I am..."

Cn!lss cocked his head, unsurprised, as the translator failed to provide any translation for the alien name. Unlike concepts such as technology, basic names and superstitions were hard to translate, no matter how capable the computers operating the system. Besides, one race's religion and naming conventions were another race's source of endless amusement.

"I would like to examine your body," the human female said. "Would that be permissible?"

"Yes," Cn!lss said. Compared to the torture he'd been expecting, a medical examination wouldn't be too bad. "I would not object at all."

— —

STEVE HAD BEEN reminded – again – of just why he'd fallen in love with Mariko. She'd stopped dead when she'd seen the alien, as if nothing she'd seen up to then had been quite real, and then she'd gone forward and started a conversation. Now, she was poking and prodding at the alien's body, all the while bombarding him with questions about how his body actually worked. Not all of the answers seemed to make sense, but at least they were learning *something*.

"They're egg-layers," Mariko said, afterwards. They left the alien in the cabin and walked out to a place where they could talk. "And they're real."

"They sure are," Steve said. "What else did you find out?"

"He's quite ignorant of how his body works," Mariko said. "I'd need a proper laboratory to do more research, but I think he knows almost nothing. It seems odd."

"These guys seem to have been kept in ignorance," Steve muttered. It still seemed absurd to him that the aliens didn't even begin to comprehend the potentials of their own systems, but he had seen human groups with similar levels of ignorance. He straightened up as Mongo and Jayne walked past, the latter looking completely stunned. "Welcome to our new ship."

"Thank you," Jayne stammered. Unlike Mariko, her family had been ranchers for the last two hundred years and had no intention of leaving their land. But that might have changed now, Steve knew. The children, in particular, would be fascinated by the starship…and the chance to live on the moon. "This is…this is…"

Steve sighed, inwardly. Mariko was adaptable, Jayne…was not. But it was hard to blame her; she'd grown up in Montana, never gone to college or anything else that might have taken her out of the state and married a man she'd known since they were both children. It was a comfortable marriage, Steve considered, but it wasn't exciting. Or maybe he was completely wrong. Both he and Mongo were gentlemen. They didn't kiss their wives and then compare notes.

"Something new," he said. Would Jayne refuse to join them? Would they have to decide what to do about someone who wanted out sooner rather than later? "And it's one hell of an opportunity."

"Yes," Jayne said. She wrinkled her nose. "It also stinks."

Steve watched Mongo lead his wife further into the ship, then nodded to Mariko and led her back towards the teleport compartment. Mariko bombarded him with questions about how the system worked, questions that produced little or no useful data from the interface. It was quite happy to teach them how to teleport into a high security zone – it crossed Steve's mind that he could simply beam into the White House – but it still wasn't prepared to tell them how the technology actually *worked*. Steve made a mental note about hiring scientists who might be able to start unlocking its mysteries, then set their destination coordinates as close to Vincent's home as he dared. Living on the edge of a town, Vincent had far more neighbours than Steve and his family.

"I wonder," Mariko said, as she eyed the teleporter, "what happens if we merge with something else that's already there."

Steve queried the interface. "Apparently," he said after a moment, "the compensators push everything out of the way."

He paused, considering it. The system would make one hell of a weapon, if used properly...or they could simply teleport bombs onto enemy ships. No, somehow he doubted that was possible. If a relatively small terminal could mess up the teleport lock, it was certain that a more advanced race had ways to block teleport signals. They certainly wouldn't share the technology with a band of barbarian scavengers if they didn't have any way to defend against it.

Mariko held herself very still as Steve joined her on the pad, then sent the signal. The starship faded away around them, to be replaced by the edges of a small farm. Steve glanced around quickly, wondering if they had been seen by one of Vincent's hired hands, then led the way towards the farmhouse. Mariko followed, her face surprisingly pale. It was clear that she didn't like teleporting, no matter how efficient it was. But Steve suspected she wouldn't be the only one who had her doubts about the system.

He smiled as he saw Vincent's small collection of older cars parked in the yard. Vincent could have expanded the farm several times over for what he'd paid for the vehicles, to say nothing of the difficulties he faced in keeping them running. But Vincent had always been a little paranoid about new technology, pointing out – when they'd teased him – just how often it had failed on the battlefield. When the Chinese dropped an EMP bomb on the US, he'd said, they'd be glad of his cars then. And, until then, they were a hobby.

Poor bastard, Steve thought, as he reached the farmhouse door and knocked. *You deserved so much better.*

Vincent's wife opened the door and peered at them, alarmed. Steve cursed, inwardly; normally, carefully-trained officers were sent to inform wives and families of their death of their husbands and fathers in combat. It was never a duty he'd wanted, nor was it one he'd ever had to do until now. And he didn't know what to say.

"Ginny," Mariko said, taking the lead, "can we come in?"

Ginny paled, but led them into the sitting room. Vincent had decorated half of it with paintings and drawings of vintage cars, Ginny had decorated the other half with paintings of flowers and her family. She was quite a talented artist, Steve had often considered, when she had time to paint. Normally, the life of a farmwife consumed all of her time. He felt an odd lump in his throat when he saw a painting of Vincent himself, then one of Mariko from years ago. There was something almost waiflike in her face that had faded over the years.

"I'm afraid we have bad news," Steve said. He hesitated, watching her rapidly paling face. What *did* one say to a wife who'd just lost her husband? And a wife who would have to help fake the conditions of her husband's death to avoid attracting attention? "Vincent…"

"Is dead," Ginny finished. She shook, suddenly. "What happened? And why?"

Steve took a breath and explained everything.

"Impossible," Ginny said, when he had finished. She didn't sound as if she believed them. "He can't have died like that, surely."

Steve wondered, suddenly, what she was thinking. He hadn't been as close to Vincent as he was to Mongo, so he had no idea how strong his friend's marriage had been. Did Ginny think that Vincent had run off with a younger woman and convinced Steve to tell his wife a cock-and-bull story to explain his disappearance? But surely no one would come up with such a story and expect it to be believed?

"It's true," Mariko said. She held out a hand as Ginny started to cry, then wrapped her into a hug. Steve watched, awkwardly, as the two women held each other tightly. Female tears had always embarrassed him. "We'll take you to see the body."

"Yes," Steve said. He send the instructions through the interface. "Brace yourself."

Once again, the world dissolved into silver light.

SIX

VIRGINIA, USA

Kevin parked the car outside the house, then took a long breath. Making contact with potential sources had always been part of his job as an intelligence officer, but it had also been fraught with danger. A source might turn out to be a double-agent or nothing more than bait in a trap. And now, even with the headband hidden under his cap, he couldn't help fearing what would happen if his target took what he said to the government. Bracing himself, he walked up the path and knocked firmly on the front door.

A middle-aged man opened it, lifting one eyebrow. Kevin felt an odd spurt of hero-worship – he'd grown up reading the man's books – which he firmly suppressed. There would be time to ask him to autograph his copies later. Instead, he held up the faked ID card and waited for the man to examine it.

"I'm Kevin, Kevin Stuart," he said. "We spoke briefly on the phone. Mr. Glass, I presume?"

Keith Glass nodded, stoking his beard as he studied the card. "That is I," he said. "What can I do for you, Mr. Stuart?"

"Just Kevin, please," Kevin said. "My...employers have a proposition for you."

Glass nodded and turned, leading the way into the house. Kevin followed, keeping his hero-worship under control. Keith Glass had spent ten years in the USN before retiring and starting a new career as an author. His work might not have won any Hugo Awards – they were delightfully politically incorrect – but they had a loyal fan base which grew larger every year. It *had* crossed Kevin's mind that recruiting Glass might put a dampener on new novels, yet they needed someone with military experience and a libertarian bent. Glass seemed to fit the bill nicely.

Once they were in the study – he couldn't help admiring the computer and the massive shelves of books – he opened his briefcase and produced a piece of paper. "I'm afraid we have to ask you to sign this before we can bring you onboard," he said. "It's a standard security agreement."

Glass ran his eyes down the agreement. "This isn't *standard*," he said. "I would be surprised if it was even *legal*."

Kevin shrugged. "Consider it a standard government-issue non-disclosure agreement," he said. "There are no protective safeguards because there is nowhere else you could acquire the data which will be disclosed to you. Should you break the agreement, for whatever reason, the consequences would be dire."

"I see," Glass said. He placed the contract on the desk and looked up, meeting Kevin's eyes. "Why should I sign this agreement?"

"Because this represents an opportunity that will never come your way again," Kevin said. He'd targeted Glass first because he admired the man's writing skills…and his innovative approach to old problems. But there were other science-fiction writers. "This is a chance to join a working group that will have a decisive effect on the world."

"I was told that before, back in 2003," Glass said. "If we had any effect on the world, beyond wasting thousands of valuable trees to print out our reports, I didn't see it."

Kevin scowled, inwardly. Glass had other qualifications than just being a writer used to considering the possibilities of space combat. He'd been involved in the Bush Administration's attempts to light a fire under NASA's collective hindquarters and get the human race heading back out into space, then a civilian attempt to work with commercial space developers to establish bases on the moon. All of those attempts had failed, killed by bureaucracy and the simple shortage of money. The experience had left all of those involved more than a little bitter.

"This is different," Kevin said. He leaned forward, throwing caution to the winds. "I tell you, sir, that this is one opportunity you won't want to miss."

He tapped the agreement. "Should you sign, you will be told the full story," he continued. "If you don't want to be involved after that, which I highly doubt, you will be free to go as long as you keep your mouth shut until full public disclosure. After that...you will spend the rest of your life wishing you'd made a different decision."

Glass met his eyes. "Alien contact," he said. "A crashed UFO?"

Kevin merely smiled. "Sign the agreement," he said. "Sign the agreement and all will be revealed."

Glass picked up a pen and signed it with a flourish. Kevin took it back, stuck it in his briefcase, and produced a cell phone. Glass eyed it, puzzled.

Kevin flipped it open, unable to resist. "Scotty," he said. "Two to beam up."

"You have got to be fucking..."

The world dissolved into silver light, then reformed.

"...Kidding me," Glass finished. "I..."

Kevin smiled. "Welcome onboard, Mr. Glass," he said. "We have a *lot* to show you."

— —

"It seems to have worked," Mongo said. "The cops haven't raised any awkward questions about the accident."

Steve smiled, humourlessly. Mariko had used the medical kits on the starship to repair the damage to Vincent's body, then they'd placed it in one of his old cars and deliberately crashed it off the road. The body had been discovered several metres from the crash site, having been hurled right out of the car and into the ground hard enough to break his neck instantly. With nothing suspicious about the corpse, it would be soon handed back to Ginny and cremated, just to make sure there was nothing left for a later investigation.

"Glad to hear it," he said, finally. One day, the world would know that Vincent had been the first casualty of a war that threatened all of humanity. Until then, people wouldn't raise too many different questions. Everyone who'd known him knew about his hobby of driving old cars. "And Ginny herself?"

"She seems to be coping," Mongo said. "Jayne's staying with her at the moment."

Steve nodded. Once the wives had been told, they'd brought in the children and a handful of relatives. They'd all agreed to keep the starship a secret, although not all of them had wanted to travel to the moon – or anywhere else, for that matter. Steve had accepted their word, then put the newcomers to work scrubbing the decks. The starship needed to be made safe for human inhabitation.

He looked up as Keith Glass stumbled into the compartment, a faintly pole-axed expression on his face. Steve smiled at him, then held out a hand and waited. Eventually, the stunned writer noticed and shook it, firmly.

"Welcome onboard," Steve said. "Will you be joining us?"

Glass nodded, frantically. Steve smiled, inwardly. Kevin had been right. What sort of science-fiction writer worthy of the name would refuse such an opportunity?

"Then let me tell you what we have in mind," Steve said. "Kevin, are you ready to proceed with stage two?"

"I think so," Kevin said. "There shouldn't be any unexpected surprises."

"Keep a teleport lock on you at all times," Steve warned. "But try not to hit the panic button unless there is no choice."

Kevin nodded and left the compartment. "We're planning to found our own nation," Steve said, turning back to Glass. "Are you willing to help us?"

THE ASHCROFT RESIDENTIAL Home was, in Kevin's droll opinion, a testament to the failure of the country to stick up for its wounded veterans. Some had been able to get the best of medical care, others had had no families or friends willing to assist them in overcoming their conditions and returning to civilian life. Kevin felt a chill run down his spine as he walked up to the doorway and stepped into the lobby. If he'd been wounded in combat – or Steve or Mongo – he might well have wound up in a similar place.

No, he corrected himself. *Steve and Mongo would never leave me here.*

The receptionist – a pretty black woman – looked up at him and smiled. "Can I ask your business?"

"I'm here to see Edward Romford," Kevin said. "It's concerning a possible placement for him in the outside world."

"I see," the receptionist said. "I'll have to ask you to fill out these forms."

Kevin sighed – there were four pages to fill in – and cursed the bureaucracy under his breath. He'd never had to rely on the VA for anything, but he'd heard horror stories about wounded ex-soldiers struggling with the paperwork or being penalised for simple mistakes that would have gone unnoticed in a more decent era. Patiently, he filled them in with his cover story and handed them back to the receptionist, who didn't even bother to look at them. Instead, she pointed him towards one of the gardens and waved goodbye.

He rolled his eyes as he walked through the building, noting just how boring it had to be for the wounded veterans. There were televisions and DVD players, but there were also large signs forbidding smoking, drinking and gambling. He had a strong suspicion that the latter two were completely ignored, provided the veterans could get their hands on drink, money and cards. Someone sympathetic might well have smuggled all three of them into the complex.

Outside, the garden was depressingly morbid, despite some attempts to cheer up the veterans with flowers. A handful of wheelchairs were parked on the grass, evenly spaced around the garden, making it harder for the veterans to even talk to one another. They ranged in age, he noted; some of them were younger than him, others were old enough to be his father. He caught sight of the man he wanted and walked forward, coming to a halt in front of his chair.

Up close, it was clear that Edward Romford was no older than Kevin himself – and crippled, crippled beyond the help of human medical science. According to the reports he'd downloaded from the residence home's computers – their security was laughable, although they had no conception of the threat facing them - Edward Romford would never walk again and, without a family to take him in, he had simply been abandoned at the home. But how long would the home be able to look after him?

"Sir," he said. "I come with a proposition."

"Married already," Romford croaked. He wasn't, Kevin knew. His ex-wife had left him long before he'd been wounded, yet another marriage destroyed by the strains deployment placed on it. "Fuck off."

He paused. "Unless you have alcohol," he added, in a softer tone. "Bitch over there says it destroys our brain cells. Why else would we want to drink it?"

Kevin smiled. "You seem to be mentally sound," he said. "Listen carefully."

He leaned closer. "There's a new residence home for veterans, in Montana," he said. It was the cover story they'd established, after they'd worked out that there were no relatives who could simply take Edward Romford away without permission. "They're pioneering a new treatment. You may be able to walk again."

Edward Romford looked up, torn between hope and wariness. He'd long since lost hope of being able to walk again, let alone have a full life.

Kevin understood just how easy it would be to give in to despair and just waste away, no matter how carefully one was treated by the nurses. Now…Romford had to wonder if this was real…or if it was just a trick. But there was no motive to trick him or anyone else.

"You can come with me, now," he added. "Or you can stay here for the rest of your life."

Romford smiled. "Take me away," he said. "Hell, just take me outside the walls and leave me there. I can get away from there on my own."

Kevin winced in pity. The residence home was hardly a prison, provided the inhabitants could walk. As it was, they couldn't get up the steps or out past the gates without help. To someone who had once walked all over Afghanistan, it was a prison, made worse by the fact the nurses were genuinely trying to help. Or were they? Kevin was a cynical person at the best of times and he couldn't keep himself from wondering if the veterans in the garden were meant to catch cold and die. It would take a burden off the residence home's nurses.

"Just don't say a word," he said, as he took the handles of the wheelchair and pushed it forward, back towards the house. "I've already cleared the paperwork."

Somewhat to his disappointment, no one tried to bar their path as he pushed the wheelchair through the building and down to the van. Finding a van designed for a wheelchair had been surprisingly tricky – it seemed that there were additional requirements to drive one – but he'd found one eventually. He helped Romford into the vehicle, secured the wheelchair in place and then clambered into the driver's seat. No one shouted in outrage as they drove out of the car park and onto the road.

"A daring commando raid," Romford observed. He chuckled, harshly. "Bitches never let us leave, even with an escort. I used to pray for terrorists or even muggers, just to put us out of our misery."

"I'm sorry," Kevin said. He felt another pang of bitter guilt – and rage. Surely their country could do better than *this* for their wounded veterans? No wonder Romford had prayed for death. Given the complete absence of security at the residence home, it was a minor miracle that terrorists hadn't attacked the building already. "But it's nearly over now."

He parked the van – they'd been warned against trying to teleport away from a moving vehicle – and then sent the command to the interface. The world became silver – he heard Romford yelp in shock – then resolved, revealing the starship's sickbay. Romford gasped and choked, then coughed violently as Mariko ran forward and caught him. Kevin watched, grimly, as she ran one of the alien scanners over his body.

"You're an angel," Romford said. He sounded dazed. "Am I in heaven?"

"You're in a starship," Mariko said, softly. She looked up at Steve. "I think he's of reasonably sound mind, but there's a lot of damage."

She hesitated. "And I'm not sure about the ethics of some of the proposed treatments."

Kevin could understand. Healing someone was one thing, but taking out their brain and inserting it into a cyborg frame was quite another. He wouldn't have wanted to give up sex and the other pleasures of being human, yet if he was facing certain death would he still make the same decision? And besides, Romford wasn't quite on the verge of death.

Romford produced a croaking sound, drawing their attention. "What sort of treatments?"

Kevin opened his mouth to respond, but Mariko beat him to it. "We can heal you, to some extent," she said. "Or we can transform you into an inhuman cyborg. You would no longer be completely human."

What an elegant sales pitch, Kevin thought, sourly. But did they really *want* cyborgs?

Romford hesitated. "You can heal me?"

"You'll be able to walk again, yes," Mariko confirmed. "It may take some time for you to get used to it, but you'll be able to walk again. And we can fix the other damage at the same time."

"Then please do so," Romford said.

Kevin watched as Mariko helped him into the tube – for all her slight build, she was surprisingly strong – and activated the medical system.

There was a long pause, long enough to make Kevin wonder if something had gone wrong, then the system came to life, scanning Romford's body. He shook his head in awe. Even under the best circumstances, no human treatment could eradicate the effects of those wounds. But for the alien autodoc it was all in a day's work.

"There would be people who would pay millions for this kind of treatment," he said, softly. "We could approach them and..."

"We will," Steve said. "But the vets come first."

"Yes, sir," Kevin said. After seeing the residential home, it had become clear that they needed to reach out for other suitable candidates. With a little effort, and some computer hacking, they could create a whole charity intent on transferring wounded veterans to the ranch, where they could be teleported to the starship. "But there are others we also need to recruit."

"You'll be off to Switzerland next," Steve said. "Don't forget your passport."

Kevin snorted. He'd have given his right arm for the teleporter while he'd been in intelligence, if only to avoid border controls and hazardous journeys across bandit-infested mountains. Maybe the Marines and the Rangers did more fighting – it was hard to argue that – but the intelligence officers were often in more danger. Kevin had been in places where a single word out of place would have ensured his death.

But Switzerland was a reasonably peaceful country.

"I won't need it," he said. "How's Keith settling in?"

"Reading as much as he can download," Steve said. "I think his fans are going to be a little disappointed this year."

Kevin sighed. "They'll tar and feather me if they ever find out," he said. Glass's fans were quite faithful. They wouldn't forgive one of their own for taking their writer away from his work. "Did we get a few samples produced from the fabricators?"

"They're ready," Steve said. "Have fun. And just think of all the air miles you're racking up."

"You mean teleporter miles," Kevin corrected. "And I don't think they really count."

"Probably should," Mariko said, from where she was watching the medical treatment. "Have you considered the long-term effects of having your body broken down to energy and then put back together again?"

"No," Kevin said.

"Nor as anyone else, as far as I can determine," Mariko said. "If it were up to me, I'd have the teleport restricted as much as possible."

"We need it," Steve said, quietly.

Kevin nodded and left the compartment.

SEVEN

Kevin had always liked the Swiss. They were a mountain folk, like some of his own family, and they had a robust attitude towards personal freedom, gun ownership and maintaining their independence despite being surrounded by stronger and often hostile nations. Indeed, they actually were more democratic – for better or worse – than much of the Western World.

They also maintained a largely-secure banking system, despite the pressures of the War on Terror. Their reputation for discretion was everything, even though it worked against the forces of freedom and liberty as much as they worked against dictatorships and tyrannies. An African despot could have a Swiss bank account, crammed with as much foreign aid funds as he could loot from his benefactors, but so could his opponents. And they had far fewer pesky laws on technology transfer than the USA. Quite a few small computing businesses had moved operations to Switzerland in the last few years.

He stopped outside the building and smiled to himself. Wilhelm Technology was a very small firm compared to the giants, but it had operations in both Texas and Switzerland. On the surface, the technology they produced was made in Switzerland, allowing it to avoid export restrictions and government interference. If nothing else, the internet made it much harder to hide when something existed the government didn't want its citizens to have. And then they could simply order it from overseas.

Idiots, he thought, sourly. Small innovative firms like Wilhelm had once been the lifeblood of the American economy. Now, they were often forced out of the market by paperwork and regulations that the bigger industries could simply pay lawyers to avoid. Maybe some of the regulations made sense, maybe they didn't...but they collectively strangled the life out of the small businessman. In desperation, some of them had even started to outsource their production facilities to other countries. Many of the major industries were already gone.

He stepped inside and smiled. There were few people working in the offices; Wilhelm Technology's factories consumed much of their manpower. The receptionist looked at his card and waved him to a seat. He'd expected a wait – most corporate big-shots preferred to keep people waiting, just to make their inferiority clear – but he was met within seconds. But then, he should have expected no less.

Markus Wilhelm had been a USAF Geek when Kevin had first met him, years ago. He'd never flown an aircraft and never would, not even one of the Predator drones, but he'd been extremely important, none the less. The fighter pilots might sneer, yet in an age of increasing technological development and deployment, the computer geek was often more important than the pilot. After he'd finished his first term, Wilhelm had taken his expertise and founded a company of his very own. And he'd seen moderate success since then. It would have been more, Kevin knew, if he'd been able to find additional capital.

"Kevin," Wilhelm said. He was a tall, but slim man, the very picture of a geek. The glasses he wore, he had once claimed, were the same style as Bill Gates had worn before he'd become a billionaire. "It's good to see you again."

"Likewise," Kevin said, as Wilhelm led him into the office. He couldn't help a trickle of nervousness. All the other people he'd contacted for Steve – and the ones Mongo was collecting – were people who could disappear, if necessary, without being missed in a hurry. Wilhelm, on the other hand, would be very noticeable if he vanished. People would ask questions. "I was wondering if you would be interested in a business proposition?"

Wilhelm turned and frowned at him. *"You* are offering me a business proposition?"

"Something like that," Kevin said. "There is a piece of...technology we wish you to market for us. We would split the profits."

"And who," Wilhelm asked, "are you working for?"

Kevin nodded, mentally. He'd expected the question. Unlike the others, Wilhelm had good reason to be suspicious of any offer, particularly with an unverifiable source. The CIA had turned more than one American business into a front operation over the years, doing serious damage to American interests when the truth finally came out. Wilhelm was hardly interested in turning his company into a cover for the Company, particularly given the pressure on his operations from the NSA.

"Someone new," Kevin said, evasively. He reached into his briefcase and produced another NDA. He'd rewritten it for Wilhelm, his wife and any of his employees he felt like inviting into the secret. "Someone who needs your assistance in selling his wares."

Wilhelm's eyes narrowed. "Tell me," he said.

Kevin had considered several cover stories, but most of them would be easily to disprove, given enough incentive to ask questions. And Wilhelm would definitely have such incentive.

"Sign," he said, instead. "And then we will discuss matters."

After a long moment, Wilhelm took the paper and sighed it.

———

"LET ME GET this straight," Wilhelm said, after he'd been teleported to the starship and given a brief tour. "You're founding your own nation and you intend to sell technology to finance your operations?"

"Basically, yes," Steve said. He found himself liking Wilhelm on sight, but it was hard to trust anyone who hadn't seen the sharp end of war completely. "We have various…gadgets we intend to sell, through you if you're interested in helping."

"A case could be made that your actions are treasonous," Wilhelm said, after a long moment. "What do you make of that?"

Steve put firm controls on his temper. "I understand that you are having your own problems with the government," he said. "What do you make of our desire to *avoid* the government?"

Wilhelm nodded, slowly. Steve smiled, recognising he'd scored a point. He wasn't sure he fully understood Kevin's explanations of precisely why Wilhelm Technology was having problems, but he was sure it was because of government interference. Besides, if Wilhelm had been completely committed to the government, he would have stayed and worked for them on a very low wage.

"We'll have to claim they came out of the factory near Bern," Wilhelm said, finally. "We were ramping up production of the new hard drives in any case, so it isn't *completely* implausible. Not being able to file a patent, on the other hand, might raise some eyebrows."

"You can file a confidential patent," Kevin pointed out.

"The government would still have access," Wilhelm reminded him. "But it might not be a bad thing if another company eventually cracked the secret of how the technology worked."

"No, it wouldn't," Steve agreed. The devices they'd intended to suggest were advanced enough to be noticeable, at least ten to twenty years ahead of Earth's finest technology. It was depressing to realise that the alien starship designers probably considered them nothing more than toys. "How quickly could you start selling them?"

Wilhelm considered. "Maybe a month or two," he said. "We *could* claim that the whole project was so secret hardly anyone knew about it — that isn't uncommon in the computer world — which would allow us to start selling in two weeks, but that would probably raise eyebrows. Few secrets remain secret indefinitely."

Steve smiled, tiredly. "Are you interested, then?"

"I'd be very interested," Wilhelm said. "But I'd also be interested in relocating to the moon once you have a colony established. What sort of laws do you intend to have covering commercial operations?"

"We haven't thought that far ahead, yet," Steve admitted.

"Better get thinking about it," Wilhelm said. "There are quite a few possibilities that don't include alien technology, if you have free access to outer space. Zero-gravity production, for one thing, would allow us to produce all sorts of improvements on current technology and machined components. And then there would be no need to worry about pollution."

He paused. "You do realise that setting up a lunar base probably contravenes the Outer Space Treaty?"

"I didn't sign it," Steve said. "And nor did the aliens."

Wilhelm blinked. "I beg your pardon?"

"There are thousands of alien races in the galaxy," Steve said. He learned forward, meeting the younger man's eyes. "As far as we have been able to determine through searching the alien database, the only law that is actually enforced regularly is a ban on genocide. And even that may be a bit iffy.

"We cannot rely on the aliens blindly accepting *our* laws when they enter *our* solar system," he added, coldly. "The galaxy appears to operate on the principle that might makes right – and they are far mightier than ourselves. If we're lucky, the best we can hope for is to become a protectorate, just like a newly-discovered tribe of natives in some godforsaken jungle lucky enough not to live near something a more advanced nation wants. If we're unlucky, we will be enslaved or crushed beneath an alien boot heel. We need to make this work, Markus, before we run out of time. And we cannot rely on the government to do anything other than impede us or smother the effort under countless studies of how to do it quickly.

"To hell with absurd treaties, to hell with charges of treason. I want to win, I want to safeguard humanity's future. And the only way to do that is to use this opportunity as ruthlessly as possible."

Wilhelm studied him for a long moment. "Very well," he said, finally. "I will join you."

"Excellent," Steve said. He nodded to Kevin. "My lovely assistant" – Kevin snorted, rudely – "will work with you to determine what would be the most...productive items to enter the market."

"I could advance you a loan now," Wilhelm offered. "I may not be Bill Gates, but I do have quite a bit of money stashed away."

"That would be very helpful," Kevin said, before Steve could say a word. "We're sitting on the largest gold mine in human history and we have barely a cent to our names."

Wilhelm smiled. "It will be done," he said. "Can I see one of the aliens?"

"Our sole captive," Steve said, standing. "Come with me."

"They don't seem very clever," Wilhelm observed, as he followed Steve through the alien corridors. "To let you take control of their ship so easily."

Kevin smirked. "How many people do you know who use ADMIN as the username and PASSWORD as the password?"

"Point taken," Wilhelm said. "Half the problems I handled while I was in the service were caused by someone neglecting basic security pre-cautions. One idiot actually took a USB stick he'd found in the trash into the Pentagon and inserted it into his computer. The Chinese must have laughed their heads off when they realised how it had happened."

Steve turned to look at him. "The Chinese?"

"They're constantly poking the edge of the electronic fence," Wilhelm said. "You won't believe just how much crap they've tried to pull, from inserting spyware into almost every computer produced in China to pay-ing officers to obtain passwords and admin permissions for them. There was a whole flurry a few years ago about a remarkably nasty computer worm that might well have come straight from China. We never really got to the bottom of that, no matter what we did."

He shrugged. "Or it could be the Russians," he added. "Asymmetric warfare is their *thing*."

"But it still seems odd for aliens not to notice the dangers."

"This race seems to be permanently trapped in the Dark Ages," Steve said, as they reached the alien's cabin. The cleaning effort hadn't quite reached this part of the ship; he saw Wilhelm wrinkle his nose as he smelled the decomposing alien meat in the air. "Just like some human groups, for that matter."

"True," Kevin agreed. "You know we used to offer laptops to school-children in Africa? The idea was that they would develop their talents and join the global information age."

Wilhelm lifted his eyebrows, but said nothing.

"We did a survey, a year after we donated the laptops," Kevin explained. "Only a handful of children ever managed to learn how to use them properly. The remainder were either junked or turned into portable lights for the women who cook. They – the laptops – were just so far outside their experience that they had no idea what to do with them."

"And these aliens are the same," Wilhelm mused. "You know, we could probably sell some crap to the aliens if that's the case."

Steve nodded. "Something to think about, if we live that long," he agreed. He opened the door to the alien's room. "Meet...the alien."

He smiled as Wilhelm gasped in shock. It was a familiar reaction by now; men who took the teleporter in their stride found themselves caught short by the mere presence of the alien. A couple who happened to be deathly scared of spiders had recoiled when they'd seen the alien, then had to be given alcohol to calm their nerves. But then, after meeting deadly spiders in Iraq and Afghanistan, the fears were actually somewhat logical.

"Let me know when you come to an agreement," Steve said to Kevin, then left the compartment. "I have to check up on Edward."

He made his way down to the medical bay, then smiled. In a handful of hours, Mariko had turned it into something more suitable for human use, scrubbing the decks clean and installing a couple of beds she'd had brought up from the ranch. The older kids had helped, captivated by the thought of learning from alien computers and neural interfaces rather than at their desks, along with the rest of the children in the region. He smiled as he saw Edward, lying on one of the beds.

"I feel fine," Romford protested. "But she threatened to cuff me to the bed if I tried to leave."

"She's the boss in this sickbay," Steve said, firmly. "How are you feeling?"

"Well, I can feel my legs and my groin," Romford said. "That's…very definitely an improvement. And I can actually walk, when she lets me."

He paused. "Does she have a sister?"

"She never talks to her family," Steve said. He wasn't surprised by the question. If he'd lost the ability to have sex and then regained it, he would have wanted to have sex as soon as possible too. "But there will be other women coming up here."

"Or there will be shore leave, I hope," Romford said. He sat upright, looking down at his hairless chest. "She says the hair will grow back in its own sweet time."

"She's probably right," Steve said. Romford was certainly *sounding* a whole lot better. The croak was gone from his voice, for one thing. "What else did she say?"

"She said he ought to stay in bed," Mariko's voice said. Steve turned to see her standing behind him, her hands on her hips. "I know this autodoc is likely to put us all out of business, but I would infinitely prefer to have you lying down until I am *absolutely* sure it does what it says on the tin."

"Yes, boss," Romford said, reluctantly.

Mariko caught Steve's hand and pulled him into the next compartment. "I don't tell you what to do on the ranch," she snapped. "Don't tell me what to do in my sickbay!"

An angry retort came to Steve's lips, but he forced it down. "What's wrong?"

Mariko sighed. "I checked him carefully," she said. "I did every test I could think of with the equipment I brought up from the ranch. And you know what I found?"

Steve shook his head.

"Perfection," Mariko said. "His spine has been repaired, several gun-shot wounds are no longer detectable, a small problem with his heart has been fixed, even the excess fat he gained since being forced into the residence has been removed. The autodoc did a *perfect* job, well beyond anything the best surgeon on Earth could do."

She sighed. "This thing will put all the surgeons on Earth out of business," she added. "And there are quite a few other things it can do. Do you realise that we could start producing cancer cures now? Or a modified virus that could destroy AIDS? Or...hell, Steve, I want to improve the kids. What sort of mother would I be if I let this opportunity pass me by?"

"Improve the kids?" Steve asked. "How?"

"All sorts of little genetic tweaks," Mariko said. "They'd have perfect eyesight for the rest of their lives. They'd live at least two hundred years with minimal age-related decay. They'd be completely immune to everything from the Common Cold to AIDS. They'd never really put on weight or lose their muscle tone; hell, I think even their mental agility can be modified and improved. And this...*thing* just did it! I asked for a list of options and it provided them, almost at once."

She looked up at him, plaintively. "Steve, honey, this scares the hell out of me."

Steve frowned. He didn't understand. "Why?"

"One thing you learn as a doctor," Mariko said, "is that, on average, there are no real differences between different races – different human races, I should say. But with this technology...it wouldn't be long until people start creating superhumans, men and women who are smarter, stronger and just plain more capable than the rest of the human race. Or you could start creating slaves, people who really are good for nothing more than grunt labour, people who are always obedient to those they know to be their masters because servitude is engineered into them.

"This is Pandora's Box, honey. And once you open it you can't stuff the contents back inside."

She hugged him, tightly. "That's why I'm scared," she admitted. "This is going to change the world. Everything will change."

Steve nodded, hugging her back. Now, he was scared too.

EIGHT

LUNAR BASE, THE MOON

"Now this," Steve declared, "is impressive."

"Glad to hear it," Graham Rochester said. "And glad you decided to look in on us."

Steve smiled. Rochester had been a British Army Combat Engineer before being seriously wounded in Afghanistan and sent back to face the tender mercies of the British National Health Service. He'd been as badly crippled as Romford – perhaps worse – and the offer of a new life had been too much for him to refuse. Unlike Romford, he'd decided to become an outright cyborg. One of his arms had been replaced by a cyborg arm that whirred and clicked at inappropriate moments, his eyes had been replaced by sensors and his skin had been coated in a material that allowed him to survive in vacuum. He claimed it was far better than mere humanity.

"I was taught it was always a bad idea to let subordinates think I didn't care about them," Steve said. "But you've done wonders in a single month."

"That's what the Royal Engineers are for," Rochester said. "You should see some of the bases we had to put together in Afghanistan at a moment's notice. Compared to that, this is a snap."

Steve nodded, his gaze sweeping across the surface of the moon. It looked oddly dirty, with modified human vehicles and mining tools scattered everywhere. The foundations of Heinlein Colony were under the lunar surface – it would provide additional protection and camouflage for the colony – but enough was visible for him to know that work was proceeding smoothly.

"We had to set up the living quarters first," Rochester continued. "Not everyone wanted to become a full cyborg, after all. Once they were done, we started to expand the base and look for sources of raw materials. Once we found ice…"

He smirked. "This base is well on the way to becoming self-sustaining," he added. "So much for NASA's little fears, right?"

Steve nodded. As soon as Heinlein Colony was ready to take a small number of settlers, he'd had two of the fabricators and their alien prisoner moved to the settlement, along with half of the supplies the Hordesmen had gathered over the years. Added to the supplies they'd purchased from Earth, Heinlein Colony would *definitely* be capable of feeding itself indefinitely soon enough, while continuing to expand under the lunar surface.

"We've actually got a couple of people who think we can *terraform* the moon," Rochester said, as he led the way through the airlock. "There's quite a bit of ice at the lunar poles; they think we can use it to create a thin atmosphere, then build up plants on the soil that will eventually thicken the atmosphere to the point humans can breathe normally."

Steve shook his head in disbelief. "Really?"

"Sure," Rochester said. "It's definitely theoretically possible, but it would also be extremely visible. And we'd have to built up a magnetic field. That's going to be the real bugger."

Steve scowled. One disadvantage of having to keep everything secret was the very real danger of being spotted from Earth. Heinlein Colony was on the far side of the moon, permanently out of sight, but the shuttles and modified tractors they used often went to the near side, where they could be seen. Fortunately, he doubted anyone would believe a word of it unless there were hard recordings of the observation. But who knew what would happen if someone on Earth did observe their presence? Maybe they'd think it was an alien settlement.

Inside, he couldn't help thinking of the abandoned mines near the ranch in Montana, the ones his father had forbidden him to go near on pain of a thrashing. The tunnels were cut from the lunar rock, carved out with automated tools then left bare and almost unmarked. Someone had carved a handful of corridor references into the crossing points, but nothing else. It would need to be made more hospitable, Steve decided, as they walked down under the lunar surface. Some of the kids would have to be hired to draw or paint pictures for the walls.

"We've set up the barracks in here," Rochester said, as they paused in front of a solid hatch. "I didn't want to take any risks with our sleeping personnel, so the barracks is actually a self-contained survival room in its own right. Should there be an atmospheric leak outside, the barracks will seal itself."

He keyed a switch and the hatch hissed open, revealing another airlock. Steve waited patiently until the first hatch had closed, then smiled as the second hatch opened, allowing him to see into the barracks. It looked, very much, like a military barracks, complete with metal bunk beds and a handful of showers at the far end of the room. The only real difference was the row of laptops on a desk along one wall and the rubber on the ceiling.

"We had quite a few people bang their heads because they weren't used to the lunar gravity," Rochester explained. "So we ended up putting rubber on the roof to ensure they wouldn't be seriously hurt. It does help, a little. I've insisted that no one gets to actually do any work for at least a week after their arrival, giving them time to get used to conditions here. We had some accidents when we were trying to use the tractors on the moon because they were designed for Earth."

He gave Steve a challenging look, as if he expected to face disagreement. Steve merely nodded. Rochester *was* the man on the spot, after all, and he'd accomplished miracles in barely a month. There was no point in disagreeing with one of his decisions, particularly one that was clearly suited to their current conditions.

"Morale is generally high," Rochester said, when it was clear Steve wasn't going to say anything. "The only real complaint comes from the unmarried men, who wish there were more women up here. Most of them are newly rejuvenated and want to put their dicks to work somewhere other than the shower."

Steve had to smile. If he'd been in his late seventies and then been returned to his early twenties, he'd start chasing women too. "Have there been any real problems?"

"No, but there will be," Rochester said. "So far, the few unmarried girls we have here have earned a lot of attention. But hormones and men and tight conditions are asking for trouble."

Steve scowled, remembering some of the stories from Afghanistan. Everyone knew someone who knew someone who had a friend who'd got into trouble with a woman on one of the bigger military bases, one of the places where it was impossible to believe that one was in the middle of a war zone. Despite all the rules and regulations, hundreds of women had been sent home for falling pregnant. The coldly practical part of him knew that brothels for the troops would have been a great idea, but it wasn't something the government could ever allow. There would have been an outcry from their more progressive factions if they'd tried.

But *Steve* didn't have to worry about that, did he?

Mariko might have a few things to say about it, he thought, a moment later. *And so might Jayne.*

"We'll have to give some thought to starting a brothel," he said, finally. "But it won't be as easy as finding veterans and space enthusiasts to work on our colony."

"Plenty of desperate young women out there," Rochester said, as they turned and walked back through the airlock. "And the guys here *will* behave. I've already threatened to tear off the testicles of anyone who sexually harasses one of my people."

Steve nodded in agreement. "Any other problems?"

"Not really," Rochester said. "There were some grumbles over restrictions on internet use at first, but we eventually overcame them once the system was properly set up. However, sooner or later, there will be a leak. Someone will say something they shouldn't on an open system."

Kevin thought it wouldn't matter, Steve recalled. They'd discussed the issue several times, when it became apparent that the alien database wouldn't be enough to distract everyone from demanding access to Earth's internet. Kevin had pointed out that there was so much fantasy online that no one would believe a claim that someone was talking from the moon. If someone could claim to be a time traveller, or a man could pretend to be a teenage girl, few people would believe the truth. Besides, sooner or later, it would no longer matter.

He leaned forward. "You have the system *completely* secure?"

"Oh, yes," Rochester assured him. "Everything going to Earth and back again goes through one of the alien systems. If someone wants to hack into our computers they won't get any further, at least not with human-level tech. We've also developed a system for scanning all files for potential problems *before* allowing them to move through the buffers. Standard precautions, naturally, but you won't believe just how much trouble carelessness has caused in the past."

Steve smiled. Two years ago, one of the kids had downloaded a pornographic video from the internet that had turned out to have a nasty virus attached. Kevin had had to fix it, while Steve delivered a sharp lecture on the dangers of downloading *anything* from the internet without taking proper precautions. And then they'd had to have the Talk. The thought of having to have it again with grown men was definitely cringe-worthy.

They stopped outside another airlock. "The alien is inside," Rochester said. "He's been quite helpful, but he's also quite ignorant. The sociologists think he truly has no idea of the depth of his own ignorance."

Steve, who had met a great many people with the same problem, nodded. "What sort of precautions have you taken against escape?"

"The room is shielded, then held on a separate system from the rest of the colony," Rochester said. "If the sociologists or anyone else wish to speak with him, they do so with guards monitoring everything that takes place inside the cell. He can't take a piss without us knowing about it."

"Good," Steve said.

"He also seems to have developed something akin to Stockholm Syndrome," Rochester added. "The sociologists think he expected to be killed as soon as he was captured, perhaps after interrogation. Instead, we've taken fairly good care of him. I've seen similar patterns among captured Iraqis and Afghanis."

Steve nodded. A distant cousin of his, an MP, had been charged with guarding prisoners in the wake of the invasion of Iraq. The prisoners had almost collapsed in fear when they'd been told to dig latrines, even though they were desperately necessary. It had taken some time before the MPs had realised the prisoners thought they were being asked to dig their own graves. Once the prisoners had realised they weren't going to be shot out of hand – their former leaders had told them the Americans would kill anyone they captured – they'd relaxed a great deal. Some of them had even gone on to lead successful careers in the new Iraq.

"Monitor me," Steve said. "I'll call when I want out."

Inside, the alien's chamber was hot and moist, as if he'd stepped right into a sauna. There was a faintly unpleasant smell, like rotting meat, in the air. The alien himself was squatting against one wall, one clawed hand tap-tapping at an Ipad and trying to play a game. It – *he*, Steve reminded himself – had requested access to the internet, or a terminal with a translator, but Steve hadn't been willing to allow either. But the alien *was* learning to read English, even if he would never be able to speak it. They just weren't designed to speak human tongues.

"Greetings," the alien said, through the translator. The security officers had suggested taking it away when the alien wasn't talking to anyone, but Kevin had argued against the suggestion and Steve had accepted his arguments. "Thank you for visiting me."

"You're welcome," Steve said. He found it hard to understand what the alien must be feeling – there were no other aliens in the colony – but he couldn't help feeling sorry for the creature, no matter what its superiors had intended to do. "How are you coping with living here?"

The alien produced a spluttering noise. "I am not being hurt or killed," he said. "But not all of your people believe what I say."

Steve had to smile. The sociologists Kevin had recruited were sensible people, men and women who had actually done field work rather than learning everything from politically-correct books. But, from some of their reports, even the most sensible of them had great difficulty in wrapping his head around what passed for culture among the Hordes. What sort of race could *live* like that, he'd asked, when there was so much potential in the galaxy?

But being poor often leads to a stubborn pride, Steve thought. *Or perhaps to a helpless despair.*

It seemed fitting, he suspected. The Horde knew, at a deep level, just how inferior they were to races that actually *produced* starships and weapons for themselves. They were dependent on those they considered their soft social inferiors, so dependent that a sudden withdrawal of support would leave the Hordesmen to fade away and die. But, at the same time, they did nothing to overcome their dependency. It would be a tacit admission that their lives were far from perfect.

"You're the first non-human they've spoken to," Steve said. The alien interface had noted that there were almost ten thousand intelligent races known to exist, a number far beyond Steve's ability to grasp emotionally. Compared to the sheer number of aliens out there, humanity's eight billion souls weren't even a drop in the bucket. "We have no experience with anyone outside our own race."

"You have been lucky," the alien stated. "Open contact might well have destroyed you."

Steve nodded. It still might, even if humanity avoided a military invasion or becoming a protectorate of a more advanced power. The sudden discovery that there were thousands of intelligent races in the galaxy, almost all of them far more powerful than humanity, would shock the entire planet. Some would see the presence of aliens as a challenge, Steve knew, others would quail away from the stars. What was left for humanity to achieve, they'd ask, if the aliens had done it all first?

"It might have done," he agreed, finally. "Is there anything we can do to make your stay more comfortable?"

The alien spluttered again. "These quarters are perfect," he said. "You do not have to improve them for me."

"If you need anything, just ask," Steve said. He glanced into the bathroom. The alien had requested a bathtub large enough for several humans to share, rather than one of the showers in the human barracks. From the reports, the sociologists were still arguing if the request constituted luxury or a simple necessity for alien life. "We are quite happy to provide."

"In exchange for answering questions," the alien said. "Why are so many of your people unwilling to believe that I am telling the truth?"

Steve hesitated, trying to put it into words. "There are some people, no matter how smart, who have a view of the universe that is focused on us," he said. "Not just humanity, a subset of humanity. They have problems coming to terms with the fact there are groups of *humans* who refuse to behave as their models suggest, let alone non-human life forms such as yourself. And when theory comes up against reality, some of them even think that reality must be wrong."

"Like one of our Horde Commanders," the alien said.

"It certainly sounds that way," Steve agreed. "Thank you for seeing me."

"I wish to learn more about your people," the alien said, as Steve turned back to the airlock. "Can you not provide me with information?"

Steve hesitated. Part of him wanted to restrict what the alien knew, part of him suspected that if they lost Heinlein Colony, they would have lost everything. But he didn't want to provide the alien with any non-human technology. It might have an unexpected sting in the tail.

The answer struck him a moment later and he swore, inwardly. "I'll have you provided with a device that will provide information," he said.

There were computers for the blind, computers that read information to their users. One of them would suffice for the alien. In hindsight, they should have thought of it earlier. "It should help answer your questions."

He stepped back through the airlock, then waited until it closed behind him. "Have them dig up a computer for the blind," he ordered. "But no internet access, nothing that can possibly provide a security risk."

"Understood," Rochester said, gravely. "Do you wish to see the Theory Lab now?"

Steve nodded. "Yes," he said. He was looking forward to hearing what Keith Glass and his band of researchers had come up with to expand their operations. They'd already proposed several ideas for making more money on Earth. "It should be interesting."

"Very interesting," Rochester said. "Do you realise we can make diamonds in orbit? There is an endless demand for diamonds of certain specifications and we can produce them, very cheaply. And then there's the supplies of raw materials from the asteroids, once we start mining them. They're even working out a Homesteading Kit for anyone who wants to set up as an asteroid miner. Once we get them out to the asteroid belt..."

He broke off as Steve's communicator buzzed. "Steve, this is Mongo," Mongo said. "You need to get back to the ship. We may have a serious problem."

Steve looked up at Rochester. "I'm sorry to cut this short," he said, "but I need to go."

"Don't worry about it," Rochester said. He gave Steve a smile that looked somehow inhuman on his modified face. "Give them hell."

NINE

Washington DC, USA

"**T**hat's odd," Jürgen Affenzeller muttered.

It was a largely unacknowledged fact that the Department of Homeland Security kept an eye on military veterans. The rationale for the policy had never been fully codified and, indeed, had started out as a sop to political correctness. Besides, veterans were trained in using weapons, they often had experience in urban combat and they sometimes suffered from PTSD and other problems after their service. It was just common sense, the DHS had argued, to keep an eye on them.

Jürgen had never really believe in the logic, if there *was* any logic in the decision. Indeed, it made much more sense, to him, to keep an eye on radical Islamic groups operating within the United States. But the simple truth was that any hint of racial profiling would cause a political shitstorm, while veterans had far fewer people willing to go to bat for them. It made little sense, but politics rarely did. Besides, he had a wife and two small daughters to feed and raising a stink about it would have cost him his job.

He'd never seen much of anything to convince him that there was a real danger. Sure, some veterans were politically active, proud members of the Gun Community and very opposed to any threats to the Second

Amendment, but few of them seemed *dangerous*. Indeed, veterans were often stanchly patriotic, unwilling to consider using violence against their own countrymen. Compared to some of the noises coming from radical groups – and *they* had expanded rapidly in the wake of the economic crisis – there was no strong reason to worry about the vets. But he didn't seem to have any choice.

But now there *was* something odd flowing into the system.

It was hard, almost impossible, to move around the United States without leaving *some* kind of electronic trace. The DHS – and NSA and several other government organisations – monitored human traces, looking for patterns that might signify trouble. It was, in many ways, a flawed replacement for having men and women out on the beat, but it did have the advantage of causing almost no disturbance at all for the suspect to pick up on. Quite a few criminal cases had been blown, Jürgen knew, because the suspect had seen the FBI agent shadowing him and panicked.

He looked down at the list of reports, trying to put them together into a coherent whole. His instincts *told* him there was a pattern, even if he couldn't see it clearly. But what did it signify?

A large number of veterans claimed benefits of one kind or another from the government. Over the last three weeks, a surprisingly high number – over three *thousand* – had stopped claiming benefits. It was an odd pattern, made all the odder by the simple fact that most of those veterans seemed to have vanished. They weren't dead, as far as he could tell; they'd just dropped out of sight. And then he'd cross-referenced the data and discovered that half of the veterans in the list were crippled. They had been unable to return to a normal life.

So where had they gone?

A call to a handful of residence homes revealed that the men had been transferred, without notice, to another residence home in Montana. Jürgen had frowned, then checked with Montana and discovered that there was no such residence home. But when he did yet another cross-reference, it became clear that the veterans who weren't crippled had *also* gone to Montana. And then they'd dropped off the grid.

He shook his head in disbelief, then started poking around the data. A man called Kevin Stuart had visited thirty of the nursing homes, then he'd been replaced by several other men...all of whom were included on the list of disappeared veterans. And veterans weren't the only ones. Keith Glass, a writer of military science-fiction, had *also* vanished...and so had a large percentage of the Space Settlement Society. Some of them were vets, others were civilians who had been very involved with NASA and civilian space programs...there was a pattern, Jürgen was sure. But what did it all mean?

Shaking his head, he put a brief report together and emailed it to his superior officer. Maybe there was nothing going on, maybe it was just a false alarm. But he honestly couldn't see how nearly four thousand men, some of them crippled, could fit into a relatively small ranch. They wouldn't have anything like enough water, for starters, or food...unless they were shipping it in by the truckload. But why would anyone do that?

Five minutes later, he received two emails in return. The first one, from his boss, ordered him to cooperate with the second email. Puzzled, he opened the second email and discovered orders to report to Fort Meade, ASAP. The NSA? It made no sense to him at all. What would a number of missing veterans have to do with the National Security Agency?

"THANK YOU FOR coming," the NSA agent said, when he arrived at Fort Meade. He hadn't bothered to give his name. "Your investigation has crossed paths with one of our investigations and we need to share information."

Jürgen kept his opinion of that to himself. The NSA wasn't known for sharing information with anyone, unless someone with real authority got behind them and pushed. It was far more likely, he knew, that they'd take what he'd found and then order him to keep his mouth shut in future. It would annoy his boss – the Department of Homeland Security desperately needed a big win, something they could use to justify their existence – but crossing the NSA was considered inadvisable. They could end his career with a word or two in the right ears.

"For the moment, you are being seconded to my team," the agent continued. "You'll be given papers to sign later, but for the moment keep your mouth shut outside the team, understand?"

"Yes," Jürgen said, tightly. "I don't suppose I have a choice."

"No," the agent agreed. "You don't."

Jürgen gritted his teeth, then followed the agent down through a series of security checks and into a SCIF facility deep under the building. It was less impressive than he'd expected, he decided, as he looked around; there was a large table, a handful of comfortable chairs and a simple projector and computer terminal. But it would be secure, he knew, as he took the seat he was offered and waited. No one outside the room would be able to eavesdrop on them, nor would any recording devices work within the room's field. It was as secure as human ingenuity could make it.

"We will be briefing a handful of *very* high-ranking officials on the progress of a monitoring program," the agent added. "Say nothing until I call on you to speak, then stick to the facts alone."

Jürgen sighed, then pasted a blank expression on his face as the officials filed into the room and made themselves coffee before sitting down. Two of them wore military uniforms, the remainder civilian suits; he discovered, not entirely to his surprise, that he recognised a handful of the civilians. But then, the National Security Advisor *was* a well-known political figure. And yet…why was he *here?*

"Over the past month, there have been several investigations into odd technology appearing from overseas," the agent said, opening the briefing. "Our investigations eventually collided with a DHS investigation, which made the entire problem considerably more worrisome."

He tapped a switch, activating the projector. A picture of a USB stick-like device appeared in front of them. "This, gentlemen, is a Wilhelm Tech Wireless Internet Dongle," he said. "The devices were introduced two weeks ago in a low-key manner, mainly through internet forums and tech sites, then sold from Switzerland through mail order. On the surface, these devices are nothing more extraordinary than any other form of internet connection system. However, they have various…attributes that made them potentially very dangerous."

Jürgen frowned. An internet dongle? How was that related to missing veterans?

"The dongles have what is probably best described as an extreme range," the agent continued. "To put it in perspective, they are capable of reaching access points located within thousands of miles of the dongle – we don't know where - and logging on. Once they have logged on, they have a *very* high rate of transmission and access to the internet, allowing downloads to be completed faster than ever before. Finally, the signals they use are almost completely undetectable except at very close range."

He paused for effect. "What this means," he said, "is that anyone using one of these systems can browse the internet without being traced or monitored by our systems."

"Anyone," one of the unnamed officers said.

"Anyone," the agent confirmed. "The packaging claims a considerable degree of improvement over previous designs, but some tests have revealed that the claims are…well, understated. *Heavily* understated. But the geek communities have already figured out how to use the dongles to surf the internet without any restrictions at all. The results have been interesting – and quite worrying."

"I see," the National Security Advisor said. "Where are these things coming from?"

"Wilhelm Tech," the agent said. "They're a small company, incorporated in both the States and Switzerland, with a good reputation for producing pieces of advanced technology at reasonable prices. We've asked the Swiss to investigate, but they're stalling. They see no reason to enforce our laws for us, nor to kill the goose that lays the golden eggs. By being incorporated in two places, they evade most of our laws governing technology transfer."

He hesitated. "Something like this should have been born secret," he said, referring to the government's rule that certain pieces of technology, no matter who produced them, were automatically considered classified. "Instead, the news is out and spreading."

One of the unnamed civilians leaned forward. "Can't you duplicate the technology?"

"Not so far," the agent admitted. "So far, we have acquired two dongles and tried to take them both apart. They both shattered on the table, leaving us with a pile of debris and a mystery. But we can tell you some odd things about the tech. For a start, while Wilhelm Tech is on the cutting edge of computer software, these devices seem an order of magnitude more advanced than anything known, even to us.

"This led to an investigation of Wilhelm Tech," he continued. "We discovered that they purchased a considerable amount of supplies from various produces in the States..."

"That's a good thing, isn't it?" The civilian asked. "It's far better to plough the money back into the States than send it to China."

"It may be," the agent said. "But their shopping list is rather odd... and it's all being shipped to a ranch in Montana. The same ranch where a number of veterans seem to be going – and then vanishing from sight."

He nodded to Jürgen. "Tell them what you told us."

Jürgen took a breath. He'd never had to brief such a high-ranking group before; hell, he'd never had to brief anyone more senior than his boss. His throat felt dry, but there was no time to take a sip of water.

"To summarise a complicated issue," he said, "a large number of veterans, some of whom should have been unable to move, have transferred themselves to the Stuart Ranch in Montana. Since then, there has been no trace of their existence on Earth, nor does there seem to be enough facilities on the Ranch to take care of them. We have been unable to determine what might be happening there."

He sat down. The agent stood again.

"We researched the ranch extensively when we realised that it was involved in the growing mystery," the agent said. "There were some worrying signs. Steve Stuart, the current owner of the Ranch, resigned from the Marine Corps in 2013, following an…incident in Afghanistan. Since them, he has been a regular commenter on conservative and liberal blogs, arguing in favour of the Second Amendment, small government and consistent law enforcement. He was involved, politically speaking, in a successful attempt to recall a local politician and force him out of office.

"Furthermore, his uncle was actually the target of an ATF investigation in the wake of the Oklahoma City bombing. Apparently, he and his family knew McVeigh personally, although the investigators concluded that they'd known nothing about the plot. The uncle in question was an army explosives expert, who would have made sure to produce a proper bomb that would have taken out the whole building."

There was a pause. One of the civilians finally broke it. "Has Steve Stuart himself come to ATF's attention?"

"Not directly," the agent said, "but he's on a watch list."

Jürgen sighed. Anyone who supported the Second Amendment publically was on an ATF watch list. It didn't matter how they supported it, or how many guns they possessed; hell, there were pro-gun campaigners who owned no guns who were still targeted for observation.

"He isn't a member of the NRA, for what it's worth," the agent said. "He *was* a member, but resigned two years ago, claiming that the organisation had allowed politics to impede its primary purpose for existence. Some of his family are members, however, while others are members of other pro-gun groups. One of them is even a member of Jews for the Preservation of Firearms Ownership.

"He's also a licensed instructor in small arms, particularly concealed carry, with an enviable safety record. So far, we have been unable to locate any complaints against him, save a report that he insisted on someone using a gun more suited to her hand. It never went any further than grousing."

The agent looked from face to face. "But we are faced with a disturbing mystery," he said. "We have a large number of men, experienced with weapons, who have vanished off the face of the Earth. We have pieces of technology that could easily be used against us, seemingly connected to the disappearing men. And we have a ranch owned by someone who cannot be counted a wholehearted friend of the government. I believe, sirs, that we should act quickly to counter this threat."

But you don't even know there is a threat, Jürgen thought. He had to admit it was odd – where *were* the men going? – but it didn't necessarily mean it was a threat. Maybe there *was* a retirement home on the ranch for the veterans. Or perhaps there was a perfectly innocent explanation, one that might be lost if the DHS troopers charged in like stormtroopers and started a fight. Somehow, he doubted the ranchers would come quietly. There were too many horror stories about ATF task forces shooting the wrong people for anyone to be complacent about surrendering themselves to their custody.

He listened as the debate surged backwards and forwards. None of the senior officials seemed inclined to rule out a raid, even though a couple of them suggested talking openly to Wilhelm Tech first. After all, maybe a deal could be made. The technology could be controlled or put to work serving the government, if enough money was made available. But instead they seemed inclined to stampede towards a fateful choice.

They need a win too, he realised, suddenly. NSA had been entwined in scandals for the last five years, ever since Edward Snowden had fled the USA for Russia, carrying with him a whole series of uncomfortable revelations about the NSA's domestic spying program. If NSA couldn't keep itself relevant, Congress and the Senate might load new restrictions on its activities…or they might simply close the agency down altogether, throwing out the baby as well as the bathwater. No, whatever was going on with Wilhelm Tech and the Stuart Ranch – and the missing veterans – they couldn't afford to talk. They had to be seen to be taking action.

— —

"THE DEPARTMENT OF Homeland Security will be supplying the SWAT team," the agent said, afterwards. "You'll be riding along with them, as will I. We'll drop a mass of troopers on top of the farm and take everyone into custody, then sort them out later. The warrants are broad enough to allow us to hold them for weeks, if necessary."

Jürgen stared at him. Years of bureaucratic infighting had finally given the DHS teeth, without having to rely on the FBI, but the SWAT team had never actually been deployed for real. "Is this even *legal?*"

"We have a search warrant for the ranch, based on the information you supplied," the agent assured him. "We even took a look at it through satellites and discovered no trace of any veterans. Indeed, there was hardly anyone in sight, apart from a handful of ranch hands. No kids, no women, no nothing. Between you and me, this is starting to look very sinister. It could even be another Branch Davidian compound."

"Maybe," Jürgen said, doubtfully. "What religion are these people?"

"Nothing registered, as far as we have been able to determine," the agent said. He reached out and slapped Jürgen on the shoulder. "Whatever is going on, someone is trying to keep it a secret and that generally means trouble. And I really don't like the presence of that advanced technology."

He strode off towards the small jet that would be carrying them to Montana. After a long moment, Jürgen followed, gritting his teeth. What the hell had he started? Armed stormtroopers were about to crash into a ranch on suspicion of…what, exactly? They could have poked around the edges of the compound, sent in a couple of agents, or even walked up to the door and asked, keeping the SWAT team in reserve. Instead, they were about to attack with loaded weapons. It was far too possible that innocent civilians were about to be caught in the crossfire, further undermining the reputation of both the DHS and NSA.

The NSA will blame it on us, he thought, coldly. *If this goes to shit, it will be our fault and our fault alone.*

And he couldn't escape the feeling that they were about to make a very big mistake.

TEN

MONTANA, USA

"All right," Steve said, as he strode into the starship's makeshift CIC. "What do we have?"

"Nine helicopters," Mongo said. "Sikorsky UH-60 Black Hawk helicopters, to be precise."

Steve swore. Black Hawks had been designed for the military, but they were also used by both the FBI and the DHS. "They've found us."

"They've found *something*, all right," Kevin agreed. "I checked the records. They're DHS helicopters."

"Right," Steve said. Clearly, operational secrecy had come to an end. Somehow – and they'd figure it out later – the DHS had cottoned on to something. There was no time to worry about it now. Instead, they had to get everyone out of the ranch and then prepare a reception. At least they had a rough contingency plan for discovery. "Send the emergency signal and recall everyone on the ranch, then prepare the combat team for deployment."

He gritted his teeth. Abandoning the ranch would be the simplest solution, but it was part of his family's history. He couldn't let the DHS goons – or anyone – just take it from him, no matter the cost. And besides, he had heard more than enough horror stories about how the

DHS treated veterans and their families. Giving them a taste of their own medicine would feel sweet.

Kevin looked up. "You do realise that whatever we do will almost certainly be noticed?"

Stuart nodded. He'd hoped for months, perhaps a year, before they were discovered, but it was clear that there had been a slip-up somewhere. One month...at least they were on their way to establishing Heinlein Colony and preparing plans for Mars and the asteroid belt. But it would ensure a rougher meeting with the federal government than he would have preferred.

Perhaps we should have gone ahead with the plan to introduce a fusion reactor, he thought, sourly. But there was no point in crying over spilt milk. Instead, it was time to mop it up.

"I'll be taking the lead down there," he said. The combat team needed to see him in command, just in case they had doubts about firing on fellow Americans. Sure, they *were* DHS stormtroopers, but that didn't make them the enemy. "Maintain teleport locks on all of us. If things go badly wrong, yank us out of there."

"Understood," Mongo said. "And good luck."

Steve nodded. They were going to need it. Not to dispose of the incoming helicopters – it would have been childishly simple to destroy them before their pilots knew they were under attack – but to push them back without actually killing anyone. Dead pilots and stormtroopers would make it harder for the government to come to terms with Steve and his buddies. They'd have to react harshly against such an overt challenge to their authority.

Shaking his head, he made his way to the teleport chamber. One way or another, the world was about to become very different.

JÜRGEN CURSED UNDER his breath as the helicopter rocketed southwards. He'd never been in a helicopter before and the experience was killing him, by inches. It didn't help that the remainder of the team, men wearing black suits and carrying assault rifles, seemed to find his near-panic hilarious. Every few seconds, the plane rocked violently, stabilised and then rocked again. He was starting to wonder if the pilot was deliberately crashing them through the worst of the turbulence.

"Just hold on in there," the NSA agent called. Despite sharing a flight, he *still* hadn't shared his name. "We're almost there."

Jürgen nodded, keeping his eyes firmly closed. It made it easier, somehow, if he didn't see the ground below the helicopter. Almost there? They'd been saying the same thing ever since they'd landed at the airfield they'd turned into a staging base and then transferred to the helicopters. He reached up and covered his eyes, adding to the darkness. Maybe that would make it easier still.

The helicopter rocked again, violently. "Whoops," the pilot called, in a thick southern drawl. "Hit a nasty spot there!"

Jürgen silently cursed him to hell.

— —

"ALL PRESENT AND correct," Edward Romford said.

Steve nodded, inspecting the first combat team. They were all veterans who had been repaired and rebuilt by the alien technology, then trained endlessly on captured alien weapons. There was still some roughness in how they acted, Steve saw, but they were getting there. It was just a shame they didn't have many combat cyborgs or powered combat suits. The ones they did have were designed for creatures the size of preteen children. God alone knew what the Hordesmen had been doing with them.

"Try not to kill anyone," he warned, once he'd finished his inspection. "You have your shield bracelets and teleport locks. If worst comes to worst, we will beam out and leave the bastards scratching their heads. Any questions?"

Romford smirked. "Phasers on stun?"

"Definitely," Steve said, rolling his eyes. The alien stunners worked surprisingly well, although the results tended to vary. A strong man might be out for a few minutes, while a weaker man or a child might sleep for nearly an hour. He still wished he'd had them in Afghanistan, though. They could have stunned everyone and then sorted the innocent from the guilty afterwards. "We don't want to kill anyone."

He ran through the tactical situation as the helicopters came into view, their rotor blades chopping through the air. It looked as though they intended to try to hover over the ranch and rappel down to the ground, a tactic that did make a certain kind of sense if they expected a hot reception. Or, perhaps, they wanted to surround the ranch and then move in. It didn't really matter, he told himself. They were in for a very rude surprise.

"Launch the screamers," he ordered, quietly.

— —

JÜRGEN HEARD THE alarms as the helicopter shook, more violently than ever before. What was wrong? Even the strong men were starting to panic as the shaking grew worse, followed by a faint crackling sound that left the air feeling ionised. There was a series of loud bangs from underneath the helicopter, then she dropped like a stone.

"We're going to have to make an emergency landing," the pilot said. He no longer sounded amused by his own daring. Instead, he sounded almost fearful. "Brace for impact!"

"They're all going down," another voice said. It took Jürgen a moment to place it as the team's commander, a smug man who'd laughed while Jürgen had been trying not to be sick. "Every last helicopter is going down…"

The noise of the craft's engines grew louder, then stopped. Seconds later, there was a thunderous crash as they hit the ground. Jürgen's eyes snapped open, revealing two of the stormtroopers forcing open the hatch and jumping out of the craft. The agent caught his arm and dragged him forward, practically throwing him after the stormtroopers. He landed badly, but there was no time to hesitate. The entire craft might be about to catch fire and explode.

"My God," the agent said. "What happened?"

Jürgen followed his gaze. All nine helicopters had crash-landed, their passengers spilling out onto the grassy field. Some of them were smoking slightly, their pilots ordering the men to run for their lives. Others seemed almost intact, utterly undamaged. It was impossible to tell what had happened to them. There had been no reason for all nine helicopters to suffer the same fault at the same time.

"I don't know," he answered. But he thought about the dongles and wondered, grimly, just what else might have been invented in secret. Something to take down helicopters? "I..."

"ATTENTION," a voice boomed. Jürgen turned to see five men standing on a grassy knoll, holding unfamiliar-looking weapons in their hands. "Discard all weapons, then proceed away from the helicopters into the field behind you. I say again, discard all weapons and then proceed into the field behind you. Resistance will not be tolerated."

The team's commander purpled rapidly. "You are under arrest," he shouted, lifting his rifle. "Put down your guns and surrender, you..."

"Discard all weapons and proceed into the field behind you," the speaker repeated. "There will be no further warnings."

"No," the commander said. He lifted his rifle and fired, once. The bullet glanced off the speaker in a flash of blue light and vanished somewhere in the distance. "I..."

The speaker returned fire. There was a flash of blue-red light and the commander dropped to the ground like a puppet whose strings had been cut. Jürgen stared, then leaned forward to examine the body. As far as he could tell, the man had simply been knocked out. There were certainly no physical wounds. Moments later, the speaker lifted his weapon and discharged a brighter shot into the ground in front of the DHS team. There was a colossal explosion, which cleared rapidly to reveal a small crater, smoking like a volcano. Jürgen gulped – just what the hell had they stumbled into? – and then obeyed orders. The rest of the team discarded their weapons and followed Jürgen into the next field.

— —

"Pussies," Romford sneered. "Big and tough when it comes to picking on unarmed men and women, but useless when their target fights back."

Steve privately agreed. In his view, the view he'd been taught by his parents, the truly brave men went into the infantry, where they matched themselves against the enemy infantry. It was true that policemen were brave too, but it wasn't the same. And the sort of people who would crash in like stormtroopers when they thought they had a cause weren't worthy of any respect at all.

"Keep them covered," he ordered. The DHS team looked thoroughly cowed, but appearances could be deceiving. Steve had seen prisoners move from cooperative to riotous within seconds in Afghanistan. "Secure their weapons, then find out who's in charge of this bunch of monkeys."

He examined the stormtroopers as his men moved to obey. They looked professional, too professional. Steve doubted his Marine platoon had looked anything like as good while they'd been in service, except perhaps when they'd been on parade. But, as Steve had been taught more than once, it was possible to look good or to be good. Few units managed both at once.

Perhaps we should have let them rappel down to the ground, he thought, snidely. *We could have seen just how well they fucked it up.*

He shook his head. There was no time for delay. The helicopters might not have managed to get off a distress signal before the screamers brought them down, but someone might well have noticed that all nine transponders had vanished. These weren't the lax pre-9/11 days. The vanished transponders would bring some sort of reaction, probably fighter jets intent on searching for prospective terrorists. And they would probably have some ground forces in the area too. Steve had done the same in Afghanistan.

Romford returned, marching a pair of men ahead of him. Neither of them looked particularly professional; one was clearly an analyst, while the other was a Washington suit. Steve saw the simmering anger, mixed with shock and terror, in the latter's eyes and smiled inwardly. A shocked man was a man who could be drained of information, then used as a messenger.

"Good afternoon," he said, with mock politeness. "And who do I have the pleasure of addressing?"

The Washington man swallowed, then looked down at the grass. "Cyril Dorsey," he said reluctantly. The man beside him let out a sound that sounded like a choked-off giggle. "I'm from the NSA."

Steve lifted his eyebrows. "The NSA?"

"Yes," Dorsey said. He railed, either through grim determination or through a sudden awareness of his companion's amusement. "And you are in a boatload of trouble."

"Try saying a *shitload*," Steve advised. "It sounds so much more dramatic."

He sighed, fighting down the temptation to start yelling at the damned bureaucrat. "What are you doing here?"

The analyst glared at him. "What are you doing with the veterans?"

Steve was momentarily nonplussed. The veterans? And then it clicked. Someone had noticed that a number of veterans were disappearing, then tracked it back to the ranch and realised that the trail ended there. Hell, he wouldn't have given the NSA the time of day, but perhaps the analyst had good reason to be concerned about the veterans. For all he knew, they could have been sacrificed to the dark gods.

"The veterans are fine," Steve assured him. He briefly considered introducing Romford, then decided against it. The veteran looked young enough to be his own son. "But you have trespassed on my property."

"We have a search warrant," Dorsey insisted. "And you *attacked* us!"

"Technically speaking, this is an embassy, which *you* attacked," Steve said. Did it really count as an embassy if the host country didn't know about it? But it didn't matter. If nothing else, the mere suggestion that it *was* an embassy would cause no end of panic in the corridors of power. Storming a foreign embassy was pretty much an act of war. "However, we are prepared to forgive your trespass in exchange for a few minor considerations."

Cyril Dorsey started to splutter again, his words tumbling over themselves so fast that Steve couldn't even begin to follow them. Instead, he waited for the man to shut up and then continued.

"You will go back to your superiors and inform them that this ranch is an embassy of another power," he said. "Furthermore, you will tell them that we expect a meeting with the President one week from today, at a location of his choosing. He may bring one companion to the meeting, if he wishes. Until then, this ranch is to remain isolated. If any federal elements are sighted within ten miles of the ranch, they will be fired on without further warning."

"Now, look here, you son of a bitch," Dorsey snapped. "You can't make threats like that!"

"Oh, those poor bastards," Steve said, looking over at the troopers. "What did they do to deserve having a fool like you in command?"

He looked back at Dorsey, dropping his facade of politeness. "Let me be clear on this, you fucking idiot," he snapped. "You are massively outgunned and you and your men are at my mercy. And, as you proposed to raid, with live ammunition, a ranch that holds my wife, children and relatives, I am not feeling very damn merciful! You could have knocked on the damn door and asked about the vets!"

Resisting the temptation to shake the man, he instead leaned closer until their faces were almost touching. "You will go back to Washington and deliver the message I gave you," he snapped. "And then you will resign, retire from federal work and go live somewhere else, somewhere where your stupidity won't risk lives. Or I will fucking hunt you down and kill you!"

The man cringed back. Steve was unsurprised – and unimpressed. He'd met too many paper-pushers who had no real awareness of the world surrounding them. Washington produced the idiots by the bucket load, then put them in charge of making government policy actually work. They never seemed to realise that they could push people too far and that, one day, their house of cards would crumble into dust. Or that their mistakes could cost lives.

"There's one thing I want you to see," Steve said, very quietly. "Turn around."

Dorsey obeyed. Steve smiled, then activated the interface and sent a single very specific command. For a long moment, nothing seemed to happen...and then a beam of red light struck down from high overhead, burning a hole into the ground. Dorsey let out a strangled cry as the ground shook, almost toppling over in horror, just before the beam snapped back out of existence, leaving a glowing crater. It was far worse, Steve knew, than the smaller weapon he'd used to make his earlier point. And it would be visible on every observation satellite in position to see it. Maybe Washington wouldn't believe Dorsey's tale, but they'd believe the satellites.

"Strip," Steve ordered. He raised his voice, addressing the rest of the assault team. "All of you. Strip."

He waited until the team was naked, then pointed towards the road leading down to the nearest town. Naked as they were, it was quite possible that the team would be arrested for indecent exposure. By the time they managed to convince the local police of who they were – or make a phone call to Washington – they would have undergone one hell of a lot of humiliation. Steve felt a moment of grim satisfaction – he hated the regular humiliations at the hands of government bureaucracy – then turned his attention back to Dorsey. Somewhat to his surprise, the man had remained on his feet.

"Remember the message," Steve said. He reached into his pocket and produced a business card. "You can call me on that number, when you're ready to let me know where you want to meet. Anywhere will do."

He paused, significantly. "And remember what I said about any federal forces near the ranch. Go."

The men fled. Steve took a look at the helicopters, then silently marked them for disassembly and conversion into something Heinlein Colony could use. If nothing else, now the secret was out, they could order whatever they wanted openly. But recruitment was going to be far harder in future. The government would try to slip a few of its own agents into the system.

"You could have handled it better," Kevin said, though the communicator. The intelligence agent sounded doubtful. In his world, there was no such thing as a dead enemy. "They're going to be *pissed*."

"It had to be done," Steve said, shortly. There was no way he would have passed up on the chance to humiliate the bureaucrats. "Washington is like a bull. Sometimes you have to hit the bastard in the nose just to make it pay attention."

"Yeah," Kevin said. "And how many idiots who try that get gored by an angry bull?"

ELEVEN

WASHINGTON DC, USA

"Let me see if I have this straight," the President said. "We have a high-tech militia in Montana that has declared itself a foreign power and has the technology to back it up?"

Jürgen swallowed as the President's gaze moved over and fixed on him. He'd never been to the White House before, certainly not as a participant in a very high-level meeting. His boss wouldn't have gone to the White House under normal circumstances. That would have been the responsibility of the DHS Director and his subordinates, not low-level analysts.

"That appears to be the only explanation that fits the facts, Mr. President," he said.

The President nodded, very slowly, then moved his gaze to Dorsey. "There are times when I wish," he said, "that I could just order someone hung. Might I ask what you were thinking when you encouraged DHS to launch a million-dollar raid on very scant evidence?"

Dorsey looked, if anything, even worse than Jürgen felt. "I...I believed that we had a serious problem that needed to be resolved," he said. "I..."

"And now we have a far more serious problem," the President said, cutting him off. "General?"

Lieutenant General Alvin Houseman, Director of the USAF Foreign Technology Division, frowned. "We picked up the blast on satellites all over the area," he said. "Our analysts worked the data and believe it was an immensely powerful directed energy weapon, fired from somewhere in low orbit. We don't have a clue what actually fired the weapon."

"A high-tech militia," the President said, softly. "What sort of militia could put an orbital weapons platform into orbit without being noticed?"

Jürgen winced, inwardly. Getting something up into orbit without being noticed was pretty much impossible. American satellites monitored every inch of the planet, watching for the tell-tale heat signature that marked a rocket launch. No rogue state could hope to put something in orbit without it being detected and marked for destruction if necessary. And yet, there was no disputing the physical evidence. Somehow, Steve Stuart and his men had put an orbital weapons platform in position to fire on American soil.

"I don't know, Mr. President," the General confessed. "The weapons system is years ahead of our best work, literally."

The same, Jürgen knew, could be said about the dongles…and whatever they'd deployed to bring down the helicopters. And the weapons they'd used. Technology that was out of this world…the thought caught at his mind, holding him still. What if the technology *was* literally out of this world? What if it was *alien* technology? But he knew that he would be committed to a mental hospital if he said that out loud.

"So we seem to have a major problem," the President observed. He looked over at the fourth man in the room. "Colonel? What can you tell us about Mr. Stuart?"

Jürgen turned to look at Colonel Craig Henderson. He was a short black man, with hair cropped close to his skull, wearing a Marine uniform. From what Jürgen had heard, he'd been at Camp Pendleton when he'd been urgently summoned to Washington. It must have been alarming, Jürgen knew. What sort of offence called for a chewing out from the President personally, rather than his senior officers. But he'd been briefed and hadn't said a word since.

The Colonel cleared his throat. "Steve…"

He swallowed, then started again. "I knew Steve when we were both going through Basic Training," he said. "He is tough, determined and often very blunt. His family has a long tradition of military service and the honour code that goes with it. When he was sent out to war, he did as well as anyone and better than most. He might have been as fearful on the battlefield as I was, during my first engagement, but he sucked it up and kept going. By the time he was promoted, he looked certain to be a lifer in the Corps."

There was a pause. "And then came Afghanistan.

"It's hard to explain to a civilian, but I will do my best. The military code, Mr. President, can be summed up as you fighting for your buddies, rather than your country. You have to be able to rely, completely, on your buddies…and, in a modern army, that can be far more than just your platoon. On deployment, you have to rely on air support, intelligence officers and the logistics officers in the rear to keep going. And you also have to trust that your political leaders won't simply abandon you when it becomes embarrassing.

"Steve and his men were caught in a Taliban ambush, Mr. President," Henderson said. "They needed fire support to get out of it, so Steve called for help. Instead of immediate assistance, they were told that the ROE prevented either long-range guns or air support from engaging the enemy. Steve was practically begging for assistance that wouldn't, not couldn't, come. In the end, he managed to lead his men out of the trap, leaving four bodies behind. We never recovered one of them. Steve retired soon afterwards and went back to the ranch."

The President leaned forward. "So…what's your impression of him now?"

"I have no idea where he got his hands on advanced technology," Henderson said. "And I have no idea if it is really him calling the shots. But if it is, I think we may be in some trouble. You would have someone with a good reason – several good reasons – to resent the federal government allied with technology that could do real damage. Steve's attitude, the attitude of his whole family, is that of someone who wants to be left alone. You didn't leave them alone."

Dorsey was spurred to respond. "They were flouting laws," he snapped. "And…"

"And you sent more helicopters than we often had in Afghanistan to storm their ranch," Henderson snapped back. "Tell me something, *sir*. What would you have said if Steve and his family had been *accidentally* killed by your people?"

"I would have demanded a full investigation," Dorsey said, weakly.

"And would that investigation," Henderson demanded, "actually have ensured that someone was punished?"

He took a breath. "Over the last five decades, there have been a whole string of incidents where people have been harassed, arrested, injured or even killed by federal law enforcement agencies, often on very flimsy grounds," he added. "And how many of those feds have been punished for it?"

The President slapped the table. "Enough," he said. His gaze moved to Dorsey, then to the DHS Director. "I shall expect your resignations… no, you're both fired. And if you leak, I'll personally see to it that you spend the rest of your lives in jail."

He looked back at Henderson. "Mr. Stuart has offered to speak with us," he said. "Do you feel we should talk?"

"Talk, yes," Henderson said. "But I would advise against trying to threaten him."

"Then we won't," the President said. He looked over at his National Security Advisor. "You were at the meeting where the raid was ordered, weren't you?"

The man paled, but nodded.

"Then consider yourself on probation," the President said. There was a pleasant tone to his voice that in no way masked the ice underneath. "And if this turns into a political disaster, I'll want your head on a platter too."

He paused. "And what, so far, has leaked out?"

Houseman was the only one to speak. "So far, nothing apart from rumours," he said. "Several bloggers in the town posted notes about naked federal troopers, but most of them seem to believe that it was a practical joke rather than anything more serious. We're pushing that forward online, helping to bury the truth under a mountain of bullshit. However, there may well be international trouble. The Russians may believe that we were testing an advanced weapon and demand answers."

The President winced. "Then we make the call and talk to Mr. Stuart sooner, if possible," he said, firmly. "I'll go, personally, even if the Secret Service objects. We need to know just what we're dealing with before we make any long-term plans."

Jürgen nodded in agreement. Clearly, the President had more steel in him than he'd suspected. And balls too, if he *was* going to meet Mr. Stuart in person. Jürgen would have liked to be a fly on the wall at *that* meeting.

KEVIN SMILED TO himself as he listened to the President. Dorsey had no idea that he and his men had carried nanotech bugs with them back to the White House, or that one of those bugs – now hidden on the ceiling – was monitoring the conversation in the White House. And yet, despite his amusement, Kevin was terrified. The sheer potential of the technology was staggering and horrific. Given enough time, the entire world could be monitored endlessly by computers. There would no longer be any privacy at all.

He looked up as Steve entered, the hatch hissing closed behind him.

"We need to talk," Kevin said, before his older brother could say a word. "Sit."

Steve sat, his face twisting. Kevin didn't give him any time to muster a response.

"Tell me," he said. "Just what were you thinking when you humiliated them so badly?"

Steve's eyes flashed. "I was thinking they deserved a little humiliation!"

"And you might be right," Kevin conceded. "But you just committed something that is arguably an act of war. You can hardly declare the ranch to be the embassy of a foreign power and then expect them to recognise it when they have never even *heard* of us!"

He went on before Steve could say a word. "You have just terrified everyone in Washington," he snapped. "Scared people do stupid things! We need them to stay out of the way, at the very least, not work to find ways to impede our plans for the defence of Earth! And what will happen to our small community if it *does* come down to a shooting war? Do you expect *everyone* to go along with it?

"Yes, you terrorised a bunch of DHS cowboys and rightly so, but what happens when they send Marines or Army Rangers or SEALS? How many of our friends will side *against* their country? Or would we have a mutiny on our hands at the worst possible moment?"

Steve glared at him. It was the look, Kevin remembered, that reminded him strongly of their father, before the old man had passed away. The look that said, quite clearly, that his children were crossing the line and heading towards disaster. But the old man had never had the sort of power that sat, now, at Steve's fingertips.

"This isn't a game," Kevin said, lowering his voice. "Military service didn't prepare you for being the leader of a new nation. Not everything is a nail that needs to be hit with a hammer."

"It worked for George Washington," Steve objected.

"Washington didn't build a new nation completely from scratch," Kevin countered. He'd read history, all history. Steve had focused on its military aspects. "There was Congress and the State Governments and quite a bit of infrastructure – and he still fucked up the slavery issue. Here...you have to build everything from scratch. You're out of your depth."

He took a breath. "I understand the urge to just hit back at the feds," he added. There had been endless talk – so far, just talk – about greeting federal agents with loaded weapons, but Steve had made it real. No matter the justification for the raid, Steve's actions were likely to have unpleasant repercussions. "But we handled the whole affair very badly. Right now, we have to look like Washington's worst nightmare. A group of irrational thugs with advanced technology and a bad attitude."

Steve looked down at the deck, then back up at Kevin. "You would have preferred to abandon the ranch?"

The hell of it, Kevin knew, was that Steve had a point. They – and Mongo – had grown up on the ranch. They'd run through its fields, climbed the mountains nearby, swum in its lakes, courted their first girlfriends in the haystacks…it was their home. And it was home to generations of Stuarts, ever since they'd first settled in Montana. The thought of federal agents swarming through the ranch, breaking furniture and searching their vast collection of books was appalling. If Kevin had been the one in charge, he didn't know if he could have coldly abandoned the ranch and set up another base elsewhere.

"I would have sent them away with their dignity intact," Kevin said. "Look, Steve, what sort of nation do you want to build?"

"A decent one," Steve growled.

"Then act decently towards other nations," Kevin said. "Particularly the nation that raised and trained most of our manpower – and the one to which many of us swore an oath."

"We swore one to protect the United States against all enemies, foreign and domestic," Steve pointed out. "What about the domestic enemies in Washington?"

"We're leaving them behind," Kevin said. "Or would you rather wage war on the United States?"

He paused, then pushed on. "Let's bomb Washington, right now," he said. "Zap the White House from orbit. Smash the military bases! Blow up the Beltway! Burn Langley to the ground! Oh, and let's make enemies of the entire American population while we're at it."

His voice softened. "I saw this before in Iraq," he added. "And so did you. Destroying Saddam's regime was easy; rebuilding a decent Iraq was hard. How many people resisted us because we destroyed their livelihoods, exposed them to their enemies and shattered their grip on power? How many others resisted us because they trusted Iran more than they trusted us? How many people fought because it was the only way we'd left them to make a living..."

Steve slapped his hand on his knee, hard. "Point. Taken."

"This isn't a fantasy any longer," Kevin said. "This is as real as reality gets."

He waved a hand at the console he'd set up, with the help of his interface. "This technology scares me," he admitted. "We have spy probes in the White House itself! It wouldn't be hard to blanket Afghanistan with bugs and track down the terrorist networks, then start obliterating them one by one. Or we could disable Iran's nuclear program, North Korea's nuclear missiles...hell, we could cripple China and Russia in an afternoon, without them ever realising what happened to their weapons. But all of those options are destructive.

"Steve, if we're going to build a new nation, we need something constructive."

Steve nodded, ruefully. "Very well," he said. "What do you propose we offer?"

Kevin had to smile. Steve had been right about one thing. Sometimes, you just had to hit the bull between the horns to make it pay attention, even if there *was* a risk of being gored by an angry bull.

"Most of what Keith suggested," Kevin said. "We have a handful of small portable fusion reactors, enough to supply the entire country's requirements. We have superconductors that would allow them to make steps forward in producing laser and other directed energy weapons. We have medical kits and cures for diseases, including some that have proven incurable by current human technology. Hell, we have quite a few other pieces of technology we could offer them."

"And we could offer assistance in going after the Taliban," Steve commented. "Do you think they'd like it?"

Kevin shrugged. Afghanistan was a major headache for the government. They couldn't commit the troop levels necessary to keep the country stabilised, which ensured that any gains made by American and local troops were often reversed when the foreign troops moved onwards to the next region. And yet the government didn't dare try to pull out completely, having built up Afghanistan as the *Good War*. Kevin had a private suspicion that Afghanistan would end up just as badly as Somalia, with the added complication of American SF roaming the countryside, wiping out small pools of Taliban wherever they found them.

And besides, the debt for 9/11 might have been paid, but that didn't justify simply abandoning the country.

"They probably would," Kevin said. He smiled, then met his brother's eyes. "We have a week before the scheduled meeting, unless they want to meet earlier. God alone knows what might happen in the meantime. So far, there hasn't been a leak, but that will change. And maybe we should ask to meet earlier, if we can. The sooner we start mending fences, the better."

Steve nodded. It was one of their father's sayings.

"Once they call, set the meeting up as soon as possible," he ordered. "I'll speak to Keith and a couple of others, then…then try to make nice with the government."

He paused. "But we won't be surrendering our independence," he added, firmly. He tapped his knee to make the point clear. "That is not on the table."

"Nor should it be," Kevin agreed.

Even with the best will in the world — and he had never believed that all government was evil — it was unlikely that the US Government could put together a plan to defend the Earth in time to save it. The Horde would notice they'd lost a starship, sooner or later, and send another one to investigate. By then, they had to be ready to take the starship out — ideally, they had to be able to capture it. A second starship would be very useful. If nothing else, it would allow them to send trade missions to the nearest inhabited star system and pick up alien tech and, more usefully, alien user manuals.

"But we do have to mend fences," he repeated. "We cannot afford having the US government trying to either impede us or even just refusing to cooperate. The consequences could be disastrous."

TWELVE

JOINT BASE ANDREWS, USA

Steve disliked having to admit that he'd been wrong, but his father had taught him – more than once – that it was worse to cling to something he knew damn well wasn't true. He *didn't* trust the government – he would *never* trust the government – yet Kevin had been right. He'd allowed his hatred to drive his actions, rather than sober cold rationality. Perhaps it was time to mend fences.

Mariko had agreed, when he'd gone to her and confessed everything Kevin had told him. She'd listened, then pointed out that men had their pride – and the more powerless a man felt, the more he would cling to his pride. Steve had humiliated the government and the government would want to push back, if only to maintain its position. But perhaps, if they talked openly, there was a chance to come to an agreement.

He smiled as he drove the van towards the gatehouse. Joint Base Andrews, the home of Air Force One, was one of the most secure locations in Washington, designated as a Presidential bolthole if the shit hit the fan. The armed Marines stepped out of the gatehouse, weapons raised, as he pulled the van to a halt. Steve couldn't help feeling a hint of nostalgia as he saw them, followed by a flicker of approval. These men were genuine combat troops, alright. They knew better than to let an uninspected van anywhere near them, not when a bomb packed in the vehicle could do real damage. Steve waited until one of them came up to the window, then removed his sunglasses.

"My name is Steve Stuart," he said. "I'm here to meet with the President."

They'd argued endlessly over how Steve should approach the base. Mongo had proposed teleporting into the base itself, but with the Secret Service on the lookout – and probably already paranoid after events in Montana – it had struck Steve as a very bad idea. Besides, as Kevin had pointed out, the idea was to try to mend fences, not rub the government's face in its technological inferiority. Eventually, one of the vans had been transported to a point near Washington by a shuttle and Steve had driven the rest of the way.

It was nearly twenty minutes before he was cleared through security and allowed to drive up to a nondescript building. There was nothing, apart from a handful of snipers on the rooftop, to suggest that anyone important was inside, something that Steve thoroughly approved of. The simplest way to avoid being targeted was to act as though there was nothing worth targeting in the area. He parked the van, then opened the door and climbed out. It felt oddly good to be standing in a military base once again.

"Steve," a droll voice said. "What *have* you been doing?"

Steve smiled when he saw Craig Henderson. They were old friends; he would have recruited Henderson, if he hadn't remained on active duty. As it was, it would be nice to have someone on his side in the meeting – or at least willing to help build links between the two parties, when the talks got heated.

"Something extraordinary," Steve said. He smiled, then jerked a thumb towards the van. "I brought a gift. You'll need to assign a team of loaders to unload it, then transport it to somewhere secure."

Henderson paused. "And what *is* this gift?"

"All will be explained," Steve said. He inclined a hand towards the door. "Shall we go inside?"

The building was surprisingly luxurious inside. Henderson kept up a running commentary about how the building was often used for secret low-key meetings between the President and foreign representatives. It was, apparently, as secure as possible, although none of the precautions seemed to block Steve's link with the starship. However, if they started to broadcast more static into the air, it might well prevent a safe teleport. He kept his expression blank as Henderson led him into a small, but comfortable room. The President was sitting on the sofa, waiting for him. He rose as Steve entered the room.

"Mr. Stuart," the President said. He held out a hand, which Steve awkwardly took and shook, firmly. "I've heard a great deal about you."

Steve nodded, feeling himself lost for words. This was the *President*, the duly elected Head of State and Government, the most powerful man in the world. He'd been brought up to respect the office, even if he had been taught that the men who sat in it were human and therefore fallible. His father hadn't spoken favourably of any President since Reagan, condemning Clinton in one breath and George W. Bush in the next. And he'd died midway through Bush's second term.

"All exaggerated, I suspect," Steve said, as the President released his hand. "Particularly the story about the Swedish woman's swim team."

The President smiled. It was a genuinely friendly smile. Up close, Steve had to admit the man had charisma. It shouldn't have been important in a Presidential election, but it was. And the man had balls. Faced with what had to look like a villain straight out of James Bond, the man had picked a meeting place and come to the meeting, without giving into the temptation to cower under his desk.

He sat down on the sofa facing the President and waited until the Navy Stewards had poured them coffee, then withdrew. Henderson stood behind the President's sofa, clearly ill at ease. Steve didn't blame him. Craig Henderson had always been ambitious, but he'd never wanted to become involved in political battles. Few military officers cared for bureaucratic engagements.

"Well," the President said. "Shall we get right to the point?"

Steve nodded and started to speak, outlining everything that had happened from the abduction attempt to the capture of the alien starship and the start of a new nation. The President listened, his face curiously expressionless; behind him, Henderson didn't even try to hide his astonishment. Steve wondered, as he came to the end of his story, just how much of it the President had guessed beforehand. After all, significant advances in technology didn't come out of nowhere.

"I see," the President said, when he had finished. "And that is all true?"

"Yes, Mr. President," Steve said.

"And you intend to found a new nation, while defending the planet," the President mused. "An interesting endeavour – and quite a worthwhile one. Might I ask how you intend to proceed?"

Steve had expected a demand that the ship and technology be instantly turned over to the government. Kevin, however, had doubted it. The government would hardly risk exposing its own weakness by making a demand it knew would probably be rejected outright. Instead, Kevin had predicted, the government would try to come to terms with the new nation.

"We intend to continue recruiting – more openly, now – and purchasing supplies and raw materials from Earth," Steve said, carefully. "Given enough time, we should be able to put together a working defence network for the planet, particularly as we unlock more and more secrets of alien technology. Eventually, we plan to settle the entire solar system and reach for the stars."

"Ambitious," the President commented. "Perhaps we can be of assistance?"

"We would prefer to do our own recruiting," Steve said. "If this became a US Government project it would cause problems with other nations, problems we would prefer to avoid."

"I would have thought that NASA might have some ideas," the President said.

Steve snorted. "If NASA had been led by men of vision, Mr. President, we would have hotels on Titan and Mars would be halfway to being habitable," he said. "Instead, trillions of dollars have been wasted on pretty artwork and feel-good diplomacy, while the Russians, Chinese and Indians move ahead with their own space programs. We don't even have a working replacement for the Space Shuttle."

He shook his head. "We will recruit people who we believe can help us, then open the floodgates to immigration," he added. "But we will deal with people as individuals, not as groups or nations. Let everyone have a chance to stand on their own two feet."

For a moment, he thought the President would ask him to explain, something Kevin had warned him to try to avoid. Ranting at the President would have been rather less than constructive, no matter how much he wanted to tell the President exactly what he thought of some of his more damaging polices.

"We have never forbidden emigration from the United States," the President said. "And, if your new nation is no threat, we will certainly not start now."

Steve nodded. "We have a great deal to offer you," he said, "in exchange for your cooperation and assistance, when we need it."

The President leaned forward, interested.

Steve allowed himself a smile. "There are three different gifts in the van, Mr. President," he said. "One of them – the large box – is a portable cold fusion reactor, capable of putting out..."

The President's jaw dropped. "A *nuclear* reactor?"

"It's perfectly safe," Steve said, with some amusement. He had to be the first person to smuggle a nuclear reactor onto an American military base. "As I was saying, the reactor is capable of putting out...well, it's capable of putting out the same amount of power as the nuclear reactor on an aircraft carrier. Anything built with purely human technology would cost at least nine *billion* dollars and take years to complete, assuming it wasn't politically sabotaged along the way. A handful of them would suffice to meet *all* of America's power requirements, without any pesky nuclear waste, political problems or even terrorist threats."

"I don't believe this," the President said, shaking his head. "A nuclear reactor the size of a small van?"

"Smaller than that," Steve confirmed. "But you don't have to take my word for it. The Foreign Technology Division will have fun experimenting with the power systems and figuring out that it does what it says on the tin. And there are two other items we brought along."

He paused, then went on. "There are a number of room-temperature superconductors," he continued. "They have quite a number of interesting applications, but the important one right now is that they can be used to build very effective batteries. One of them could be used to power a car for weeks, replacing gas…which would sharply reduce the West's dependency on Middle Eastern oil. We could meet the requirements of the United States and our allies from local production, once the batteries were used to replace gas everywhere."

"There would be political problems," the President said, sourly.

Steve wasn't surprised. The wealthy oil corporations and Arab states had worked hard to ensure that possible alternatives to oil were marginalised or simply disregarded. Introducing the fusion reactors and the batteries would have a whole series of effects on American society, perhaps even knocking over the oil corporations, which would render millions of people unemployed. It was unlikely that they would *all* want to go to space.

"We will not interfere in your decisions, Mr. President," Steve said. "Or those of your successors, as long as they don't threaten us.

"The final item is a set of medical treatments designed to eradicate cancer," he added. "We can only produce them in small quantities so far, so if the CDC or someone else manages to figure out how to duplicate them we would be very pleased. Again, you don't have to take my word for this. You can take the gifts, all of them, and test them freely, as you see fit. And how you use them is up to you."

The President gave him an odd little smile. "You don't have political ambitions?"

Steve hesitated, trying to put his thoughts into words. "Mr. President, I was raised to be independent, to live my life without support from outside the family," he said. "My family's motto might as well be *Live and Let Live*. Ever since I became politically aware, I realised that both the Republicans and the Democrats were intent on expanding the government's authority, without expanding the political oversight. Politicians in Washington were acting more and more like untouchable aristocrats than elected leaders of our nation. Both parties were pushing for laws that divided society and turned Americans against one another.

"I was taught that everyone deserved a chance to seek their own place in society and to be considered on their own merits. The best and brightest would rise to the top, Mr. President, but that is no longer true in America. Every single person claims to be a victim now, claiming to face discrimination when they don't get a job or when someone is mean to them or they see something that offends them. I could give you a hundred examples of policies put forward by politicians, from Affirmative Action to Don't Ask Don't Tell, that have only undermined the positions of groups they were intended to help.

"But why have groups? Why insist that two people are different because of skin colour, gender, race or religion? Why not just have individuals?"

He paused. "We're not interested in waging war on America, Mr. President, nor are we interested in attempting to reform the United States. I simply don't believe the country *can* be reformed. Instead, we're building a new society where those who wish to join us and live life on their own merits can do so. An escape hatch, if you like, from a society that is rapidly becoming intolerable."

The President pressed his fingertips together. "You know, when I was younger, I used to read *Atlas Shrugged*. A guy I knew, a few years older than me, actually tried to set up a Galt's Gulch of his own. It lasted barely a year, then fragmented."

Steve nodded. "Why didn't you go?"

"Because the system Rand suggested was unsustainable," the President said. "She admired the men who spearheaded the production of goods to trade, but thought little of the men who made it work. The machinists, the factory workers, even the floor sweepers. All of them had their own role to play in making the production work.

"And my friend wasn't the only one who tried to set up his own little commune. California is littered with the remains of such places. The only ones that succeeded, that achieved any measure of success, were the very low tech ones. And life there was hard.

He paused. "How do we know that your grand society is going to be different?"

Steve considered his answer carefully. Two days ago, he would have angrily denied that could ever be a possibility. But now...the President did have a point. Their society had already trembled, as tiny as it was, in the aftermath of the attack on the ranch. Another shock like that could destroy the nation he was trying to build.

"We don't, Mr. President," he admitted. "It is possible that our society *will* come apart. But unless we try, we will never know. We have high technology, we have a stream of recruits and we have plenty of ideas for expansion. And if we fail...at least we will have tried."

"True enough, I suppose," the President said. "Do you intend to go public?"

"I was hoping to remain secret a while longer," Steve confessed. In hindsight, embarrassing so many federal agents might not have been a bright idea. Rumours were already spreading rapidly. "Why do you ask?"

"I would prefer to try to manage how the information is released to the public," the President said. "We're talking about the entire world being turned upside down."

"True," Steve agreed. He paused. "There is one other card we would like to put on the table."

He leaned forward. "I understand that you are preparing one final push in Afghanistan," he said. "We have some...devices and personnel that might be of assistance."

"I believe that should be coordinated through the military," the President said. He looked up at Henderson. "Colonel Henderson will act as the liaison officer between us, at least for the time before there is any public announcement. Colonel, I'll get you high clearance and whatever else you need to get the job done properly."

He stood. "It's been an interesting meeting, Mr. Stuart. And if things were different, I might have joined you myself."

Steve doubted it. The President was a professional politician, born into the political class and never experienced life outside it's charmed circle. He had no idea what it was like to live, literally, on less than a dollar a day. Or how hard it was to struggle with government bureaucracy. Would he really have tried to make a go of it on his own?

But he kept the thought to himself. Kevin was right. There was no point in making enemies for no good reason. And the President could help them get everything they needed to succeed.

"I'd like to see your starship, one day," the President added. There was an oddly wistful note in his voice. "My eldest daughter keeps talking about becoming an astronaut."

"She'll have her chance," Steve said. He had a sudden mad impulse to teleport all three of them to the starship, to give them the grand tour. But he forced it down ruthlessly. If blocking the DHS raid had had unpleasant repercussions, what would kidnapping the President do? "They'll all have their chance, if they are willing to try."

He watched the President go, then turned to look at his old friend. "Ready to see a whole new world?"

Henderson nodded. "Are you...is all of this for real?"

"Have the van taken to somewhere safe for the FTD to examine," Steve said. It would be brilliant if the FTD *did* figure out how to produce their own reactors. The interface had been far from helpful about how they worked. "And then I will take you somewhere that will really blow your mind."

THIRTEEN

SHADOW WARRIOR, EARTH ORBIT

"This ship is really unbelievable," Jürgen Affenzeller said. "And you can do so much from up here?"

Kevin had to smile. He rather liked Affenzeller, even if he *had* been the person who'd seen through the cloak of secrecy and realised that *something* was up. It was a pity he worked for the DHS, yet with some careful nurturing perhaps Affenzeller could be convinced to switch sides and join the growing lunar settlement.

"Yes, we can," he said, keeping his doubts to himself. "And just wait until you see some of the stuff the *aliens* can do."

He tapped a switch, accessing the live feed from thousands of nanotech drones scattered across Afghanistan. The level of access was just unbelievable, so much so that he doubted he could even *begin* to analyse it all, even with the help of the ship's computers. Each of the Taliban fighters lying in ambush in yet another mid-sized Afghani town had a tiny drone firmly fixed to his head, without any clue the drone was there. Even the larger models were far too small to be seen with the naked eye.

Piece by piece, they were putting together a picture of the enemy network that had simply never existed beforehand. Couriers were identified, tagged and tracked as easily as tracking wild animals in the jungle.

Each of their conversations were recorded, then scanned for incriminating keywords. When certain keywords were used, a second flight of drones would be dispatched to tag the next group of insurgents and continue the process. It had only been two days since Steve and the President had come to an agreement, of sorts, and the Taliban were already on the verge of defeat. But they didn't know it yet.

He made a face as he looked down at some of the other reports. There were local policemen who weren't Taliban, but preyed on the people they were meant to protect without even the fig leaf of religious justification used by the Taliban. Some of them were simple thugs, others were drug addicts, rapists or even paedophiles. Kevin shuddered at one particular memory, then silently blessed the Hordesmen who'd brought the starship to Earth. The new settlement would never have to compromise with evil just to make progress.

And they hate us because we support one set of their enemies while claiming to fight the other set, he thought, bitterly. *No wonder the Taliban sometimes looks better than the alternative. They actually have a nose for government, even if it is harsh and brutal.*

It was worse, he knew. The Afghani Government was corrupt, so much so that nearly half of the foreign aid poured into the country had vanished into Swiss bank accounts. Most of the ministers were put into office based on who they knew, rather than the results of any election, and were more interested in feathering their own nests than helping to fight the Taliban. No wonder half of them were left carefully alone by their enemies. They were better advertisements for the Taliban than anything the insurgents could do for themselves.

Affenzeller coughed. "Sir?"

"I got distracted," Kevin confessed. On the display, the drones had also carefully marked the positions of over five hundred IEDs. "Are they ready to proceed."

"Craig says so," Affenzeller confirmed. "He's with the front line, ready to advance."

Kevin nodded. Over the past two months, Coalition forces had steadily surrounded the nondescript town, trapping over three hundred insurgents inside the net. Naturally, the insurgents had prepared themselves for war, using the civilian population as human shields and press-ganged labour while they rigged their homes for demolition. And, with the human shields preventing the Coalition from simply bombing the town to rubble, the insurgents had an excellent chance of killing a few American or British soldiers.

Or so they think, he reminded himself. *Let's see how this goes.*

He checked the location of the civilians again, carefully. The insurgents had pushed veiled women and children forward, using them to shield their positions. Kevin shuddered – if the women survived the engagement they would almost certainly be killed by their menfolk afterwards – and then keyed a switch. One by one, the drones attached to the insurgents reported back. Everything was in position, ready to move.

"Remote controlled warfare," he muttered. "The dream and the nightmare."

He cleared his throat. "Tell the Colonel that we will trigger the drones in ten minutes," he said. "And then he should advance with care."

— —

ALMENA WAS FOURTEEN years old and terrified out of her mind. Once, her life had revolved around cooking, cleaning and trying to learn as much as she could from her schooling, after the old restrictions on girls going to school had been removed. Now, she was a helpless prisoner, caught in the arms of a strange male. The school had been destroyed, her teachers had been killed, her brothers had been taken away and her life had become a nightmare. All she wanted now was for it to end.

She twisted, slightly, in the man's grasp. He was older than her, wearing flowing white robes that were badly stained with something, perhaps human blood. He'd already told her that they would be married, once the battle with the infidels was over. Almena knew that he could make his promise – his threat – come true. She'd always known, from the moment she knew the difference between males and females, that one day her father would decide a suitable match for her. Her opinion would barely have been considered. But now…her father had lost his power to someone even worse.

He muttered something in a language she didn't recognise, then slapped her head. Almena saw stars and almost threw up, only swallowing the urge out of fear of another beating. The man snickered unpleasantly, then pointed a finger towards the edge of the town. Out there, the infidels were gathering. Almena was almost as scared of them as she was of the men who had taken her town and destroyed her family. Even if she survived, what would happen to a girl without a family? The younger girls had whispered dark stories about girls who were thrown out into the streets. Almena had never wanted to discover if any of them were true…

The man holding her jerked, then let go. One hand clutched his forehead, then he staggered and hit the ground. Almena jumped backwards, almost tripping over the edge of her dress, unable to take her eyes off the twitching man. He convulsed once, violently, then fell still.

She looked up. All along the line, insurgents had fallen, their captives pulling themselves free. It was a miracle, as if the hand of Allah had swept down from the heavens and wiped out the infidels who were holding them prisoner, the infidels who would have forced the girls into loveless marriages for their own pleasure. Moments later, she heard the first explosions in the distance and scrambled for a place to hide. Maybe the infidels were coming anyway, but it no longer mattered. They could hardly be worse than the insurgents.

Finding a hole, she crawled into it and closed her eyes to wait.

— —

STEVE HEARD A faint whine as the drones moved forward, searching for IEDs. The quickest way to get rid of one was simply to detonate it in place, so the drones were vibrating the ground to trigger the weapons. Those that refused to detonate were marked down for later attention, while the advancing troops were steered around them. Inch by inch, the troops moved closer to the occupied town.

It looked fairly typical for the region, he noted, as they closed in on the edge of the defences. A large number of primitive huts and hovels, a handful of more modern buildings in the centre and a single stone mosque, rising above the buildings and gleaming in the sunlight. It had been used as an Observation Point by the Taliban, Steve knew, trusting that the American infidels wouldn't fire on the mosque. But the ROE hadn't saved the men inside. The drones had killed them the moment the command was given, leaving their lifeless bodies on the ground.

A chill fell over him as he realised what was missing. No one fired at them as they entered the town, not even a single shot. Most of the human shields looked to be in shock as they stared down at their former captors, others had probably grabbed weapons and fled for their lives. The Taliban had told them, Steve guessed, that the American troops would kill the men, then rape the women and children. They'd told the same story everywhere, hoping to encourage the locals not to cooperate with the Coalition. And, given the behaviour of some local policemen, the bastards might even have a point.

The chill grew stronger as he looked down at one of the bodies. There was a tiny hole in the side of his head, smoking slightly. His AK-47 lay beside him, abandoned and useless against an attack they hadn't even seen coming. Kevin had been right, Steve told himself, as he looked up towards the mosque. The world had changed and he could no longer be the person he had been, when he had nothing to worry about but the ranch.

"Dear God," Henderson said. "What have you done?"

Steve shook his head as he looked back at the body. "Opened a whole new world," he said. "And a whole can of worms too."

"You never spoke a truer word," Henderson said. "Have you grown up a little now?"

Steve shrugged.

The afternoon was almost surreal. Normally, evicting the Taliban from a mid-sized town would take days of hard fighting, particularly if the ROE refused to allow close fire support for the advancing troops. But now, all that remained was carting out the bodies and then clearing out a handful of homes that had been turned into massive IEDs. The locals looked to have been reduced sharply by the insurgents; civil affairs teams spoke to the handful of male survivors and discovered that most of the men had been butchered as soon as the siege had begun. Steve wasn't too surprised. The insurgents had only had a limited supply of food and the town's menfolk, watching their wives and children starve, might have turned against the Taliban.

He watched a platoon of Royal Marines transporting bodies towards the mass graves, then looked up at the sun setting in the sky. Life in the village would never be the same again, even if the ones who had fled in time to escape being taken captive managed to return. The whole district had been traumatised, first by the Taliban and then by the Coalition's counter-attack. Maybe they should just offer to take the women and children with them, maybe offering them a place to live on the moon. But it would be a problem when there were no quarters available for them.

"You'd better make yourself scarce," Henderson warned. "The media is on the way."

Steve sighed. At his request, the media had been kept away from the front lines, in hopes of keeping the secret a little longer. But they'd finally broken through the bureaucratic cordon and convinced the officials to allow them to move up to the town. Hell, with resistance crumbling so quickly, it was quite possible that they thought the Taliban was finally on the verge of breaking and wanted to be there when it did.

And it will break, Steve thought, bitterly.

But most of the men who'd died today weren't the true monsters. They'd been pushed into fighting, either out of religious conviction or because they simply didn't have anywhere else to go. As always, the true brains behind the terrorists and fanatics had remained out of battle, hiding on the other side of the Pakistani border. But not any longer, Steve told himself. The network of drones was already picking its way through the networks, isolating the true monsters at the heart of the Taliban. They were all doomed. They just didn't know it.

He caught sight of a young girl, staring at him from the darkened entrance to a tiny hovel, her face no longer hidden behind a veil. It was hard to guess her age; in America, he would have confidently guessed that she was still preteen, perhaps ten at the most. But in Afghanistan, where so many children were malnourished and treated badly, she might well be old enough to marry by local standards. Her face was bitterly pale, her eyes fixed on his face. Steve felt a wave of pity, tinged with bitter helplessness. It was girls like her who had borne the brunt of the war, massively oppressed by the Taliban and then caught in the middle of savage fighting as the Coalition fought to shatter a grassroots insurgency. Somehow, he doubted she would survive the coming winter.

I could take her, he thought. It would be simple enough; walk over to her, take her arm and teleport them both to orbit. But what would happen then? *But I couldn't take them all.*

He keyed his communicator. The girl vanished into the shadows as soon as she saw it, perhaps assuming it was a weapon. They'd recorded footage of the Taliban shooting their weapons randomly, purely for giggles. Or perhaps it had been intended to convince their prisoners that they were too irrational to be negotiated with.

"Kevin," he said. "Round up a few volunteers for medical services, if you can find them, and send them down here. There are people who need help."

"Understood," Kevin said. There was an odd note in his voice. "Do you think that any of them are likely recruits? We could find space for a few dozen, if necessary."

Steve swallowed, understanding – finally – the guilt he'd dismissed as a liberal delusion. He had so much and the locals had so little. He lived in peace; the locals lived in permanent war. His wife and daughter were safe; the women and children here might be married off against their will or simply raped, if the town fell to the wrong occupation party. And the

American government, despite its flaws, was far better than anything the locals had produced or had designed for them. It was hard *not* to feel guilty.

"I believe some of them might be suitable," he said. It was hard to know when everyone in the town had almost no practical schooling at all. "But others...others are unlikely to fit in."

He sent a command to the interface. The teleporter activated and the world faded away in silver light.

— —

GUNTER DAWLISH HAD had enough run-ins with the military bureaucracy to know when he was being fed a line of bullshit. As one of the veterans of freelance journalism – it was a point of pride that he didn't take any regular pay from any newspaper or TV broadcaster – he'd heard enough spin to have a nose for it. And where someone was trying to sugar-coat a shit sandwich, it generally meant that someone had something to hide.

But what?

Gunter had gone to a great deal of trouble to be embedded with the 1st Marine Division. It did have a certain element of risk – reporters had been killed in Afghanistan – but it also allowed him to earn respect from the soldiers, who were the true heart and soul of the war in Afghanistan. But without respect, they wouldn't talk to him and most soldiers regarded reporters as the enemy. It was very hard to win their respect. Not being linked to any established part of the Mainstream Media did help, he knew, but so did bravery.

He jumped out of the AFV and looked around. It should have taken weeks, at best, to reduce the town's defenders to the point where the Coalition could just walk in. Instead, it had taken barely an hour to take the entire town. There hadn't even been a major battle, his sources had whispered, and the only causality had been a soldier who'd triggered an undiscovered IED...it just didn't make sense.

The town's remaining inhabitants were gathered at one end of a field, being tended by a group of medics and Civil Affairs specialists. For once, there seemed to be no attempt to hide the women, something perhaps encouraged by the shortage of males in the group. Indeed, the more Gunter looked, the stranger it seemed. The defenders seemed to have been wiped out…or had they fled? Had the military, having laid its plans for a great battle, discovered that its enemy had retreated and then claimed victory anyway? Or…?

He followed the soldiers out towards the mass grave and swore, sucking in his breath as he saw the bodies. The defenders had died, he realised, and clearly no one in the local community had felt like burying them, a clear rejection of their ideology. But what had killed them? Most of the bodies seemed strangely unmarked. Indeed, there seemed to be very few insurgents who'd died conventionally. It just didn't make sense.

His imagination went to work. *Gas? Something new and untried? But how could it have left one group untouched while others died?*

Shaking his head, he removed his small camera and started to take pictures, then uploaded them to his storage site through the dongle his assistant in New York had procured for him. Sending messages through the military internet was always risky, particularly if they *were* trying to spin something into a victory. But the dongle seemed to allow him to bypass all of their precautions. And maybe a few people he knew might have an idea what happened to the bodies.

By the time they were escorted back to the base, he had half of his story already written in his head.

FOURTEEN

"**W**elcome to your first dose of guilt," Mariko teased. "It's what being human is all about."

Steve snorted, but he couldn't escape the image of the girl staring at him. She had haunted his dreams for the past week, ever since he'd laid eyes on her for the first time. It wasn't romantic, he hastened to tell himself, it was a grim awareness that she was human, that she was real, that she had thoughts and feelings of her own. She wasn't just a statistic any longer.

He sat up in bed and looked over at his partner. Mariko had spent most of the last few days in Afghanistan, working in the refugee camps. From what she'd said, conditions had been hellish, particularly when some of the villagers who'd fled ahead of the Taliban started to return and assert their authority. Eventually, Steve had provisionally authorised a number of children – and teenage girls – to be moved to a camp and placed in line to go to the moon. It was a drop in the bucket, but his conscience would allow no less. Besides, he knew – all too well – what fate awaited them if they remained in Afghanistan.

"I thought I was human," he said, bleakly. "I didn't know I wasn't."

Shaking his head, he swung his legs over the side of the bed and stood, making his way towards the shower. Whatever else could be said about the decor the Subhorde Commander had considered appropriate – the interface said it was alien porn, but it looked like nothing more than splashes of paint – the showers were wonderful. He stepped inside, allowed the warm water to wash the sweat of nightmares away from his skin, then waited for the hot air to dry his body. Outside, Mariko was already pulling herself out of bed.

She looked gorgeous, Steve realised, once again. Part of him wanted her right away, to take her back to bed and prove to both of them that life went on, but he knew there was no time to waste. The meeting was scheduled to take place in thirty minutes. Instead, he walked over to the food processor, picking up pieces of clothing along the way, and ordered them both breakfast. There was a ding from the machine as it produced its latest version of something edible for humankind.

"They won't starve, down there," Mariko said. "And they won't die of thirst either."

Steve nodded. He'd sent two biomass processors down to the sur-face, along with a portable water cleanser. It was probably best not to think about where some of the biomass was actually coming from, but the locals wouldn't starve. So far, they were so grateful to be fed that no one had started to complain about the tasteless food. The cynic in Steve suspected that it wouldn't be long before that changed.

He passed her one of the plates and tucked into something that looked like scrambled eggs, although the eggs were gray and the bread a faint pinkish colour. It tasted fine, despite its appearance. Kevin and Mongo kept experimenting with the food processors, trying to produce something that both looked and tasted good, but there were just too many variables in a system designed to feed individuals from over a thou-sand different races, each one with their own requirements. The sections on interstellar diplomacy he'd accessed through the interface had warned of problems in serving dinners when two or more races met to talk. One race's food might be literally sickening to the other race...

Once they were finished, Steve returned the plates to the proces-sor and walked out of the cabin, heading down towards the conference room. It was astonishing just how much like home the giant starship had become, now they'd cleaned the decks and removed most of the more disturbing alien artworks. The interface seemed to believe that some of them were worth considerable amounts of galactic currency in the right places, but Steve found it hard to believe that it was right. But then, if someone could stick a piece of wood in a glass of urine and claim it was modern art, perhaps the Horde had their own sense of aesthetics. Or, for all he knew, there were races that collected their art.

The conference room was an odd mixture of human and alien technology. Steve had moved the heavy wooden table from the ranch into the compartment, then surrounded it with chairs from the closest office store. One of the alien projectors sat on the table, ready to project images into the air; another was placed near the door, allowing people outside the starship to attend the meeting virtually. The system was so remarkable that it made videoconferencing look like a piece of crap. Kevin hadn't taken long to point out that it would also add a whole new dimension to pornography.

He sat down at the head of the table and waited, accessing files from the interface to bide the time. Kevin, having the shortest distance to go, arrived within minutes, then sat down at the other end of the table. Charles, who had teleported up from Earth, took a seat next to Steve, while Mongo and Wilhelm sat down at the middle. Steve couldn't help wondering if they were already picking sides, in anticipation of the moment they developed factions. It hadn't taken the newborn American Republic long to develop political parties.

Steve shook his head, inwardly. As long as he had influence, he would make damn sure there were no political parties, no one voting the party line against their conscience. Maybe parties had an important role to play, but they eventually became more intent on ensuring their own survival than actually representing their people. And that was the death knell of democracy.

"I call this meeting to order," he said, cheerfully. "Coffee's in the processor, smoke them if you have them, etc, etc."

There was a brief pause as the group found cups of coffee for themselves and Wilhelm lit up a rather large cigar. Steve, who had given up smoking years ago, watched it with some amusement. Now, with alien medical technology, smoking posed no health hazard at all. But it was still banned on the moon, outside the smoking room. The CO of Heinlein Colony wasn't inclined to take chances with the rapidly expanding base.

"It's been a week since we intervened in Afghanistan," Steve said, once they were sitting again. "It's been ten days since we came to a preliminary agreement with the United States Government. I believe, therefore, that this is a good time to take stock of our position and bring us all up to date. Kevin?"

"I get to go first, do I?" Kevin asked. He smiled, rather dryly, then sobered. "At the moment, both the Afghanistan and Pakistani Taliban are in disarray. Their senior leadership has been effectively wiped out, shattering their command and control structures. In some places, this may allow for local accommodations and even surrender talks, as the Pakistani Taliban absolutely refused to allow any form of compromise between the Coalition and insurgent fighters. We have successfully created a window of opportunity for the local government and the Coalition to re-establish their authority over the nation.

"However, we have not tackled the underlying conditions that brought the Taliban into existence and gave them so many supporters. Corruption in the government has not been brought under control, tribal issues remain untouched and there is still a growing humanitarian crisis in large parts of the country. In the long run, we may see a resurgence of the Taliban insurgency – or something else, something more local.

"A further problem is that we may have accidentally destabilised the Pakistani Government," he added. "They had ties to the Taliban, despite our protests, fearful of what would happen after the inevitable American withdrawal. Now, several of those agents are dead and the Pakistani Taliban is unravelling. The government may take advantage of the situation to eradicate the last traces of the insurgency or it may become more inclined to host them, as the geopolitical realities have not changed."

Steve sighed. Like most American officers, he had rapidly grown
to distrust and despise the Pakistani Government during his service in
Afghanistan. They had played a double game, helping NATO with one
hand and protecting the Taliban with the other. Maybe they did have
good reasons for acting in such an underhand manner – although it wasn't
something Steve would willingly have tolerated – but they also undermined American trust and support for their government. And there were
far too many questions about just how Osama Bin Laden had remained
in Pakistan without being discovered. Had he been hidden and protected
by Pakistani intelligence?

"We are proceeding to track down Al Qaeda links from Afghanistan
and Pakistan to the Middle East," Kevin concluded. "As Langley warned,
AQ has fragmented into several dozen franchises that are both cooperating and conflicting with one another. We can work out ways to identify
most of them, but it's going to be a long hard slog."

Steve nodded, slowly. "Keep working on it," he said. "What about
the cooperation you've received from the government?"

Kevin smiled. "Which one?"

He went on before Steve could say a word. "I've got a team of analysts
from NSA and Langley assisting with the intake," he added. "Most of
them are doing a wonderful job, although the sheer torrent of information is often overloading our capacity for analysing it, let alone turning
it into actionable intelligence. Still, we have some advantages. For one
thing, once we tag someone he stays tagged."

Steve felt a chill running down his spine. Kevin had been right. The
sheer potential for abuse was terrifying. As long as they held control, it
wouldn't happen...or would it? Would there come a time when he'd be
tempted to use the technology to rid himself of political enemies? He
thought of some of the politicians in Washington and gritted his teeth.
Would he be able to resist the temptation?

"Good," he said, finally. "Charles?"

Charles nodded and leaned forward. With Kevin detailed to intelligence, Charles had effectively taken over recruitment.

"Now that we can move more openly, we have around five thousand prospective candidates in mind," Charles said. "Half of them are military veterans, some crippled, others are various civilians who may be able to assist us. Quite a number are research scientists on the cutting edge of technological development, several are theorists who can be added to Keith's group. However, the wider we cast our net, the more likely it will be we pick up a spy."

Steve nodded. The DHS had already put together a profile of the people Steve was recruiting, even if their imagination had failed to deduce the existence of the starship or Steve's long-term plans. He had already confirmed that they wouldn't try to recruit serving military personnel, but the government could probably find a likely candidate and try to brief him first. Who knew where *that* would lead?

"Run them all through the lie detector first," Kevin said. "So far, no one has been able to fool it. If they turn out to be spies, we can either restrict their movements or tell them we'll pick them up later."

"That leads to another problem," Charles said. "Two, actually; where do we draw the line?"

Steve lifted his eyebrows. "The line?"

"Ninety percent of our recruits, so far, are American," Charles said. "The remainder are British, Canadian and a handful of others from NATO countries. I'm planning to expand operations in Britain once the British Government is briefed into our existence. But where do we draw the line?"

He leaned forward. "Once we go public, there will be millions of people wanting to immigrate," he added. "Not all of them will come from the West. Do we refuse to take Muslims? Or Russians? Or Chinese?"

Steve looked down at his hands. America had been built on immigration, he knew, hundreds of thousands of immigrants forced into a melting pot that had produced a semi-united culture. But now immigration was often a threat, to both America and the West, when the immigrants refused to integrate and the government refused to force them to comply. One immigrant was hardly a problem, a whole community – often isolated, not always speaking English – was a major headache. He'd heard too much from the south to take the problem lightly.

"Let me see if this makes sense," he said. "We take people who are willing to work – no handouts for anyone on the moon – who speak English and are prepared to follow our laws, such as they are."

"That *does* require that we codify our laws," Kevin said. "So far, all we have are a handful of regulations on the moon. We'll need a constitution, we'll need a civil code, we'll need some form of police…hell, we probably need some form of the Pledge of Allegiance."

"We'll write one out," Steve said. "It's a problem we will have to tackle over the next few months, I suspect."

He shrugged. "Markus?"

Wilhelm leaned forward. "The US Government has requested ten fusion reactors," he said, "and as many superconductors as we can produce. So far, we have provided five reactors, three of which have vanished into Area 51. The remaining two have been quietly attached to the national power grid, replacing a number of purely human power plants. I think they're running experiments with the superconductors right now, concentrating on trying to produce batteries and directed energy weapons. The latter, in particular, will be very useful.

"In the meantime, the Internet Dongles have been a fantastic success and the world is waking up to their potential. Internet geeks all over the United States have been unlocking their functions, including several we didn't anticipate when we produced them. By now, I imagine that NSA is having kittens. It's simply not possible to trace the dongles through modern human technology. Several of them have even spread to China, despite – I'm sorry to say – the Chinese government slapping an immediate ban on them. Anyone would think they didn't want their people to have unlimited and unmonitored access to the internet."

He smiled. "Suffice it to say that the next few years should be very interesting," he said. "I suspect that modern file-sharing software is about to be replaced with something else, something far faster. Hollywood and the other producers are going to go ballistic when they realise that someone can download a complete copy of *The Avengers II* in less than five minutes. In the long term, we may destroy Hollywood completely."

"What a shame," Steve said, dryly. He had scant regard for Hollywood. "What about our imports?"

"We've been able to expand more," Wilhelm said. "It turned out that one small company was producing inflatable space stations for NASA. They…"

"Hold on," Kevin interrupted. "*Inflatable* space stations?"

"It's quite a sound piece of technology," Wilhelm assured him. "As always, the real problem is getting the bubbles up to orbit. We can do that, which will allow us to expand our operations in space and start working towards producing asteroid homesteading kits. Give us five years, sir, and the asteroid belt will be full of tiny settlements."

"Another good reason for laws," Charles commented. "How do we tell when someone's been claim-jumping?"

Wilhelm shrugged. "Other imports are proceeding well," he said. "Now the government isn't going to get in our way, I've started to order more specialised space equipment as well as vast quantities of supplies we need for the colony. The cost is quite staggering, but we're raking in money from the dongles."

Steve smiled. "Keep a sharp eye on it," he said. "We don't want to wind up in debt to the government."

He looked over at Keith Glass. "And our long-term plans?"

"The alien database suggested several ways to terraform Mars," Glass said, calmly. "I suspect we will need to use the quickest way, which will take just over a hundred years, once we produce the right equipment. However, the database also warned that it would destroy any prior traces of life on Mars…assuming, of course, there ever was any. And it will hardly be unnoticed on Earth when we start slamming ice asteroids into the planet.

"Tech-wise, we've made some progress on understanding alien weapons and defensive systems," he continued. "They do have force shields protecting their starships, but they can be broken down by sufficient energy. Unfortunately, the energy needs to be a ravening needle, not a simple explosion. I suspect that a modern alien starship could simply take a nuclear blast and shrug it off. Right now, we're preparing plans to convert modern nuclear warheads into bomb-pumped lasers. However, without a large-scale nuclear warhead production program, it might take us years to build up enough weapons to defend the Earth."

Mongo snorted. "And if they made a fuss over Iraq perhaps having nukes," he said, "what will they make of us building nukes on the moon?"

Steve shrugged. "Could we purchase warheads from the Russians and adapt them?"

"Perhaps," Glass said. "However, I don't know if they could be adapted. Russian tech is…crude, to say the least. We might be better off constructing our own breeder reactors on the moon, at least in the long term."

"We can work on that," Steve said. He had never been irrationally terrified of nuclear power – the alien interface spoke of antimatter power plants and even stranger ideas – but he knew enough to treat it with extreme care. "And perhaps recruit some more experts from Earth to assist us."

"Perhaps," Glass agreed. "In the meantime…"

He stopped as an alarm rang.

Steve checked the interface, then swore. "We have one contact, perhaps two, coming towards the solar system," he said. Their time had just run out. "I think we're about to be put to the test."

FIFTEEN

SHADOW WARRIOR, EARTH ORBIT

Steve had spent days studying how the aliens waged war, only to discover that there were as many ideas on how to fight as there were spacefaring alien races. Only a tenth of known intelligent races, according to the database, had actually developed spacefaring technology on their own – and only a handful had developed FTL before they were discovered by someone else – but there were still quite a few ideas. The only reassuring note was that the Horde didn't seem to be very competent at space combat, no matter how capable they were on the ground. But with two starships – if there *were* two starships – coming towards Earth, they would definitely have the numbers advantage.

"Sound red alert," he said, as he sat down in the chair he'd fabricated to replace the Subhorde Commander's throne. "All hands to battle stations."

Mongo smirked. "How long have you been waiting to say that?"

Steve glowered at his back, then linked into the interface, accessing the starship's tactical systems directly. They weren't designed to actually fight the ship, he'd discovered, but they did handle issues that moved too rapidly for organic brains to comprehend. The two contacts were still racing towards the edge of the solar system, the gravity-waves announcing their arrival speeding out ahead of them. It would be nearly an hour, the interface noted, before the enemy starships arrived at Earth.

He disengaged, then looked over at Charles. "Bring the assault teams onboard and issue weapons," he ordered. "And then prepare them, as best as possible, to board and storm another alien ship or two."

"Understood," Charles said. He hesitated, then leaned forward. "Are you going to alert the President?"

Steve hadn't considered it until Charles brought it up. *Should* he alert the President? But what could the President do? It would take days to bring the American military to full alert – and besides, it wasn't as if it posed any real threat to the Hordesmen. All they'd have to do was stay in orbit and drop rocks on any centres of resistance. After a few hours of constant bombardment, the remainder of the human race would be begging to surrender. No, there was nothing the President could do. But should he be told anyway?

It would be a gesture of trust, Steve knew; the President *had* wanted to be kept in the loop. But it would only worry him when there was nothing he could do…and yet he'd be outraged if he heard, afterwards, that Earth had been in grave danger and he hadn't known a thing about it. No, he probably should be told. And, if *Shadow Warrior* was lost, he might be able to swear blind that he'd never heard of the ship or its human crew. Maybe the Horde would accept it.

Steve made a face. "I'll talk to him," he said, finally.

He keyed into the interface, then opened the link to the communicator they'd given the President. The Secret Service, those few in the know about the starship and the new colony, had been frantic with worry, pointing out that there was no way to prevent the President from being kidnapped from under their very noses. But the President had overruled them, showing more balls than Steve had expected from him. Or maybe he was smart enough to understand what had happened to the Taliban and deduce that Steve could easily do the same to him anyway, even if he didn't carry the communicator.

It was late night in Washington, he realised, a moment too late. But the President was probably used to being woken in the middle of the night. Besides, Steve's first Drill Instructor had been confident that being woken late at night was good for the recruits character, the bastard.

"Mr. Stuart," the President said. "What can I do for you?"

"There's one, perhaps two, alien starships heading into the system," Steve said, quickly. "We may just have run out of time."

He heard the President gulp. The man had only had ten days to come to terms with the reality of aliens and a group of former US servicemen in control of an alien starship and a growing lunar settlement. He'd been the most powerful man on Earth, but now Earth was merely a drop in the galactic bucket, a tiny and utterly insignificant world protected only by its isolation from any gravity point. And nemesis was fast approaching.

"You need to call a very quiet alert," Steve said. He knew it would be useless, but at least it would convince the President he was doing something useful. "And pray for us."

"I will," the President said. "Good luck."

"Thank you," Steve said.

He broke the connection and returned his attention to the main display, now reformatted for human eyesight. The two contacts were reducing speed, slightly, as they entered the solar system, apparently trying to avoid the outermost planets and their gravity wells. From what Keith Glass and his theorists had deduced, partly from clues in alien fiction, the alien ships actually bent gravity around them and surfed through space at FTL speeds. A sufficiently large gravity well would break up the gravity waves and force them to return to normal space, if indeed they'd left it. Glass's reports hadn't been too clear on that topic.

Perhaps we need to hire more theorists, Steve thought, coldly.

It burned at him that the Hordesmen, despite being primitive barbarians, had access to the technology of his dreams. But they'd bought, begged or stolen it for themselves. No wonder, Steve considered, they were trapped in cultural stasis. The gulf between them and the Galactics – or humanity – was simply too wide to cross easily. They'd have to change their very mindset to start making advances and *that* would be tricky, if not impossible. In many ways, they were simply too conservative for their own good.

"They're not leaving a ship on the edge of the solar system," Mongo commented. "You'd think they'd consider it a wise precaution."

"They don't think Earth is dangerous," Kevin countered. "Remember just how casually they moved into the atmosphere and kidnapped us?"

Steve nodded, bitterly. Every year, thousands of people in the United States went missing, never to be seen again. Some of them had probably just wanted to vanish, others had been murdered and their bodies hidden beyond easy discovery...and some of them might just have been abducted by aliens. God knew there were plenty of *stories* about alien abduction in the United States. Could some of them have been taken by other aliens? He hadn't seen anything resembling the tiny grey aliens of *X-Files* myth in the database, but that didn't mean they didn't exist. There were *thousands* of spacefaring aliens in the galaxy.

"No, they don't," he agreed. He leaned forward. "Do we have the decoy ready to go?"

Kevin smiled. "It's ready," he said. "And they won't be expecting it at all."

Steve had to smile. As if to make up for being outnumbered, trawling through the files had revealed the security codes the Hordesmen used to assure one another that they were safe and not under enemy control. The latter codes, it seemed, were rarely used, as the Hordesmen preferred death to what they saw as dishonour. But, with some ingenuity, *Shadow Warrior* ought to be able to convince the newcomers that everything was fine until it was too late.

"We just got a message from Heinlein," Mongo said. "They're going dark now."

"It won't be enough," Kevin said, grimly. "Maybe we should have fled after all."

"No," Steve said. He hadn't been able to abandon the ranch and he wouldn't be able to abandon Earth. It was home, despite its flaws. "We couldn't leave our homeworld and billons of people to burn."

He sucked in a breath. There hadn't been a truly existential war in American history since the Civil War – and *that* had been against fellow

Americans. The last time the American Republic had faced total defeat had been in 1812, when the British might have managed to tear the newborn republic apart and reabsorb it into the British Empire. Even Hitler or Stalin wouldn't have been able to land troops on American soil and occupy the country. The logistics of such an invasion would be staggering, utterly beyond comprehension…

But they were fighting an existential war now, he knew. The Hordesmen wouldn't hesitate to bombard the planet into submission, reducing humanity to a wave of slaves…slaves who might just take over, given time to learn more about their masters from the inside. No one on Earth, outside a tiny select group, knew about the coming engagement. But their lives depended on it. If Steve and his family lost, a nightmare would descend upon Earth.

Maybe Kevin was right, he thought. *Perhaps we should have fled.*

It had seemed a cowardly solution at the time. *Shadow Warrior* could easily carry a few thousand humans and their children to another star system and provide the base for a high-tech civilisation. Given time and alien medical technology, they could build up a massive population without needing immigrants from Earth, while the Horde would be faced with a disturbing mystery. Somehow, he doubted that lost Horde starships were uncommon…and with no trace of Galactic technology on Earth, it would be hard for the Horde to blame humanity for the loss. But would that really stop them bombarding the planet into submission?

He pushed his thoughts aside as the alien starships drew closer. It wouldn't be long now.

"Picking up gravimetric fluctuations," Kevin said, softly. "I think they're decelerating."

There was a *ping* from the display. "They're dropped out of FTL," Kevin added. "And they're coming our way."

"On screen," Steve said. He chuckled, dispelling the tension. "I thought of that one yesterday."

"Keith was saying that *Star Trek* was a poor excuse for an SF show," Kevin joked. "We should have gone with *Babylon 5*."

Steve considered it. He'd watched all five seasons of *Babylon 5* in Iraq, between patrols through dangerous cities and countryside. "Nah," he said, finally. "I hated the fifth season."

He looked up at the display as the two alien starships came into view. One of them looked to have been built by the same designers responsible for *Shadow Warrior*, as it looked like a large dagger ready to stick itself into its enemy's heart. The other looked rather alarmingly like a giant crab, except it had three claws instead of two. With some imagination, it was possible to see how they might both be able to land on a planetary surface.

"Small ships," Kevin commented. "But armed to the teeth."

Steve had to smile. The smallest ship was over a hundred metres long, bigger than anything humanity had put into space. Were they so jaded that such a wondrous creation seemed *tiny*?

"Send them the distress call," he ordered. "Let them think we're in trouble."

He watched as the holographic image of the Subhorde Commander's second-in-command started requesting help from the newcomers. The original Subhorde Commander, according to their alien captive, would have killed himself out of shame, an act that would somehow allow his subordinates to remain blameless. Steve couldn't help wondering just what sort of society would insist on suicide for something that was hardly the person's fault, but he feared he already knew the answer. The Hordesmen hated having to admit that they needed assistance from anyone else.

Just like us, he thought, remembering his grandfather's stories about the Great Depression. The family had gone hand-to-mouth for years, but they'd never accepted government help or even local charity. *We're stubborn bastards too.*

"They're altering course and coming towards us," Mongo said. "Their weapons are charged, but they're not targeting us – or anyone else."

"Good," Steve said. The ships might be smaller than his ship, but they packed a nasty punch…assuming, of course, the Hordesmen knew how

to use the weapons. Did they? It seemed impossible that they didn't...
and besides, he didn't dare assume so unless he had very clear proof of
their failings. "Are our assault teams ready to go?"

"Aye, sir," Kevin said. "Edward is ready to go; I've uploaded starship
specifications into his combat implants, so he and his team won't be lost."

"Excellent," Steve said.

"Picking up a response," Mongo interrupted. "They're demanding
more details."

"Tell our spoiled brat to start whining," Steve ordered. The simulated
Subhorde Commander wasn't any more intelligent or knowledgeable
than the one Steve had killed. He wouldn't know what was wrong, any
more than the rest of his people. They probably thought that kicking the
equipment would start it working again. "And then request immediate
transhipment of emergency supplies."

"Enemy ships entering weapons range," Mongo said. "I'm passive-
locking our weapons onto their shield generators."

Steve smirked. One idea that seemed to have come straight out of *Star
Trek* was aligning the teleporter to beam its people through the shields,
provided one knew the shield frequency. The Hordesmen probably didn't
know it was possible, but the interface had helpfully provided details
when asked. Once their shields were battered down, the assault would
begin...if, of course, they *had* to batter down the shields. As long as the
Horde had no idea that *Shadow Warrior* was in human hands, they'd come
in fat and happy.

"Keep passive target locks at all times," he said. "If we go active,
they'll smell a rat."

The seconds ticked away as the two starships converged on *Shadow
Warrior*. "Enemy ships are entering teleport range now," Mongo said.
"They're requesting permission to board."

Steve checked the weapon at his belt, then keyed the alarm.
Throughout the ship, the entire crew would be drawing weapons, ready
to engage the aliens if they managed to teleport onto the ship. The human
crew couldn't risk alerting the aliens, Steve knew; they'd have to wipe out

the unsuspecting aliens as quickly as possible. At least they now knew how to configure their stunners to stun Hordesmen, rather than butchering them like animals.

He took a breath. "Grant it," he ordered. "And prepare to lower shields."

If the timing worked…if the timing worked…

"One ship has lowered shields," Mongo reported. There was a grim note of frustration in his voice. "The other is keeping its shields in position."

Steve gritted his teeth. The ambush, it seemed, was about to get bloody. "Beam the first set of assault teams to the enemy starship," he ordered. "And then target the other ship's shield generators and open fire!"

Mongo keyed a switch. "Aye, sir," he ordered. "Phasers engaging…now!"

On the screen, the second enemy starship was suddenly wrapped in a bubble of glowing light as the directed energy weapons burned into its shields. Its companion was already partly disabled – the attackers had beamed stun grenades and modified screamers as well as the assault team itself – but Steve kept an eye on it anyway. Maybe someone had been wearing a mask or a spacesuit, something that would provide enough protection for them to rally the troops and counterattack.

"Enemy ship is returning fire," Mongo said. The starship shuddered a moment later as pulses of energy slammed into her shields. At least none of the consoles seemed inclined to explode as the starship was hammered. *That* always happened on *Star Trek*, but it was more than a little unrealistic. "They're coming right towards us."

Ramming speed, Steve thought. If the Horde Commander thought he and his crew were doomed, he might as well try to take the captured starship down with them. It would fit in with what they knew of the Horde's Code of Honour, although Steve wouldn't have called it *Honour*. More like bloody-minded stupidity.

"Evasive action," he snapped. It wasn't going to be easy. The smaller ship was considerably more manoeuvrable than the Warcruiser. He hastily checked with the interface and discovered that a small cruiser ramming a full-sized Warcruiser would almost certainly result in mutual destruction. "And continue firing."

"Target their drives," Kevin advised. "Slow them down!"

"It doesn't fucking matter," Mongo snapped. He didn't look up from his console. "We either board them or destroy them or we're thoroughly fucked."

Steve cursed under his breath, feeling helpless as the smaller ship converged on his starship. They were evading, but the smaller ship was easily altering its course to ensure that it would still manage to ram the larger ship. Statistics raced up the side of the display, charting the damage to the enemy ship's shields and the time to impact, when the two ships would collide.

I kept Mariko on the ship, Steve thought, with sudden bitter regret. He didn't mind risking his own life – it ran in the family – but risking the life of his partner and children were quite another matter. And, with Mongo and Kevin on the ship, there would be no one left to look after the children. *All* of their children. *I've killed her.*

Mongo let out a cry of delight. "Their shields are fluctuating...one shield hexagon is down!"

"Beam the assault team onboard," Steve ordered. The enemy commander was clearly no slouch, even if he didn't really understand the technology at his command. He was already rolling the ship, trying to put another shield hexagon between his ship and *Shadow Warrior*. But it was too late. "And then prepare fire support, if necessary."

"Understood," Mongo said. *Shadow Warrior* rolled again, evading the suddenly uncontrolled alien craft. Steve fretted for a long moment before confirming that the ship's course would take it nowhere near Earth. "Assault team one reports that they have secured their target."

"Good," Steve said. With the Hordesmen stunned or dead, there would be nothing standing between the humans and control of the starship. "Have them take control of the ship, then steer her to the reception point. And continue to monitor assault team two."

SIXTEEN

Shadow Warrior, Earth Orbit

umping into a combat situation had always given Edward Romford the shakes, even before he'd been crippled and forced to face the fact that he'd never walk again. He was fine walking to the line of battle, or driving a Bradley towards the sound of the guns, but dropping from an aircraft and parachuting into the combat zone scared the pants off him. In that sense, the teleporter was actually worse, with a brief interval when the enemy could shoot at him and he couldn't even *see* them.

The silver light faded away, revealing the bridge of an alien starship. Like the first starship, it was a strange mixture of technology, with several pieces that might come from a previously unknown race. The aliens were already staggering as the stun grenades took effect, but several of them had managed to don masks before it was too late. Edward silently gave them points for earnestness, even though he hated what he'd read of the Horde. He'd hated wearing MOPP suits too.

He lifted his weapon as soon as he orientated himself and opened fire, spraying stun pulses over the entire compartment. The stunner was a fantastic weapon, he decided, as the remaining aliens hit the deck. It was easy enough to point and shoot, then sort everyone out afterwards. Indeed, he had a feeling that police departments across the USA would be trying to buy stunners as soon as they went on the market. But that would be years in the future.

Bracing himself, he stepped forward, hunting for the alien in charge. The starship's commander had fallen off his throne, somehow; Edward couldn't help thinking of a spider that had been flipped upside down by a cruel human as he rolled the alien over and tried to remove the neural interface. It stubbornly refused to budge and, despite its apparent frailty, wouldn't come free when he pulled at it. As far as he could tell, it had merged with its owner's flesh.

He keyed his communicator as the rest of the team spread through the starship, stunning the handful of remaining aliens. "Sir, I can't disengage the neural interface."

There was a long pause. "I killed the last one," Stuart said, grimly. "They don't disengage unless commanded to do so or if their owner is dead."

Edward gritted his teeth, then drew his knife from his belt and sliced open the alien's throat. Foul-smelling green blood cascaded out, pooling on the already scarred and tainted deck, as the alien breathed its last. The interface hummed slightly, then withdrew from the alien's skull. As soon as it was free, Edward felt an odd compulsion to take it for himself and place it on his head.

He fought it off as he picked the headband up and passed it to the volunteer. The volunteer took it and placed it on his head, then winced as the interface made contact with his brain. From what Edward had been told, the experience was painful, but the volunteer's face looked as if he were on the verge of collapsing into madness. Eventually, finally, he brought the link under control.

"I think this one was made by different people," he said, as he took control of the starship. "The operating system appears to be completely different."

"I see," Edward said. "Does that mean you can't handle the ship?"

"I can handle it," the volunteer assured him. "It just took some time for the device to adapt to a human brain."

Edward nodded, then keyed his communicator again. "Target secured," he said. "I say again, target secured."

It had been easy, he knew, but the Hordesmen had suspected nothing until it was far too late for them to escape. If they realised that the Sol System was becoming a black hole for their ships, they'd either give the system a wide berth or send a much more formidable fleet to challenge Earth's defences. By then, humanity had better be ready to defend itself.

"Understood," Stuart said. "Take the ship to the reception point. We'll deal with the prisoners there."

— —

"WELCOME TO ALCATRAZ," Graham Rochester said. "Our primary penal centre for alien POWs."

Steve had to smile. Alcatraz was nothing more than a dome of lunar rock, covering an area big enough for a dozen football fields. The only way in and out was through an airlock that wouldn't open unless a modified shuttle or tractor had already docked there and exchanged security codes. In the unlikely event of the prisoners managing to force their way through the airlock, they'd find themselves breathing hard vacuum. If they weren't careful, the entire prison would decompress.

"We've included a sizable supply of their food," Rochester continued. "Once they wake up, we'll send a holographic projection into the prison and explain the state of affairs. I don't think they can kill themselves with what they have on hand, but..."

He shrugged. "Overall, given their honour code, they probably *will* try to end their lives," he warned. "But we can't guard against that without keeping them stunned indefinitely, which will eventually kill them anyway."

"Understood," Steve said. On the display, the alien prisoners were sleeping peacefully. None of them had been particularly injured, but four had died when they'd collapsed at the wrong time and injured themselves when they fell. Their bodies had been shipped to a medical centre, where they would be examined carefully by human scientists. "Do you have any other concerns?"

"The Hordesmen don't treat their prisoners very well," Rochester said. "It occurs to me that we could try to convert some of the POWs to our side. They'd be killed if we sent them home, sir. They have to know it."

"Bastards," Steve said. What sort of idiot would blame someone for being taken prisoner when there had been literally no opportunity to resist? But there had been human cultures like that too, ones that had treated the prisoners they'd taken shamefully. "But if you can get it organised, feel free to try."

"Yes, sir," Rochester said. "I'd also like to get a few military policemen up here to help take care of the prisoners. We'll treat them under the Geneva Conventions as much as possible."

Steve looked up at him. "We *cannot* afford to allow them to send messages home," he said. "That would be far too revealing."

"Assuming that their bosses are interested in any messages from prisoners," Rochester commented. "But apart from that, we will treat them fairly well."

Steve nodded and turned away from the display. "On to more serious matters," he added, "how are you getting along with Heinlein Colony?"

"Expanding faster and faster," Rochester said. "The new supplies from Earth really helped, sir. But we are going to need more personnel soon enough. And some proper cooks."

"I understand," Steve said. "Just don't tell me you want to open a McDonald's franchise up here."

"It would be better than the crap from the food processors," Rochester pointed out. Steve had his doubts, but held his tongue. "But I was thinking more of someone experienced in operating a small eatery, rather than a fast food place. Hell, get three or four of them and let them compete for customers. Of course, we'll need a monetary system first..."

He eyed Steve expectantly. "At the moment, we're effectively operating a system where people work and we take care of them," he said. "Alarmingly like communism, really. But that is going to have to change."

"Another headache," Steve admitted. He rubbed the side of his forehead, then nodded. "Perhaps we should just pay everyone in American dollars. Or gold."

He smiled. His father had always gone on and on about the value of gold, but Steve knew that gold's value depended upon having someone willing and able to purchase it. Gold would work, he suspected, if it were sold down on Earth, but if the bottom dropped out of the market there would be a colossal economic disaster.

"I was thinking a kind of Lunar Credit," Rochester said. "We could pin it to the dollar, for now, but we don't want something that is pegged by forces outside our control. That almost fucked Greece."

Steve nodded. If nothing else, the economic troubles in Greece meant that the country had plenty of young men and women willing to emigrate to find work. He was sure that, once the public announcement was made, hundreds of thousands of them would apply to join the growing colony. The only difficulty would be training programs and *those* were just a matter of time. As the colony expanded, experienced men could start training inexperienced men, who would then train newcomers in turn.

And, as they set up more homes below the lunar surface, there would be room for people who didn't want to live on Earth, but couldn't work on the moon.

"I'll work on that, along with a constitution," he said. "Have you had any major trouble just yet?"

Rochester scowled. "One idiot with more initiative than common sense built himself a still and nearly poisoned a couple of workers with bootleg alcohol," he said. "I clobbered him, then put the idiot on punishment duty for a couple of weeks. But we will probably face something more serious later on, as we keep expanding. We need some kind of law, sir, rather than just my fists."

He waved a cyborg arm under Steve's nose. "That could be very dangerous in the future."

"It will be done," Steve said. "Somehow."

He shook his head. He'd seen more than a few attempts to rewrite the constitution or devise a completely new one, but they were either simplistic or excessively detailed, full of *ifs*, *buts* and *exceptions*. There were people who wanted to restrict the franchise to those who had served a term in the military and people who thought that only those who paid tax should vote. Both ideas sounded reasonable, but they had flaws that would become disastrous if the system suffered a serious breakdown.

And most of the other ideas boiled down to *I should get a vote. Here is the list of people who shouldn't get a vote.*

"Good luck," Rochester said. He paused. "For the moment, we're largely operating under Queen's Regulations, with some exceptions for off-duty hours. But that will have to be clarified soon."

Steve nodded, tiredly.

"Markus Wilhelm was talking about moving his factories up here, as soon as we have cleared space for them," Rochester continued. "I imagine that other corporations will want to follow suit, particularly if our regulations are nowhere near as tight as the States. But that will cause problems too. What happens if we don't over-regulate and we have an industrial accident?"

"All right, all right," Steve said. He held up his hands in mock surrender. "You've made your point. I'll speak to the alien, then go back to the ship and start working on a constitution. And then Kevin and Mongo can read through it and decide what they think of it. How long did it take the Founding Fathers to draft the constitution?"

"Around one hundred days, but it depends on just what you use as the starting point," Rochester said. "Just try and keep the lawyers out of it. We don't want a monstrosity like the European Constitution."

Steve nodded. The Constitutional Convention had included lawyers – or at least people trained in the law – but they'd also been statesmen. He wouldn't have trusted any modern-day lawyer to draw up a Constitution to govern a kids playground, let alone an actual country. Hell, perhaps they should have a law banning lawyers from government altogether...

"We'll make it happen," he said. Had Washington and Franklin felt so tired, even as their work came to fruition? "Somehow, it will happen."

— —

CN!LSS HAD FALLEN in love with the human laptop as soon as it had been gifted to him by one of the humans charged with watching him. It was clunky, compared to some of the computers he'd seen when he'd been trying to study Galactic technology, but it was also remarkably simple. He'd read through countless files on humanity, researched aspects that puzzled him...and discovered that humans seemed to like nude photographs of themselves. When he'd asked, his guards had muttered something about human sexuality and changed the subject.

The more he studied humanity, the more impressed he became. Humans were...odd, both a technological race and yet a divided race. Almost every Galactic power had unified their homeworlds before reaching out into space or shortly afterwards, when they discovered that they weren't alone in the galaxy. Even the Hordes had an overarching structure, although it was more symbolic than real. No Horde would happily accept the domination of another Horde indefinitely.

But humanity...they'd come so far, despite so many different attitudes and cultures. Human religion was a strange mixture, utterly beyond his comprehension, while human government perplexed him. There were societies that reminded him of the Hordes – and yet they were technological while there were others he simply couldn't understand. What sort of ruling family ruled indefinitely? What sort of society operated by giving everyone, strong and weak, a vote? Half the time, he would read one website and then discover that the next website contradicted it. If he believed all he read, the human race was in a permanent state of civil war.

He looked up when the door opened, revealing the human commander. Cn!lss pulled himself to his feet, then slipped into the Posture of Respect. Maybe the humans didn't really expect him to prostrate himself, but there was no point in taking chances. He hadn't seen any of the humans beheaded by their superiors, yet even the most brutish Horde Commander tried to keep such discipline away from Galactic eyes. After all, they might disapprove and suggest trade sanctions on the Hordes.

"Greetings," the human said. As always, it was hard to read emotion on the alien face. They simply didn't have anything like the Horde's range of expressions. "Two more of your ships have been captured."

Cn!lss wasn't sure how he felt about two more ships falling into human hands. On one claw, two more Horde Commanders had been humiliated – and he *hated* his superiors with a passion he couldn't have hoped to convey to his human captors. But on the other claw, it suggested that the humans were steadily growing more and more powerful...and, combined with their technological inventiveness, would soon be in a position to leave their star system and wage war on the Hordes. Would his entire people be exterminated?

"Good," he said, finally. At least it didn't *seem* as if the humans would commit genocide against the Hordes. "Did you take prisoners?"

"Most of the crews," the human said. "Do you wish to speak with them?"

"No," Cn!lss said, hastily. "They would reject me as a traitor."

"I expected as much," the human said. "Our sociologists will wish to discuss them with you later."

"I have nothing to add," Cn!lss warned.

"We will see," the human said. "And there is a second issue we would like to raise with you."

Cn!lss waited, expectantly.

"We will be sending a trade mission to the nearest settled star," the human said. "What do you think we could offer them?"

Cn!lss considered it. The nearest settled star to Earth, as far as he knew, was a multiracial colony on the end of a dangling chain of gravity points. There was almost no form of overall government, merely dozens of small settlements on the planet's surface and asteroid belts. Indeed, it was commonly believed that, sooner or later, one of the larger galactic powers would eventually swallow it up. But, for the moment, its political insignificance was incredibly useful to the shadier sides of galactic society.

"Guns," he said, finally. "And probably quite a few other things, if you give me some time to consider it. Or you could sell slaves."

The human made a spluttering noise. "As nice as the idea of selling the" – he spoke a word the translator refused to handle – "into slavery is, I think it would be a very bad idea."

"That may well be true," Cn!lss agreed, reluctantly. Given the use some humans were put to by outside powers, they'd probably be reluctant to let more humans out of their control. "I think you could also offer mercenary groups. They are big business on the edge of galactic society."

"We might have to do just that," the human said. "I wonder what" – another untranslatable word – "would make of it."

"Much of your technology is primitive, but so are many of the races along the edge of society," Cn!lss offered. "It's quite possible that they would be happy to buy technology from you, even though it isn't the best in the galaxy."

"That would probably be a good idea," the human said. "Anything else?"

"Rare metals would be useful," Cn!lss offered. "But I don't know what else."

He paused. "And you would have to be careful. The other Hordes might realise you're flying one of their starships."

The human made the gesture he had come to realise meant agreement. "It's a problem," he agreed. "One final question, then. Would you be willing to accompany the mission as an advisor and native guide?"

Cn!lss hesitated. He was being *trusted*? The Subhorde Commander had never trusted him, not after he had studied the Galactics. Why, he might have been secretly intent on subverting the Horde and destroying its way of life! One word out of place and he would have been beheaded on the spot. But the humans were prepared to trust him?

"If you will have me, I will happily come," he said. How could he refuse the chance to show his loyalty? "And I will be very useful."

"Good," the human said. "My people will speak to you soon."

He turned and left the cell, closing the hatch behind him.

SEVENTEEN

WASHINGTON DC, USA

The world had changed. Gunter Dawlish knew it, even though he could never have put the feeling into words. It was as if something was just lurking under the world's collective awareness, something big enough to leave hints of its presence even as it remained unseen. He knew it was there. But what *was* it?

He'd spent long enough as an embedded reporter to know when he was being fed a line of bullshit. Hell, his report suggesting that some kind of new weapons system had been deployed against the Taliban-held town had earned him some more enemies in official Washington. But the next set of reports were even stranger. The Taliban leadership had started dying in large numbers.

There was always someone, he knew, who had pulled the trigger. It was a media age, after all, and few things remained secret indefinitely. If a weapon was fired, someone had to have fired it and that person would want his ten minutes of fame. Hell, several of the SEALs who had gone after Bin Laden and killed him had talked, within the year. But there was no one talking about the sudden drop in Taliban leadership.

It puzzled him. If drones had been deployed in such vast numbers, there would have been an outcry from the Pakistanis. Gunter knew better than to believe the Pakistani Government gave a damn about women and children killed in the northern parts of their deeply divided country, but they would have to make a public statement just to avoid more unrest. But they'd said nothing…and nor had anyone flying the drones. Or had the SEALs been sent over the border to slaughter their way through the Taliban leadership? It was a heartening thought, a display of nerve he'd thought missing from the President's administration, but as far as he could tell no one had been placed on alert.

He finally passed through the TSA checkpoint – they always paid close attention to anyone coming back from Afghanistan and the Middle East – and headed for the taxi rack. The driver chatted endlessly about the latest baseball statistics as Gunter opened his laptop and skimmed his emails. As always, there were a hundred pieces of junk for every tip he received from his sources. Being a reporter meant that everyone and their dog felt they could feed him a line, whenever they felt like it. But he still went through every email. Watergate had started as a minor break-in, after all. Who knew where the next story of the century would come from?

He'd made it his business to cultivate relationships with a number of military officers in various positions, providing advice on handling the press and keeping them calm. In exchange, they sometimes fed him tips, although nothing classified. Asking for classified information was a good way to lose a contact altogether; they might not report him to anyone, but they certainly wouldn't want to risk their careers any further. After Snowden, the White House and the Pentagon had become more than a little paranoid over unauthorised leakers in senior positions. It was ironic – most of the leaks in Washington came out of the bureaucracy, trying to sway political opinion one way or the other – but unsurprising.

Four of his contacts claimed – and, with collaboration, he believed them – that a covert military alert had been called a day ago. Military bases across the United States had rushed to full alert status, recalling troops, launching aircraft and generally preparing for war. It looked like some kind of exercise – God knew that the military had been caught on the hop before – but if so, his contacts noted, there hadn't been a single whisper that it was coming from higher up. And there was always a tip-off from higher authority…

"Here you are, man," the driver said. "Long flight?"

"Very long," Gunter said, as he closed the laptop. He'd stopped telling people he was flying from Afghanistan after several of them had eyed him suspiciously for the rest of the drive. "Thank you for the ride."

He paid, then climbed out of the cab and walked up to his house. It was in one of the better parts of Washington, a gated community with a very effective security service. Part of him disliked the idea of having to hide behind a wire fence and armed guards, but there was little choice. Crime in Washington had been on the rise for years, with the police seemingly helpless to do anything about it. And there was almost no crime within the community. The owners screened all their new residents, ensuring that children could play in the streets freely without fear. Shaking his head, he opened the door and stepped inside, looking longingly at his bed. It still felt like late night in his head.

Instead, he sat down at his desk and continued going through his emails. Several more had arrived while he'd been paying the driver, including one odd report of a series of high-energy bursts in outer space, alarmingly close to the planet. From what his source said, civilian astronomers were going berserk trying to understand what had happened. Was it a solar flare or something like it…or was it unnatural as hell? Gunter looked down at the dates and shivered, suddenly, as realisation struck him. The event in outer space matched the date and time of the unscheduled military alert.

But was there something really there? Carefully, he started to look though the rest of his files, all the tips shared between independent reporters who couldn't call on the vast resources and influence of the Mainstream Media. Over the last week, stocks and shares in companies that produced space hardware had risen, sharply. Someone was apparently buying enough of their produce to ensure their shares rose quite significantly. But who? NASA wasn't doing anything, as far as he could tell, and even the military space program had been cut back sharply. Or was there a program so secret that most government officials didn't know a thing about it?

There had been one odd whisper from a friend in Afghanistan. Apparently – and it could easily have been rumour – there had been a new black ops team inserted into the country from an unknown nation. And yet they'd had near-complete access to American intelligence and resources, something not offered to any nation. Maybe they'd been an American team, so secret that they'd been mistaken for foreigners, or maybe there was something else going on. Were they connected with the Taliban deaths?

Shaking his head, wondering if it was all the result of jet-lag and tiredness, he started to try to put the pieces together. But none of the results he got seemed to make sense.

— —

THE PRESIDENT LOOKED haggard, Jürgen realised, as he stepped into the Oval Office. He had spent an uncomfortable night in the bunker underneath the White House while his wife and children were whisked away to an highly-classified location. Behind him, Craig Henderson looked concerned. He didn't think much of the President – Jürgen could read his body language, even if his voice was nothing but respectful – but he was still their Commander-in-Chief. And he'd spent the night wondering if Earth was on the verge of being destroyed.

"Be seated," the President said, as the CIA and NSA directors entered, followed by two more officials Jürgen didn't know personally. "We have received a communication from the Russians. They know that *something* happened in orbit."

Jürgen wasn't surprised. Whatever Mr. Stuart and his men used to keep their shuttles undetected by purely human technology – and he had some theories about how that technology worked – it hadn't managed to hide the brief and violent battle in orbit. NSA's network of satellites had picked up the energy flashes, as had a number of civilian systems and – apparently – the Russians. There was no point, Jürgen suspected, in trying to cover the whole affair up. After all, there was nothing so conspicuous as a man ducking for cover.

"I received a very tart note from the Russians earlier this morning," the President continued. "They out-and-out accused us of violating several treaties, including the one forbidding the deployment of nuclear weapons to orbit. Reading between the lines, they don't have the faintest idea of what actually happened, but they think we do."

"The emergency alert," Jürgen said.

"Yes," the President said. "They know we called an alert before the fireworks started in orbit and they don't believe in coincidences."

CIA nodded. "They won't be the only ones, Mr. President," he said. "There isn't another government in the world who knows about Mr. Stuart and his band of…lunar settlers. They will *all* be demanding answers."

It was funny, Jürgen reflected, how CIA could make settling the moon sound like a crime worthy of good old-fashioned hanging. But then, the CIA had been thoroughly embarrassed by the near-complete extermination of the Taliban leadership. *They* hadn't been responsible for it. If they had, the news would probably have leaked right now. No more than the DHS, the CIA *needed* a success to secure their position in the world.

"There will be others putting the pieces together," one of the unnamed men said. "I've had several calls from various independent reporters, the ones willing to take chances on something…a little out of the ordinary. So far, there's nothing from the mainstream media, but I wouldn't expect that to last. There's just too many sources of information for them to assume that someone is trying to hoax them into making an embarrassing mistake."

"Not to mention the Russians threatening to lodge protests at the UN," the President muttered. "So…what do we tell them?"

"The truth?" NSA suggested. He smirked. "Let them lodge their complaints with Mr. Stuart?"

CIA eyed him, nastily. "There are two problems with that," he said. "Either they would believe us or they wouldn't. If the latter, they would assume that we were covering up something and take the whole affair public. If the former, they would believe that a group of Americans has taken over the moon and declared themselves an independent nation. They'd start panicking, then they'd start blaming us for the whole affair."

NSA looked back at him. "How – exactly – can Washington be blamed for Mr. Stuart's actions?"

"He's American – or he *was* American," CIA said. "Whatever, the Russians will have good reason to blame us. And if they decide that he's acting completely without restraint, Mr. President, they are likely to do something drastic."

"But if we lie to them," the President said, "eventually the truth will come out and we'll look dishonest."

He snorted. "And what is to stop Mr. Stuart announcing himself to the world?"

"Nothing," Jürgen said, simply. "They were planning a public announcement soon enough in any case."

"And what," the President said, "will happen when the news gets out?"

There would be panic, Jürgen knew. Maybe not over Heinlein Colony, but over the existence of aliens, aliens who had come alarmingly close to bombarding Earth. Hell, there was definite proof – now – that aliens had abducted humans from the planet and turned them into cyborg soldiers. There would be colossal panic right around the globe. And then…who knew what would happen then? How would humanity cope with the thought of no longer being alone in the universe?

He recalled the files Kevin Stuart had given him to read. They were immensely detailed, too detailed for him to believe them a hoax. There were upwards of ten thousand intelligent races known to exist – at least, known to the starship's designer – and most of them were far more advanced than humanity. At best, Earth was a tiny primitive tribe in a jungle, utterly unaware of the surrounding world. The shock of discovering just how badly humanity was outmatched would shake the world to its core.

He'd read some of the scenarios devised over the years concerning alien contact. The writers had been more than a little paranoid, pointing to the prospect of humans adopting alien religions or abandoning homebuilt tech and becoming entirely dependent on alien technology. Or there would be humans who would embrace xenophobia and attack everything alien, to the point they accidentally started a war, a war humanity couldn't hope to win. Even the most optimistic scenarios had been thoroughly ominous. The very foundations of human society were about to shake and shake badly.

The President cleared his throat. "I will speak with Mr. Stuart later today," he said. "However, we need a contingency plan to release the information as soon as possible."

CIA leaned forward. "I agree that we should level with the Russians and the rest of the world governments," he said. "Or at least the ones we can trust to keep a secret. However, I do not believe we should tell the general public just yet."

The President lifted his eyebrows. "You propose to keep it a secret indefinitely?"

"Mr. Stuart's people have been hellishly effective against the Taliban," CIA pointed out, carefully. "And most of the involved governments don't have the slightest idea of what happened in Afghanistan. But if we reveal the truth, the Pakistani Government – among others – will tremble, perhaps fall. And they're not the only ones."

He took a breath. "Fusion power and super batteries, Mr. President, offer the chance to break the oil dependency once and for all. If that news leaks, we will see a sudden upsurge in trouble from the Middle East. Nations like Saudi Arabia and Bahrain, nations dependent on oil revenue, will do whatever it takes to delay the introduction of fusion power. They will stroke the fires of anti-nuclear feeling, throw money at political candidates who will pledge to delay the introduction of fusion indefinitely and probably finance terrorist attacks aimed at Mr. Stuart and his people."

The President smiled. "And your real concern?"

CIA smiled back, humourlessly. "Right now, we have a chance to exterminate the senior terrorist leadership all over the world," he said. "I would prefer not to risk giving them warning of what we could do."

The President looked at Jürgen. "Is that a valid point?"

Jürgen swallowed, nervously. He would have preferred not to take sides in a dispute between two people who were both immensely senior to him, but he had no choice.

"I do not believe the terrorists could escape the bugs," he said, carefully. "And if they go underground, Mr. President, their ability to strike at us will be minimised anyway."

"True," the President agreed. He gave CIA a droll look. "Sorry."

CIA shrugged, seemingly unbothered.

Craig Henderson leaned forward. "Mr. President?"

The President nodded, inviting him to speak.

"There will be panic, Mr. President, whatever we do," he said. There was no doubt whatsoever in his tone. "I would suggest placing the military and police on full alert before making the broadcast."

"We will," the President said, grimly. "And how will your friend react to all of this?"

"People like him, Mr. President, believe in getting the matter over and done with as quickly as possible," Henderson said. "He wouldn't pussyfoot around, but just tell the world and then let everyone work through their panic."

He shrugged. "But we do have some encouraging news," he added. "We *did* turn back the alien attack on Earth."

"You mean Mr. Stuart and his friends turned back the assault," CIA said. There was a sardonic tone to his voice. "The government isn't going to look very good, no matter what we do."

"Then we may as well make it look as though we are cooperating with them," the President said. "We can spin that to our advantage, if necessary. Congress will probably accept it, provided they don't interfere with our affairs. And we can let the foreign affairs take care of themselves."

On that note, the meeting ended.

— —

GUNTER FELL ASLEEP over the laptop and only woke up, several hours later, when one of his cell phones started to shrill loudly. Pulling himself upright, he reached for the phone just in time to miss the call. Cursing under his breath, he put the phone down and yawned; moments later, the phone vibrated. Someone – he didn't save numbers in the phone, knowing it could be confiscated - had sent him a text message.

He frowned. It read WHITE HOUSE MEDIA STATEMENT, 1800HRS. GLOBAL BCAST. BE THERE.

Frowning, Gunter glanced at his watch. It was 1600 and he'd slept for over five hours. The laptop had placed itself on standby, conserving power. Unsurprisingly, he discovered when he moved the mouse, a couple of hundred more messages had arrived while he'd been sleeping. One of them insisted that the United States Government – or the Russians or Chinese – had been testing secret weapons in orbit. Another, a press release from a well-known researcher, stated that the whole event was nothing more than a series of zero-point energy releases. Gunter couldn't understand the technobabble the researcher had included, but it looked far too much like someone was trying to squash all opposition through scientific-sounding gibberish.

Shaking his head, he stood up and pulled off his clothes, then headed for the shower. There was just time, by his watch, to shower, shave and then call a taxi to take him to the White House. As an independent reporter, he might have some problems getting in, but if it was a global broadcast there would be little point in impeding him. There would be no exclusive scoop for anyone. It was irritating, yet it couldn't be helped.

Besides, if there were any exclusives coming from the White House, they'd be given to the reporters who kissed up to the administration.

Or spend all of their time writing paeans to the President, he thought, as he turned on the tap and water cascaded down over his body. *But how could I compromise my independence so badly?*

EIGHTEEN

"Smile," Mariko said. "You're on television."

"The *President* is on television," Steve muttered. The President was welcome to it, as far as Steve was concerned. If he had to face a horde of reporters shouting inane questions, he might just have started screaming at them or ordering the Secret Service to turn their guns on the mob. He was all in favour of grace under pressure, but there were limits. "And he's trying to spin this in his favour."

He snorted. The President's logic, when he'd called, had been unarguable. Too much had been seen for any sort of cover-up to work, the President had pointed out, and it was better to release the information while they could still control it to some extent. Steve would have preferred to wait until they had a working constitution and a legal code, but events had moved out of his control. They'd just have to grin and bear it.

"The planet was defended," the President said. Mentioning the alien attack had worked a miracle. The reporters had been struck dumb. "And humanity is reaching out towards the stars."

Steve rolled his eyes as the President came to the end of his speech. It wasn't a bad one, as political speeches went, but it glossed over quite a few details. For a start, the President had implied that Heinlein Colony was an independent nation, yet he hadn't quite come out and said it outright. And then he'd hinted the US Government had access to alien technology without suggesting that it didn't have *complete* control over alien technology. And he'd finished by promising that more information would be revealed soon.

"It could have been worse," Kevin said, mildly. "Can I upload the data packet now?"

Steve nodded. In the time between the President's decision to go public and the actual broadcast, Kevin had worked frantically to put together a data packet for the internet, starting with a brief overview of the whole story and ending with a statement about their plans for the future. Unlike the President's broadcast, the data packet made it clear that Heinlein Colony was an independent state, as were the planned future colonies on Mars, Titan and the asteroid belt. He'd also included a great many photographs of Heinlein Colony and a number of other lunar sights, as well as selected data from the alien files.

"Make it so," he ordered.

Kevin rolled his eyes, then sent the command through the interface. "It should be interesting to watch," he said. "I rather doubt that most people will believe it at first, even with the President vouching for us."

Steve shrugged. The politics in the US had grown poisonous long before the current President had taken office. Republicans wouldn't believe a word that came out of a Democratic President's mouth and vice versa. Hell, most people assumed automatically that politicians lied whenever they started to speak. It was hard, given the number of scandals that had washed through Washington one day only to be forgotten the next, to fault anyone for believing that politicians were out for themselves, first and foremost, and to hell with the rest of the country.

"That isn't our problem," he said, as he stood up. "Keep an eye on it; let me know if something happens that requires immediate attention. I'm going to work."

Kevin lifted an eyebrow. "You are?"

"We need a constitution," Steve reminded him. "And a legal code. It's time I started writing them both."

"Let me read it before you start uploading it," Kevin called after him. "And make sure Mongo and a few others read it too."

Steve nodded as he stepped into his office and closed the hatch. It had once belonged to the Subhorde Commander, although Steve had no idea what the alien actually *did* in his office when he was so rabidly anti-intellectual. If there had been Horde females on the ship, he would have wondered if he'd used it for private sessions, but there had been none. Females, according to the files, were restricted to the very largest ships.

He sat down at his grandfather's old desk – he'd had it shipped up from the ranch – and activated the interface. Downloading hundreds of actual and theoretical constitutions hadn't been difficult, but he found himself returning time and time again to the Founding Fathers greatest piece of work. It had a simplicity that most later versions lacked. Pulling up Keith Glass's recommendations, he read through them and then reached for a sheet of paper. He had been taught by his mother, while she was homeschooling her children, that something written down physically would last longer in his mind than something typed. Besides, it *felt* right to use pen and ink for the first draft.

It was a more complex task than he'd realised, somewhat akin to editing his writings, but on a far greater scale. The sheer weight of history – future history – pressed down on him. He wrote out the first section, then crossed it out completely and wrote out something different, asking himself if each and every human right had to be guaranteed by law. And yet, if the rights known to exist at the time were included specifically, would that automatically *exclude* any rights still to be discovered?

Carefully, he outlined the structure of government. Keith Glass had pointed out that small government was best – Steve was hardly going to disagree with *that* sentiment – but there was also a need for a unified government. Very well; instead of a handful of large states, there would be hundreds of small cantons. The Solar Union – as Glass had termed it, after a government in one of his books – would not be an entirely coherent entity. It would be more like the Culture than *Star Trek's* Federation.

We'll have to see how it works in practice, he noted, as he finished writing out the government design and sent it to Kevin and Glass for comments. It would have the advantage of allowing the local governments to remain in touch with their populations, but it would also take time for them to come to any decisions. In the meantime, the overall government would be responsible for defence and foreign affairs. *We might have to modify the system later if it doesn't work properly.*

The Bill of Rights was simpler than outlining the government, he decided. Anything that took place between consenting adults in private, whatever its nature, could not be considered a crime. There would be a right to bear arms, but there would also be a responsibility to use them carefully. Everyone, no matter the offence, would have the right to a jury trial and/or the right to insist on being tested under a lie detector. There would be total freedom of religion for individuals, but religion could not be used as an excuse for criminal or terrorist acts. Extremists of all stripes would very rapidly find themselves removed from society permanently.

Defining a citizen was simple enough, he decided, as he wrote out that section. A citizen would be someone who had lived in a canton for two years, paid taxes and chosen to join its voting register. People could refuse to become citizens if they wished, but they would have no voting rights and no say in government. It struck him, a moment later, that some people would probably move between cantons regularly, so he rewrote to say that someone had to have a canton as his permanent residence for two years. There would be no joint citizenship of cantons. One person, one vote.

He was midway through drafting the legal code when Kevin called him. "There are some quite interesting responses," he said. Steve glanced at his watch, then down at the sheets of paper. Had it really been three hours since he'd started work? "I'm afraid the Russians, Chinese and French have lodged protests at the UN and are demanding we turn the starships and the lunar base over to them."

Steve snorted. "Them and what army?"

Kevin chuckled. "The UN is calling an emergency meeting to discuss the situation, scheduled for tomorrow afternoon," he said. "They're undecided if they want to treat us as an independent state or not, but we have been invited to participate."

"I'll think about it," Steve said.

The thought made him grit his teeth. He *hated* the UN and considered it worse than the federal government. At least the feds could sometimes find their asses with both hands when they went looking. There was no war or natural disaster, no matter how unpleasant, that could not be made worse by the United Nations. Hell, the fighting in Libya might have ended sooner if the transnational ICC hadn't put out a warrant for the dictator's arrest, making it impossible for him to back down.

But then, what could one reasonably expect from an organisation that didn't even have a majority of democratic states? The whole concept had been fundamentally flawed from the beginning.

"They're also demanding access to the alien prisoners," Kevin said. "In fact, they're not the only ones – and quite a few of the others have been much more respectful."

"They're not going to be paraded around Earth," Steve said. Quite apart from the violation of the Geneva Conventions, it would probably be considered cruel and unusual punishment. *And* it wouldn't help any attempt to convince the Hordesmen to join humanity. "But if there are scientists who feel they can add to the research program, see if they're worth recruiting."

"Understood," Kevin said. "By the by, did you read the report from the two new ships?"

Steve shook his head. He really needed to recruit more staffers. But maybe that was how bureaucracy had begun, back in days of yore. The guy in charge, unable to do everything himself, had recruited more and more people to help him do his work. And then the whole process had just snowballed out of control.

The bureaucrats will be held to account in the cantons, he told himself, firmly. *They will not be permitted arbitrary power.*

"We have four new fabricators and nine new shuttles, as well as quite a few other supplies," Kevin said. "If we put them all to use, we should be able to double our output of fusion reactors and other vital supplies for the new colony. Keith thinks we might even be able to try to fiddle with one; we might even be able to unlock the command codes."

Steve had to smile. Overcoming the restrictions on the fabricators would be useful, but it needed to be balanced against the risk of putting one of the fabricators out of commission permanently. The technology involved in producing one was far in advance of anything from Earth, although the researchers were starting to have an idea of how they worked. Duplicating one without a clear idea of what they were doing could take decades.

"Tell him to be very careful," he said. "If nothing else, we can use the fusion reactors as bribes. Give them only to nations that recognise our independence and agree to respect our dominance in space."

"The UN wants to talk to the aliens," Kevin said, "but no one can agree on what message to send. If the Hordesmen come back, Steve, they're going to be very confused."

"Poor bastards," Steve said, unsympathetically. As far as anyone could tell, the only time the Hordes bothered to be diplomatic was when they were facing vastly superior force. And even then, the Hordesmen who had made whatever diplomatic concessions were necessary were expected to kill themselves after making the deal. "But we won't be bound by any promises the UN makes to the Hordes."

"I'd like to set you up with a reporter or two," Kevin added. "Like it or not, we have to shape the public relations battleground to our advantage..."

"Why?" Steve asked. "What does it matter what sort of crap the reporters spew out about us?"

"I wasn't thinking of going to the MSM," Kevin said. His voice tightened. "It matters, Steve, because we still need to recruit people from Earth. If they think of us as some new-age version of *The Authority*, they're going to be fearful. We need them to consider us rational agents, not monsters. And if we can get public opinion on our side, it will make it harder for the governments to move against us."

Steve scowled. He had to admit that Kevin had a point, but he didn't *like* it.

"Very well," Steve said, finally. "But someone *reasonable*. I want to see the name before you make the arrangements."

"Of course," Kevin said. "And the meeting at the UN?"

"I will not be sucking their cocks," Steve said. "You make it damn clear to them that if they treat us as naughty children who need a spanking we will simply walk out and to hell with the UN. We are an independent nation and will be treated as such."

"They let the Libyan nut lecture them for hours," Kevin said. "I think they can put up with you."

He paused. "One other thing?"

Steve sighed. "What?"

"Take a break from trying to write the constitution in a day," Kevin advised. "The Founding Fathers took over a hundred days. You cannot be expected to write a complete document for the ages in less than a couple of months. Frankly, you really need a carefully-selected committee and a complete absence of pressure."

Steve snorted, but he took his brother's point. "Read through what I've written so far, then let me know what you think," he said. "And I'll try to keep up with the news."

━ ━

"THAT'S DEFINITELY YOUR face on television this time," Mariko said, an hour later. She'd taken one look at his face and ordered him into bed, where she'd massaged him until he'd started to relax. "I think that's your photo from Boot Camp."

"It is," Steve said. He couldn't help noticing that the tagline claimed it was his High School graduation photograph, which was definitely a critical research failure. He'd never been to High School. "And I bet that reporter is coming down against me."

"Or maybe he has a crush on you," Mariko teased. "It's not *that* bad a photograph."

Steve gave her a doubtful look. The photo had been taken four weeks into Boot Camp and he looked *ghastly*. His eyes were sunken, his face was pale and he looked suspiciously like a drug addict trying to resist the temptation to start taking drugs again. All things considered, it was a minor miracle Mariko managed to like it. But then, she did have strange taste in men.

He flipped through the channels, shaking his head. Both FOX and CNN seemed to have their doubts about the whole affair, suggesting their senior management hadn't quite decided which way to jump. The BBC reported the whole thing in tones that suggested that it was all a giant joke, despite the President's speech, while Al Jazeera seemed to believe it was all a Western plot with dark motives. Online, some bloggers were tearing apart the President's speech while others were pointing out the clear evidence of extraterrestrial life. It was a complete madhouse.

Turning back to the original reporter, it was clear that news teams were already heading towards the ranch. Steve had largely shut down family operations there, but there were still supplies moving towards the area for transport to space. Activating the interface, he sent orders to keep the reporters out of the ranch if possible – and, if not, to pull out completely and abandon the ranch. It would be painful, but he didn't want another incident. In hindsight, embarrassing the DHS so thoroughly might just have been a major mistake. There were already leaks from the Department, now the President had opened the floodgates.

He started to flip through channels again. A preacher he vaguely recognised was screaming about the End of Days, predicting fire, floods and nuclear disaster. In Washington, a crowd was gathering in front of the

White House, although it was impossible to tell what – if anything – they wanted from the government. A handful of Congressmen and Senators were being interviewed, but it was clear that they knew little about what had been going on. Most of the comments included threats to impeach the President for not telling them about the starship and the existence of aliens.

"Business as usual, really," he said.

Mariko nodded, then pushed him back on the bed and straddled him. "I'm a doctor," she said, "even though I've felt as ignorant as a new intern over the last month or two."

Steve nodded. Mariko had had to get used to using alien technology that did just about everything for the doctor, including mending old wounds and removing scars. It was so far in advance of human technology that all she really was in the ship's sickbay was a button-pusher. Steve could understand her frustration with not really *knowing* what was happening when she used the technology, but there was nothing he could do about it.

"You are pushing yourself too hard," Mariko continued. "You're in the prime of health for a man your age – and the alien treatments will ensure you remain youthful for quite some time. But you are still pushing yourself too hard. The Head of Government *cannot* do everything on his own. You need to delegate more to your friends and allies."

"I could appoint you Minster of Heath," Steve said.

He gasped as Mariko poked a finger into his chest. "Be serious," she said. "You've already had to hand recruitment over to Charles. Start handing over some other matters too. You won't do anyone any good if you work yourself into an early grave. Or don't you want to give up control?"

Steve gritted his teeth. She was right, he knew. Part of him didn't want to give up control over the fundamentals of their new society. How could he trust anyone else to write the constitution? But, at the same time, he was pushing himself too hard.

"I understand," he said. "I'll see who I can find to help."

NINETEEN

After some careful diplomatic negotiation, it had been decided that Steve could beam directly into the United Nations itself, rather than face the gathering crowds outside the building. All of New York seemed to have come to a halt as protesters, in favour of Steve or against, had descended on the city. According to the reports Steve had seen, the NYPD – completely overwhelmed – had called for reinforcements from all over the State and convinced the Governor to call up the National Guard. It was still proving hard to control the crowds.

The silver light faded away, revealing a UN staffer who looked rather shocked by what he'd seen. Steve smiled at him, noted the man's nametag – KOMURA – and then allowed the Japanese man to lead him towards the waiting room. According to Kevin, who had slipped bugs into the UN after the emergency session had been called, several ambassadors had been replaced in a hurry by more senior representatives, while hundreds of deals were being struck under the table. But then, Steve acknowledged, they'd done the same themselves. His representatives had spoken to several democratic governments, offering fusion and other technological goodies in exchange for recognition. He had a feeling that the overall response relied upon the outcome of the coming session.

"The Secretary-General will summon you in ten minutes," Komura informed him. He looked as though he wanted to ask a few questions, but held his tongue. "Nothing about this is normal, I'm afraid."

Steve nodded and waited until the man had made his escape, then checked the bracelet at his wrist. The force shield should protect him from anything up to and including an IED, but he was grimly aware that human ingenuity might find a way to break through it. Light passed through the shield, after all, and a teleport lock could be blocked fairly easily, even with human technology. The Secret Service had already started to broadcast radio signals through the White House, ensuring that Steve couldn't kidnap the President if the whim struck him.

He rolled his eyes at the thought. Why would he *want* the President?

It was nearly an hour before Komura returned and invited him to proceed into the General Assembly Chamber. Steve, who had been monitoring Kevin's observations of the diplomats, wasn't surprised at the delay. The Russians had already lodged a strong complaint with the Security Council, backed up by China, while they were trying hard to line up other backers from the rest of the Assembly. In the meantime, the French seemed caught between the Russians and the promise of fusion technology, while Britain and Canada were reserving judgement. From what the President had said, there was too much political strife in America itself to make any promises about which way the United States would jump.

Steve had grown up in the countryside and he had never been able to understand why New Yorkers chose to cram so many people into so small a place. The old hints of claustrophobia came back in full force as he stepped into the chamber and faced the stares of the gathered diplomats, ambassadors and world leaders. Part of him wanted to trigger the emergency signal and teleport out, vanishing in a haze of silver light. Surely, facing the Taliban armed with only his fists would be easier than facing so many hostile stares.

They can't do anything to you, he told himself, firmly. *And they can't stop you either.*

But somehow the thought didn't help.

The silence shattered with an angry demand from the Russian Ambassador in Russian. It took the interface a few seconds to provide a translation – the Russian was complaining about the violation of the Outer Space Treaty – and in the meantime several other ambassadors started shouting too. The Chinese Ambassador seemed to believe that Steve had undermined his country's laws, something that puzzled him, while several African ambassadors were railing against the white man. But it was hard to be sure. Everything was just blurring together into a god-awful racket.

There was a loud banging from the General Secretary's seat. "Order," he snapped, as the room started to quieten down. "Mr. Stuart. You have been...invited here to give your side of the story."

Steve smiled. "You make it sound as though I am on trial," he said, gathering himself. He wasn't naive enough to believe that the General Secretary had any real power. If the five permanent members of the Security Council agreed, they could do whatever they damn well pleased. "Might I ask what the charges are?"

There were some titters from the reporters, but the diplomats remained silent.

"It is our intention," Steve said, when it became clear that no one else was going to speak, "to establish a new nation covering the solar system, one capable of defending the human race against alien threats and taking humanity to the stars. We do not intend to become embroiled in affairs on Earth, nor do we recognise the existence of treaties intended to limit the development of outer space."

"Those treaties were signed by *your* country," the Russian Ambassador bellowed.

"The human race is not alone," Steve continued, ignoring him. "There are over ten thousand alien races out there, some of whom have already kidnapped humans from Earth and turned them into living weapons.

Others will see us as a threat...or a prize to be won. And, right now, Earth's defences rest in our hands. There is nothing the massed might of the United Nations" – he fought down the urge to let loose an undiplomatic snigger – "can do to protect the planet, if one of the Galactics decide they want it.

"You speak of international treaties and accuse us of breaking them. The Galactics are not signatory to any of our treaties, nor should we expect them to respect our legal positions. We do not, yet, have the force necessary to hold our own. It is our priority – and it should be the priority of the entire planet – to build both that defensive force and a society capable of facing the galaxy calmly, but confidently. *That* is our task.

"We invite other humans, individual humans, to join us. Give us those who want to build a new world, those with the dreams that will take them to the stars, those who wish something more than the hidebound governments of Earth can provide. We will take all who are willing to fit into our society and work to defend Earth."

He paused, long enough to realise that he had captured the attention of everyone in the vast chamber. "You have demanded that we hand over the ships and technology to you," he said, looking at the Russian and Chinese representatives. "We must refuse to comply with your request. Quite apart from the grim awareness of just what you would do with the technology that has fallen into our hands, we have no faith in the governments of Earth. How could this organisation, an organisation that produces little beyond corruption and paperwork, hope to coordinate the defence of the entire world?

"We make you this offer. Recognise our right to exist, place no bar in the path of anyone who wishes to join us and we will trade technology to improve your lives. Fusion power will transform your societies, medical technology will help cure your ill...there are no shortage of possible pieces of technology we can offer you. But we only offer it on the condition you stay out of our way.

"If you refuse, you will get nothing. We will not interfere with you. But we will not grant you our technology either."

There was a long silence, broken – eventually – by the representative from Iran, who started ranting about American interference and infidel lies. This time, Steve understood; Wilhelm Tech had openly admitted their alliance with Heinlein Colony and Iran had banned the dongles, which hadn't prevented Iranians from smuggling them into the country. The Chinese, he realised, probably had the same concerns. Their firewalls, intended to prevent their citizens from plotting resistance to their rulers, had been neatly circumvented.

We will have to do something about their nukes, Steve thought, coldly. But it wouldn't sit well with the pledge of non-interference. *Or perhaps we should just leave the Middle East to them.*

Komura beckoned to Steve frantically as the roar grew louder. UN security forces were rushing into the room, hastily preparing to separate the ambassadors if the threatening riot actually materialised. Steve hesitated, then allowed the Japanese man to lead him out of the chamber and into a small antechamber. Inside, there was a comfortable pair of armchairs and a small tray of expensive alcohol. Steve took one look, then dismissed it.

"There are some diplomats who wish to talk to you," Komura said. "In private, I should add."

He hesitated, then leaned forward. "Are you interested in recruiting a semi-professional diplomat?"

Steve turned to look at him. "And you're interested in being hired?"

"Yes," Komura said. "Have you ever *tried* to work here?"

"No," Steve said. He gave the young man a long considering look, then nodded to himself and produced one of Charles's cards from his pocket. "Call this number, then go to the address they give you for pickup. You'll have to undergo a security check first, but if you pass you'll be welcome."

Komura nodded. "And if I don't pass?"

"Nothing bad will happen," Steve said. "But you won't get to see the stars."

BY THE TIME he finally found time to move to the hotel and meet the reporter, Steve felt utterly exhausted. As he'd expected, several nations had attempted to strike private bargains with him, the French and Israelis being the most persistent. The latter had good reason to need Steve's technology – they'd offered everything from diplomatic recognition to outright military support – but the former seemed to be playing both ends off against the middle in hopes of coming out ahead. It was a typically underhand dealing for diplomats in the UN.

Gunter Dawlish had started to report from Afghanistan after Steve had retired from the military, but his name wasn't unfamiliar. Steve had read a few of his articles before the attempted abduction, what now felt like years ago. He'd spoken to Craig Henderson and a couple of others he knew who had stayed in uniform and they'd all confirmed that Dawlish was a straight-shooter. Maybe not inclined to take everything said by the military for granted – Steve could hardly blame him for that attitude in an age of spin – but not an ideological or personal enemy of the armed forces.

"Mr. Stuart," Dawlish greeted him. "Thank you for agreeing to meet me."

Steve smiled. Before Dawlish had finally been accepted as the first reporter to get a private interview, Kevin had interrogated him thoroughly. The reporter had agreed to let Steve and Kevin read his article before it was posted, then make changes if any were suggested. Steve had agreed, in turn, that the whole interview would be recorded and the only changes would concern his own words, rather than the editorial slant. Later, the record would be released on the internet in any case.

"You're welcome," he said. "And thank you for agreeing to meet something private."

"I wouldn't do anything to risk this scoop," Dawlish assured him. He took a seat and then motioned for Steve to sit down facing him. "First question, then. Where you responsible for events in Afghanistan?"

Steve lifted his eyebrows. "Yes," he said, finally. "We were."

Dawlish nodded, then changed tack. "How much of the official story is actually true?"

"Almost all of it," Steve said, without going into details. So far, the President had managed to cover up most of the DHS raid and he wasn't going to broadcast the story unilaterally. "All you really need to know is that we were kidnapped by aliens, turned the tables on them and took control of their ship."

"And that there really is an alien threat," Dawlish said. "Do you believe we can build a defence in time?"

Steve met the reporter's eyes. "I believe that if we don't try, right now, we will never know," he said. "Earth is small beans, by Galactic standards. Most of them don't even have the faintest idea we exist and care less. But that is about to change. We will be...*protected*, if we're lucky, or enslaved if we're not. Building a formidable defence is our only hope of salvation."

Dawlish nodded. "There's been a lot of speculation on the internet about what kind of society you intend to build," he said. "Some people have been expecting a redneck paradise, with only WASPs allowed, while others think you're going to build a Objectivist dream, with you as John Galt. What do you really intend to build?"

Steve frowned, inwardly. The President had also mentioned John Galt. Coincidence?

Probably, he decided. "I don't have time to explain all the flaws in *Atlas Shrugged*," he said, after a moment. "Unless you want to turn the rest of the interview into a literary criticism session?"

Dawlish shook his head, hastily.

Somewhat amused, Steve went on. "The short answer is that we intend to build a democratic state built on individual rights and responsibilities," he said. "Generally, anyone who is willing to accept the rights and responsibilities of being a citizen will be welcome to join us as a voting citizen. We don't really give a shit – pardon my French – about age, race, sexual orientation or religion. As long as someone is prepared to uphold their rights and responsibilities, they are welcome."

"That's interesting," Dawlish said. "There's a preacher in Montana claiming you're going to build a world without homosexuals, Jews, Muslims and Catholics."

Steve shrugged. "I'm not a member of any church," he said. "I can't be held responsible for a loudmouth who just happens to share the same state as myself. If anyone else thinks I should be…"

He shrugged, again. "That's their problem," he explained. "Basically, we intend to uphold personal rights and responsibilities. You have the right to do whatever you please as long as you don't hurt non-consenting adults. If you do, you will be tried by a jury and punished as the jury sees fit. We expect there will be some teething problems along the way, but that's the basic idea."

"*Some* teething problems," Dawlish said. "I used to study the opening of the Wild West. Just establishing law and order took years."

"We may well have the same problems," Steve said. "I have several people looking at legal issues for homesteaders in the outer solar system. Upholding their rights requires a force capable of doing just that, but such a force could easily turn into a major problem in its own right. Just look at the federal government."

Dawlish leaned forward. "Are you anti-government?"

Steve had expected the question, but it was still tricky to answer. "I believe that as long as humans are imperfect beings, we need some form of government," he said. "A lawless anarchy might sound ideal, but it would rapidly devolve into the stronger picking on the weaker. At the same time, I believe that the government can grow *too* big and *too* powerful and become a bully itself. That, I think, is what has happened to our federal government.

"I could cite any number of cases where federal authority has been abused, without any recourse for the victim of federal mistreatment. There are farmers who have been raided for daring to sell untreated milk, small businesses ruined by pointless petty regulations, political correctness allowed to drive wedges between people, policemen abusing the general public, lives torn apart and people jailed because of the tiny difference between a legal and illegal weapon. And, if you look at the laws the right way, everything the government does is perfectly legal.

"But it sure as hell isn't *right*.

"I don't promise paradise," he concluded. "Our hopes of creating a post-scarcity society have faded when we discovered the colossal power requirements for constructing matter out of raw energy. Building our society will be a long and bumpy road, but we have the experience of previous societies to guide us and help us avoid mistakes."

"But you'll create new ones of your own," Dawlish commented.

"Oh, certainly," Steve agreed. "But we'll try to learn from our mistakes."

Dawlish nodded. "How do you intend to relate to nations down on Earth?"

"Ideally, we won't have anything more than friendly trade relationships," Steve said. "Maybe not even that, for non-democratic states. Our intention, as always, is to build an off-world society capable of facing the challenges of the stars. We have no intention of building an empire on Earth."

"I'm sure the federal government is relieved to hear that," Dawlish said.

Steve nodded, but said nothing.

"However, there are worse states than the United States," Dawlish added. "Don't you think you have a moral responsibility to deal with them?"

"I really hate it when people suggest I have a moral responsibility to do anything," Steve admitted. "On the face of it, I suppose you do have a point. But let's face it — we overthrew Saddam and, partly because of problems in the federal government, we wound up fighting a bloody war for six years. There's still a striking lack of gratitude in large parts of the Middle East."

He held up a hand before Dawlish could say a word. "I know, we didn't help them as much as we had hoped," he added. "But it put me off future interventions even before we captured the alien ship. In future, our only interventions will be against governments that refuse to allow their people to leave their states and go to space."

"I see," Dawlish said. "I have quite a few other questions…"

Steve grinned. "I've a better idea," he said. "How would you like to see the moon?"

Dawlish grinned back. "I'd love it."

TWENTY

HEINLEIN COLONY, LUNA

G unter Dawlish had never really wanted to be an astronaut. They did nothing, beyond flying to orbit and then landing back on boring old Earth. There was no drama in the space program, in his view, nothing particularly exciting. But now...he took a step forward and gasped as he realised just how weak the gravity on the moon actually was. He could jump into the air and fly...

"It gets everyone," Rochester called after him. "We give new arrivals a few days to get used to it before we put them to work."

"It's bloody fucking fantastic," Gunter said. He knew he sounded like a kid and he didn't much care. "you could make a mint just letting people come to the moon for a few days."

"We're working on it," Rochester assured him, as Gunter dropped back down to the ground. "Heinlein – the author – talked about people flying under the lunar dome. We're actually planning to build a stadium for such games in the next few months. Maybe even build some form of antigravity broomstick and play Quidditch."

Gunter snorted. "Just how big is the colony now?"

"Oh, we're expanding all the time," Rochester said. "We have some alien laser cutters to dig into the ground, then human technology to expand and keep expanding. One of our processors turned lunar rock into something we can use to line the colony edges, then we just build the rest of the structure up piece by piece. At worst, all we have to do is dig out a cave, install an airlock and Bob's the bloke who buggers your auntie."

He shrugged. "We have around two thousand people working here now," he added, "with new chambers and living accommodation added all the time. Someone had the bright idea of installing a fish farm, so we're hopefully going to get some better food in the next few weeks."

"And we have millions of requests – literally – for places on the moon," Steve Stuart said. "I think the colony will expand at terrifying speed. But it won't be the only place."

Gunter turned to him and lifted an eyebrow. "Where else?"

"We have plans underway to start terraforming Mars," Steve Stuart reminded him. "And there will be thousands of asteroids to turn into small homesteads. The stars are the limit, quite literally."

The tour of the colony took longer than Gunter had expected, but he couldn't help admiring just how much work had been done in just over a month. Rochester put it down to an absence of idiotic bureaucratic safety regulations and the skills of a dozen former combat engineers. They were very good at improvising, he explained, detailing some of the problems they'd had in adapting Earth technology for the lunar surface. Even trucks and tractors designed for very cold environments had needed heavy modification before they could be placed on the moon and put to work.

"That's one of the few laws we have," Rochester said, as they passed through a large airlock and into an underground chamber. He pointed at a sign on the rear of the hatch. "And common sense reigns supreme."

Gunter had to smile. The sign read ANYONE STUPID ENOUGH TO NOT CHECK THEIR SPACESUIT BEFORE PASSING THROUGH THIS HATCH DESERVES TO DIE.

"It seems rather blunt," he said. "What do your people think of it?"

"They put it up," Rochester said. He shrugged. "On Earth, you have idiots winning the Darwin Awards by sneaking onto railway lines and getting killed...and then their relatives try to sue the train operators. Or criminals breaking in and then suffering an accident and trying to sue the person they tried to rob. Here...if there genuinely is someone to blame, they *will* get hammered, but if it was a genuine accident or the victim's stupidity we will learn from it and move on. We certainly won't shut down the whole program for years while politicians beat their breasts and cry crocodile tears for a TV audience."

He smiled. "We do take care to keep the children well away from the airlocks," he added. "There aren't many kids up here, but those we do have are supposed to stay in the lower levels without their parents or another adult accompanying them."

Gunter looked over at him. "You have *kids* here?"

"This is a city, or it will be," Rochester said. "You'd be surprised by just how many people on my team wanted to move their families here."

He shrugged. "Setting up the school took some time," he added. "But once we hired some decent teachers the kids started to settle down and study properly. And they *love* the low-gravity environment."

"I recall at least one science-fiction novel where Luna-born children could never return to Earth," Gunter said, slowly. "Is that actually going to be a problem?"

"It could be," Rochester said. "We give everyone muscle-building stimulants, but someone who stays in Luna gravity long enough will have problems when they return to Earth. Ideally, of course, everyone should exercise frequently to keep building up their muscles, but some people will probably fail to keep up with it."

He shrugged, again. "As we say, time and time again, you are responsible for your own behaviour," he reminded Gunter. "If someone doesn't exercise...well, the condition of their body is their responsibility."

Gunter shook his head, then looked over at Steve Stuart. "What sort of taxes are you going to have here?"

"We plan to insist that no one is charged more than ten percent of their earnings," Steve Stuart said. "Both personnel and business; if a business is based here, on lunar soil, it won't be taxed more than ten percent either. We want to avoid the endless problems people have with filling in tax assessments back in the States. If you earn a thousand dollars, you owe one hundred dollars to the government."

"I might move here," Gunter said. "Would you take me?"

"We'd take anyone who was willing to accept the rights and responsibilities of citizenship," Steve Stuart said. "If you wanted to be based here, you would be welcome. But I did have a different job offer in mind for you. I think I'll need a press secretary."

Gunter shook his head, quickly. "I hate dealing with the press," he said. "Sorry."

Rochester snorted. "You *are* the press."

"And that's why I hate it," Gunter said. "Being a reporter can be fun, being someone who has to handle the reporters is far less...interesting. But I would definitely like to move here."

"We'll let you know as soon as the first apartment blocks are up and running," Rochester assured him. "Now, if you'd like to see the aliens...?"

"MR. KOMURA PASSED the test with flying colours," Kevin said, when Steve returned to the starship. "He was something of an idealist when he joined the United Nations, but he isn't any longer. Apparently, actually dealing with the politicians and diplomats is bad for one's hero-worship."

"I'm not surprised," Steve said. "Does he have any divided loyalties?"

"He'd probably have something to say about it if we moved against Japan," Kevin said. "Other than that, he will be loyal enough to us, as long as he isn't mistreated. I explained the rules on working for us and he accepted them."

Steve blinked. "We have rules?"

"He's the first employee of our new State Department," Kevin reminded him. "I would prefer not to start building a monster like the *old* State Department, one full of bureaucrats, leakers and people who know nothing taking the lead."

He shrugged. "Anyway, most of the Western Governments are prepared to recognise us as being an independent state provided we share fusion technology and a handful of other technological advances with them," he continued. "They've also agreed not to stand in our way as we recruit, but they've requested that we don't go after serving military personnel. And they want us to buy supplies from them in bulk."

"We'd have to do that anyway," Steve pointed out, as he took a cup of coffee from the food producer. It tasted just right for him, but he knew there had already been plenty of complaints from civilians who were not used to military coffee. "Don't they know that?"

"Of course they do," Kevin said. "This is just their way of saving face. They can't stop us from doing whatever the hell we like, so they ask us for concessions we intend to give them anyway..."

Steve rolled his eyes. "So it's all playacting for the media," he said. "Wonderful."

"I seem to recall mom smacking you for deciding you didn't need manners any longer," Kevin said, snidely. "Or have you forgotten her lecture?"

Steve felt his cheeks heat. Their mother had been strict, homeschooling her children in-between the hours they worked on the farm. Steve still recalled the thrashing she'd given him after he'd been unjustifiably rude to one of her guests...and how she'd explained, afterwards, that manners were the lubricant that kept society together. If everyone said what they meant, all the time, society would break down. Or so she'd said. It hadn't been until he'd joined the Marines that Steve had truly understood what she'd meant.

"It's the same basic idea," Kevin explained. "They ask for concessions, we grant them...and it looks as though they got something out of the deal. It will soothe their pride."

He paused. "I did have a set of private conversations with the President," he added. "He's having problems with the Senate. None of them are very happy about us just...taking the starship and setting up on our own. A few have even threatened to revoke our citizenships."

"Fuck them," Steve said, sharply.

"It's a valid point," Kevin said. "You might want to consider renouncing yours anyway, along with the rest of us. Just by being American, we cause problems for the American government, which gets the blame for our existence."

Steve snorted. "I'm sure the British didn't get the blame for anything George Washington did after independence," he countered.

"Washington was President of an independent America," Kevin said. "He was no longer even remotely connected to Britain."

He sighed. "Overall, the President thinks we'll get recognition, as long as the US clearly benefits from the arrangement, but he would like a couple of other concessions."

Steve rolled his eyes. "What does he want?"

"First, he wants us to continue the antiterrorist program," Kevin said. "We would have done that anyway, I think, but this will make it official. Second, he wants us to send medics to the United States, armed with alien medical technology. If we helped people who needed it, we would build up a lot of goodwill."

Steve made a mental note to check who the President wanted them to help, then nodded. "I think Mariko would chop off my balls if I refused," he said. "Very well. We will give the President his bones."

"An excellent decision," Kevin said.

Steve eyed him darkly.

"The bad news," Kevin continued, "is that almost all of the non-democratic states have been less keen to recognise us. China and Russia are taking the lead, but much of the Middle East is united in its disapproval and, between them, they might be able to delay formal UN recognition. The bigger nations are worried about the effects of the dongles, the smaller nations are worried about losing oil revenues. And then there's the request for asylum we received."

Steve blinked. "Asylum?"

"There's a Christian in Egypt who is facing official displeasure," Kevin said. "He wants out. And he won't be the last one, either. There are millions of people around the world who would want to get out of non-democratic states."

"I see," Steve said. "And they won't let them go?"

"Not without being pushed," Kevin agreed. "You will need to worry about that, Steve."

They both looked up as the hatch hissed open, revealing a tired-looking Wilhelm.

"Good news," Wilhelm said. "We're in business."

Steve smiled. "We are?"

"So far, we've got over two hundred companies, mainly small technological and computing companies like my own, applying to set up shop on the lunar surface," Wilhelm said. "Some of them are actually quite big, really; placing their factories on the moon would give us a growing industrial base. A number of bigger corporations have also expressed interest in moving some of their operations to the moon, but they want more details of what we can offer them first. I think they'll expect first glance at any unlocked alien technology."

He paused. "But many of the smaller companies have hundreds of brilliant people working for them," he added. "Some of those people are even on the list of people I want to recruit."

Steve had to smile. "It will still take months to get them to the moon," he pointed out. "And what about their personnel?"

"Oh, nothing is finalised yet," Wilhelm said. "But they're quite keen to move ahead."

He hesitated, noticeably. "We've also had literally thousands of requests for server space," he continued. "As the alien servers are capable of holding billions upon billions of terabytes, this isn't a problem. But it's raised a whole new problem – two of them, in fact."

Kevin smirked. "How many of those requests come from pornographic sites?"

"I'm shocked you could imagine using the internet for porn," Wilhelm said. He looked down at the deck, irked. "Half of them, as it happens."

Kevin's smirk grew wider. "We could have some fun sampling it."

Steve had a more practical concern. "Is this likely to prove a problem?"

"We have become, to all intents and purposes, a data haven," Wilhelm said. "Quite apart from the porn, what happens when someone stores criminal or terrorist information on our servers?"

He shrugged. "I've copied the user guidelines from the servers I used to run in Switzerland," he added. "Child pornography is completely banned. All other pornographic material is to be stored in one particular subset of the servers, so they can be excluded from search results fairly easily. Some of what we've been offered is…sickening."

Steve wasn't surprised. He'd served in Iraq and seen Iraqi business-men offering American and British soldiers pornography that would have been shocking in America, let alone in what was meant to be a strictly Islamic country. There hadn't been anything remotely *tasteful* about it, insofar as porn could ever be tasteful. He'd never been sure if the Iraqis genuinely did like watching men having sex with animals or if someone was trying to sneer at the outsiders by selling them disgusting porn.

"Criminal operations – and I include mass spamming in this – and terrorist operations are completely banned," Wilhelm added. "I'd prefer not to get into a legal tussle over what defines a criminal act, particularly as we don't have a working legal code yet, so everyone who sets up a web-site on one of our servers has to accept the user guidelines. Anyone who breaks them afterwards can get a hammer dropped on him."

"Good work," Steve said. "What else do we need to know?"

"There are millions of requests for lunar accommodation, if not citi-zenship," Wilhelm said. "I've had to hire new staff just to work my way through them. So far, anyone who might be useful to help build the col-ony has been forwarded to Charles, while everyone else is being examined on a case-by-case basis. We've got several hundred requests from authors who wish to live on the moon and work there – and they can, as long as they have access to the internet. Once we have the accommodation blocks up and running…"

"Quarters won't be very nice, at least for a few years," Kevin commented.

Wilhelm shrugged. "I don't think that matters," he countered. "They want to be part of something great. And they also want to get their foot in on the ground floor."

He smiled. "Speaking of which, we have several hundred thousand requests for tours of the Apollo landing sites," he added. "If we charged them each ten thousand dollars, we'd have much more cash to spend on Earth. Hell, give us a few months and we would probably drag the world economy back out of the dumps."

Steve understood. He hadn't been able to resist the temptation to go take a look at where Neil Armstrong had set foot on the lunar surface either. The human tech looked primitive, compared to the technology they'd captured from the Horde, but it had been built without alien assistance. That, according to the databanks, wasn't entirely common in the galaxy. A large number of races had bought or stolen spacefaring technology from other races. Not all of them had mastered it for themselves.

Us too, I suppose, he thought. *But we will figure out how the technology works and how to improve it.*

"Keep working on it," he said. "Maybe we can detail a shuttle to transporting tourists to the moon."

"We should," Wilhelm said. "We need ready cash, Steve. Right now, we don't have as much as we will need in the future."

Steve rolled his eyes. By any standards, his government was the most powerful one in the entire solar system. But they were also among the poorest, at least for the moment.

"Kevin, I want you to work on *Captain Perry*," he said. They'd renamed one of the captured starships, as its original name sounded thoroughly absurd to human ears. "Ideally, I want you ready to depart within the week."

"I understand," Kevin said. He sounded both excited and terrified. Steve couldn't blame him. Neil Armstrong had stepped onto the moon, but Kevin would be flying well outside the edges of the solar system. "I won't let you down."

"Just remember that you're representing humanity," Steve warned. "Don't let any of us down."

TWENTY-ONE

CAPTAIN PERRY, EARTH ORBIT

"You don't look a bit like Captain Kirk," Carolyn Harper said. Kevin rolled his eyes. A week of hard labour had cleaned out most of the starship and allowed the human crew to move in, leaving them all tired and irritable. Edward Romford and his men would provide a security team, but Carolyn and her fellow scientists had their own role to play. If they were lucky, they might be able to understand the theoretical basis of the alien FTL drive and then start working out how to duplicate it.

"That's good to hear," he said. "Who do I look like?"

Carolyn considered him for a long moment. "Truthfully, I'd be hard put to say just *who* you looked like," she said, finally. "That fake Native American from *Voyager*?"

"*Thank* you," Kevin said, crossly. He'd only watched a handful of *Voyager* episodes, the ones that had featured the Borg. Discovering that alien technology could easily create something like the Borg Collective had led to a few sleepless nights. "I don't want to act like him."

He snorted, then pretended to examine Carolyn. "You look like..."

"Shut up," Carolyn said, without heat. "I'm not the one playing starship commander."

Kevin had to smile. Carolyn looked, in no particular order, young, pretty and nerdy. Her blonde hair was tied up in a shapeless bun, but he had the distinct impression that she would clean up nicely if she ever let her hair down. But from what he'd read of her file, she'd probably deliberately cultivated the nerdy look to ensure she was taken seriously at her former company. Like most of the others, she'd had one look at the alien technology and practically begged to join the team. It was the opportunity of a lifetime.

"I suppose," he said. Perhaps, during the month they would be spending in transit, he would make a pass at her, just to see how she responded. Or maybe it would be unprofessional. It wasn't as if they didn't have plenty of other entertainments. "But you're playing Mr. Spock."

The banter came to an end as Commander Rodney Jackson entered the bridge. He was a Royal Navy submarine commander, recently retired after thirty years in the navy. Kevin, looking for someone with experience of long voyages in completely isolated ships, had snapped him up like a shot. Once Jackson had checked with the British Government, he'd accepted the post of XO without hesitation. It too was the opportunity of a lifetime.

"We have everything stowed onboard, sir," he said. If he resented reporting to someone who wasn't even a naval officer he kept it to himself. Like most submariners Kevin had met, he was short, stocky and permanently calm. "And the starship appears ready for departure."

Kevin nodded. Like *Shadow Warrior*, *Captain Perry's* systems were largely controlled through the interface, but there were also command consoles on the bridge. It was astonishing just how many training programs there were, programs that had allowed the human crew to practice operating the ship time and time again until they were far more capable than the Horde's pilots. Kevin had long since lost his astonishment at just how ignorant the Horde really was of such matters. But it was an advantage the human race desperately needed. The Horde still possessed far more starships than their human enemies.

"Very good," he said.

Choosing potential trade goods had been tricky. The alien captive – currently in a cabin on the lower decks – had recommended weapons, particularly ones that could be reconfigured for non-human hands, so Kevin had loaded the starship with hundreds of different weapon designs. They had also picked several items of human technology, various movies that might be worth selling and a handful of food and drinks. And they'd even taken several bottles of maple syrup.

But there was no way to know what, if anything, they'd be able to sell them for.

They *had* recovered some galactic currency from the Horde, but it was difficult to say just how much it was actually *worth*. The alien rate of exchange fluctuated constantly, while the more isolated planets seemed to prefer trade goods to currency that might be worthless by the time it was shipped to somewhere it could actually be *spent*. Kevin knew that, if they failed to make some sales, they might have to start offering human mercenaries, purely to build up a stockpile of galactic currency. But that offered its own risks. What if one alien power chose to take its irritation with the mercenaries out on Earth?

He grinned as his crew took their places. "Open hailing frequencies," he ordered. "I want to speak to *Shadow Warrior*."

It was nearly two minutes before Steve's holographic face appeared in front of him. "Kevin," he said. "Are you ready to depart?"

"Yes," Kevin said, flatly. A week of intensive effort had left them all exhausted, but they would have a month to recover while the starship was in transit. According to the databanks, the risk of interception was very low. "We've said our last goodbyes, written our last letters...we're ready, sir."

He sobered. Never, not since radio had been invented, had a human crew been so far out of touch. Sailing in a wooden ship had run the risk of simply never being seen again, but modern technology had removed most of those risks, even as it made it possible for politicians and bureaucrats to peer over the ship's commander's shoulder. It was quite possible, he knew, that *Captain Perry* could set out on her epic voyage and never be seen again. There were pirates out there as well as interstellar terrorists and great powers waging outright war against their opponents.

Perhaps Steve had the same thought. "Good luck, Kevin," he said. "If you don't come back we'll all be very upset."

Kevin had to smile. Where Steve had set out to build a new society, Kevin might well have taken the starship and vanished out into interstellar space. There was a whole galaxy waiting for the human race, after all. But he wouldn't be tempted to take *Captain Perry* on a long voyage of exploration. They needed to collect information and return it to Earth. If they failed, unlocking the secrets of alien technology might take longer than Earth *had*.

"We will," he promised. "Or die trying."

He took a long breath. "Give my love to Mongo and the others," he added. "Goodbye."

Steve raised his hand in salute. A moment later, his image vanished completely.

"Prepare the drive," Kevin ordered.

"The drive is online and ready to go," Jackson reported. "All systems appear to be in optimal working order."

Kevin wasn't surprised. The Horde's concept of basic maintenance was terrifying – he had a feeling that they lost at least one or two ships a year – but at least they'd stockpiled a reasonable amount of spare parts. Guided by the interface, the human crew had carefully replaced everything that had been threatening to break and then sent the damaged components to Heinlein Colony. Some of them, he hoped, would be duplicable by human technology.

"Good," he said. He braced himself. "Engage!"

He hadn't been sure what to expect when the FTL drive activated. Some races suffered badly, according to the databanks, and needed to be sedated or held in stasis for the entire trip. Others seemed to find it exciting or felt nothing. Kevin...felt a flicker of *unreality* for a long moment, followed by a strange kind of queasiness. And then everything seemed to return to normal.

But the display were black, showing the unblinking nothingness of FTL.

"We are currently heading away from Earth at several times the speed of light," Jackson said, in hushed tones. "No man has ever been this far from Earth."

"No human-crewed starship," Kevin corrected. *Aliens* had taken quite a few samples from Earth over the years. God alone knew what had happened to their descendents. Some would have been turned into mind-burned cyborgs, but the others? Were there brothers of mankind out among the stars? "But we will not be the last."

He settled back into the command chair. "We will run drills for the first half of every day," he added. "And then we will spend the rest of our time researching the galaxy."

The next two weeks fell into a pattern. They ran emergency drills every day, learning more and more about the sheer variety of threats in the galaxy, then researched the vast datafiles on the starship. Kevin was used to the interface by now, but even he found it hard to keep track of everything it had to show the human users. And then there were the little hints they found that might just suggest ways to duplicate alien technology. The official files might be long on elaborate superlatives and short on details, but there were plenty of hints elsewhere. But could they be turned into working technology?

It was astonishing just how used they became to flying through space in an alien starship. Boredom started to sink in rapidly after the first week, followed by a form of claustrophobia as the researchers realised that they were truly cut off from Earth. They could no longer email their friends and research partners, nor could they go elsewhere if they wanted a break from their work. Jackson, who admitted that half the trainee submariners felt the same way too, organised an endless round of games and contests to keep everyone distracted. On a submarine, he pointed out, there were far fewer distractions.

Kevin privately understood. Anything could be happening, back on Earth. The Horde could have attacked again, he knew, or terrorists could have successfully struck at Heinlein Colony or one of the recruiting cen-tres on Earth. There were just too many people volunteering to go to the moon for them all to be screened, even with alien lie detection technol-ogy. All they could really do was make sure that no one who hadn't been properly screened got access to the starships or other pieces of alien tech-nology. But his understanding didn't make it any easier to bear.

He spent a surprising amount of time talking to the alien. Cn!lss, once he'd overcome his slight fear of the utterly inhuman alien, was a strange conversationalist. On one hand, he seemed quite willing to share everything he knew with his human captors. But on the other hand, there were large gaps in his knowledge that seemed utterly implausible. If Kevin hadn't studied the records on the Horde so care-fully, he would have assumed the Hordesman was keeping something from him. But ignorance of the greater galaxy seemed to be part of their worldview.

"The world we're visiting will not twitch a claw at your presence," Cn!lss assured him. "They are used to visitors who do not wish to share anything of themselves with strangers."

Kevin nodded. He'd given serious thought to wearing something that completely covered their forms, but it seemed pointless. The human race wasn't *that* different to several other galactic races, including some who looked almost identical as long as they didn't remove their clothes. They'd be likely to be mistaken for one of those races, Cn!lss assured him, provided they didn't undergo a medical examination. *That* would have revealed their humanity beyond a shadow of a doubt.

"You have contacts," he said, softly. "People we can talk to?"

"Quite a few who do business with the Hordes," Cn!lss said. "They will sell to anyone, provided the price is right."

"How very human," Kevin muttered.

He sighed. It looked very much as though they would have to hire a local to help them sell their wares, giving the local a chance to cheat them out of half of their profits. If, of course, there *were* any profits. He couldn't help worrying about what would happen if their produce turned out to be completely worthless. Or, for that matter, if they were simply cheated so badly they wound up with nothing. It seemed alarmingly possible.

The thought still nagged at him as he walked into the research lab and met Carolyn. His half-hearted attempts to lure her into bed had failed, but she seemed friendly enough. Kevin had sighed and given up, more or less. Maybe she was just worried about bedding her ultimate superior on the starship.

"I think we have a rough idea of just *how* the alien drive works," she told him, as she took her eyes off the screen. "It actually folds space around it, allowing the starship to cross large volumes of space almost instantly. Or at least we *think* that's what it does."

She picked up a sheet of paper and held it up in front of his nose. "Imagine you start here," she said, pointing to one end of the paper. "You want to get to the other end, which is quite some distance away. If you have to walk normally, it will take you some time."

Carefully, she started to fold the sheet of paper up like a concertina. "By folding the space around the starship, the FTL drive ensures that the distance the starship has to travel is much shorter than it seems. But... the more space is folded, it seems to create gravity waves that allow the ship to surf towards its destination and..."

She paused. "You're not following this, are you?"

Kevin shook his head. He was, he knew without false modesty, pretty smart. It was why he'd gone into Intelligence in the first place. But Carolyn was far smarter than him, even though she had very little practical experience. As a theorist, she was first-rate. And yet...could she actually turn theory into technology that would make FTL a practical reality?

"We know it can be done," Carolyn said, when he asked. "The aliens can make it happen, after all. And we also know that chinks in space-time form naturally, allowing the aliens to expand through space without FTL drives. If we'd had one of those in our star system..."

"I know," Kevin said. "We'd have been overwhelmed *long* ago."

He shivered. When he'd realised that there were over ten thousand intelligent races known to exist, he'd wondered why Earth hadn't encountered them openly centuries ago. The answer had finally emerged from the databanks, only to give rise to more questions. Galactic society preferred to concentrate on the gravity points, even though there was a working form of FTL drive. It was odd to realise that such a towering civilisation looked so strange, when viewed on a standard chart, but it did make sense. Earth had been ignored simply because she was too far from the galactic mainstream.

They don't have infinite power, not yet, he thought. *Without it, there are limits to how far they can expand without the gravity points.*

It was odd. The aliens had all the tools to create a post-scarcity society, yet they lacked the power sources necessary to make that final jump. If they managed to gain access to an infinite source of power – zero-point energy, perhaps – they would be able to transform themselves into *Star Trek's* Federation or the Culture or something even more powerful. But they couldn't, not yet. Humanity still had a chance to catch up.

Or do we? The thought was a bitter one. Humanity had fought wars that had claimed millions of lives. The Galactics had fought wars that had killed *billions or trillions*. They thought nothing of building starships large enough to carry an American aircraft carrier in their holds or of converting an entire star system into a warship production plant. Or they could use nanotechnology to enslave hundreds of millions of people... no matter how he looked at it, humanity's survival would depend, very much so, on keeping their heads down and not making any enemies. But they already had one merciless set of enemies in the Horde.

Carolyn elbowed him. "Penny for your thoughts?"

"Just thinking about how far we have to go," Kevin said. The vast majority of humanity – at least in the West – had absorbed the reports from the moon...and then gone onwards, living their lives as if Steve and his family had never existed. He rather envied their ability to stop thinking about what it all meant. "How long until you can produce a working FTL generator?"

"Probably years," Carolyn admitted. She rubbed her forehead as she sat down. "I can see the bare bones of an FTL drive, but actually making it work would be tricky as hell. If we could open up the drive on the ships..."

Kevin shook his head, firmly. The whole system was sealed, a sensible precaution where Hordesmen were concerned. Besides, it was fairly clear from the instruction manual that any attempt to open the drive section would almost certainly disable it permanently. They couldn't risk being stranded in interstellar space.

"I understand," Carolyn said. She yawned, suddenly. "But it will be years before we make any real progress."

"I know," Kevin confessed.

"Tell you one thing," Carolyn said. "We may be halfway towards artificial gravity and thus antigravity. It will take some work to produce enough superconductors, but once we have them we might be able to produce our own antigravity systems."

Kevin smiled. The real problem with human spaceflight was lifting cargo out of Earth's gravity field. Every piece of weight had to be accounted for, somehow. The giant rockets that had propelled Apollo 11 to the moon had been discarded as they expended their fuel and became deadweight. But if humanity could master antigravity technology...

"Good luck," he said. "Make it happen and you'll be famous right across the world."

"That's tiny, now," Carolyn said. "Do you think anyone is ever famous right across the galaxy?"

"I doubt it," Kevin said. "The galaxy is really staggeringly huge. And besides, not all of the aliens share the same tastes. Who knows – they might actually *like* listening to the Screaming Singer of the Week."

"Nah," Carolyn said, after a moment's thought. "They couldn't be that perverse."

TWENTY-TWO

HEINLEIN COLONY, LUNA

"**H**ere he comes," Mongo said, as the shuttle swept down towards the lunar surface. "Are you ready?"

Steve shrugged, unsure. Arranging the state visit had been tricky, to say the least. Every world leader who considered himself important – something they all seemed to have in common – had demanded to be the first to visit the moon. And it hadn't just been them, either. The Secretary General of the UN, the Pope and hundreds of other significant political figures had also demanded to be the first to visit. In the end, Steve had ruled that the American President would be the first, if the Secret Service let him come. They'd been horrified when they realised they wouldn't be given complete access to the colony, even though it was their duty to protect the President.

But the President had come. Steve had to smile at the thought. He had thought – and still thought – that the President's politics were appallingly bad for America, but he definitely had to admit the man had balls. But then, what sort of politician would pass up on a chance to make history?

There was a faint flicker of energy around the shuttle as it passed through the force field and settled to the ground. The force field was keeping the atmosphere in, allowing Steve and the rest of the reception party to stand in the open without spacesuits. But part of him really didn't like being so badly exposed. One glitch with the shield generator and they'd be dead before they could hope to escape.

The hatch opened, revealing the President and his youngest daughter. She'd wanted to be an astronaut, Steve recalled; she was staring around the lunar surface as if she'd never quite expected it to be real. The Secret Service had thrown another fit at the thought of letting the First Daughter – one of them, at least – go with the President. But they'd been overruled, again.

Steve nodded to Mongo, who stepped forward. "Present...ARMS!"

The small group of soldiers, armed with modified alien weapons, snapped to attention. Steve hadn't wanted a big ceremony, but he'd agreed – reluctantly – that some form of ceremony was probably required. In the end, they'd made it as simple as possible.

"Welcome to Heinlein Colony, Mr. President," he said, as the President reached the end of the line. "And you, young lady."

The President's daughter looked up at him, eagerly. "Are we going to see Apollo 11?"

"We are," Steve confirmed. Had he ever been so eager as a child? Probably. "But first we have to tour the colony."

He allowed Rochester to take the lead as they stepped through the airlock and into the rapidly-growing underground colony. It had been a month since they'd make their public debut and the response had been astonishing. The lunar population had more than quadrupled, while several new factories had been set up on the moon and more were on the way. Indeed, with another starship at their disposal, they'd even started pointing water asteroids towards Mars to start the terraforming process. The protests from environmentalists on Earth had simply been ignored.

"This is an incredible place," the President said, as they came to the end of the tour. "You must be very proud."

"We are, Mr. President," Rochester said. "We've built quite a community here over the last two months."

They entered Baen's Bar and sat down at a reserved table. The owner had operated a diner in Montana Steve had patronised, but he'd gratefully moved to the moon when Steve made the offer. It was growing harder and harder to run a small business in America these days, thanks to the bureaucrats. Steve knew there would be no shortage of recruits for the foreseeable future.

"Beef, chicken and other kinds of meat are expensive up here, at the moment," Steve explained as menus were passed round the table. "We're still working on setting up farms for animals, so we're having to bring it up from Earth. But, on the other hand, there are fewer overhead costs for small businessmen."

The President laughed. "Point taken," he said. "And retaken. And taken once again."

Steve shrugged. "I'm afraid the food isn't as fancy as you might get in a state dinner," he added. "But it is very good food."

"That will be something of a relief," the President joked. "Do you know how difficult it can be to endure a ten-course dinner?"

The cook took their orders, then vanished behind the counter. Steve smiled to himself as the sound of frying burgers echoed over towards the table, then allowed his smile to become obvious as a young girl served the drinks. The President's daughter had chosen a colossal milkshake, which had arrived in a weirdly-shaped glass that had been produced in zero-gravity. Unsurprisingly, the President had settled for coke.

"You've done quite a bit over the last month, if the reports are accurate," the President said, as they waited. "Are you planning to slow down?"

"Not at all," Steve said. "The first asteroid homesteading kits are being completed now, so we hope to set up the first asteroid mining stations within the next month. Despite the naysayers, we had an astonishing number of applicants volunteer to enter the training program, even though there are significant risks and a very real possibility of death millions of miles from home. And we're placing orders for components that will be used to construct the first base on Titan..."

He smiled. "We have a very long way to go."

The young girl returned, carrying a large tray of burgers, fries and other unhealthy foods, which she placed on the table. Steve sensed more than heard Mariko click her teeth in irritation as he took one of the burgers and started to eat it, savouring every bite. It was a genuine burger, nothing like a piece of recycled cardboard from a global fast food company. The meat blended well with the cheese, mustard and catsup. And the fries were just perfect.

"My wife is going to be irked with me," the President observed. "I'm not supposed to eat such foods."

"It could be worse," Rochester said. "You could be eating recycled food."

"Most of the bloggers on the moon seem to complain about it," the President observed. "You'd think they'd be able to produce something that tasted good as well as provided the right nutrients."

"Some of our people have a theory about that," Steve said. "The whole system is designed to encourage its users to either grow foodstuffs for themselves or work out how to reprogram the system to produce something tasty. We're working on the first option."

"Once we have a proper farming system set up here, our food will probably taste a lot better," Rochester agreed. "It will probably do wonders for morale too."

After they had finished the meal – the President insisted on thanking the cook and his daughters personally – they walked back to the airlock and boarded the very first lunar hovercraft. It had been a pain to build on Earth because it was next to useless in the low gravity; eventually, once the truth had come out, the designers had promised to produce a far better version. The President's daughter seemed to fall in love at once, running forward and sitting in the pilot's chair. Mariko had to gently push her back towards the passenger seats, allowing Mongo to take the helm.

"This is actually a covered bus, allowing us to operate without spacesuits," Steve explained, as Mongo started the engine. The hovercraft moved forward, balancing on a stream of gas, then inched out of the hanger. "And we added an antigravity generator, but apart from that the system is all human. We could have settled the moon years ago."

Silence fell as the bus made its way through Heinlein Colony. There were few signs of habitation above the ground, but there were dozens of men in spacesuits and converted tractors, working to set up a mass driver. Given time, lunar rock could be shipped back to Earth for conversion into space stations – or HE3 could be shipped to Earth for the fusion power plants.

"That's going to be the first aboveground apartment block," Rochester said, pointing towards an excavation site. "Once its sealed, crews will install everything from plumbing to internet cables, then we'll invite people to move into it. Half of the apartments have been marked down for long-term lunar residents, the other half will be sold to people who can support themselves on the moon."

The President's daughter looked up. "Could *I* have one?"

"Only if you come and work here," Rochester said, not unkindly. "Or if you manage to put down the rather large sum we're demanding from anyone who won't be working for us."

Steve nodded. Heinlein Colony simply couldn't afford freeloaders. People who could work anywhere – authors, artists, consulting technicians – could settle on the moon, even if they weren't working for the colony. Or people who were prepared to pay the down sum. But someone who couldn't work, or wouldn't work…it was going to be a right little headache for quite some time to come.

"I will," the President's daughter said, firmly.

The President and Steve exchanged glances. Having the President's daughter on the moon would be one hell of a publicity coup – and a practical nightmare. She was young enough to adapt, presumably bright enough to learn to live on the moon…but if it became public, it would be extremely difficult for her. If nothing else, she'd be yelled at by men and women who disliked her father's politics.

"We shall see," the President said.

We should slip a bug into that conversation, the mischievous part of Steve's mind commented. *And see precisely how that goes.*

He pushed the thought aside as the President looked over at Mariko. "I understand that you will be leading the medical teams?"

"I will," Mariko said. "Now the whining has come to an end, that is."

Steve winced. Mariko had been quietly furious about the endless series of delays, caused by her fellow doctors. The American Medical Association had filed complaint after complaint, questioning everything from the true nature of alien technology to the credentials of Mariko and her fellow doctors, even though the alien technology did all of the work. In the end, the AMA had only relaxed its opposition after it became clear that it was costing them politically and public opinion was turning against them.

And that people were threatening to sue them, Steve thought, cynically. *A terminally-ill rich man won't hesitate to sue when he thinks the AMA is standing between him and healthcare he desperately needs.*

"Politics," the President said. "And will you be offering treatments to all?"

Mariko tossed Steve an annoyed look. "Adults who can pay and children will get priority," she said. "Adults who can't pay will have to wait in line."

Steve winced, again. They'd come close to a screaming row after he'd insisted on taking paying customers first, even though the colony desperately needed the money. Mariko had objected, violently, to denying *anyone* medical care, even if they couldn't pay. He'd eventually given in on treating children, knowing that Mariko would practically strangle him if she wasn't allowed to help kids. It was necessary, he knew, but it didn't make it any easier for either of them to handle it.

"There will be hundreds of rich men waiting in line too," the President said. "People are funny that way."

Steve couldn't disagree.

"Here we are," Mongo said, breaking into their thoughts. "Apollo 11."

Steve stared out of the porthole as the sight came into view. The American flag was still standing, looking faintly uncanny; NASA had treated it to ensure it looked unfurled, even though there was no wind on the moon. Beyond it, the landing stage stood on the lunar surface, utterly unmarked by the passage of time. But then, there was no atmosphere on the moon either.

"We won't be going any closer," Mongo said, as the bus came to a halt. "I don't want to risk damaging the landing site."

The President said nothing. Beside him, his daughter was twitching with excitement as she stared at Apollo 11. Steve felt an odd lump in his throat as he took in the magnificent scene before him. *Americans* had done that, he knew. *Americans* had reached for the moon and landed on the surface of another world. But would Armstrong and his fellow moonwalkers have imagined that mankind would fumble the ball so badly? That no one would set foot on the moon again using purely human technology?

They didn't know, Steve thought. *They never thought that we would lose our nerve.*

It was a purely human achievement, yet it was so trivial compared to what the Galactics had done. A single large starship, manned by competent aliens, could smash all three captured ships and overwhelm Earth's defences in a moment. Earth's teeming billions would vanish without trace amidst the trillions upon trillions who thronged through the galaxy, never sparing a moment to think of a primitive blue world called Earth.

"This is a mark of what humans can do," he said, out loud. "We built this on our own; we cracked the secret of producing rockets, nuclear fission, steam engines and so much more on our own. The Horde did not. We have the basics of scientific enquiry; the Horde does not. They have no hope of duplicating Galactic technology for themselves, we can and we will. And we will reach for the stars."

"Fine words," the President said. "Do you plan to run for election?"

Steve gaped at him, then realised he was being teased. "I think we will be holding elections in two years," he said. "That should give us a large enough population to make them meaningful, while giving us time to finalise the constitution and the legal code. I...don't know if I will stand for election."

The President leaned forward. "Who elected you now?"

It was an awkward question, Steve had to concede. But he had a rejoinder. "Who elected the leaders of over half the states with membership in the UN?"

"You need to hold yourself to higher standards," the President said.

"There will be elections," Steve said. "At that time, I will decide if I want to stand for office or gratefully retire to the moon. There's a whole universe out there to explore, after all."

He looked over at the back of Mongo's head. "Can you take us back now?"

"Just a moment," the President's daughter said. She plucked a cell phone out of her pocket and started taking photos of everything from the bus's interior to the view outside. Steve sighed as she took a photograph of him and the President seated together, then one of Mariko standing against the large porthole. "These will go on my facebook tonight."

Steve rolled his eyes. He'd always disliked watching his children post their pictures on facebook – or anywhere else online for that matter. He was mildly surprised the President's daughter was even *allowed* to use facebook. Quite apart from the threat of her being stalked, her posts and check-ins would pose a definite security risk. Terrorists would be able to follow the President and his daughter wherever they went.

"I'm sure you will get lots of likes," he said, finally.

He waited until the bus had returned to the colony, then invited the President to join him in the secure room. "I need an update on weapons delivery," he said. "Has the USAF thrown another fit?"

"Congress is making a fit instead," the President said. "They're not keen on transferring nuclear warheads to *anyone.*"

Steve snorted. Once, there had been a time when he would have adamantly opposed sending weapons to any country, at least unless it was a genuine ally. And nukes shouldn't go anywhere outside American control. But now he needed those nukes. The plan to set up a breeder reactor on the moon – or even out in space – was going slower than he would have liked. Most of the people with experience in producing modern nuclear weapons were unable or unwilling to leave their home countries.

"You need to make them listen," he said, urgently. "Bomb-pumped lasers might be the only surprise we can produce before the Horde comes back."

"I've already pushed things as far as I can," the President said. "You do realise just how badly you shocked the world?"

Steve nodded, sourly.

"Congress isn't sure just where it will all lead and they're getting mixed messages from their constituents," the President continued. "And there are fears that it will change the demographic map of America permanently."

Steve rather suspected they had a point. The culture wars had turned America into a deeply divided country. If all the conservatives or libertarians left to set up home on the moon, he asked himself, what would it do for the rest of America? They'd be talking about millions of people, but it was quite possible that there *would* be a major demographic shift. And what would happen then?

"It will definitely change the map if the Horde bomb America into radioactive ash," Steve said, tartly. "And besides, maybe they should learn to think of America ahead of their own interests."

"And exactly how," the President said, "do you intend to ensure that *your* politicians put the interests of your...colony ahead of their own affairs?"

"Carefully," Steve admitted. "Very carefully."

"Best of luck," the President said, cheerfully. "And thank you very much for this tour."

His expression softened. "My daughter really enjoyed herself, Mr. Stuart, and so did I."

"Thank you," Steve said. He couldn't fault the President for pointing out the elephant in the room. How *did* one screen for integrity in one's politicians? "And please tell everyone that it's a good place to live up here."

TWENTY-THREE

CAPTAIN PERRY, YING

"**R**eady to disengage drive," Jackson said. "All stations are standing by."

Kevin nodded, feeling tension running through his body. They'd prepared as best as they could for a month, but none of them had ever set foot on an alien world before. Even those of them who had experience with different human cultures had never experienced anything so completely *alien*. It was quite possible that they would make a very simple mistake and doom their mission.

"Disengage drive," he ordered. He'd made the decision not to come out of FTL with shields up and weapons ready to fire, but all stations were ready to snap to alert if necessary. Who knew how the system's authorities would react to a starship coming out of FTL at full battle readiness? And yet, there was no overall authority in the Ying System. "Take us out of FTL."

There was a faint indescribable sensation and then the display suddenly filled with light. The stars didn't look too different to the stars from Earth, at least to Kevin's untrained eye, but the system was *crammed* with starships and industrial stations. There were thousands of starships and spacecraft making their way to and from the system's inhabited planets, while the entire system seemed to be thoroughly developed. Each planet had at least a dozen habitable asteroids surrounding it, while countless more drifted in free orbits around the primary star.

Cold awe threatened to overwhelm him. This was the dream, a solar system so heavily developed that nothing could threaten to exterminate its inhabitants. The human race would be safe from all harm once the Sol System was as heavily developed as this one. And yet it was a very minor system by alien standards, their version of a free city, somewhere without an overall authority. Who knew just how heavily developed an alien core system would be?

"Send the locals our IFF," he said. It had been carefully modified, although the alien had advised them that hardly anyone on Ying would care. "And request permission to approach the planet."

He looked down at the display while waiting for the response. A stream of alien starships were making their way through normal space towards the gravity point, a tear in the fabric of reality. The aliens, masters of gravity and antigravity, had concluded that streams of gravity between stars created natural folds in the fabric of space-time, allowing spacecraft to hop from system to system without an FTL drive. Many of the oddities of galactic history, Kevin suspected, came from the simple fact that FTL was a comparatively recent invention. Before then, they'd been completely dependent on the gravity points.

"There's no defences around the gravity point at all," Edward Romford pointed out. "You think they don't consider the system worth defending?"

"Or maybe they think it would be pointless," Kevin said. "There's no single authority in this system to coordinate a defence."

He shrugged. Prior to the invention of FTL, the gravity points had provided a bottleneck that had forced any aggressor to appear in a known location if he wanted to attack. The defenders might be outnumbered, but they would be able to counter with fixed defences and minefields. But FTL had completely undone the defender's planning and allowed the aggressor to appear from anywhere. It must have been an awful surprise, Kevin considered, for the defenders when FTL had first been invented.

But the whole system was yet another illustration of just how colossal the galaxy actually was, compared to Earth. Kevin had been in lawless cities, in places where enemies met and traded despite mutual hatred, yet they had always been isolated places where no outside power wanted to establish control. Here...it was the same, but scaled up to a whole solar system. Part of him just wanted to collapse in horror, his mind unwilling to grasp what he was seeing. The rest of him just wanted to get on with the mission.

"They've assigned us an orbital slot," Jackson said, shortly. "And they've sent us a full set of charges too."

Kevin accessed the interface, then smiled. They weren't being charged for being in high orbit, but moving to low orbit would cost...as would hiring a hotel on the planet's surface or hiring a heavy-lift shuttle. He smiled at just how *human* it was, despite the inhumanity of the planet's settlers. Planetary orbit might cost nothing, but everything else came with a pretty steep charge. He'd been on holidays where the flight was cheap, yet everything else was expensive as hell. The basic idea was the same.

"Understood," he said. "Take us into orbit."

It was easy to see, as they approached the planet, why no larger interstellar power had laid claim to Ying. The planet might have been habitable once, but it had suffered a massive ecological disaster centuries ago. If there was a native race, it had died out as the surface slowly turned to desert. Even now, sandstorms rolled across the planet's surface, far more powerful than anything recorded on Earth. The planet's authorities, such as they were, seemed reluctant to invest in terraforming their homeworld.

But it makes a certain kind of sense, he told himself. *If they made the system more attractive, someone might come in and take it.*

"Entering orbit now," Jackson said. He grinned, nervously. "We're here."

"So we are," Kevin said. An odd feeling gripped his chest. It took him a moment to realise it was nerves. He'd been in tight spots before, but this was very different. There would be no hope of rescue if the shit hit the fan. "The away team will gather in the teleport chamber."

"Good luck, sir," Jackson said.

"Don't forget your orders," Kevin said. "We'll check in, every hour on the hour; if you don't hear from us for over four hours, assume the worst. And if you don't hear from us in a day, take the ship back to Earth. No heroics, Commander."

"None will be taken," Jackson assured him.

Kevin smiled as he walked through the ship's corridors and into the teleport chamber. The alien was already there, standing somewhat apart from the five humans who made up the rest of the away team. Kevin nodded to each of them in turn, hoping and praying that they would be capable of maintaining their calm on the planet's surface. None of them had any real experience with aliens, apart from the Horde. And the Hordesmen were hardly typical Galactics.

"All present and correct," Edward Romford said. "And we're all armed to the teeth."

"Just be careful not to start something unless absolutely necessary," Kevin warned. There were no gun control laws on Ying, but the humans would be badly outnumbered. On the other hand, from what they had been told, if they shot their way out of trouble no one would bat an eyelid. "Onto the pads."

He stepped onto the final pad and activated the interface. "Energise."

The world faded away in silver light, then reformed as something different. The heat struck him at once, a wave of warm air as hot as anything he'd felt in the Middle East, but carrying with it a whole series of unfamiliar scents. He felt his body start to sweat as he stood upright,, fighting against the planet's stronger gravity. Despite the augmentations he'd had inserted into his body, he had the uncomfortable feeling that they were going to have real problems until they managed to adapt to the planet's environment. It was nothing like Earth.

He looked around. They were standing in a small stone chamber, bright light pouring through two open windows. An alien clicked impatiently, motioning with one long tentacle for them to step off the pads and out of the room. Kevin stared at the alien for one long moment, then remembered his manners and led the humans past the alien and through the door. Who would have thought that an octopus-like creature could develop the ability to walk on land?

Outside, the smell was stronger, much stronger. Hundreds of thousands of aliens teemed through the city, moving between dozens of buildings that seemed to be built from stone, but in countless different styles. All of them seemed larger than life…it took him a long moment to realise they were designed to accommodate all different races. A doorway sized for humans would have problems allowing a Hordesman to step through, he suspected. No wonder the Hordesmen had so disliked their starship. It hadn't been designed for their race.

Down one long street, there was something rather like a market. Here, aliens seemed to gather together in small groups of their own races, rather than mingling with other races. It struck him as odd until he recalled just how hard it was to find something that could be eaten by more than a handful of races. One race's food might be another race's poison - or worse. Here, where there were no laws to prevent accidental poisonings, it was well to be careful. Further down the street, there were stalls that seemed to be getting attention from everyone, even a handful of aliens that looked like giant spiders. Kevin couldn't see what they were selling.

"We're going to need to get a hotel room," Romford said. "Somewhere we can use as a base."

"Yes, the alien chirped. "This way."

KEVIN HAD EXPECTED problems with getting a room suitable for human habitation. In hindsight, such fears had been completely groundless. The hotel managers wouldn't have any problems configuring their rooms to suit people from just about any race, from the walking lobsters to the giant spiders. Kevin assumed, as a matter of course, that the rooms were bugged, even though his check had revealed nothing. He rather doubted that the Horde had had access to up-to-date galactic surveillance technology.

Once they'd set up the room and sorted out how to use the facilities – the bathtub had clearly been designed for a much larger creature – Kevin, Romford and Cn!lss set out again, looking for the nearest library. It hadn't been too hard to find on the planet's datanet – access, once again, cost a surprisingly high sum – but when they found it Kevin couldn't help feeling disappointed. Instead of row upon row of books, there were a handful of alien computers and a librarian who looked like a giant monkey, complete with tail. It was silly to be disappointed, he knew, when countless races couldn't use human books. But it still felt disappointing.

Once they'd paid – again – the librarian paid them no heed as they accessed the terminal and started to hunt for tech manuals. Kevin had practiced endlessly with the interface he'd taken from *Shadow Warrior*, but it was still difficult to search through the sheer mass of data someone had uploaded into the alien system. It was nearly an hour before they managed to download a whole bundle of tech manuals the aliens probably considered primitive, too primitive to bother to classify. But then, would the United States try to classify the secrets behind producing a World War One-era dreadnaught? Or the secret of producing gunpowder? Somehow, Kevin doubted that anyone would bother.

We can work our way through the more primitive technology the aliens built, then use it to understand the underlying principles, Kevin told himself. The grave danger was becoming completely dependent on alien technology. But once humanity understood how it actually worked, they could start producing it for themselves – and maybe even improving on it. It was alarmingly clear that humanity would need to do more than just match the alien technology. They'd have to make improvements of their own.

He hesitated, then started the next series of searches. One of the concepts noted in the Horde databanks had been of cultural uplift, of a primitive race being helped to spacefaring status by a more advanced race. The Horde databanks hadn't actually gone into details – they'd certainly not been given any such assistance – but the library did have some files on the topic for anyone to see. Kevin copied them all, then sat back and waited while the information was transmitted to *Captain Perry*. If nothing else, they would have retrieved something the human race could use.

"We'll have to come back," he said, straightening up. The alien chair might have adapted to fit his posterior, but it still felt uncomfortable. "Carolyn and the others will have to go through it and see how the search can be adapted and improved."

"Maybe we can establish a direct link from the ship to the library," Romford suggested. "They could search the computer for themselves."

"It would cost," Cn!lss stated.

Kevin rolled his eyes.

He couldn't help feeling nervous as he followed Cn!lss through the streets, into what the alien had described as the premier trading ground for good and items that were illegal in certain parts of the galaxy. There were more and more aliens around, most of them carrying weapons and looking grim, while the skies were rapidly darkening as another sandstorm moved over the city. He looked up as sand started to pelt the city's protective forcefield, causing flashes of brilliant lightning to glitter out high overhead. There was definitely nothing like it on Earth.

But the building they approached was surprisingly familiar, even though it was completely alien. Two guards, both monkey-creatures, eyed them suspiciously, then listened as Cn!lss explained they wanted to meet with the merchant. There was a long pause – Kevin's interface warned him that they were being scanned – and then the door opened, revealing a darkened room. The two humans exchanged glances, then followed Cn!lss into the warehouse.

Inside, the cold struck him at once. There had to be a forcefield keeping it inside, he thought grimly, as he struggled to pull his clothes around him. The floor was covered with ice, as if the inhabitant of the building wanted to sleep on it. Slowly, the darkness receded, just enough for him to see the outline of a colossal creature sitting in the centre of the room. For once, Kevin had some problems matching it to anything on Earth.

From what little he could see, he had a feeling he should be very glad he couldn't see the entire creature.

"Greetings," a voice said. The creature shivered, very slightly. "You have items to sell?"

"Weapons," Cn!lss said. "Very crude, but very effective weapons."

There was a long pause. "You will supply details," the toneless voice said. "Now."

Kevin's interface reported that it was being asked for a file. Kevin hesitated, then sent the file containing the weapons information and specifications. AK-47s, he had been told, were crude compared to Galactic technology, but simple enough for the Horde to operate without breaking them regularly. But the downside was that the Galactics would have no trouble in duplicating the weapons. A few hours with a fabricator would be all they needed.

"Primitive," the voice stated. "But effective."

"Yes," Cn!lss said, quickly. "And they can be reconfigured as necessary."

"Indeed," the voice agreed. "How many can you supply?"

Kevin stepped forward. "We can supply a thousand weapons and ten thousand rounds of ammunition right now," he said. "More can be produced later, upon demand."

The negotiation process went backwards and forwards for nearly an hour, as the humans showed their wares and waited to see how the alien reacted. Kevin wasn't too surprised to discover that most of their wares were almost worthless, but the alien seemed oddly impressed by some of the alcohol and human artworks. Eventually, the alien made an offer, which Cn!lss turned down and countered with one of his own. It was clear, Kevin decided, that Cn!lss had been doing the bargaining for the Horde. Or maybe that he *should* have been doing it, if he hadn't been *allowed* to do it. Eventually, they came to an agreement.

"I'll have the weapons shipped down to the planet's surface tomorrow," Kevin said. They'd have to hire a landing strip, of course. That too would be expensive. "You can pay us the remainder of the balance then."

"I may take some of your cargo on spec," the creature offered. There was still no hint of feeling in its voice. As it inched forward, Kevin had a sudden impression of claws – lots of claws. He had to fight the urge to jump backwards. "It may be worth something to others."

Kevin nodded. The alien had a very good reputation, according to Cn!lss, for driving a hard bargain, but he didn't try to cheat his clients once the deal was made. Indeed, if he did manage to find a market for anything else the humans had brought, he could be relied upon to set up the deal...taking a commission for himself, of course. Shaking his head, he bowed politely to the alien and allowed Cn!lss to lead him out of the building. The two guards nodded their heads as they stepped past. Clearly, Kevin noted, they'd moved from potential problems to valued customers.

Outside, it was as hot as ever, but darkness had fallen over the city. It took him a moment to realise that the sandstorm had grown stronger, strong enough to block out the sun. Most of the aliens seemed to have fallen back into their buildings, leaving the streets almost deserted. A cold chill ran down the back of his neck as they started to make their way back to the hotel. Something didn't feel right...old instincts, honed in Afghanistan, sprang to life. Something was definitely wrong. Mentally, he started scouting for ways to evade possible enemy contact...

Cn!lss let out a noise as four aliens, four very familiar aliens, stepped into view. Kevin froze as the Hordesmen lifted their weapons, pointing them right at the humans. Their eyes scanned the humans quickly, then there was a brilliant flash of blue light...

...And then Kevin crashed down into darkness.

TWENTY-FOUR

HEINLEIN COLONY, LUNA

"**T**hank you for coming," Rochester said.

Steve scowled at him. It had been 0300 on the starship when his interface had jerked him awake – and, for good measure, woken Mariko too. If it hadn't been an urgent call, he might just have given in to the temptation to go right back to bed. Instead, he'd taken the shuttle from Earth orbit to Heinlein Colony. If something had gone badly wrong, bad enough for Rochester to call him, it probably demanded immediate attention.

"You're welcome," he said, trying to remind himself not to snarl. Just because he was tired was no excuse for snapping at a subordinate. He'd heard plenty of stories about commanding officers who'd refused to allow their subordinates to wake them, even when the enemy forces were on the advance. It was one of the reasons Adolf Hitler had lost World War Two. "What happened?"

"A crime," Rochester said, as he turned to lead the way into the colony. "Quite a bad one, I'm afraid."

Steve winced. He'd been expecting *something* to happen ever since they started expanding the circle of recruitment wider and wider. Ex-military personnel tended to have some common sense, particularly the ones who had served in combat, but civilians could do some damn silly things from time to time. Or maybe it was an ex-military person. Some of them could be idiotic at times too.

"Shit," he said. The legal code they'd devised was about to be tested, badly. "What happened?"

"From what we've put together," Rochester said, "Daniel Witherspoon managed to get very drunk last night, probably from one of the illicit stills. While drunk, he started an argument with his wife that turned into a fight; he beat her pretty damn badly. And then his daughter tried to intervene and got beaten too. They're both currently in the medical bay."

Steve sucked in a breath. "How bad was it?"

"They would both have been sore for several days, according to the medics, if they hadn't been treated," Rochester said. "The lack of any real damage is quite indicative."

"Bastard," Steve said. If Witherspoon had been so completely drunk he'd forgotten himself, it would have almost certainly resulted in considerably more serious damage. Instead, he'd managed to hurt both his wife and daughter without inflicting any permanent harm. Or, at least, without inflicting any permanent physical harm. Who knew how they would react after being beaten so badly? "Where is he?"

"In the cells," Rochester said. "Jean is keeping an eye on him."

Steve hastily accessed the interface and retrieved the file on Daniel Witherspoon. He'd been discharged from the army four years ago and, since then, had spent most of his time trying to hold down a succession of part-time jobs, while drinking heavily. Someone would probably claim, in hindsight, that recruiting him had been a mistake. But, looking at the file, it was clear that Charles had felt sorry for him. Witherspoon, out of the army, had had few skills that any civilian employers wanted or needed. He'd certainly never really tried to develop himself.

But there was no point in feeling sorry for him, Steve rebuked himself sharply. Maybe Witherspoon hadn't been able to get a break until now, but it didn't excuse beating his wife and child. Or…had he turned aggressive *because* of his success? Steve had wondered, sometimes, what would have happened to him if he hadn't had the ranch? Would he have drunk himself into an early grave? Or would he have sucked in his pride and stayed with the military?

They reached the handful of holding cells and stopped. Jean D'Arcy looked up at them, then smiled. Tall, black, with hair cropped close to her skull, she looked formidable even without combat implants. And she'd held down a position of sheriff in Texas long enough to be utterly confident in her own abilities. When she'd been offered the post of Lunar Sheriff, she hadn't hesitated before accepting the job.

"It's good to meet you at last," she said. "I wanted to thank you for this opportunity in person."

"We can talk later," Steve said. "For the moment, I want your impressions of our friend in there?"

"He's claiming to be totally repentant," Jean said. Her mouth twisted with distaste. "He's lying, sir."

Steve lifted an eyebrow. "How do you know that?"

"I've seen it before," Jean admitted. "Some guy goes and drinks himself into a maddened state, then goes off and beats his wife. But the truly repentant ones act differently. This guy...weeps and wails when he thinks he's being watched, but goes quiet when he thinks he's alone and unobserved."

She shook her head. "And there's also the injuries," she added. "This was no maddened beating, sir. This was as deliberate as a spanking."

"I thought as much," Steve said. He hesitated, then asked the next question. "Have you spoken to the victims?"

"The wife is confused," Jean said. "The daughter...is torn."

She shrugged. "Sir, when someone is married, when the relationship is still there, people are often torn between wanting the husband back and wanting to be rid of him," she continued. "So far, despite the beating, Mrs Witherspoon hasn't reached the point where she just wants him out of her life. His daughter...she wants her old father back, but she also wants to be rid of the drunken lunatic who's taken his place."

Steve gritted his teeth. One of his family's friends had been in the National Guard, rather than the regular army. He'd been called up for service in Iraq, been wounded there and returned a broken man. Two years afterwards, following screaming fits and threats against his family's life, he'd put a gun in his mouth and killed himself. His children had wondered, out loud, just what sort of devil had stolen their father's body. The kind man they'd known had died in Iraq.

"I thought he would have been treated for alcoholism," he said, sharply. "Did he evade the tests somehow?"

"No," Rochester said. "But while we handled the physical need for alcohol, we didn't – we couldn't – handle the mental addiction to drink. It's possible that even one sip of moonshine or rotgut tipped him back over the edge."

"We will need to be more careful with our screening tests in future," Steve said, darkly. "For the moment…"

He turned back to Jean. "What would you advise we do with him?"

Jean met his eyes. "Right now, we have a legal code that is largely untested," she said. "And we really need to make it clear that we are not engaging in arbitrary punishment, no matter how deserved. We can't use his fists any longer."

Rochester clenched the fists in question. "This isn't one miner beating the shit out of another miner," he said. "Nor is this a fight that broke out over gambling. This is this…*asshole* deliberately beating his wife and daughter, without any cause I care to recognise. There is no bloody way this can be excused."

He looked at Steve. "Give me five minutes alone with him, please."

Steve was tempted. He was *very* tempted. Mariko would not have allowed him to lay a hand on her, not unless she wanted it. And his partner would be furious with him if he allowed the man to escape without punishment. A savage beating might teach him a lesson. But, at the same time, Jean was right. They needed to test their legal code.

"Select a jury," he ordered, finally. "There wouldn't be any lawyers; someone would have to speak with Witherspoon, then explain his rights under the legal code. "Make sure they're people who don't know him personally, if possible. Let them be unbiased."

"Show them the images and there won't be a single unbiased person in the colony," Jean muttered. "The girls were quite badly battered, sir."

"I know," Steve said. "I know."

In the end, he ended up explaining Witherspoon's rights himself. The man seemed torn between repentance and a cold self-satisfaction that sent chills running down Steve's spine, something that he was tempted to mention when the jury finally assembled. Pushing his feelings aside, he explained that Witherspoon could either admit to the charges or deny them and present a countervailing argument of his own. The jury would either accept his arguments or find him guilty. If the latter, they would also devise their own punishment.

"But I didn't mean to do it," Witherspoon whined, when Steve had finished. "Really, I didn't mean to do it."

"Then I suggest you tell that to the jury," Steve said. "They're the ones who will decide your fate."

He had never been fond of lawyers – viewing them as a plague on mankind – but he was starting to realise they might serve a useful purpose. Someone would have to be appointed as the Public Defender, to advise suspects of their rights under the law and assist them in producing their defence. Someone else would have to sum up the case for the jury...no, that someone might wind up leading the jury one way or the other. And there would have to be someone to present the case against the suspect.

The jury assembled in the largest available chamber in the colony, a room that had once served as a dining hall and then turned into a store-room for supplies brought from Earth. A handful of colonists, including three lunar bloggers, took seats where they could see everything, then Witherspoon himself was brought into the court in handcuffs. Jean, who would be presenting the case for the prosecution, had pointed out that she really needed extra staff or a dedicated prosecutor. Steve had to admit she had a point, although it would raise problems of its own. What would happen when the prosecutor found winning more important than justice?

"The charges facing Daniel Witherspoon are serious," Jean said. "The previous night, Witherspoon drank heavily, then went home to his chambers. There, he fought with his wife, which ended with him beating her quite heavily. When his daughter attempted to intervene, she was beaten too. Both women are currently in the medical bay."

Witherspoon looked reluctant to speak when it was his turn. Indeed, he hadn't even attempted to suggest if he would be pleading innocent or guilty. Steve rolled his eyes, then waited, as patiently as he could, for the man to present his defence. He had hours, if necessary. There would be no attempt to cut his defence short.

"I was drunk," he said, finally. "I did not mean to hurt either my wife or my daughter."

Jean rose to her feet. "You inflicted no permanent harm," she said. "That implies, very strongly, that you were in perfect control of yourself."

She showed the jury images taken by the doctor. "As you can see, the bruises look very bad," she continued. "But they would have faded, naturally, over the coming week if they hadn't been treated already. There would have been no permanent physical harm. But the scars you inflicted on their minds will never heal."

Witherspoon offered no defence. Eventually, the jury withdrew to a secure room to debate Witherspoon's fate. Steve watched them go, wondering if he was doing the right thing. A word from him could have condemned Witherspoon to death, or return to Earth, or a lifetime of hard labour. What if the jury took the view that no permanent harm wasn't as bad as something that *did* cause permanent harm? Or felt that they'd heard too much about mental harm from courtrooms down on Earth? It was so hard to prove that anyone had really suffered mental problems or depression from anything.

The jury returned, fifty minutes later.

"It is a principle of lunar law," the foreperson said, "that a person is responsible for their own actions. If they should happen to be under the influence of drugs or alcohol, they are still responsible for themselves as they chose to enter a state of diminished rationality. As such, your attack on your wife and daughter was your responsibility.

"Furthermore, you have presented no excuse for your actions, no suggestion that they might somehow have been justified. Accordingly, we find you guilty of the charges brought against you."

There was a long pause. "We debated sentencing for quite some time," the foreperson continued. "Some of us felt you did not deserve to live, or that there was a strong possibility that you would reoffend. Others felt you simply did not deserve to live here. However, we have decided that you will spend four years at hard labour instead, assuming you wish to remain on the moon. If not, you may return to Earth."

Steve wondered, absently, if Earth would take him. Witherspoon was an American citizen, technically, but the precise legal status of the lunar colonists was somewhat vague. It was arguable that they held joint citizenships, yet it was uncertain how it would all play out. As Kevin had said, it might be better if they all renounced their American citizenships. But Steve hadn't been able to bring himself to do that, not really. He still clung to the ideal of America in his heart.

Witherspoon, after being told that he had a day to decide, was marched out of the room and back to the cells. Steve sighed, then walked over to the bloggers, most of whom were just finishing their articles. As the first trial on the moon, it would set precedent for the future…although Steve had no intention of allowing precedent to rule unchallenged. The jury would always have the final word on just what happened to suspects.

"Mr. Stuart," Gunter Dawlish called. He'd moved to the moon, a decision that had boosted his popularity on Earth. "Do you have any comment on the case?"

"Justice has been served," Steve said, after a moment's thought. "The guilty man has been offered a choice between punishment or permanent exile from the moon."

"Which is likely to be exile from his wife and daughter too," Dawlish said. "Or will they be exiled too?"

"No," Steve said. "They are not to blame for Witherspoon's actions, so they will not be held to account for them. Should they wish to go with him, if he leaves, we will honour their request. If not, they will always have a place here."

Another blogger stepped forward. "Don't you feel it was handled a little too fast?"

That, Steve had to admit, was an awkward question. "I think we had all the facts established," he said. "If there had been a requirement for more investigations, we would have delayed the trial until they were carried out. If necessary, we would have used lie detectors to ensure that everyone involved was telling the truth."

"But the prosecutor was also the policewoman," another blogger asked. "Does that not create a conflict of interest?"

"She wasn't the one who passed sentence," Steve said, with a shrug. The blogger had a point, but they didn't have a legal staff yet. One would be needed, sooner rather than later. The next trial might be far less open and shut. "And now, if you will excuse me..."

He followed Rochester back to his office and sighed. "That could have gone better."

"It went about as well as could be expected," Rochester said. "Drink?"

Steve let him pour two cups of coffee, then took one gratefully. "Are there any other problems I ought to know about?"

"There's one that may turn into a problem," Rochester said, carefully. "You know we have a number of homosexual men on the moon?"

"I know," Steve said. "So?"

"Two of them want to marry," Rochester said. "Should we allow it?"

"What we want doesn't actually matter," Steve said. "Let them call themselves husband and husband if they want. If they want to register a partnership, let them do that too. It's not as if we give any incentives to married couples."

Or disincentives, he thought, in the privacy of his own mind. One of the reasons he had never actually married Mariko was out of fear of what would happen if the marriage failed. Judges granted women all the rights in America these days, while leaving the man permanently tied to her. He'd known two retired Marines who had been unable to remarry or even have more children because their income was being garnished to keep the wife in house and home, while they could only see their children from time to time. He had just never felt like taking the risk.

He shook his head. "It doesn't cause any harm to the rest of us if they get married, does it?"

"Not really," Rochester said. "Their teams will have to be resorted – I try to keep brothers apart, just to keep emotion out of the picture. But that isn't a problem now we have plenty of people on the surface teams."

"Then let us not stand in their way," Steve said. He couldn't understand homosexuality, but he imagined they had the same problem with heterosexuals. Besides, everyone deserved a chance to seek happiness wherever they found it. "Any other problems?"

"The teachers want the kids to have more afterschool activities," Rochester said. "They think the kids spend too long in VR worlds, so I'm planning to expand the sporting complex for them. But not all of the kids are interested in remaining in school. Some of the teenagers have even been caught roaming the upper levels."

Steve sighed. "Give them another lecture," he said.

"I have," Rochester said. "I've even threatened to have the next teenager caught up there publically paddled. It doesn't seem to have done any good."

"Of course not," Steve agreed. "I was an idiot when I was a teenager too."

He shrugged, expressively. "We'll just have to keep playing with the problem," he said. "And as we expand, the problem will solve itself."

Rochester smiled. "And someone wants to set up a brothel," he added. "She even has girls lined up and everything."

"Best not to talk about it," Steve said. "Mariko would *kill* me."

TWENTY-FIVE

YING SYSTEM

It was a curious fact - Cn!lss attributed it to the stubbornness of the average Hordesman – that stunners didn't have quite the same effect on them as they did on most other races. They were immobilised, sure, but they could still hear and feel what was going on around them, even though they were helpless. He could hear the Hordesmen chattering as they picked up their victims and carried them off, then picked up Cn!lss himself.

An odd sense of fatalism fell over him as he was carried away. Maybe he hadn't been captured – recaptured – by his own Horde, but he had no reason to expect anything other than an inglorious death. Hordesmen who were captured were expected to kill themselves – and Hordesmen who didn't kill themselves were generally killed anyway by their captors. No one would seriously believe a Hordesman to know anything worth sparing their lives.

He listened, carefully, as they were carried through the city. He knew better than to expect rescue; part of the reason he'd recommended Ying in the first place was because it was almost completely lawless. No one would object to the humans scanning the libraries for information, but no one would move to protect them too. They were captives now... where were they going? And why had they been targeted?

Cn!lss found it hard to believe, as he heard the sound of a door opening ahead of them, that the Hordesmen had been watching for humans in particular. Had they been watching for the missing starships? But they weren't a part of Cn!lss's Horde…he pushed the thought aside and waited, feeling a brief spurt of pain as he was dropped on a stone floor. Moments later, his entire body jerked as someone zapped him with an shocker. His eyes snapped open, revealing five armed Hordesmen and a single small blue alien.

There was a groan from beside him. Cn!lss turned to see the human – *Kevin*, he reminded himself – sitting upright, clutching his head. The small alien snapped his fingers and another alien appeared from the shadows, carrying a bottle of water. A servitor, Cn!lss realised, someone from yet another race that had no hope of standing on its own two feet. He would be a servant all his life, just as the Horde were nothing more than brutish mercenaries, slaves to the races that could and did build their own technology. Would the humans, too, end up like that?

"I believe we should talk," the small blue alien said, addressing Kevin. "We may have made something of an error."

— —

KEVIN HAD BEEN concussed once before, during a mission in Afghanistan that had very nearly been the end of him. It wasn't an experience he'd enjoyed. Now, he had to fight hard to keep from throwing up as the tall green alien offered him water to drink. The alien was oddly cute, pretty much a green-skinned alien space babe. But the genitals, if they were genitals, were completely different from anything human. Staggering slightly, he managed to pull himself to his feet and stared at the smaller alien confronting him.

He couldn't help thinking of a mutated Smurf. The alien was short, barely taller than Yoda, with bright blue skin, no hair and eyes that were as dark as the inky blackness of space. He – Kevin assumed it was a he – wore a loincloth and nothing else, revealing a bare and utterly hairless blue chest. He couldn't help thinking of the alien as a child, yet there was no doubt that he was the one in command. The Hordesmen clearly deferred to his authority.

The Horde are mercenaries, he thought. *I'm looking at one of their masters.*

"An error," he repeated. Beside him, Romford was still stunned. "What sort of error?"

"It was our assumption that you were allies or slaves to the Varnar," the alien said. "Their willingness to use your people as cannon fodder suggested the latter. We were therefore prepared to go to some distance to locate your homeworld and recover samples of your people for analysis. It simply did not occur to us to attempt to contact you openly."

Kevin felt his eyes narrow. *That* showed an alarming awareness of events on Earth. Had the aliens hacked the starship database? Or was it simply a coincidence? Or a deduction?

"We maintained a watch for all traces of human life," the alien continued. "When you arrived, you were noticed. The fact you had a Hordesman with you suggested that you took one or more of their ships."

"Indeed," Kevin said, feeling sweat pouring down his back. "And who, might I ask, are you?"

The alien leaned forward. "My name does not fit well into any galactic tongue," he said. "I am called Master by the Hordesmen, but I hope you will come to think of me as *Friend*."

"Right," Kevin said, doubtfully. "I need to call my ship, *Friend*, and inform them that we are safe."

Friend made an elaborate bow. Kevin hesitated, then reached for the communicator and tapped in a code to signify that they were alive and well, but the situation was as yet uncertain. There was a brief response, then silence. Kevin nodded, then turned back to the alien.

"We clearly have a lot to tell each other," he said. "Why don't you start at the beginning?"

"We should move to a more comfortable location first," Friend said. "This building is not entirely...*friendly*."

Kevin nodded, but allowed the aliens to shock Romford awake and then lead them through a set of twisting corridors into a large dining room. Everything seemed designed for children, he realised, as the alien motioned them to a table. One of the stools was barely large enough for an adult human man. Two more of the green-skinned aliens appeared from nowhere, carrying trays of food and drink. Kevin eyed it doubtfully, then picked up something that looked like a potato wedge, just to be sociable. It tasted rather like fish and chilli.

"I will start at the beginning," Friend informed him, as he took a swig of something that looked rather like green beer. It smelt faintly unpleasant. "The Varnar were appointed" – there was a pause as the translator struggled to provide a translation – "satraps of this region of the galaxy, as the Tokomak didn't care enough to do it for themselves. Since then, they have waged war on the remaining spacefaring races."

He paused, significantly. "We believe that the Tokomak deliberately chose to start wars that would prevent us from becoming a major threat to their beloved *status quo*," he admitted, thoughtfully. "The race they chose as their representatives didn't have the strength to do more than fight, rather than crush us all like bugs. Even if that wasn't their desired outcome, it was what they got. For the past" – another pause – "three hundred years, this sector has been locked in a bitter war."

Kevin frowned. There hadn't been *that* much mentioned about the Tokomak in the datafiles they'd captured, apart from the fact they'd developed FTL and used it to bind large sections of the galaxy together. There was no hint they were an empire, let alone that they assigned other races to serve as their subordinates in certain parts of the galaxy. But then, given that the files had been intended for the Horde, it was possible that large parts of galactic history had simply been overlooked.

Friend scratched his right ear. It took Kevin a moment to realise that it was intended as a smile.

"Things have changed, recently," Friend continued. "The Varnar have been deploying a new set of cyborgs, constructed from human brains, flesh and blood. Those cyborgs have proven distressingly effective on the battlefield, allowing them to finally start making gains against their enemies. In short, the war might be lost in as little as two hundred years."

Kevin sucked in his breath. Humans had fought the Hundred Years War, but it hadn't been an endless series of military campaigns. Indeed, there had been long periods of peace between bouts of fighting. And besides, the technology for decisive advances and battles simply hadn't existed at the time.

But, on an interstellar scale, two hundred years was nothing.

"We decided we needed to recover samples of our own," Friend admitted. "We chose to use deniable assets for various reasons."

Ensuring that the Varnar didn't know you knew, Kevin guessed. The story did seem to match with what they'd been told, although he wasn't sure how much of it they could take for granted. Friend might have his own reasons for telling a version of the story that wasn't entirely true. But he had to accept it, for the moment.

He leaned forward. "Why us? What makes our brains so special?"

"We believe, from what little intelligence we recovered, that the Varnar did not need to do much modification of your brain tissue to turn you into combat cyborgs," Friend said. "It is possible that your race is unusually comparable with standard neural interfaces, or that that the Varnar performed genetic modification on the samples they captured and then force-cloned tissue from them. Or it is vaguely possible that they did something else and convinced us that your race was particularly special to hide what they'd done."

"Humans would prefer to believe that," Kevin said. The thought of seeing Earth turned into nothing more than a reservoir of genetic livestock was terrifying. Or destroyed. The Varnar, if they realised that humans were breaking out into space, might strike first. "Let us cut to the chase then, as we humans say. What do you want?"

"Your assistance," Friend said. "We would like humans to fight with us against the mutual foe."

"Human mercenaries," Kevin said. There were humans who would volunteer to fight, he knew, purely for the adventure. Hell, if worst came to worst, he had authority to discuss the prospect of selling human military services. But this…this would get them involved in a war they knew next to nothing about, even if Friend was being completely truthful. "And what would you offer in exchange?"

Friend pressed his fingertips together, then spread them out. "What would you *like* in exchange?"

Kevin took a breath. "Starships and technical support," he said. "And help in developing a modern industrial base."

There was a long pause. "You wish to become more than just soldiers?"

"Our race is very – very – inventive," Kevin countered. "But we can only be inventive in your favour if we have the tools to do it."

"So it would seem," Friend said.

Kevin could understand the alien's fears. They might be exchanging one enemy for another…but, even so, it would take years for humanity to match the Varnar as a threat. The aliens had to know that, didn't they?

"We wish the services, then, of five thousand human soldiers," Friend said, finally. "As a down payment, we will provide certain forms of support right now."

He paused, again. "We will provide you with five large freighters, fifty shuttles and ten unlocked fabricators. And some technical advice you can use to start producing your own technological base. Would that be sufficient?"

Kevin gambled. "Twenty unlocked fabricators," he said. How desperate were the aliens for human help? The longer they delayed, the harder it would be to stave off defeat. But would human help really prove decisive? "And we want some warships too."

"We can extend you a credit line so you can buy older ships," Friend said. "There is no shortage of vessels comparable to the one you captured. But we cannot sell you modern warships."

"Understood," Kevin said. "And the fabricators?"

"They will be provided," Friend said. "In exchange for this, we want the humans on this planet within" – another pause – "four months, five days. Once they are here, they will be transported onwards to the war front. We will provide weapons, care and feeding."

"They'll want to be able to write home," Kevin said. He couldn't help wondering what was he sending humans into. What sort of role would a mere five thousand humans play on the battlefield? Or were the aliens thinking that they would serve as shock troopers? "And go home from time to time."

Friend blinked at him. It was a disconcertingly human gesture. "Why?"

"Because they need that lifeline to fight," Kevin said. He gambled, again. "It will make them far more effective soldiers."

"Then it will be done," Friend said.

There was a long discussion over the precise terms of the agreement. The humans would serve for five year terms – the aliens had wanted twenty years, but Kevin pointed out that few humans would be prepared to make a lifetime commitment. Then the aliens wanted the humans to become cyborgs; Kevin countered by pointing out that they'd need volunteers for that, but there would probably be no shortage. Steve had already created quite a few from volunteers. Combat intensity was up for discussion, but Friend noted that there could be no promises. Kevin wasn't too surprised.

"Health care will become a major issue," he added. "And pensions."

That sparked another debate. The alien seemed confident that anything that wasn't immediately fatal could be cured – and they would pay for it, if necessary. Pensions puzzled him, but he eventually agreed that human mercenaries would be paid a large lump sum upon their departure. And dead bodies would be returned to Earth if conditions permitted.

"Thank you," Friend said, when he had finished. "We will honour your terms."

Kevin hoped he was telling the truth. It would be difficult for Earth to haul the aliens into a court of law and sue them.

Friend stood. "Your supplies will be delivered to your ship, while the promised starships will be sent directly to your star system. And then you will send the troops here."

He turned, then walked out of the room.

After a moment, one of the green aliens motioned for them to walk out of the building and back onto the streets.

It isn't rude, Kevin reminded himself, as they started to walk back to the hotel. *It's just how they do things, really.*

He said nothing until they were back at the hotel, where they stripped down and swept their bodies carefully for surveillance devices. Nothing was found, but as he reminded himself – again – that didn't necessarily mean anything. The tools he'd used against the Taliban were primitive compared to the latest cutting-edge technology the Galactics deployed regularly. Grimly, he reminded himself to be careful what he said, then called the ship and made a full report.

"We will be sent the down payment," he concluded. "I think we should spend several more days here, then head back to Earth."

"We have to offload the other supplies anyway," Jackson reminded him. "I've had to pay out quite a few bits of currency just to hire the shuttles. If we'd brought our own…"

"We would just have been charged for the landing pads instead," Kevin said, rolling his eyes sardonically. Somehow, he doubted that Ying would become a noted holiday destination for human tourists. Or maybe it would. People went on vacations to dangerous places all the time. Some of them never came home. "Finish offloading the goods, then keep an eye on things."

He looked over at Cn!lss. "Are you all right?"

"They could have killed me," Cn!lss said. It was always hard to tell, but the Hordesman looked miserable. "They could have ended my life right there and then."

Kevin felt a flash of sympathy. He'd never been the weak and friendless nerd – growing up on a farm had given him muscles and homeschooling had allowed him to avoid the worst of High School culture – but he understood just how intelligence could isolate someone from the less fortunate. Steve and Mongo were hardly *stupid*, yet they had a directness about them that Kevin lacked. But then, that very directness had worked out in their favour more than once. Kevin wouldn't have had the sheer nerve to set up his own country, no matter how much he wanted it.

"They didn't, though," he said. "They won't hurt you, ever again."

He had a sudden impression of what life must have been like for the alien techie. He was needed, desperately, and yet he was also disdained, because the Horde weren't smart enough to realise how much they needed him. It had never surprised Kevin that so many intelligence officers – particularly the lower-ranked ones who never left America – were so socially stunted and awkward. Or that they were easy prey for manipulation by outside intelligence agents.

They want to be part of something – anything – greater than themselves, he thought. *But they lack the skills to make themselves part of that something, to pretend to blend in with the crowd.*

He shuddered. It was impossible to be sure, but most intelligence officers Kevin had spoken to had believed that Edward Snowden was a Russian agent, no matter what he claimed to be. There were just too many KGB-style fingerprints over the whole affair to suggest otherwise, ending with Snowden's flight to Russia. Had he chosen Moscow because he believed the Russians would never surrender him...or had he been pushed into choosing it by his masters? There was no way to know.

The isolated children, the outcasts, had always been easy prey for manipulators. And it was far too hard to counter it in each and every specific case. He felt a twinge of bitter guilt. What, if anything, had they done to Cn!lss? They'd practically made him the same offer of a home where he *didn't* run the risk of dying because some Horde Commander was having a bad day. To him, it had to seem like an offer of paradise.

But it had to be worse than any merely human intelligence coup. Americans and Russians were human. Humans and Hordesmen were very different races. Cn!lss might never see his own kind again. He would never have a mate...well, he probably wouldn't have had one anyway. Horde society assigned mates to the strong, not to the intelligent. And abducting wives was considered good sport.

"We will make a home for your people and change their society," he said. "There will be Hordesmen raised in a very different culture, one that values intelligence rather than brute force and stupidity. And you will have a home there."

"Thank you," Cn!lss said. It was always hard to be sure, but he seemed unconvinced. "But my people do not change."

Kevin had his doubts. The tests had suggested that most Hordesmen, like humans, shared the same basic level of intelligence. It was just stunted, quite deliberately, by their upbringing. Given a very different upbringing, there would be more Hordesmen learning to use their intelligence, rather than fighting their way through a finishing school that looked absolutely murderous. And who knew what they would become then? Perhaps, instead of building their own empire, the human race could build a United Federation of Planets.

He smiled. If nothing else, laying plans for the future would help to pass the time on the voyage home.

TWENTY-SIX

NEAR RIYADH, SAUDI ARABIA

The mansion had been designed to resemble nothing less than a desert tent, as if the occupants still clung to the lives of their ancestors. It was a lie, of course; the occupants enjoyed riches and luxuries the ancient desert clans would have found completely beyond their comprehension, when they weren't sneering at them. Oil wealth had warped Saudi Arabia's society out of all recognition; social unrest threatened every time the government tried to reduce benefits to its population, while the unemployed and unemployable young male Saudis had plenty of time to consider both the finer points of Islam and their own royal family's adherence to those values.

And now those thoughts will become sharper, the Foreign Minister thought, as he climbed out of the car and walked towards the mansion. His bodyguards fanned out around him, watching for trouble. The Pakistanis were loyal as long as they were paid, he knew. But how long could they be paid?

It might not matter, he knew. Part of their contract was an agreement they could stay in Saudi Arabia if necessary, along with their wives and children. Pakistan looked to be on the verge of civil war, even though large chunks of the Taliban leadership had simply been wiped out. But he didn't care to gamble with his family's safety – and their grip over the country they ruled as a private fiefdom. It was already shaky enough after the Americans had started to develop new technology.

He gritted his teeth as they reached the doors and stepped inside. The American infidels didn't fool him, not really. They wanted – they needed – to break the oil monopoly, particularly now their country held an increasing hatred for Saudi Arabia and the Middle East. No matter the vast sums of money spent on shaping political and public opinion in the West, it was becoming increasingly clear that the flood of off-world technology would eventually shatter the monopoly completely. And once that happened…

The Foreign Minister had no illusions about his family's popularity. They were *hated*, increasingly so, by the people they claimed to rule. Any step towards democratic government, no matter how slight, ran the risk of becoming disastrous, while they could hardly become more Islamic without risking an eventual takeover by the religious leaders. Hell, it would be damn near impossible to force his family to become more Islamic. Very few of them even bothered to fast on Ramadan, let alone honour the other tenets of Islam.

There was a long pause as the bodyguards met other bodyguards and exchanged glares, then the Foreign Minister stepped past them and into the meeting room. Three other men stood there, one from Bahrain, one from Dubai and one from Iran. He couldn't help wondering just what was going through the Iranian's mind. Iran and Saudi Arabia hated each other so thoroughly that, absent the presence of Saddam and later the Americans, they would have gone to war years ago. But the Foreign Minister had no illusions about the military balance of power either. If the Americans stayed out of the war, Iran would almost certainly win within a year.

It was the age-old problem for any Arab ruler, he knew. If they actually trained their men to be competent soldiers, part of a much larger army, they ran the risk of being deposed in a coup. Allah knew there had been hundreds of coup plots over the last fifty years, some of which had come alarmingly close to being launched. But if they kept their militaries weak and divided, commanders fearful to talk to one another because of the risk of being taken for spies, they would lose all military effectiveness. If the Americans hadn't protected Saudi Arabia for so long…

He pushed the thought aside as he greeted the Iranian, reminding himself firmly to be diplomatic. The Iranian had been invited, after all, as had the other two. All four nations ran the risk of being completely marginalised, thanks to the influx of off-world technology. If they worked together, they might manage to save themselves. And if they didn't, they were all thoroughly screwed.

Perhaps I should start sending my family out of the country, the Foreign Minister thought, as he sat down on the rug. *Getting Saudis and Iranians to work together will be like herding cats and dogs.*

There was a pause as serving men appeared from the side doors, carrying trays of coffee, rice and meat, then – once they were gone – the diplomats started to eat. It felt oddly surreal to the Foreign Minister, who would never normally have chatted to an Iranian in such relaxed surroundings, but it was necessary. Leave it to the Americans to be blunt and direct. The Arabs had a different way of looking at the world. But then, he reminded himself, the Iranians were not Arabs. Indeed, they would find the claim they were rather insulting.

"We have a problem," he said, when the meal was finished and their coffee was replenished. "The new influx of technology threatens us all."

"It threatens you more than us," the Iranian pointed out. "Our country is stable."

Economically speaking, the Foreign Minister thought, he had a point. Iran had a self-reliance that Saudi Arabia would never be able to develop for itself. But if it couldn't export oil at all, it would still take a major hit in the pocketbook. The long-term results would be devastating.

"There is also the influx of new computer technology," the Foreign Minister countered. "What is *that* doing to you?"

The Iranian glowered, then nodded. Saudi Arabia had had its own problems with the new dongles, despite a hasty religious ruling from the clerics that buying and using one was against Islamic Law. Getting that ruling had cost the family dearly, but it seemed to have had little effect. Several dozen dongles had been confiscated by the Security Ministry, while Allah alone knew how many others were drifting through the country, completely undermining the computer firewalls the government used to prevent its citizens from accessing large parts of the internet. Officially, the firewalls were meant to protect innocent minds from pornography, but everyone knew the truth. The firewalls were intended to keep people who might disagree with the government from talking to one another.

But the dongles were almost completely undetectable...

No matter what the security forces did, this particular jinn was out of the bottle and wouldn't be put back in a hurry. Half of the religious police were illiterate morons whose sole claim to any form of piety was memorising the Qur'an. They probably wouldn't recognise one of the new dongles if they laid eyes on it, even without some computer genius taking off the plastic covering and installing the transmitter in his computer. It had already happened, in the West...and Middle Eastern computer nerds had far more reason to hide. He would have been very surprised if the same problem wasn't happening in Iran.

"Not to mention other problems," the Iranian continued. "Do you realise they sold Israel a working laser system?"

The Foreign Minister nodded. Iran's long-term plan for war against Israel was a war of a thousand cuts, using primitive rockets and terror attacks launched by Palestinian groups to undermine the Israeli will to resist. The laser system from outer space – it sounded like the title of a bad movie – simply swatted the missiles out of the air, leaving nothing but dust to drift down to the ground. If nothing else, the whole affair exposed just how hypocritical the lunar settlers were. They claimed not to interfere...and yet they protected a country many of their own people regarded as a menace to world peace.

But he had his doubts about the independence of the lunar settlers. The American Government could have stopped them, if it had seen fit, or simply impeded their operations on Earth. Instead, they seemed to be taking a hands-off approach, which suggested something rather more sinister to a conspiracy-minded thinker. The whole lunar settlement was nothing more than a false flag operation on a gigantic scale. Instead of being actually independent, the whole affair was an American plan to change the world, while the American Government escaped all blame.

A devilishly cunning plan, he thought. *The President makes changes he desperately needs to make, all the time protesting his innocence. How very clever!*

The Bahraini leaned forward. "We have agreed there is a problem," he said. "But what do we do about it?"

"You should start thinking about running for your lives," the Iranian sneered. "Your master may not be able to protect you for much longer."

The Foreign Minister sighed. "We're here to discuss possible courses of action," he said. "I don't think backbiting helps very much, does it?"

"No," the Iranian said.

The Foreign Minister sighed. Bahrain was effectively under Saudi military occupation, even though few in the West were genuinely aware of it. The Sunnis might run the semi-island, but the vast majority of the population were Shia...and they wanted change. And Iran, he knew, had been quietly fuelling the flames ever since the damned Arab Spring. It caused no shortage of headaches for their enemies, while making it harder for the West to take its normal sanctimonious approach to the problem. After all, the Royal Family of Bahrain *were* tyrants.

"Most of our normal tools seem to have been disabled," the Foreign Minister admitted. "I think American public opinion is moving in favour of fusion power."

He sighed, again. The environmentalist movement had been quietly funded by the Middle East, in the hopes it would prevent any move to energy independence for the West. They'd spread horror stories about nuclear power, coal power and natural gas fracking...and now, with fusion power promising an unlimited supply of completely clean energy, the environmentalists had seized on it as *mana* from heaven. They might be useful idiots, but they weren't paid agents. It would be incredibly difficult to convince them that fusion power was just as dangerous as fission power.

And if they see our fingerprints, they will use it to discredit the whole movement, he thought.

The discussion raged backwards and forwards, but nothing was really decided, apart from the agreement that they *did* have a problem. If the lunar settlers truly were independent, pressuring the American Government would be pointless. And even if they weren't, the American government was big enough to make it difficult to pressure, particularly – as the Iranian pointed out – as Saudi Arabia's influence was dropping fast. *And* there was the very real danger of picking a fight they couldn't hope to win.

But, if fusion power continued to spread, they were doomed.

The Foreign Minister had no illusions. American oil companies would be hurt, true, but Americans were incredibly adaptable. They would survive. His country, however, would not survive if they couldn't export vast amounts of oil. About the only other thing they exported in large quantities was Radical Islam and that was very much a two-edged sword. It was possible, he supposed, that the Chinese would want oil…

"The Chinese have their own problems with dongles," the Iranian said, sardonically. "They may not be able to *take* your oil."

The Foreign Minister winced. He'd met several Chinese technicians, men working in Saudi Arabia for princely wages, and they'd been incredibly clever and inventive. He had no doubt that Chinese technicians would be able to use the dongles themselves, even though the Great Firewall of China was far more capable than anything the Arab states had built for themselves. And then the simmering Chinese unrest might come out into the open and start demanding open change.

But that only took them back to the final question. What were they going to do?

"We need to take decisive action," the Foreign Minister concluded. "And we will need your help."

Carefully, he outlined the plan they'd devised.

It was a measure of their desperation, he realised afterwards, that no one – not even the Iranian – raised a serious objection. If the current state of affairs continued, they knew, all of their nations were doomed. Iran might end up with a new government, with the previous government purged by victorious rebels, but Saudi Arabia would sink without trace. The mansions and cities they'd built required constant maintenance to keep them in order. If they couldn't afford to maintain them any longer, they would rapidly start to fall apart. Water supplies would come to an end. And then vast numbers of people would simply die.

"Desperate," the Iranian said. "Desperate, but necessary."

No one disagreed.

WASHINGTON DIDN'T SEEM to have changed much in the two months since the UN debate in New York, Gunter decided. There were a large mob of protesters outside the White House – several different groups, according to the Washington PD – and lobbyists were still making their endless rounds between Congress and their corporate employers. The only big difference, according to his sources, was the addition of a force field generator to protect the White House, even though the President was no longer Terrorist Target Number One. That honour had been taken by Steve Stuart.

He smiled at the thought as he stepped into the lobby of the hotel and waited for security to buzz him through. Senator Cavendish seemed to prefer to use hotels, rather than establish his own home in Washington, although – as he was quite wealthy in his own right – Gunter suspected this worked out in his favour. He had room service at all hours, a discreet place to meet allies and enemies and a reasonable level of security. And, if someone didn't take a close look at his expenses, it looked more humble than buying a mansion in one of America's most expensive cities.

"Ah, Mr. Dawlish," the Senator said, as the maid waved Gunter into the Senator's suite. It was practically a luxury apartment in its own right. "Would you care for coffee?"

"Yes, please," Dawlish said. He waited for the Senator to finish pouring two cups of coffee, then took a seat. "I was surprised you called me today."

"I much prefer reading your work to that of the MSM," the Senator said. "It's either endless abuse or crawling, depending on which side you're on. The bloggers are much more even-handed."

That, Gunter knew, wasn't entirely true. Bloggers could have a political slant just as easily as a hired reporter. But when there were no editors, it was easier to *see* the political slant for what it was and disregard it. And besides, most bloggers certainly *tried* to be even-handed, even if it didn't quite work out.

"Thank you," he said.

"I won't lie to you," Cavendish said, as he sat down. "Recent events have quite unsettled the GOP – and the Democrats too. Who knows what will be the end result of all this new technology?"

Gunter smiled. "A better world?"

"Perhaps, or a worse one," Cavendish said. "What will happen to America if our best and brightest go into space? Would we be losing the talent we need to keep ourselves a First World nation?"

"Perhaps," Gunter said. "Or perhaps we would be securing our future instead."

He shrugged. Years ago, he'd read a research paper that asserted that Americans came from hardy stock. The first Americans – or at least the first settlers, seeing the paper didn't seem to recognise the existence of the Native Americans – had been willing to leave Europe and make a new life in America, even though there had been a very high risk of death. Their descendents had a fire, the author had claimed, that their relatives in Europe lacked. He'd concluded by asserting that America needed an improved immigration policy to ensure that only those with the drive and determination to succeed were invited into the country.

There was no way to know if the author was actually correct, but he'd heard the rumours winging their way through the political mainstream. Young men and women with the drive and determination to succeed were signing up for lunar settlement in vast numbers; the waiting list, he'd heard, already included millions of names. And these men and women wouldn't just be determined to succeed, they'd also be natural supporters of the GOP. The party was watching its natural voter base threaten to erode.

But it was likely to cause other problems too. What would happen, he asked himself, if he tax burden on the average American citizen continued to rise?

"The transition has to be carefully managed," Cavendish said. "We must elect a new government that will guide America through the next few years."

Gunter lifted his eyebrows. "Are you planning to run for President?"

"I think so," Cavendish said. "But matters are undecided at the moment."

"Because half of the GOP thinks that most of their representatives in Washington are RINOs," Gunter said. "Or traitors."

He sighed. It was another problem, one that bedevilled all political parties. At base, they were political *consensuses*, compromises between different attitudes and viewpoints that allowed them all to stand under the same banner. But when large parts of the organisation felt betrayed, they tended to make their displeasure felt. Even without Steve Stuart and the alien technology, the GOP would probably have had a few uncomfortable years. But then, it was probably true of the Democrat Party too. Hope and change had simply not materialised.

"I would also like to open up talks with Mr. Stuart directly," Cavendish added. "His endorsement would be very useful."

Gunter doubted that Stuart would offer anything of the sort. "I can certainly give him your number," he said. "But he was pretty alienated from mainstream politics even before he started his own country. He might have nothing to say to you."

"There's no harm in asking," the Senator said. "And besides, I have other plans for the future."

Sighing inwardly, Gunter settled in for the long haul.

TWENTY-SEVEN

"**B**ack on Earth, there are people – know-nothings – protesting about what we are doing here," Steve said. He hated giving speeches, but he had to admit there was a certain satisfaction in giving *this* one. "They think what we're doing is morally wrong. They think that we're the bad guys for slamming a few asteroids into Mars. They think we're" – he held up his hands to make quotation marks – "damaging the environment."

There were a handful of chuckles from several of his listeners. They'd all suffered at the hands of environmentalists or environmental regulations, regulations designed by bureaucrats who knew next to nothing about farming or anything else they sought to regulate. And the whole idea of *opposing* the terraforming of Mars, they all agreed, was absurd. Humanity needed more places to live.

Steve smiled and went on. "But we are the *builders*, the ones who make it possible for humanity to live," he continued. "Mars is a dead world, utterly dead. There are no giant slugs or rock snakes crawling over the surface, nor are there any traces of a long-gone civilisation. What is the harm, I ask you, in turning Mars into another homeworld for mankind?

"There isn't any harm," he concluded. "Let the protesters exhaust themselves shouting and screaming down on Earth. Let them bemoan what we're doing, here and now, just as they bemoan our ancestors who settled America. But somehow I doubt they will refuse to visit Mars in the future, just as they don't go home to Europe and abandon America. Today, the future belongs to those who dream and build a better world."

He lifted his glass. "Ladies and gentlemen," he said. "I give you the future."

On the display, seventeen asteroids tumbled towards Mars. They'd been carefully selected, then nudged towards their targets with nuclear bombs Steve had purchased from Russia. The environmentalists had howled about that too – nukes in space, they'd wailed – but the whole system had worked perfectly well. Mars would get its first infusion of water, the Russians would get a handful of fusion power plants and a number of nuclear weapons would be removed from Earth. The Russian weapons had been crude, according to the techs, but perfectly functional. And they'd been used to build rather than destroy.

But we're going to need more of them, he thought. Talks with America over the production of additional nuclear devices – they'd been trying to stay away from the word *bomb* – were going nowhere fast. *We're going to have to set up breeder reactors of our own.*

They did have several advantages over Earth, he knew. Nuclear waste – always a problem – could be simply launched into the sun, where it would vanish without trace. He'd actually offered to take the nuclear waste from various countries on Earth and dispose of it, although those negotiations weren't proceeding any faster. Fear of a shuttle accident, it seemed, was delaying the talks. Never mind that there hadn't been a single shuttle accident in three months...

He shook his head, then looked back at the display. It *did* look destructive, he had to admit, but the icy asteroids would melt within Mars's scant atmosphere and increase the water content of the dead world. The water would match up with seeds the terraforming crews had already scattered, starting the slow development of a breathable atmosphere. Brute-force terraforming, as the aliens called it, would still take upwards of a hundred years, but by the time it had finished Mars would live again. The only real problem was warming the planet long enough to develop a proper greenhouse effect.

I wonder if the environmentalists will stop screaming about the asteroids long enough to start screaming about the greenhouse effect, he wondered, nastily. *That's another evil buzzword for them.*

But it was necessary, he knew. Mars was a cold world. The heat of the sun was already diluted by the time it reached the planet, forcing the engineers to develop an ozone layer to keep as much heat as possible trapped on the planet. There was a perfectly natural version of the greenhouse effect on Earth, after all, and it had worked very well for thousands upon thousands of years. Duplicating it for Mars was an urgent requirement.

The small crowd fell silent as the first asteroid plummeted into the planet's atmosphere. Even though the atmosphere was thin, it left a fiery trail as it fell downwards and eventually slammed into the planet's surface. Steve sucked in his breath sharply as the display pulled out, revealing the atmospheric patterns slowly spreading out over Mars. They were oddly beautiful, even though he knew that anyone within a hundred miles of the impact would be very unlikely to survive. He couldn't help wondering if they had created a new art form.

We should have learned from the asteroid that wiped out the dinosaurs, he thought, remembering one of Keith Glass's impassioned anti-NASA rants. Nothing NASA could have done would have saved humanity, if a large asteroid had plummeted towards the Earth and smashed into the planet. Indeed, reading between the lines in the alien files, it seemed that asteroid impacts were often used to depopulate worlds, with everyone involved swearing blind that it wasn't actually deliberate genocide. Not that the victims would have cared by then, he suspected. Anyone lucky enough to survive the impact would die soon afterwards, killed by environmental change or the destruction of civilisation.

Hell, the environmentalists should have gotten behind NASA and pushed, he thought, dryly. *Or is it only bad if humans are responsible for environmental change?*

The second asteroid had a longer trajectory through the planet's atmosphere before it finally struck the surface and exploded. Steve watched, staring in awe, as the next few asteroids slammed down in quick succession, each one adding more water droplets to the planet's atmosphere. Time seemed to slow down as the atmosphere changed, great clouds of dust rising up into the higher levels, then slowly drifting back towards the planet's surface. The engineers had predicted that, Steve knew, and they'd welcomed it. Dust in the atmosphere would help trap the heat from the explosions.

He heard a cheer as the final impact slammed home, then relaxed. He'd known that nothing could go wrong, yet he'd worried endlessly. Mars wasn't quite as important, economically, as the asteroids, but humanity needed a new home that wasn't dependent on life support. If the aliens came calling before Earth was ready...he shook his head, dismissing the thought in irritation. They wouldn't stand a chance if someone more advanced than the Horde turned up, not for several years. If that happened, Steve's only real option was to run.

Shadow Warrior could keep a small human population alive for centuries, if necessary. They could make their way to a far distant star system and start again, using the vessel's technology to rebuild human society. They could make it...but he didn't want to abandon Earth. It would be the ultimate failure of his long-term plan.

"The spectacular part is over," he said, as the ripples from the last asteroid slowly faded away. "But, right now, it's raining on Mars for the first time in eternity."

He accessed the interface, then displayed the view from the sensors they'd placed on Mars. Droplets of water were falling from the sky and splashing on the ground, then slowly sinking into the planet's soil. The drones were already deploying the first seeds, seeds that would take root and start producing oxygen as well as bringing life back to the soil. Given ten years, Mars would look green rather than red as the plants spread rapidly. But that would only be the start of the terraforming process.

Smiling, Steve looked towards the members of the Mars Society. They'd drawn up endless plans to colonise Mars, plans that had never been put into action...until now. Steve had seen some of their work and admired it, even though he knew that alien technology and communications would fundamentally change some of their plans. But it would be interesting, he told himself, to see what sort of society developed on Mars.

It will still be decades before proper colonisation can begin, he told himself, as he stepped over to meet them. *And by then, the world will have changed beyond all recognition.*

"We wanted to thank you in person," the leader said. Steve hated being mobbed, but the society members didn't seem to care. "What you've done today is remarkable."

"Thank you," Steve said. "And your work is pretty impressive too."

"But not quite in the same league," the leader said. "When can we begin actually settling the planet?"

Steve shrugged. "When we get more transport organised," he said. The Americans, Russians and Europeans had started producing spacecraft for the Earth-Mars journey, they just needed to be lifted up into orbit. If some of the ideas about duplicating alien antigravity technology actually worked – and could be done with purely human engineering – the whole process would expand rapidly. "And then you can start organising the first colony mission."

It would be a more controlled process, he knew, than the plan to settle the asteroids. Mars was a whole planet, after all. And there were more legal issues; technically, settling Mars was also illegal under the Outer Space Treaty. But Steve was not inclined to care about a piece of ill thought out legislation he hadn't signed...and nor were the other developed countries, now. They were more interested in getting all they could from the lunar settlement and its monopoly on alien technology.

"We look forward to it," the leader assured him. "And thank you for the space station."

Steve had to smile. The space station in question was purely human technology – and inflatable, much to his private horror. Combined with a small amount of alien technology, however, it had rapidly proven a viable concept. The Mars Society would be able to maintain a watch on the planet and the automated sensors on the surface indefinitely. But if the Horde decided to use it for target practice, he knew, it wouldn't stand a chance.

"You're welcome," he said. Actually, all *he'd* done was provide transport. "And I wish you the very best of luck."

He moved through the compartment, exchanging a few words with each of the people, several of whom had paid through the nose to be allowed to watch from the starship. It still perplexed him that people, even sensible people who had made their own fortunes, were willing to throw so much of it away on a whim, but he'd stopped complaining. If nothing else, it helped fund the endless demands of the lunar colony.

"I've got plans to move most of my plants to the moon, if you will have me," one computer tycoon said. He'd built up several plants over the last few years, trying to ride the cutting edge of computer development. "We think we can use the lunar gravity and the planned stations in space to improve the technology remarkably."

Steve nodded. It would bring more industry to the moon, which was always important, but it would also allow them to continue researching alien technology. One secret, at least, had already been cracked. It was incredibly difficult to produce a perfect room-temperature superconductor on Earth, but it was quite possible in zero-gravity. It was also possible to produce perfect diamonds, which were likely to cause their own problems. The diamond cartels would probably start hiring assassins when they realised that they were about to be fatally undercut.

Not that we would waste our time on it, he thought. *We need the diamonds for industrial processes.*

He smiled at the tycoon, then moved on to the next couple of viewers. One of them was an extraordinarily successful romance writer, who was a millionaire despite her books being – in Mariko's opinion – little more than glorified pornography. Steve had taken a look, purely out of scientific enquiry, and decided the woman was a hack. But she got paid for it, so she must have hundreds upon thousands of fans. Maybe, the cynic in him added, the outfit she wore helped. It was supposed to be a spacesuit, he guessed, but it was so tight that he could see her nipples quite clearly.

"This is quite inspiring," she gushed, as she took his hand and shook it, firmly. Steve was hard-pressed to place her accent. "I really feel someone could write an extraordinary story on Mars."

"I'm sure someone could," Steve agreed, deciding not to mention just how many writers had set books on Mars without actually setting foot on the planet. "Do you plan to move here?"

"I think I will stay on the moon, for now," the writer said. "It has great atmosphere – and besides" – her face suddenly hardened – "the tax is minimal. And *far* less confusing."

Steve couldn't disagree. Tax forms were one of his pet hates.

"But this is really romantic, in a way," the writer continued. "Do you think your partner would be interested in an interview?"

"I'm sure she would," Steve lied. He had barely seen anything of Mariko over the past week, despite the teleporter. She was busy with the medical clinic in New York. "Now, if you will excuse me…"

"But there's so much room for a story," the writer said. "Just imagine it; two people find love and romance among the asteroids. Perhaps two people who hate each other have to mine an asteroid together. Or perhaps they're trying to be together, despite their parents…"

"I'm sure I saw a movie like that once," Steve said. "But if you put two people who hate each other into the same tight space, they'll probably wind up *killing* each other instead of falling in love."

"But if they were smart enough to realise that they would only get arrested," the writer said, "wouldn't there be a chance then? There could be all forms of sex in it as they slowly grow accustomed to each other…"

Steve felt his temper snap. "You can write whatever stories you like, provided they are about fictional people," he said. "But I don't think it would be very realistic."

The writer looked offended. "I'm just trying to get ahead of the curve here," she said. "I thought there were already applications for sex in zero-gravity. Or isn't it as good as it sounds?"

Steve glowered at her, then stomped off. He'd tried sex in zero-gravity with Mariko, but it hadn't been quite as interesting or exciting as space opera pornography had suggested. It was more of an exercise in orbital docking than anything else. But if someone wanted to try it...the writer was right, he had to admit. There were no shortage of requests for private compartments in the planned space hotel.

He shook his head, tiredly, as he approached the porthole and peered down at Mars. The red planet looked tired and worn, not unlike how Steve himself felt. There were just too many things that needed his attention, even though he'd started to build up a staff and hand as many responsibilities to his subordinates as possible. Recruiting newcomers, placing orders for technology and supplies on Earth, keeping an eye open for possible trouble from the planet...and ducking requests, pleas and demands that he share his technology with everyone. He couldn't help wondering if this explained why so many bad ideas had been allowed to enter the American system. The idiots who wanted them had just kept whining until the sensible people had given in. And then the ideas had been very – very – difficult to remove.

It had been much easier managing a ranch, he told himself, sourly. Or even commanding Marines in combat. Instead, he found himself signing papers, making deals with governments and corporations and trying desperately to find some time for himself. No matter how capable his staff was becoming, he was still overwhelmed.

Maybe this is why CEOs keep fucking their secretaries, he thought, dryly. *They're so stressed by their work that they really need the sex.*

He let out another sigh, wishing that Kevin was back in the Sol System. But it would be another two weeks, at the very least, before he could return. Steve had no way of knowing what was happening outside the Sol System, or just what the Horde was doing. Were they considering another attack on Earth? Or were they still unaware that they'd lost three ships, instead of just one? There was no way to know.

Shaking his head, he strode back towards the bridge, avoiding the remainder of the guests before they could speak to him. Let them wait, if it was urgent; he didn't need more prattling congratulations. Did the President ever feel this way, he asked himself; did he ever feel like just walking away from the job? It would have seemed absurd, years ago, that he would have anything in common with the President. But he understood, now, the sheer weight of power that the President had assumed. It would be easy, far too easy, to make mistakes...and then refuse to accept failure. When someone was so powerful, every little failure would feel like a complete disaster.

On the bridge, the sensor crews were monitoring Mars. Everything was proceeding according to plan, he noted. There might be a need for more asteroids in the future, but not for several months at least. They'd also have to unlock the water in the ice caps...

His interface buzzed, reporting an urgent message from Earth.

"Steve," Mongo's voice said, "you have to get back here urgently. The shit has hit the fan."

Steve blanched. It took seventeen minutes for a message to travel from Earth to Mars. Not long, by Galactic standards, but far too long by humanity's standards.

"Take us back to Earth," he ordered. The Mars Society was already onboard their space station, monitoring the planet below. "Best possible speed."

TWENTY-EIGHT

NEW YORK, USA

Mariko had always wanted to be a doctor. It had been an obsession of hers ever since her father had introduced her to *Doctor Who*, even though she hadn't been entirely clear on what a doctor did at the time. As she grew older, her enthusiasm had refused to fade, even after she discovered that actually *working* as a doctor brought unpleasant risks in ligation-prone America. Sometimes, someone died, no matter what the doctor did to prevent it. And then the doctor would be sued by the grieving relatives. It had been a relief to leave the big cities for the countryside, where people were generally more sensible, and fall in love with a man who didn't mind her working as a vet rather than a doctor.

But she'd never lost her desire to *help* people. The alien technology worried her – an autodoc could become the most effective torture machine in history – but it also galvanised her to use it to save lives. She'd had to watch too many people die through untreatable injuries or incurable diseases, both of which could now be handled by alien technology. It did irritate her that she didn't have a clear idea how most of the technology worked, but in the long run she had faith in Steve and his friends to solve the mysteries. For the moment, all that mattered was that it *did* work.

The clinic had once belonged to a doctor who, like her, had abandoned the city in the wake of soaring healthcare costs and laws written for the benefit of the lawyers, rather than doctors or their patients. She hadn't been too surprised to discover that it had been shut down, rather than the city finding another doctor. It was just the sort of stupid decision that came from having more concerns about money than public health. Or control, for that matter. The medical authorities hated it when someone challenged their control.

She smiled to herself as she watched the next set of patients entering the waiting room and take a seat. Some of them were wealthy enough to pay the fees – she'd had bankers, lawyers and politicians pass through her clinic over the past two weeks – and others were children, unable to comprehend what was happening to them. Her heart broke a little every time she saw them and, despite the suggestions she should concentrate on paying clients first, she tried to make sure the children were healed quickly and efficiently. Few dared to complain, at least openly. The last time someone had, she'd ordered him flung out of the clinic and told never to come back.

"All right," she called. "Send in the first patient."

A young girl entered, half-carried by her mother. The AMA hadn't quite finished running through its stockpile of delaying tactics, but it didn't really matter. Alien tech could scan a body quicker than Mariko could read a medical file, allowing her to both diagnose and cure the disease in one fell swoop. Mariko examined the girl, decided she was about eight years old, then motioned for her to climb up on the bed and lie down. Judging from her appearance, her father was either white or Hispanic. The mother was very definitely black.

"They said there was nothing they could do for her," the mother said, tearfully. "She wasn't important or wealthy."

Mariko looked at the scan results and nodded in understanding. The girl was suffering from AIDS, which suggested that one or both of her parents also had the disease. A quick glance revealed no evidence of abuse, let alone rape; she gritted her teeth, then keyed the machine to produce the cure. Given the right treatment, AIDS could be held in remission indefinitely, but those treatments were expensive. Who was going to offer them to such a poor child?

"You'll need treatment too," she said. Up close, the girl's mother didn't look very good either. "I'll scan you too, then prepare treatment. What happened to her father?"

"I have no fucking idea," the woman snarled. The hatred in her voice was overlaid by misery. "He just up and left. Doesn't even know he has a daughter."

Mariko sighed. The woman could have requested help, but that would have resulted in a long series of intrusive questions from the administrators. Mariko had dealt with social workers before; some of them were good and decent people, doing their best for their charges, but others seemed to assume they had licence to pick apart their charges' lives. Big Sister, with all the power and almost no accountability. Who were the poor and destitute going to complain to, faced with the might of the federal bureaucracy?

"No, probably not," she said. She picked up a scanner and pressed it against the woman's arm, then nodded as she saw the results. Her HIV hadn't yet become AIDS, but it would soon enough. "What do you do for a living?"

The woman glowered, but said nothing.

Prostitute, Mariko thought. She produced two pills, one of which she passed to the girl. She hesitated, eying it doubtfully, then swallowed. Mariko gave her a glass of water, then passed the other pill to the mother. It would, assuming that everything went well, cure her completely. But it would do her no good if she went out and caught it again.

"I'd like you both to wait two weeks, then take one of these a day for the next week," she said, reaching into a cabinet to produce the immune boosters. "If either of you show any reaction to the first set of treatments, come back here at once. But you shouldn't."

She looked down at the girl. They were always cute at that age, she knew, remembering her own daughter. But with AIDS it was unlikely –

it had been unlikely – that she would have reached twenty before she died. And, given her circumstances, by then she would probably have slipped into prostitution like her mother. Mariko wanted to take her away from it all, but to where? She pulled the mask of dispassion over her face, refusing to admit to her feelings. Later, she knew she would curl up in bed and cry.

"Good luck," she said, as she helped the girl off the table. "Come back if you have any problems."

The girl hugged her, then followed her mother out of the examination chamber. Mariko took a long moment to gather herself, then called for the next patient. He was a balding middle-aged man, who seemed surprisingly dignified despite his illness. A quick check revealed that he had paid his fee without fuss, so Mariko scanned him quickly. He was suffering from a nasty form of cancer that would be hard for human technology to remove.

"Stay still," she said, as she pressed a piece of alien technology against his head. "This will only take a few minutes."

She shook her head in awe as the cancer was rapidly broken down into harmless debris, which would be expelled from the body soon enough. The man – he turned out to be a Wall Street Stockbroker – thanked her loudly, then offered whatever help she required to make the clinic a success. Mariko thanked him for the offer, then sent him out and called for the next client. The small boy who entered looked thoroughly miserable.

"He's been behaving oddly all year," his mother said. Her voice was frustrated enough to convince Mariko not to snap at her for bringing an undiagnosed patient to her clinic. "He won't take a bath, he's been throwing screaming fits whenever we go out and he's…well, he's been trying to harm himself. I really don't know what's wrong with him!"

Mariko was starting to have a very nasty idea. The way the boy cringed away from her was worrying, despite her decidedly non-threatening appearance. And not taking a bath…she could smell him from several metres away. Hell, that might have been why her receptionist had sent the mother and her son in as soon as possible. His smell would have been very unpleasant in small quarters.

"Let me see," she said, and scanned him. There was surprisingly little overt damage, at least on the surface, but there were quite a few internal telltale scans. She carefully adjusted the scanner so it was covertly scanning the mother, then looked up at her. "Do you have any idea what might be wrong with him?"

"No," the mother said. The scanner indicated she was telling the truth. "We wanted to take him to a psychologist, but they cost..."

"You should take him to the police," Mariko said, sharply. It was her duty as a doctor to report signs of abuse. If the woman didn't take her kid, Mariko would have to make a report herself. "Someone has been abusing him."

The mother's mouth dropped open. "But..."

Mariko sighed. She'd seen child abuse before and quite a few parents missed the signs completely. The problems normally built up over time, so the parents overlooked them as they materialised, while an outsider saw them at once.

"He's trying to make himself unattractive," she said, bluntly. "That's why he refuses to wash. Maybe that alone wouldn't be significant" – she'd once come across a girl who'd read *The Witches* and refused to take baths for several months – "but there are other worrying signs. One of them are internal scars in his anus. Something forced a penis or a finger in there."

She carefully copied her results onto a USB stick, then passed it to the stunned woman. "Go to the police," she said, as she healed the damage. There would be a permanent record for the police, even though there would be no physical damage any longer. "Find out who did this to him and make them pay."

It didn't sound like it was the father, thankfully, she noted as she called for an escort for the woman and her child. If the boy wanted to go with his parents, it suggested the real cause of the problem was the baby-sitter...if there was a babysitter. A girl, perhaps; it was quite possible that the boy had flinched from Mariko because his abuser was also a girl.

She watched them go, then sunk down on her chair and put her head in her hands. There were times when she really hated being a doctor.

"Poor bastard," she muttered.

There were things she could do, she knew. She could offer to transport them to the moon, if the husband had skills the colony could use. Or she could erase memories from the boy's mind, allowing him to grow up without having his development stunted. Or...perhaps she could track down the abuser herself and ensure that Steve and a few of his friends administered some very real justice. But she knew she couldn't do any of them.

She stared down at her hands for a long moment, then stood and called for the next patient.

— —

ABDUL AL-KAREEM HAD never really expected to get the call. He and his brothers had been inserted into America five years ago and told to be American in every way they could, as long as it didn't compromise their ability to do the mission when the time came. They'd opened an Iranian restaurant, introduced thousands of Americans to the joys of Iranian food and generally acted like model Americans. Abdul himself had a steady stream of relationships, while one of his brothers had married an American girl and the other had a steady relationship going that might turn into marriage. There had been no reason to expect that the world would turn upside down.

But it had. He'd seriously thought about refusing, when the message finally arrived, but he knew there was no escape. Agents had gone native before, he'd been told, and they'd always been betrayed. The lives they'd built for themselves would be shattered, whatever happened, and they'd never be able to resume them. All they could do was serve their home country and pray they managed to escape there before the Americans reacted.

He parked the van near the clinic and glanced back at his two brothers. Both of them had been trained intensely for covert operations and urban insurgencies – it would have seriously upset the Americans if they'd realised that all three brothers were veterans of the Iraq War, Iranians who'd fought on the other side – and knew just how to act. Besides, New York might take terrorists seriously, but America was still an open society. It would take time for them to clamp a ring of steel around New York and, by then, he hoped to have their target well and truly out of the city.

"God is Great," he said, softly.

He saw the look in his brother's eye and cringed, inwardly. They'd all been tempted by America, but Abdullah had truly fallen. His wife and children would not get out of the city, no matter what happened. They knew nothing about Abdullah's past or his secret mission, but the American authorities wouldn't take it into account. Abdullah's family would be very lucky if they didn't vanish into a secret prison where they'd be tortured, then murdered. It had happened before.

"Don't worry," he said. It was a lie, but it had to be said. Somehow, he doubted Abdullah would ever see his family again. "We'll get them out too."

Abdullah eyed him nastily, then opened the case at his feet. It hadn't been hard to sneak the weapons into the city, let alone the high explosives they'd bought for the diversion. He'd thought about trying to purchase additional weapons from American sources, but there was too much chance of running into either a patriotic gun dealer or an FBI sting operation. That, too, had happened before.

It had surprised him, when he'd gone to look at the clinic two days ago, that there was almost no security at all. The Americans were truly a proud folk. But, given the capabilities of their new technology, perhaps it wasn't that surprising. They probably thought they could teleport their people out before it was too late. And if the Americans were right, Abdul knew, his team was about to expose itself and destroy their American lives for nothing.

He picked up the cell phone and pushed a button. "Open the doors," he ordered. "Go."

The explosions bellowed out in the distance as he jumped out of the vehicle, followed rapidly by Abdullah. Americans, New Yorkers with long memories of terrorism, scattered as he fired a handful of shots above their heads, then crashed into the clinic. He bellowed orders for the Americans to get down on the ground – better they believed it to be a simple hold-up as long as possible – and led the way into the inner room. The doctor was easy to recognise, thanks to the endless newspaper articles on her. She was Japanese-American, surprisingly short compared to her famous husband…

And she was reaching for something at her belt. Abdul threw himself at her and slammed a fist into her face, knocking her to the ground. The device, whatever it was, fell and hit the ground with a sharp crash. Abdul searched her rapidly, depositing everything she was carrying on the ground, then picked her up and fled back into the waiting room, tossing a handful of incendiary grenades behind him. If they were really lucky, the assumption would be that the doctor had died in the fire, rather than kidnapped, although he wasn't holding out any hope. The Americans were experts at forensic science.

He'd feared Americans trying to stop them, but the explosions and gunfire seemed to have left the witnesses thoroughly unmanned. No one tried to bar their path as they jumped back into the van. Amir, who had kept the engine idling over while his two brothers raided the clinic, gunned the vehicle forward as soon as they slammed the doors closed. Abdul let out a sigh of relief, then carefully searched the doctor again, resisting the temptation to grope her small breasts. This time, he found nothing.

"Tie her hands," Abdullah suggested. "And pray the van performs as advertised."

Abdul nodded and bent down to secure the doctor's arms behind her back. The delay had been caused by the need to prepare the van for its mission. If their intelligence was accurate, no one could teleport through a haze of electronic static – or, they hoped, spy on them. The Taliban leadership had relied on stealth rather than heavy shielding and paid for it. If the intelligence was accurate, they had a chance of getting away. But if the intelligence was inaccurate...

"Poor little thing," Abdullah suggested, as the van moved through panicky streets. They'd have to change vehicles before they headed down to the docks. The explosions might have shocked the NYPD, but it wouldn't be long before they realised they were nothing more than a diversion. "She doesn't deserve this."

"That's the American in you talking," Abdul snapped. "Have you forgotten what we are?"

But they'd had to, he knew. They couldn't afford to comport themselves like strict Muslims, not when it would draw attention. They'd grown lax, relaxing into American ways, eating pork and drinking alcohol. But it was time to put such things aside and remember what they were.

He put his hand on his brother's shoulder. "You are an elite member of a special unit, fighting an age-old war," he reminded him. "I would suggest you kept that in mind at all times."

The thought made him scowl. If their handlers realised that Abdullah was having problems, it would be unlikely he would ever be allowed to leave home again. Instead, if he were lucky, he would be permanently retired. And if he were unlucky...

"Besides, we're committed now," he added. "But then, we always were."

TWENTY-NINE

SHADOW WARRIOR, EARTH ORBIT

"You should have been fucking keeping an eye on her!"

Steve glared at Mongo, feeling his hands clenching into fists. "Why the hell was she left so exposed?"

Mongo somehow managed to keep his voice very calm. "She didn't want an army surrounding her," he reminded Steve. "And she didn't want any form of additional protection."

Steve stared down at the deck, feeling an odd helplessness he hadn't felt since 9/11. Mariko was his lover, his partner, his wife in every way that mattered…and she was missing, presumed kidnapped. Stave had no illusions about just how many enemies he'd made since he'd stepped up to the UN and rubbed their collective faces in their helplessness. One or more nations might well have decided to kidnap Mariko to avenge their humiliation, or to try to gain leverage over him, or…merely to show that he could still be hurt. If the latter, he knew, it was unlikely that Mariko would survive much longer.

"They took her, right," he said. "They didn't kill her?"

"Yes," Mongo said. "We have footage of her being yanked out of the clinic, before the grenades started to detonate. She's a prisoner, Steve, but she isn't dead."

Steve hastily reviewed the footage through the interface. The whole attack was breathtakingly simple, which was probably why it had succeeded. No attempt to sneak into the clinic, no attempt to pose as someone terminally ill, just a simple smash and grab. It was very *professional*, with all the variables cut down as much as possible. That, he decided, suggested that whoever was being the attack represented a country, rather than a terrorist group.

"Bastard disarmed city-slickers," he growled. "Not *one* of them did anything."

He cursed them under his breath. In the country, there would be someone with a gun, someone who would offer armed resistance to terrorist attack. But in New York, famed for restrictive gun laws, the entire population had been unmanned. It was unfair – and he knew it was unfair – but he found it hard to care. His partner was missing – and helpless. Her captors could do anything to her…and Steve's imagination filled in too many possibilities.

"Find her," he growled. If only she'd agreed to have a tracking implant inserted in her body. But she'd declined. Steve would have declined too, if he'd had the option, but still…he wanted to scream at her for refusing and at himself for not forcing the issue. She could have been found by now if she'd had an implant. "Whatever it takes, find her."

He wished, desperately, that Mongo had gone to Ying and Kevin had stayed behind. His younger brother might not be a Marine or any other form of infantryman, but he was one of the smartest people Steve had met. Kevin could have deployed all the bugs and drones and taken out all the stops to find Mariko, then acted to recover her while everyone else was still dithering.

"And call on the NYPD," he added. "Tell them we want them to put every effort into finding her."

"They can't," Mongo said. There was a bitter tone to his voice. "The explosions in New York saw to that, Steve."

Steve gritted his teeth, feeling another wave of helpless fury. The terrorists had bombed New York, forcing the NYPD to divert resources to deal with the aftermath. Even if the dispatchers realised that the bomb-ings were just diversions, they might still be unable to redirect their people. There were dead and dying on the streets of New York, once again. He wanted to call the Mayor personally and scream at him, but what good would it go? The Mayor could hardly refuse to tend to his own citizens.

"Then we take care of it ourselves," he said, accessing the interface and staring down at New York from high overhead. The terrorists might have accidentally outsmarted themselves, he realised. Their divisionary bombings would have snarled traffic pretty thoroughly, which meant they would either go to ground somewhere within the city or be delayed as they tried to smuggle Mariko out. "Use everything we have and *find* her."

He scowled, remembering kidnapped soldiers and the desperate manhunts American forces had launched when they realised the soldiers were missing. It was a race between terrorist and soldiers, he knew; the terrorists had to get their captives out of the zone before the soldiers had blockades and barriers in place to prevent them from escaping. Holing up somewhere within the zone was risky, even in a shithole like Iraq or Afghanistan. The searchers might not stumble across the hiding place, but the locals might well betray the terrorists, either out of hatred or simple irritation with American troops stamping around and disturb-ing everyone. New York would be even worse, from their point of view. *Someone* was bound to see something and call the NYPD.

They'll want to get her out of the city, he thought, morbidly. *But where will they take her?*

— —

JÜRGEN AFFENZELLER WAS no stranger to sudden, intensive demands for action, but this was something else. The nightmare scenario – a terrorist attack on representatives of a foreign power – combined with a sudden awareness that the foreign power might well blame the United States for the lapse in security. It would be unfair, Jürgen knew, but he also knew the world wasn't particularly fair. By any standards, Steve Stuart's partner should have been given the same level of protection as the First Lady.

But the First Lady is about as useful as tits on a bull, he thought, as he hastily deployed the covert sensor apparatus to New York. The President had authorised it personally, even though there would probably be lawsuits and threats of impeachment afterwards. *Steve Stuart's partner is a doctor. She couldn't work with a small army surrounding her.*

He brought up the footage from the security sensors and hastily scanned through it. The terrorists had not only hidden their faces, they'd worn dark ill-fitting clothing, just to make it harder for them to be tracked. It hadn't worked too badly, Jürgen had to admit, but it had its limitations. For one thing, their body language was still readable. And, for another, the van they'd brought could be tracked through the streets.

Few citizens really realised just how formidable a public monitoring system New York had built up in the years since 9/11. It was questionable just how much of it was actually useful for tracking terrorists and it *did* invade civil privacy to a truly disturbing degree, but when the time came to retrace the terrorist footsteps it allowed their movements to be backtracked across the city. The van itself didn't seem to have been rented – its plates suggested it was a rental, but a quick check revealed that the plates had been stolen in Washington – which implied that it had actually been brought into the city at one point. Carefully, he started backtracking through the records.

It took nearly twenty minutes for the cross-referencing program to find a match. Three brothers, all from Iran, refuges according to their DHS file. They'd made it over the border into Pakistan, then applied for settlement in the United States. Their relatives in America had vouched for them, so few red flags had been raised beyond their origins in Iran. The DHS had conducted an interview, decided there was nothing to worry about and then just let them vanish into New York. In hindsight, Jürgen suspected, the DHS was going to be blamed for allowing the terrorists to enter the country.

He placed a call to the NYPD's anti-terrorist division and asked them to check up on the brothers. If he was wrong, he would find out very quickly – and innocent people would not be swept up in a police dragnet. But if he were right, he was confident the brothers would not be at home and, indeed, their wives and children would be wondering what had happened to them. Terrorists these days were advised not to confide in their wives and families, not after quite a few had been betrayed by their relatives, who didn't see death in the cause of *jihad* as a worthy aspiration.

While waiting, he uploaded the details of the van into the cameras and scanned through the thousands of eyes watching New York. Hundreds of matches came back at once, most of them wildly out of place; thankfully, the traffic snarl would have made it harder for the terrorists to make their escape. But which one was the terrorist van? Or had the terrorists already abandoned their vehicle? There was no way to know.

Not yet, he told himself.

The phone rang. "Yes?"

"This is Captain Aldridge," a voice said. He sounded brisk, mercifully professional. "All three of the suspects are missing, sir."

"I see," Jürgen said. It wasn't conclusive proof of anything – the DHS had tracked men it had believed to be terrorists before, only to discover that they'd been having affairs – but it was suspicious. "Take their families into custody, *gently*. Have them interrogated, then explain to them that their menfolk may be in serious trouble."

He winced as he put down the phone. Maybe the families *did* know what was going on, maybe they were guilty as sin – at least of keeping their mouths shut – but it was quite possible that their lives were about to be upended through no fault of their own. They'd be held as suspects, then treated as pariahs, idiots too stupid to realise there was something wrong with their relatives. As always, the terrorists left a trail of broken lives and shattered souls behind them.

Pushing the thought aside, he looked back at his computers. There had to be a clue somewhere, buried within the records. All he had to do was find it.

"Maybe put out a full alert," he muttered. "Let the public know what we're looking for."

He shook his head, a moment later. A simple white van...there were hundreds of thousands of the vehicles within the State of New York. They'd be utterly overwhelmed with false positives. The terrorists had played it smart, so far. But their flight would be frantic enough for them to make mistakes. And he'd be there to pick up on them.

— —

"YOU WILL HAVE my full support," the President said. "We will do everything within our power to look for her."

Steve nodded, bitterly. Mongo had told him, in no uncertain terms, to sit down, shut the hell up and *wait*. There was nothing else he could do, despite increasingly unpleasant suggestions concerning random bombing of terrorist-supporting countries. The NYPD investigation was proceeding slowly, far too slowly. They had too many other problems to deal with right now.

He wanted to take action, he wanted to do something, *anything*. But there was nothing to do.

"All traffic in and out of New York is being stopped by the National Guard," the President continued. "The airports have been placed on alert. Everything will be searched, no exceptions. We're working on inspecting shipping too, Steve. We *will* find her."

Steve gritted his teeth. New York's National Guard had been a military disaster until after 9/11, whereupon they'd managed to redeem themselves and perform excellent service in Iraq, but he had no illusions about the sheer difficulty of the task facing them. Searching every single vehicle that might want to enter or leave the city would be immensely complicated, while it would cause huge traffic jams and considerable bad feeling. Hell, he had a feeling the Mayor would find himself caught between the President's orders and the very real risk of losing his job.

"Thank you, Mr. President," he said. The cynical part of his mind wondered if the President was genuinely concerned or if he was worried about the looming diplomatic disaster. Or both. Meeting the President in person had convinced Steve he wasn't quite the liberal idiot Steve had believed him to be, before the world had turned upside down. "Everything you can do will be welcome."

He paused. "Have you heard anything diplomatically?"

"Just a protest from Chad's Ambassador to the UN," the President said. "He wanted to fly out, but his plane was grounded in the wake of the bombings."

An ass in ambassador, Steve thought. He'd met several diplomats on military service and most of them had been conceited assholes. Or was it something more sinister? Did the terrorists plan to sneak Mariko out on a diplomatic plane, relying on diplomatic immunity to keep her hidden?

"I want diplomatic planes searched," he said, and explained his reasoning. "Feel free to blame us for the imposition."

"It will be more than just an imposition," the President said, after a moment. "It will be seen as an attack on diplomatic formality itself."

Steve sighed. The President's concern was understandable, but he wasn't about to let someone sneak away under the cover of diplomatic immunity.

"Make it clear to them, Mr. President, that we consider this an act of war," he said, firmly. He had no intention of showing weakness to anyone. "If a nation or a group of nations is implicated in this act, we will crush them like bugs."

～ ～

IN WASHINGTON, THE President rubbed his eyes as soon as the connection closed, feeling suddenly very tired.

Few people truly realised it, but the power of the Presidency was hedged around with a series of checks and balances. The President was powerful – the most powerful man in the world – yet he was far from all-powerful. He couldn't bomb a country back to the Stone Age because he'd had a bad morning and wanted to take it out on someone. Nor could he grossly overreact to terrorist attack, no matter how vile. In the aftermath, he would have to deal with the mess.

But Mr. Stuart...

The President honestly wasn't sure what to make of him. Power seemed to have matured the man, at least to some degree, as he tackled the problems in forming a government. But he still enjoyed a certain immunity from blowback, from repercussions from his actions. What would he do with the vast power at his disposal if he had definite proof that a foreign nation was behind the attack on his partner? The President knew what *he'd* be tempted to do – and he knew what the system would prevent him from doing.

But who would stop Mr. Stuart if he decided to take brutal revenge on the terrorists?

ABDUL LET OUT a sigh of relief as they finally made it down to the shipping company and pulled into the giant warehouse. He'd anticipated some delays, but he hadn't realised just how many Americans would act like headless sheep and drive somewhere – anywhere – rather than remain at home. The radio talked of martial law, of blockades on the roads and endless delays at airports. It was far too likely, he knew, that they would be caught even after changing the van.

He climbed out of the vehicle and nodded to the four men waiting for them. Like Abdul and his brothers, they were long-term sleeper agents, among the handful in the Greece-registered shipping company who knew it's true function. Most of the workers were East European, men and a handful of women who provided cover through their sheer ignorance. They knew nothing they could betray.

"She's in the van," he said. He looked up at the giant shipping container sitting at one end of the warehouse. Inside, there were food, drinks, blankets, a portable toilet and a handful of books. "Remember to keep her under cover at all times."

He watched grimly as the men carried the girl – she looked almost childlike in her current state – out of the van and into the shipping container. She would wake up soon enough, Abdul judged, just in time to discover that she would be spending the next few weeks in the company of all three brothers. By the time they reached their final destination, she would probably be suffering from Stockholm Syndrome.

Or perhaps she'll hate all three of us, he thought, ruefully. His brothers and he had spent years together, but their captive wouldn't know them at all. *But her feelings hardly matter.*

Bracing himself, he stepped into the shipping container, followed by Amir and a reluctant Abdullah. His brother had gloom and misery written all over his face; Abdul silently promised the ghost of their dead mother that he'd take care of his younger brother. The last thing she would have wanted was for her son to be sent to a re-education camp.

"Make sure she's secure," Amir said. "We don't want her breaking loose."

Abdul snorted, rudely. The American girl wasn't a superhero. Even if they released her hands, even if she managed to kill all three of them, she still wouldn't be able to get out of the container. Still, he cuffed her to the side of the container anyway, then braced himself as the hatch slammed closed. Inside, even illuminated by a powered light, it was still thoroughly unpleasant. They were going to be sick of each other by the time they reached their destination.

"You may as well get some sleep," he said, as he inspected the girl. She would probably recover without problems, he told himself. If they'd inflicted permanent damage, there was no way to deal with it in the container. "We'll be on our way, soon enough."

Moments later, the container started to shake as it was transported towards the boat. Abdul shuddered, trying hard to keep his reaction under control. He'd had nightmares ever since he'd had his first trip in a container, nightmares where the crane broke and sent the container falling towards the ground…or into the ocean. Or nightmares where the ship sank and they all drowned, helplessly.

He knew, all too well, that they could easily come true.

THIRTY

*T*he break came forty minutes after the terrorists were identified. A vehicle fire had been reported in downtown New York, but largely ignored in the wake of the bombings. However, when it became clear that a white van had been deliberately set on fire, Jürgen became very interested indeed. Further checks revealed that the vehicle had been carefully parked out of sight of any CCTV cameras, ensuring that there was no footage of the van or whatever vehicle the arsonists had used to make their escape.

But *that* wouldn't stop him from identifying the vehicle.

He carefully went through all the records, working out the timing piece by piece. Logically, the terrorists would have left a timer on the van to ensure they had time to make their escape, but it would be a risky move. An abandoned van would attract attention, particularly now. It suggested that the terrorists had departed maybe five to ten minutes before the van caught fire, which meant...he went through the records and identified a number of suspect vehicles, then set the system to backtracking them through New York. Three of them vanished off the grid, but the fourth had gone directly to a shipping company.

Clever, he thought. The airports might be closed, the roads might be blocked, but it was much harder to stop and search even a small container ship. One of the many nightmares plaguing the Department of Homeland Security was a terrorist smuggling in a nuclear bomb in a shipping container, secure in the knowledge that even the best detection systems would be unlikely to pick up any traces of radioactivity. And this time the container ship was heading out of the country, back to Greece.

It would not normally have attracted much attention, he knew. Greece wasn't on the list of countries to be viewed with deep suspicion, even though it was alarmingly close to North Africa and the Middle East. The ship might meet up with another ship during its voyage or simply move the container onwards when it reached Athens. And it wouldn't be noticeable unless the ship was searched from end to end.

He cursed under his breath as he realised the ship was already on her way out to sea. They'd clearly planned it for quite some time, assuming he was right. The ship wasn't leaving urgently, she had been scheduled to depart on this precise day for several weeks. There was simply nothing, other than a minor mistake, to use to identify her as a potential suspect.

Shaking his head, he reached for the phone. The Coast Guard would have to intercept the ship and escort her back into harbour, where she could be searched *thoroughly*. There would be complaints, he knew, and probably genuine ones too. Holding a ship long enough to be searched would be immensely costly to the shipping company. Ships simply didn't make money when they were at anchor. But there was no alternative.

Besides, there were no other leads to follow.

— —

"Sleeper agents, it looks like," Mongo said. He'd been following the progress of the interrogations, but they'd yielded little of interest. "People who blended so well into our society that they remained well below the radar."

Steve nodded, feeling cold rage replaced with icy determination. The brothers had been model immigrants, pretty much. They paid taxes, took part in community activities and never went to any of the more dubious mosques. Hell, from what the youngest brother's American wife was saying, they never prayed at all. But it had all been a lie. They'd waited until they received their orders, then moved into action.

And they carried it off flawlessly, he thought, bitterly. *Damn bastards.*

He looked down at the reports. Iran was probably the prime suspect, either out of a desire for revenge – he'd given Israel the laser defence system, after all – or out of a desire to influence the off-world development of space. The Iranians had a long history of training insurgents and sleeper agents, as well as meddling in Middle Eastern affairs and trying to undermine their rival governments. But they weren't the only suspects. The remains of the Taliban had good reason to want to hurt him, while the oil monarchies of the Middle East hated his guts. They'd spent billions of dollars at the UN, trying desperately to prevent the introduction of fusion technology. And they'd failed.

"Got something," Mongo said. "A Greek ship – the *Karaboudjan* – may well be their getaway vessel."

"Show me," Steve ordered.

He looked at the image from the drone, then scowled. The *Karaboudjan* was a medium-sized freighter, large enough to carry hundreds of shipping containers. He remembered some of the rumours about the Al Qaeda Navy and shuddered, inwardly. Had New York been clutching one of those vipers to its bosom? Or had the *Karaboudjan* been serving as a perfectly innocent freighter up until now?

"The Coast Guard is calling for military assistance," Mongo said. "I believe they're putting together a team of SEALs now."

Steve shook his head. "Tell them we want to scan the vessel first," he said. "And if she's on it, we can get her back quicker than them."

He had no illusions about what orders the terrorists would have in the event of capture. If there was a strong risk of falling into enemy hands, they would first kill their captive and then kill themselves. Ideally, he

knew, they would have to stun the terrorists, then sort out the mess afterwards. But if Mariko wasn't onboard the ship, he didn't want to attack it
and cause another major incident. There would be enough repercussions
from destroying the terrorist network and the country backing them.

Slowly, the nanotech drones started to search the vessel, their reports
building up a holographic diagram in front of Steve. As far as he could
tell, most of the crew seemed European and there were even a handful of
women, something very unusual for a terrorist ship. But then, it could
just be cover. If the vast majority of the crew were unaware of their ship's
true purpose, it would be harder to find someone willing and able to
betray the rest of their comrades.

"Here," Mongo said. "Those guys don't look like shippers."

Steve couldn't disagree. The six men in a lower room looked more
like soldiers than sailors, although they were wearing civilian clothes. A
quick check revealed that they had a small arsenal with them, enough
weapons to stand off pirates or a commando offensive. Mongo checked
the records and noted that the *Karaboudjan* often went near the east coast
of Africa, where the pirates occasionally came out to prey on Western
shipping. Armed guards and a willingness to shoot one's way out of trouble were often the only true barrier to pirate attack.

"Soldiers or terrorists," he mused. "Probably trained soldiers. Do we
have any records of them?"

"They're listed as armed guards from a Greek company, but nothing
past that," Mongo said. "Kevin would probably be able to dig up more
information."

"Probably," Steve agreed. He watched as the drones started to enter
the containers, rapidly scanning the contents. Most of them held pieces of
technology or clothing that couldn't be found in Greece these days, from
what he'd read online. Others were completely empty, something that
puzzled him. Surely empty crates were inefficient? Or was more coming
out of Greece than going into the country? "I..."

He swore as one of the drones reported back, after entering yet another
container. "Got her," he said. "She's there!"

Mongo peered over his shoulder as other drones converged on the container. Inside, Mariko was lying against one wall, her hand cuffed to the metal. Three men, two of them sleeping, were sharing the container; Steve felt his teeth clench in rage as he realised just how helpless his partner was, if one of her captors decided to have some fun. She wasn't a soldier, not even a combat medic. And she had never learnt to fight with her bare hands.

"Teleport her out," Mongo urged. "Then the SEALs can take the vessel in peace."

Steve checked the interface, then shook his head. There was just too much metal and electronic interference to allow a successful teleport. Mariko wouldn't thank him if she rematerialised with her head sticking out of her ass...and that was only if she was lucky, he knew. Most teleport accidents, according to the files, were instantly lethal and there was rarely a body to bury. The quantum uncertainty principle would see to it.

"We need to stun them all, then board the ship," he said. "The SEALs can have her afterwards."

He stood up. "And I'll be leading the mission in person," he said. At least they had a strike team on alert, composed of a handful of augmented soldiers. "I will not..."

"Steve," Mongo said, sharply, "you shouldn't be leading the mission. You shouldn't even be there. You're far too personally involved."

Steve glowered at him. "And would you be happy if Jayne was on that ship and you had to remain behind?"

"No," Mongo said. "But I'd accept it."

He pushed Steve back into his chair, then headed towards the hatch. "I won't let her get hurt," he said. "And we *will* get her back to you. Just get ready to stun her captors upon command."

Steve nodded, reluctantly.

— —

ALANNAH THEODORI STOOD on the deck and watched America fading into the distance. She hadn't been sure what to expect of her first voyage across the ocean, but she had to admit she enjoyed it despite the cramped working conditions and the sometimes crude language of the older sailors. But then, she knew there were only handful of jobs in the shipping industry and she was incredibly lucky to get this job. Besides, it was a stepping stone to greater things.

She took a breath, tasting the sea air, then turned to head down to the hatch. As always, there was no shortage of work for the crew, even when they were miles away from land. Her duties weren't difficult, but they were tedious and her supervisor got very snippy whenever she and her fellow crewmates got bored and started to play with their smartphones instead of working. But she couldn't blame him for that, not really. They had to keep everything shipshape onboard ship — he made the pathetic joke at least once a day — and slackness would be a grave mistake.

A funny feeling flickered through the air, as if they were about to be struck by lightning. She looked up and saw a strange silver light appear along the deck, rapidly growing into the shape of a man. No, several men. She stared, unable to quite believe what she was seeing, as the man came into view, all wearing black uniforms and carrying strange-looking weapons. And then one of them pointed a weapon at her...

There was a flash of blue-white light and everything went black.

— ⌐

MONGO WATCHED THE girl fall, then keyed his communicator. "Have you got them?"

"Stunned them all," Steve said. The tiny drones could stun as well as kill, thankfully, even though it had never been tested in combat. "Hurry up."

Mongo nodded, then rapidly issued orders to his men. One group would secure the bridge, the other would go after the armed guards, then the hold. Anyone they encountered would be stunned without warning. Stunners had one definite advantage over automatic weapons; they could be used without fear of accidentally killing an innocent person. The safest course of action was to stun everyone on the ship, then transport them all back to shore and sort them out with the help of lie detectors and truth drugs. Afterwards, the innocent would be released and paid compensation, while the guilty went to the moon.

The six guards – or terrorists – didn't have the faintest idea the assault team was there until it was far too late. Mongo wasn't particularly surprised; if they'd hoped to hide their true nature from the crew, they wouldn't have been patrolling the decks in full armour this close to the United States. They threw a stun grenade into the room, then followed up as the terrorists dropped to the deck. Mongo checked them rapidly, then marked them down for later attention and moved down towards the hold. Unsurprisingly, the hatch was locked. A quick burst from his alien-designed weapon burned right through it.

It wasn't the first container ship he'd searched, but it was the first he'd actually known where to look for something. Deliberately or otherwise, the terrorists had placed their container on the second level, making it very hard to search. Mongo, undeterred, organised a set of ladders, then burned his way into the container. Inside, the air already smelt rank. He couldn't help wondering just how the terrorists had intended to endure at least two weeks of an increasingly foul stench.

They've probably been in worse, he thought. Back in Basic Training, he'd been pretty rank too. And he'd crawled through sewage in Iraq. It was astonishing, he knew, just what one could get used to if there was no choice. *And Mariko wouldn't have been offered one.*

He released the girl and carefully lowered her out of the container, back to the deck. Behind him, his team grabbed the three terrorists and moved them out too, using rather less care with their bodies. Mongo snapped at one of them who deliberately banged a terrorist head against the deck. He understood the impulse to just *hurt* the dishonourable bastards, but they needed evidence. Besides, it was unlikely that lunar courts would show any mercy to the fuckers.

"Steve, we got her," he said, as he carried the girl back up to the deck. "Can you get a lock on her now?"

"Yes," Steve said. "Are you coming up too?"

"Not yet," Mongo said. In the distance, he could see a pair of Stealth Hawks flying towards the ship. Seal Team Six would no doubt be outraged that the crew had already been stunned, leaving them with nothing more than clear-up duties, but it hardly mattered. Once the ship was taken into a naval port, the SEALs would have plenty to do. "Let me hand the ship over to the newcomers first."

He would never admit it, certainly not to the SEALs themselves, but they had always impressed him. Perhaps he would have considered trying to transfer if it had been possible, yet there were no guarantees. Outside cross-training, he would have had to enlist in the Navy and work his way through training a second time. And he'd been reluctant to do anything of the sort after Steve had left the military.

The SEALs dropped down from the helicopter and looked around, weapons at the ready. It was hard to tell – their faces were hidden behind masks – but they seemed to be rather surprised at the sight before them. Mongo grinned, then saluted the team leader. After a moment, the SEAL returned the salute.

"Everyone on the vessel is stunned," he said. "We'll be taking the terrorists with us, but everyone else should be treated gently. Most of them were not aware of any wrongdoing on this vessel."

"Understood," the SEAL said, gruffly.

Mongo nodded, picked up Mariko and triggered the teleporter. The world vanished in a shimmer of silver-white light.

—

"Is she going to be all right?"

"Physically, I believe so," the medic said. He'd been in the French Foreign Legion before retiring and then applying to join the lunar settlement and he still had a faint French accent. "Mentally... it is always questionable after such a shock."

"I know," Steve muttered. Mariko had been scanned, intensely, using alien technology. She had suffered no physical damage, apart from a handful of bumps and bruises. Mercifully, she hadn't been molested or raped. "Can you wake her up?"

"I'd prefer to let her wake up naturally," the medic said, firmly. "These sort of injuries need to be watched, carefully. I understand how you feel, sir, but her safety should come first."

"Understood," Steve said, irked.

It was nearly forty minutes before Mariko opened her eyes and stared up at the ceiling. Steve was at her side instantly, unsure of how best to proceed. Should he take her in his arms or would that produce a panic attack? Or...what should he do?

"Steve," she said. "What happened?"

Steve hesitated, reminded himself that she was a grown woman and briefly outlined everything that had happened. "We tracked you down and recovered you," he concluded, after detailing the desperate search. "And here you are, safe and sound."

"Thank you," Mariko whispered. She gave him a long look. "Is it always going to be like this now?"

"I plan to make sure it never happens again," Steve said, firmly. "If you go back to the clinic, you'll have a small army protecting you."

Mariko nodded. Steve eyed her, worriedly. He'd never liked the idea of submissive girls, no matter how attractive it seemed. Mariko was certainly not submissive...or, rather, she *hadn't* been submissive. But now, she was accepting his suggestions without argument, even though she'd refused them earlier. It didn't strike him as a very encouraging sign. What would she do, he wondered, if he ordered her to stay on the ship? Or the moon?

"You should take a few days to rest," he said, instead. "That should give us plenty of time to rebuild the clinic."

She nodded, again. Steve felt suddenly helpless. She hadn't demanded that she go right back to New York to help deal with the bombing aftermath or even that he stop treating her as an invalid. Had her spirit been broken by the kidnappers?

He ground his teeth together in silent fury. Whatever else happened, he was *damned* if he was letting the bastards get away with it. And heaven help anyone who tried to stand in his way.

THIRTY-ONE

"**G**oing by the latest reports, Steve, New York suffered fifty-seven dead, ninety-five wounded, some critically," Mongo said. "All that for a fucking diversion."

Steve nodded, unsurprised, as he stared at the terrorists through the one-way force field. "I think we can arrange for the wounded to be treated in one of our clinics," he said. "They were injured in an attack on us, after all."

Mongo nodded back. "We scanned them all pretty thoroughly," he continued. "They all had suicide capsules in their teeth, ready for immediate use. We removed them before we woke the bastards up, Steve, and they all tried to go for the capsules. These guys are pretty damn hardcore."

"I know," Steve said. "And the ship's crew?"

"All innocent, according to DHS," Mongo said. "They used the lie detectors we provided – as far as everyone knew, apart from the Captain, the terrorists were just a hired security team. The Captain was the only one who knew the truth…"

Steve looked over at him for a long moment. "And the truth is?"

"They're Revolutionary Guards, Steve," Mongo said. "The attack came from Iran."

Steve gritted his teeth, remembering briefings on the Revolutionary Guard during his military service. They were partly a Praetorian Guard, charged with keeping the Mullahs in power, partly a terrorist group and partly a business in their own right. Like the KGB and other security organisations with a complete absence of public accountability, they had acquired land, businesses and countless other interests in their name. By now, they were probably – directly or indirectly – one of Iran's major employers.

They'd done worse than just hold 'death to America' marches too, he knew. Iran's fingerprints had been found on weapons and explosives in both Iraq and Afghanistan, with the country trying to ensure their chosen tools gained control in both regions. And, for that matter, to bleed the Americans white. Steve recalled one Marine wondering out loud if the Mullahs hoped their more fanatical followers would go to Iraq and get killed by the Americans. It was so hard to balance a theocratic regime with the compromises that had to be made, just to keep the country on an even kneel.

But there was something about the whole affair that puzzled him. The Mullahs were careful poker players, never overplaying their hands. So why had they risked losing everything in this manner? Iran would suffer, badly, as fusion tech became more widespread, but they were in a far better position than Saudi Arabia or the tiny oil kingdoms dotted around the Middle East. Or were they convinced that Steve would one day turn his attention to them?

Or maybe they were afraid of losing power, he thought. *They wouldn't want their own people to start questioning their values.*

"Start the interrogation," he ordered, wishing – again – that Kevin was with them. *He* could have handled the whole affair without fuss. "I want to know everything they know."

It was nearly an hour before they had some clear answers. The guards on the ship were there to serve as a security team, but they were also there to provide support to terrorist groups and sleeper agents at the ship's ports of call. Steve made careful notes of the details they provided, intending to pass them on to the various security forces. If nothing else, the whole affair would lead to the uncovering of a number of sleeper cells.

The kidnappers themselves were long-term sleeper agents, intended to remain in reserve until the United States finally attacked Iran. Steve listened to their conversation carefully; one of them seemed genuinely repentant, the others seemed more sorry they'd been caught than anything else. But the repentant one had had the wife and children in the United States.

Steve shrugged. Even if he were freed, it was unlikely he would ever see his wife and children again. They'd be interrogated once more, than probably put into a witness protection program. They hadn't known about what was coming, but it wouldn't stop people blaming them for it.

He turned and strode out of the room, back to the CIC. After a moment, Mongo followed him.

"Iran is going to be destroyed," he said, flatly. He activated the interface, bringing the ship's weapons online. It wouldn't be too difficult to destroy Iran. A handful of large kinetic warheads would smash most of the cities, while smaller missiles would take out the military bases and oil installations. "They're all going to die."

"No," Mongo said.

Steve blinked in surprise. It was *Kevin* who would have argued for mercy – no, not mercy, a more subtle revenge than mass destruction. But Kevin was light years away.

He leaned forward. "Why not?"

Mongo met his eyes evenly. "Do you remember Jock Hazelton?"

Steve nodded, puzzled. Jock Hazelton had been a young lad living near the ranch, only a year or two younger than Mongo. He'd been a quiet, withdrawn child, so no one had suspected him of being responsible for a series of thefts and pieces of vandalism all over the countryside. Steve still recalled the angry interrogation from his father when he, as one of the rowdier children, fell under suspicion. It hadn't been until he'd been caught in the act that everyone had realised that Jock Hazelton had been to blame for all of it. His embarrassed family had left the region soon afterwards.

"Do you remember," Mongo demanded, "how we were all blamed for it?"

"Yes," Steve said. It had rankled; the threats, the sharp eyes following them wherever they went, the awareness that their father had come far too close to thrashing all three of his sons on suspicion. By the time the truth had come out, distrust had seriously damaged the community. "I remember."

"So tell me," Mongo said, "how you can hold the entire population of Iran to blame for what their leaders have done?"

Steve took a breath. "They didn't overthrow the government," he protested. "They..."

Mongo snorted. "I seem to recall you spending most of your time bitching and moaning about the feds," he said. "But you didn't take up your rifle and go Henry Bowmen on them."

He pushed on before Steve could say a word. "You know that life in Iran isn't *comfortable*," he said. "But you also know that Iranians are held in terror by scumbags like that lot" – he jerked a thumb towards the holding cells – "and any resistance is severely punished. How can you blame them for not rising up when resistance seems futile?"

Steve glared at him, trying to think of a response. Nothing came to mind.

"I hate those bastards as much as you do," Mongo snapped. "But is it *right* to destroy their entire country, taking out millions of innocent people, just because you're angry at the fuckers in charge? You have the power to punish those who are truly guilty, to hold them to account for their sins, yet you intend to flail around like the idiots who never suspected poor little Jock!"

He took a long breathe. "Steve...you're building a government here," he said. "The last thing you want is to convince everyone that you're a power-mad monster on a scale worse than Hitler. Because that's what you will be, if you slaughter everyone in Iran."

"Our Great-Grandfather *died* fighting Hitler," Steve said.

"And what," Mongo demanded, "do you think he'd make of you?"

He sighed. "Steve, you need to think about more than just revenge," he said. "I know you're hurting, I know you're angry and I don't blame you for being either. But you have to think about the future too. What sort of impression does it give the rest of the world if you commit genocide?

"The tech monopoly will slip, sooner or later," he added. "There are already plans to produce more superconductors with purely human technology. Then there's the guys who think they can produce a primitive fusion reactor. Antigravity might not be too far away, thanks to the theorists – and if they do manage to master superconductors, they can probably produce antigravity too. What will happen if the world governments fear and hate us instead of agreeing to work with us? Your dream will die!"

Steve fought to keep himself calm. His love for Mariko demanded revenge; his love for what he'd created agreed with Mongo and insisted that something more subtle had to be done, instead of mass slaughter. But would it be enough to make the point that acts of terrorism would not go unpunished?

"Yes," Mongo said, when he asked. "Kill a few thousand soldiers and evil bastards like the theocrats of Iran won't give a shit. They're just chattel to them. But kill the leaders, show them there's no place to hide, and they will be scared. And, while you're at it, destroy Iran's nuclear program once and for all. Let the world see what we can do without bombing a country into radioactive dust."

Steve took a long breath, suddenly feeling very tired. "Make the target selections," he ordered. "I want the entire government wiped out."

"I was going to suggest taking them as prisoners," Mongo said. "We can find some hard labour for them to do, once we've finished interrogating them. God alone knows what else we might find out along the way."

He paused. "And who knows what Iran will become without the Mullahs holding them back?"

GUNTER DAWLISH HAD spent most of the afternoon trying to get a read on just what had happened in New York. There had been explosions, he knew, and over a hundred people were dead or wounded, but there were also thousands of rumours flying around. A ship had been boarded, the crew had been captured, and Iran was involved somehow. The internet, source of millions upon millions of rumours, had even suggested that the explosions in New York were the first steps in a war between America and Iran. But there had been no other military moves as far as he could tell.

His cell phone rang. "Mr. Dawlish," Steve Stuart said. "Would you care to join me?"

"Of course," Gunter said. He might be a lunar citizen now, but an invitation to Mr. Stuart's flagship was still a rarity. "What can I do for you?"

"I'm bringing you up now," Stuart said. "Brace yourself for teleport."

Dawlish closed his eyes. When he opened them, he was standing on a teleport pad, facing Stuart. The man looked as if he had aged ten years overnight, although Dawlish wasn't sure where that impression came from. It was hard to be certain, but Stuart had always looked to be in his late thirties.

"Come with me," Stuart said.

He didn't say another word until they were in his cabin, looking at a holographic image of Earth. Small icons moved around, each one – Gunter realised slowly – representing a ship, an aircraft or a satellite. He couldn't help admiring the sheer detail of the image, even as it started to focus on Iran.

"I want you to pass on a message," Stuart said. He sounded in control of himself, but Gunter could hear the edge of rage underneath his words. "The Government of Iran launched the terror attacks in New York City as a diversion, so they could kidnap...kidnap one of my people. With the assistance of the American Government, we tracked down our missing person and captured the kidnappers. We have clear proof that they came from Iran and that their mission was ordered at the very highest levels."

Gunter sucked in a breath. "Do you have proof of this?"

"We will give you full access to the recordings," Stuart said, "but understand; we are not asking you to judge. Nor are we asking the United Nations for permission to go after the bastards who killed fifty-seven American citizens and kidnapped one of *my* people. We are going to go after them right now."

He looked Gunter in the eye. "Right now, the senior government ministers of Iran are being taken from their country," he said, "along with their entire council of religious leaders. They will be interrogated; the results of their interrogations may lead to the identification of others who need to be taken into custody. Instead of a full-scale invasion and the deaths of countless Iranians, the guilty – men who have held their own government in a state of tyranny since the revolution against the Shah – have been removed. They will be tried for their crimes and, if found guilty, executed."

Gunter hesitated, unable to take in the sheer scope of what he was being told. "You are kidnapping the entire government?"

"We are taking its senior leadership," Stuart said. He nodded to the display. "We are also eradicating every last trace of Iran's WMD program. Their nuclear sites, their chemical weapons stockpiles and even their small selection of biological weapons are being removed and destroyed. The scientists will also be taken. They will not be permitted to return to Iran.

"Given what we could have done, in response to an outright act of war, this is a comparatively mild response," he concluded. "But we want you to take a message to the world.

"Over the last seventy years, it has been extremely difficult to hold rogue states accountable for their actions. Their leaders don't give a shit about random bombing raids or cruise missile attacks; no, they use them as propaganda to make us look like the bad guys. It took a full-scale invasion to hold Saddam to account for his actions, which forced us to fight a bitter insurgency in the country for eight years. Now, we have determined the best way to proceed, one that genuinely does hold the leadership of such states to account.

"For every attack we can trace back to a country, we will go after that country's leadership," he concluded. "We're not interested in trying to force them to surrender, we're not intent on claiming land for ourselves, we're merely interested in punishing them for supporting terrorism. None of the arguments against sparing a country's leadership will hold any ice with us. Such attacks will be avenged.

"There are those who will say, perhaps out of fear, that we are over-reacting. But really, is our way not better than slaughtering thousands of innocents?"

"It certainly seems that way," Gunter said, finding his voice. "But I know many governments will disagree."

"Of course they will," Steve said. "It isn't *sporting* to go after your fellow leaders. It might give the bastards ideas."

He paused, then went on. "This attack killed over fifty American citizens, citizens who just happened to be in the wrong place at the wrong time," he added. "Does it seem right to let it go unavenged?"

"I don't think so," Gunter said. "But I think you've opened up one hell of a can of worms."

"I know," Steve said. "But we couldn't leave it hanging either."

— —

"AND THAT'S ALL that happened," he concluded, as he sat next to Mariko. "The government is being interrogated now, while the rest of Iran seems stunned. They'll react, sooner or later, but not for a while."

He paused. "Am I a hypocrite?"

Mariko considered it for a long moment. "I don't think you preached against war and devastation while *unleashing* war and devastation, so you're not a hypocrite," she said. "It's no sin to change your mind or even admit that you might have been wrong."

"I'm not good at that," Steve admitted. Flexibility might be one of the watchwords of the Marine Corps, but he knew they couldn't be *too* flexible. "I was prepared to burn Iran to ashes before Mongo…"

"Gave you a speech telling you that you were being a damn fool," Mariko said, without heat. "And he was right."

Steve sighed. "Whatever happened to girls that always supported their men, no matter what?"

"They only existed in fevered male imaginations," Mariko said, dryly. "And besides, wouldn't you prefer me to tell you when you're being an asshole?"

"I suppose," Steve said.

They sat for a long moment in silence, then Steve opened his mouth. "I didn't really think through what I was doing, did I?"

"There comes a time when you have to act, rather than think," Mariko said. "I've handled operations when the plan, as detailed as it was, suddenly went to hell and I had to improvise on the spot. And you're very good at reacting to the unexpected."

She paused. "But you're also in a position where you have ample time to stop and think about what you're doing," she added. "And that is what you will have to do from now on."

"I'm not going to run for President," Steve said, suddenly. "After we hold elections, I'm going to find a place to set up a homestead and stay there. Someone else can take the reins for a while."

Mariko reached out and touched his hand. "Wherever you go, I will be with you," she said, softly. Her hand felt very warm against his coarse flesh. "Why don't we set out as traders?"

Steve had to admit he was tempted. There was a whole universe out there, after all, and starships that could support a small number of humans indefinitely. They could take a small amount of trade goods and move from system to system, selling their wares. No one would know or care about their lives on Earth, assuming they cared about Earth at all. Instead, they'd just be two aliens among uncounted trillions.

"We could do that," he said. But there were other problems, other issues. Did he have the right to take even a small trading starship for himself. "Once Earth is ready to defend itself, we could leave."

"Oh, Steve," Mariko said. She shook her head slowly, then reached out and pulled him towards her for a kiss. "You'll never allow yourself to put down your work."

THIRTY-TWO

CAPTAIN PERRY/SHADOW WARRIOR, EARTH ORBIT

Kevin couldn't help feeling nervous as *Captain Perry* returned to Sol. They'd been away for over two months and anything could have happened in that time. The Horde could have launched another attack, another alien race could have arrived…or all hell could have broken loose on Earth. It was a colossal relief, when the ship finally slipped out of FTL some distance from the moon, to exchange signals and counter-signals with *Shadow Warrior* and confirm that everything was fine.

He looked down at his display as the ship entered orbit around Earth. A number of dead satellites and pieces of space junk were gone, plucked out of orbit and taken to the moon to serve as raw materials. In their place, there were a handful of inflatable space stations and a couple of odd-looking spacecraft. It took him several moments to realise that they were intended to transport large numbers of colonists to the asteroid belt. And they were built with purely human technology.

Smiling, he keyed his display. "All hands will need to go through debriefing before starting shore leave on Earth," he said. "Please don't try to leave before then, as you also need to be briefed on conditions on the planet itself."

He looked over at Jackson and nodded. "You have the bridge."

"Aye, sir," Jackson said. "I have the bridge."

Kevin stood, walked through the hatch and down towards the teleport chamber. Flying back to Earth had felt quicker than travelling into unknown space, although he knew there was no real difference. Perhaps it was the effort of digging through the vast quantities of data they'd recovered from the alien world. The scientists had barely been seen outside their cabins and research compartments, where they had been working their way through technology the aliens considered primitive and pre-contact humanity would have considered incredibly advanced. In the meantime, Edward Romford and his staff had been working out the details for hiring troops from Earth. They seemed to believe there would be no shortage of volunteers.

He paused outside Carolyn's door – they'd become closer on the return flight, although he still hadn't managed to talk her into bed – then shook his head and walked on until he stepped into the teleport chamber. Inside, the teleport operator was already inspecting the system, as if he knew precisely how it worked. Kevin nodded to him, stepped up onto the pad and sent the command directly through the interface. The silver haze rose up around him, then faded away, revealing *Shadow Warrior's* teleport bay.

"Steve," he said. His brother was standing by the hatch, a grim half-smile on his face. "It's good to see you again."

"You too," Steve said. "Quite a bit has happened since you left."

Kevin eyed him, worriedly, as Steve turned and led the way out of the compartment. His brother looked...*tired*, as if he had been working far too hard. Normally, Steve was brimming with energy, ready to do whatever he thought he had to do. But now...he was acting as if he had no energy at all. But Steve said nothing more until they were back in his cabin and the hatch was firmly closed.

"Take a beer from the fridge," he said. "And pass me one while you're at it."

Kevin opened the fridge and discovered a handful of bottles of beer, rather than the cans he'd been expecting. Each of the bottles was marked with an image of the moon, etched into the glass, and a name he didn't recognise.

"They were produced on the moon," Steve said. "One of the moonshiners I knew from the ranch asked permission to set up a small brewery. I gave it to him and…well, those are the first results."

"Lunar beer," Kevin said. He opened his bottle and took a swig. It tasted faintly nutty, but it was better than most of the canned beer he'd drunk in his life. "A very small brewery?"

"For the moment," Steve said. "He's actually been talking about expanding his operations and trying to sell lunar beer on Earth."

"I'm sure it would be a hit," Kevin said, taking another sip. "Do you get free beer as his patron?"

Steve snorted. "I forgot to write that into the contract," he said. "All I get is a dollar or two off the price."

Kevin chuckled, then put the beer down on the table. "All right," he said. "What's been happening since I left?"

"I almost destroyed Iran," Steve confessed. "And Saudi Arabia."

Kevin stared at him. "What?"

He had no love for either country, although – if pressed – he would have had to admit that he preferred Iran to Saudi Arabia. The Iranians might hate America, but it was a honest hate, while the Saudis were torn between covert hatred and a desperate attempt to maintain the balancing act between the United States and their own religious fundamentalists. He knew just how much Saudi money had gone to support terrorists over the years…and lobbying efforts in Washington. The Jewish lobby was utterly overshadowed by the sheer power of the Arab lobby.

"They kidnapped Mariko," Steve said, morbidly. "We tracked her down, took her back and dealt with the terrorist filth."

Kevin held up a hand. "Wait," he said. "Start at the beginning."

The story didn't seem to make much sense at first. According to the Iranian officials who had been captured, they'd worked with Saudi Arabia to counter the introduction of new Galactic technology on Earth. It seemed to make little sense – the Iranians were not given to gambling, no matter how fanatical their regime seemed – but Kevin had a feeling that they knew they were risking substantial unrest in the very near future. And besides, they'd believed they could count on the Saudis and the other Middle Eastern countries to prevent American retaliation. They simply hadn't taken Steve and his new country seriously.

And the Saudis might have expected them to take the fall, Kevin thought. *That would be just what they would consider ideal.*

"So they sent kidnappers after Mariko," Kevin said. They clearly didn't know Steve very well. He might not have been married to his partner, but she was his wife in all the ways that mattered. Steve would move Heaven and Earth to find her – and he had the technology to take a ghastly revenge for any harm they did to his lover. "And you found them?"

"We had a bit of help from the DHS," Steve confessed. He looked down at his bottle of beer, then back up at Kevin. "I never thought I would be grateful for the bastards."

He shrugged. "We found the ship, raided it and took her back," he added. "And then we kidnapped the governments of all of the involved nations."

Kevin couldn't help it. He giggled.

"Funny," he said. "And what happened to them?"

Steve smiled. "You won't believe what turned up in the interrogations," he said. "Quite apart from involvement in international terrorist activity and suchlike, we caught quite a few war criminals the ICC never bothered to charge with any crime. A few of the Iranians were responsible for the violent purge of pro-democracy activists, one of them was responsible for ordering his men to fire into gathered crowds...the Bahraini officials we captured were responsible for selling their country out to the Saudis. Naturally, we put all of the evidence on the internet."

Kevin smiled back. "And how did you reach people whose opinions actually matter?"

"I think we did just that," Steve said. "There's almost no support for them on Earth, apart from a handful of *pro forma* protests."

Kevin nodded in understanding. Whatever nations might say in public, it was very rare for dictators or religious theocrats to be held accountable for their crimes. Their subordinates could die like flies, if necessary, but it was rare to go directly after the dictator. Maybe there was some logic to it – the dictator was the only one who could actually surrender – yet it had always struck him as sick. Why kill the men who were forced to stand against American troops or carry out ghastly atrocities when the dictator himself remained immune?

It was the age-old problem, he knew, for anyone serving a dictator. Carry out the dictator's orders and commit war crimes, wipe out entire villages, kill the men, rape the women and children…or take a suicidal stand against him? The moralists in the West expected the latter, but Steve knew better. Why would a random soldier in the Iraqi Army have refused an order to kill Kurds in job lots when he *knew* that Saddam would kill him and his entire family, while the West was unlikely to hold him to account? People willing to stand up and say *no* were very rare. Most of them did it from a safe distance.

Often a very safe distance, Kevin thought. He remembered Trotsky and shuddered. *But sometimes not far enough.*

"I see," he said, finally. "And what's happened in those countries now the leaders are gone?"

"Bahrain's remaining government has been overwhelmed," Steve said. "So far, they're still arguing over the composition of their new government and eying both the Saudis and Iranians nervously. Saudi itself is having major problems with riots in the streets, Iran seems to be in a state of shock. Thankfully, as they are a much more established nation, the loss of the senior government hasn't crippled their ability to feed their population."

"Good," Kevin said. "And what about yourself?"

Steve met his eyes. "I came far too close to obliterating half the Middle East," he said. "What sort of monster does that make me?"

Kevin shrugged. "Do you know how many times I dreamed of something that would exterminate the population of Afghanistan?"

He stood up and started to pace. "I had this romantic vision of tribesmen sweeping majestically across the mountains, even though I knew it to be nonsense," he admitted. "I lost it very quickly, when faced with a people who seemed to consider deception second nature. Everyone lied to us; civilians lied because they feared Taliban retaliation, soldiers lied because they didn't want to admit they didn't know what they were doing. It wasn't long before I was thoroughly *sick* of the sheer hypocrisy underlying everything they said and did.

"Rape is illegal, but they force girls into marriage that is rape by any other name. Prostitution is illegal, yet the Taliban was quite happy to run brothels for its fighting men. Homosexuality is illegal, but catamites and outright male rape are common throughout Afghanistan. Drug abuse is illegal, yet they grow poppies to produce opium to help fund their war. Oh, there were times when I would have gladly slaughtered the bastards in job lots.

"But I didn't, and you didn't," he concluded. "Having the thought doesn't make you evil, it's carrying it out that would take you across the moral event horizon. How many times have you considered homicide and never actually done it?"

Steve nodded, wordlessly.

"It's good that you've learnt some of the limits of power," Kevin added, returning to his seat. "But I don't think you've crossed the line into outright evil."

"Mongo chewed me out," Steve said. "If he hadn't..."

"Mariko would have done it," Kevin said. "Or Charles. Or Vincent's ghost would have risen from the grave to condemn you for committing genocide. Instead...you removed the guilty and gave their victims a chance to take the freedom they deserve."

"Or plunge into civil war," Steve said. "Saudi *really* doesn't look good these days."

Kevin smirked. "Fuck the bastards," he said. "Now...my turn."

He braced himself, then started to give a complete report of everything that had happened since they'd left Earth. Steve leaned forward, interested, when Kevin reached the section about the meeting with Friend and the deal to send human mercenaries to fight beside the aliens. They'd considered the possibility, ever since realising that humans had been abducted and turned into warriors by one alien race, but it was still an unpleasant surprise. Steve took a copy of the agreement, read through it very carefully, and then looked up.

"This is better than I expected," he said. "Is there a sting in the tail?"

"As far as I can tell, there's nothing wrong with any of the supplies or technical support they gave us," Kevin said. He wasn't blind to the implications of the aliens producing so much so quickly. From their point of view, it had to be a relatively small payment. "And we will progress much faster if we have help."

He paused. "The terms and conditions are part of the agreement," he added. "They're not bad at all, at least from our point of view. I think they're desperate."

"It certainly looks that way," Steve agreed. He looked up, suddenly. "But would the introduction of a handful of humans turn the tide? It sounds like the plot of a bad space opera."

"It actually makes a certain kind of sense," Kevin said. He'd down-loaded texts on interstellar warfare from the alien database and read through them on the way home. "Their major planets are heavily defended, Steve. They have planet-based energy weapons, heavy force fields and plenty of other surprises. Taking the high orbitals would be tricky, to say the least; they're forced to land troops and take out the planetary defence centres on the ground."

He shivered, remembering some of the records they'd found on Ying. Invading a heavily-defended planet was incredibly difficult – and bloody. It made the greatest battles of the United States Marine Corps look like minor squabbles…which, from the alien point of view, he supposed they were. A race that counted hundreds of stars amid its empire wouldn't be too impressed by either America or Japan. Why, even the British Empire at its height had only claimed a quarter of the world's surface.

"But it also explains, I think, why we were left alone for so long," he added. "The major powers in this part of the galaxy are involved in a long slow war."

He'd read through the political notes too, although he had his doubts over how complete they actually were. One major power, backed by a far distant empire, was trying to dominate the rest of the sector, which seemed to be set to keep the wars going indefinitely. Kevin's original thought – that the far-distant power had set out to create an endless war deliberately – seemed to have been right. As long as the minor powers were fighting, they weren't threatening their far-distant power.

"Which leaves us with the problem of which side to support," Steve mused.

Kevin slapped the table, hard. "Steve...these races...even the smallest of the interstellar powers is far more powerful than all of humanity put together," he said. "Our best bet for survival, I think, is to ally ourselves with the side that *hasn't* been force-cloning human tissue and use the time to build up our own position. We are, at best, a microstate. The major interstellar powers will laugh at us if we try to hold any pretensions to power."

He shrugged. "Hell, the Horde has more starships than us."

"I know," Steve admitted.

Kevin sat back in his chair. "I propose we send them the mercenaries – or, rather, humans who are trained in observing and learning as much as possible from their surroundings," he said. He'd spent a lot of time considering the practicalities on the flight home. "They come back to Earth for leave, we debrief them and learn everything they know. In the meantime, we use this the money we will be paid to build up our own forces. Eventually, we will be able to take the risk of stepping openly onto the galactic stage."

Steve frowned. "There's one problem with this," he said. "Once the Varnar realise they're facing human soldiers, and they will, they will attack Earth. Destroying our planet would cut off the supply of human troops."

"That's the risk we have to take," Kevin said. He paused. "But we can use one of the ships we're being sent to set up an isolated colony far beyond the edge of galactic civilisation. The human race will live on, even if Earth herself is destroyed. And we will come back for revenge one day."

"I hope you're right," Steve said. He paused. "We could probably round up five thousand experienced soldiers, but if it's going to be more than that we will need help from the planetary governments."

Kevin nodded. "They'd want to have some involvement," he agreed. "But I think we have very little choice."

He stood. "There is some good news," he admitted. "Between what we discovered on the trip out and the alien files we downloaded, we might be able to start mass production of human-built antigravity units within a year or two. And then the solar system would lie open in front of us."

"The Mars Society will be delighted," Steve commented. He grinned. "Assuming, of course, they stop arguing over the political structure of Mars to actually take note."

Kevin smiled back. "Is Mars going to be one of the cantons?"

"I suspect we will end up with several cantons on Mars," Steve said. "The *real* problem is dealing with the prisoners. Perhaps we can find them some hard labour on Mars."

"I'm surprised you let them live," Kevin commented.

"Oh, the ones who were truly guilty are dead," Steve said. "As are the ones who committed foul crimes against their own people. But the others…finding them something to do is a little harder. Maybe we should just have them breaking rocks."

"Good idea," Kevin said. He smiled at the thought of fundamentalist clerics actually forced to work with their bare hands. "Make the bastards work for a living."

THIRTY-THREE

WASHINGTON DC, USA

The Secret Service had objected, strongly, to someone teleporting into the White House, even with permission from the President. They'd compromised, eventually, with an agreement that Steve could teleport into the Treasury Department and walk though the underground tunnels to the White House without being seen by the protesters gathered outside the building. Steve couldn't imagine why they honestly thought they were doing any good – he wasn't about to stop the terraforming of Mars, no matter what they said – but the President had felt it was best to keep his visit low-key. And he was probably right.

It wasn't the *first* White House, he knew. That building had been burned by the British during the War of 1812 and then replaced with the structure that had represented the heart of American government ever since. It was an impressive building, Steve had to admit, but it was grander than he felt the government should have wanted. Successive Presidents, each one almost a prisoner within the White House, would have developed delusions of grandeur, perhaps even dreams of absolute power. Perhaps a smaller building would have served the United States better.

A log cabin, perhaps? He asked himself, sarcastically. *Or a simple farmhouse?*

He couldn't help looking around like a yokel as they came out of the tunnel and walked up towards the Oval Office. The White House *was* like a palace, at least in the parts that were used to impress foreign visitors. He couldn't help wondering if some of the odder First Ladies had been warped by living in the house, both mistresses of the building and, at the same time, prisoners of their husband's career. But then, it was only recently – comparatively speaking – that women were expected to be more than just wives and hostesses.

The President rose to his feet to greet Steve as he stepped into the Oval Office. Steve held out his hand and shook it firmly, then sat down facing the President's chair. The sofa was sinfully comfortable, he decided, as the President sat down. Perhaps he should buy a few for the moon.

"The world seems to have turned upside down yet again," the President observed. "But at least people seem supportive of your decisions."

Steve nodded, shortly. The capture of Iran's government had been greeted with cheers in the streets of America, particularly after the blame had been placed for the bombings in New York. A handful of politicians who had openly questioned Steve's actions had been hit with a colossal backlash from the voters and several of them looked likely to be recalled or lose the next election. The rest of the world had been a little more cautious in their responses, but it was hard to argue against the evidence. Some of the clerics had been shaming their religion in ways Steve had always considered only theoretically possible.

But the entire world seemed to be holding its breath, waiting for the next change in the global situation. God alone knew what would happen next.

"My brother returned from an alien world," Steve said. In the five days since *Captain Perry* had returned to Earth, the news had leaked and spread widely. Everyone wanted to interview the commander and crew of the captured starship. Kevin had given a handful of interviews, but mainly kept himself out of sight on the moon. "Among other things, he obtained several more fabricators and plenty of alien tech manuals."

"Allowing you to unlock the secrets behind alien technology," the President said. Once, Steve would have suspected the President hadn't actually read his briefing notes. Now, he knew the man was far from stupid. "How long do you think it will be before you produce your own fabricator?"

"Probably several years," Steve admitted. "Reassembling molecules is a little more complex than producing fusion power or even antigravity. But the new fabricators will allow us to expand by leaps and bounds. Unfortunately, it comes at a price."

He paused, then explained about the alien demand for mercenaries.

"We don't seem to have much else to market," he concluded. "And we need your help."

The President frowned. "I believe that much of your population is made up of ex-military personnel," he said, after a moment. "It was one of your criteria for early recruitment."

Steve nodded, remembering how the DHS had seen vanishing veterans and panicked over nothing. But then, he would probably have asked a few hard questions if he'd seen veterans disappearing without explanation.

"It is," Steve said. "Their first request is for five thousand soldiers, Mr. President, but we believe they will want more. Hundreds of thousands more."

The President's eyes narrowed. "You want to borrow American military units."

"Yes, Mr. President," Steve said. "Maybe not for the first deployment, but certainly for others."

"I have a feeling Congress will not be pleased," the President said. "There was a reason mercenaries became so popular in Iraq."

"Cowboys," Steve muttered. The government had been worried about the effects of losing troops on American public opinion, so they'd hired mercenaries to fill some of the gaps. But the mercenaries had ranged from genuinely competent to idiots and they'd caused a lot of political problems for the government. He didn't blame the Iraqis for wanting to prosecute some of the former mercenaries. They'd killed people without any good cause. "But we're going to do better than that, Mr. President."

The President sighed. "And if I refuse?"

"We intend to recruit anyway," Steve said. "But we won't recruit from serving formations."

He left unspoken the simple fact that quite a number of serving soldiers would consider moving to the mercenary force rather than reenlisting in the United States military. There were soldiers who had enlisted for adventure, rather than anything else, and what better adventure than fighting on a whole different world? And there would be a high rate of pay, generous benefits and other advantages, even if most of the alien currency they earned would be taxed heavily to help fund Earth's expansion into the galaxy.

"I was also planning to buy up one of the private training complexes and turn it into a recruitment and training depot," he continued. "But if you think that would cause political problems..."

"It would," the President said. "Unless, of course, we got something in exchange."

Steve leaned forward. Now the bargaining could begin. "What do you want?"

The President studied him for a long moment. "Assistance in producing our own fusion reactors," he said, simply. "And superconductor batteries."

"American firms are already involved with the research efforts," Steve pointed out. "And some of the components cannot be manufactured on Earth."

"Then we would want additional supplies of both," the President said. "And some military assistance."

Steve lifted his eyebrows. International terrorism was reeling, both under the sudden loss of their leadership cadres and their financial backers. For once, the War on Terror had come genuinely close to being won. But there were growing problems in the Middle East and Pakistan, which was experiencing a terrifying level of civil unrest. It was quite likely,

Steve knew, that the Pakistani Government would fall soon enough. And it wasn't the only major headache.

"What sort of assistance would you like?" He said, finally. "And why?"

"We believe that North Korea is undergoing severe economic problems," the President said, softly. "Their Chinese patrons have been distracted and the Russians aren't interested in feeding them these days. It is quite possible that their government will consider making a lunge for South Korea, unleashing a bloody war."

Steve scowled. He hadn't seriously considered Korea, but he had to admit the President had a point. "We could wipe out their leadership too," he said. "And yet that would certainly result in civil war."

The President shook his head. "We would like some military assistance if the North Koreans do start attacking the South," he said. "And we would like their nuclear program destroyed."

Steve nodded. "Very well," he said. "It will be done."

———

"AN APPROVABLE DECISION," Romford said, four hours later. "Getting rid of North Korea as a nuclear power will definitely make the world safer."

"I suppose," Steve said. He looked around the training complex. It was surprisingly impressive, reminding him of Camp Pendleton. "These guys didn't miss much, did they?"

"I believe they were retired Marines," Romford confirmed. "The training program had its limits, but it certainly did a good job at turning out cohesive teams. And they proved themselves in combat."

Steve nodded. International Warriors had been one of the large private security companies in the world, recruiting soldiers from all over the world and hiring them out as everything from bodyguards to local police forces. Steve had met a couple of their recruiters back when he retired from the Marines and he had to admit that he had been seriously tempted. If he hadn't had the ranch, he might well have signed up and been deployed to Africa or the Middle East as part of a private bodyguard team.

But that might have gotten me killed, he thought. The last report from Saudi Arabia had suggested that a number of hired bodyguards had been slaughtered by the Saudi National Guard. No one was quite sure why. *Or I might never have seen the starship.*

He looked around the training complex, thoughtfully. The owners had designed it to simulate every possible field of combat, from house-to-house fighting to jungle or naval combat. It wasn't too surprising, he knew. They'd supplied guards for freighters cruising near the coast of Africa as well as private security teams. The former Marines or SEALs who made up such teams wouldn't want to let their skills slip. Besides, lacking the endless government bureaucracy, the company had been able to adapt, react and overcome quicker than some aspects of the Pentagon. Rumour had it that they even paid bonuses for soldiers who spoke foreign languages.

"So tell me," he said. "Is this suitable for our purposes?"

"More or less," Romford confirmed. "We can run basic medical checks here, give everyone a translation implant, then start running through training cycles until we get used to working as a team. We'll probably run into problems when we start recruiting people from outside the United States, but we will overcome them. It will help, I think, that we won't give a shit about political correctness."

Steve nodded. The agreement with the President, which was currently being examined by a select group of American politicians, would effectively turn the training camp into a private fiefdom. As long as the soldiers entered willingly and signed the right contracts, they could be put through the most intensive training possible without worrying about bureaucratic rules and regulations. Knowing the dangers of abuse, Steve had been careful to hire training officers he knew and trusted...with the private thought that he could do almost anything to a training officer who failed his trust.

Something lingering in boiling oil, perhaps, he thought. *Or maybe simple exposure to hard vacuum.*

"Give us a couple of months, I think, with the first volunteers," Romford added. "Then we can start recruiting others. But we're going to have to experiment a bit with the training programs."

"True," Steve agreed. This wasn't a standard military deployment, no matter what it looked like on the surface. The soldiers would be travelling to alien worlds and fighting there. "It wouldn't do to recruit an xenophobe."

"Or someone with a deathly fear of little blue men," Romford agreed. He smiled, brightly. "Anyone who read *Green Lantern* will probably be very suspicious of our...noble benefactors."

Steve gave him an odd look. "I would never have fingered you as a comics fan."

"There was a kid who came to see his granddad in the damn residence," Romford said. "I think he was bored out of his skull, so he used to show me the comics and try to read them to me. The last few issues had the Guardians creating a Borg rip-off and sending them to turn the entire universe into thoughtless monsters. And then they all died."

"A likely story," Steve said. It wasn't uncommon for soldiers to enjoy reading comics as a form of escape from their lives. Hell, he'd been a great fan of *Doctor Who* for precisely that reason. The episodes were unrealistic, but that was the point. War movies would have been a bit too close to home. "I think you bought them for yourself."

Romford looked away. "Anyway, we will be watching for people with an adverse fear reaction," he continued, changing the subject rapidly. "Part of the training program will include holograms of many of the nastier-looking alien races, particularly the ones that look like spiders or movie monsters."

"Exposure will probably help," Steve said.

He winced at an old memory. He'd once been deathly scared of scorpions, to the point where he hadn't even been able to *look* at the creatures. Iraq and its legions of deadly scorpions had cleared that right up, even though he still found them creepy. Hell, they'd spent the boring days before crossing the border capturing scorpions and watching them fight each other for entertainment. But what if there were soldiers who literally went to pieces when confronted with alien life forms?

"Let us hope so," Romford said. He smiled, suddenly. "We've also started constructing a holographic training room, where we can test people to the limit. A few more days and we should be able to start offering training that is as close as possible to reality."

"Good," Steve said. He took one last look around the training field. "They're willing to sell?"

"They've been having legal and financial problems lately," Romford said. "There's some problems with operating a mercenary company these days – and the UN really didn't help, when it bitched and moaned about guards doing their damn jobs. And yet, everyone in an unstable place wants trained bodyguards to watch their backs."

He shrugged. "They're willing to fold themselves completely into us," he added, "or continue to operate, as long as they can base themselves on the moon. Our taxes are lower and our regulations pretty much non-existent."

"It will do," Steve said. The more businesses that had interests on the moon, the harder it would be for Earth-bound politicians to interfere with the settlers. "What about recruitment?"

"I will be going," Romford said, shortly. His tone didn't invite disagreement. "I'm building an army here, sir. I'm damned if I won't lead it into battle."

"Or at least some elements of it into battle," Steve commented. The aliens hadn't been too clear on what they actually wanted from their human mercenaries. Reading between the lines, Steve had a feeling they didn't know themselves. "We still don't know precisely what they want from us."

"Shock troops, I suspect," Romford said. "I've studied recordings of enemy cyborgs in action, Steve. They're hard to kill – they're amazingly durable – but apart from that there doesn't seem to be much about them that an unaugmented soldier with intensive training couldn't duplicate."

Steve frowned. "Implanted weapons and neural links?"

"The former we can match with handheld weapons, the latter we may not need," Romford disagreed. "They also don't seem to be long-term thinkers. I suspect they're programmed to be instinctive fighters, but not to think past the current battle. Which could cause us problems, sir. They don't seem to have any concern about committing small atrocities."

Steve winced. "And we will get the blame?"

"Perhaps," Romford said. He looked thoughtful for a long moment. "Or at least we will be considered tainted. But how much freedom of choice do they actually have?"

"Maybe too much," Steve said, remembering just how close he'd come to committing genocide. "Or maybe they're just not programmed to give a damn about civilians in their way."

The thought made him shudder. Someone who grew up in a brutal and ruthless society would probably become brutal and ruthless himself, but there would always be an element of free will. The cyborgs, on the other hand, might have certain fundamentals hardwired into their heads. They might not be able to question their orders, or hold doubts about the justice – or even the expediency – of mass slaughter of innocent civilians. Did that make them guilty? Or was it the aliens who bore the guilt? How could one blame a gun for firing when it was its user who pulled the trigger?

Didn't stop people being afraid of guns, he thought, cynically. *Or trying to ban them…and hanging out their own people for slaughter.*

Romford cleared his throat. "We have two thousand volunteers so far from people who applied to join the lunar society," he said. "Charles has sent out a general request to the other people waiting in line, with the promise of lunar citizenship for them and their families if they accept. Quite a few old-timers have accepted in exchange for rejuvenation treatments, so I've authorised them. I've limited recruitment to Americans, so far, but I would like to change for the second batch. There are quite a few potential recruits in other NATO countries. After that…"

He shrugged. "We'll have to start inviting Russian, Chinese and Indian soldiers," he added. "And probably soldiers from quite a few other countries. There will be problems."

"I know," Steve said.

"But we're not the UN," Romford concluded. "Anyone who causes minor problems will be booted out – and sent back home, if they have been real assholes. And anyone who breaks the ROE will be interrogated, then summarily shot if they fucked up badly enough."

"Just make sure you devise a sensible set of ROE," Steve advised.

"The aliens might devise them for us," Romford said. "But as long as we have a say in the decision, we shouldn't have a problem."

Steve nodded. "Keep me informed," he ordered. "I want to know about any problems as soon as they appear."

"Understood," Romford said.

THIRTY-FOUR

HEINLEIN COLONY, LUNA

"You do realise," Kevin said, "that this is still quite distressing."

Steve looked unsurprised. He'd grown up a little in the last few weeks, Kevin noted, even though he was still being far too casual about his decisions. But at least this would – should - cause fewer immediate problems. The nanotech had hunted down North Korea's stockpile of nuclear warheads and casually disarmed them. It would take a careful inspection to reveal there was a problem and, somehow, Kevin doubted the North Koreans would dare to report any problems if they found them. The Dearest Leader was far too fond of lopping off his subjects heads for them to dare to face him with bad news.

Idiot, he thought, as he stood up. *If you kill the messenger, the only thing you get is less mail.*

"But it's done," Kevin said. "The North Koreans will be unable to fire nukes in all directions, should war break out."

The President had been right, he'd decided, after catching up with the torrent of information from Earth. North Korea *was* starving, there were threats of revolution and the Chinese were completely distracted. Why wouldn't the Dearest Leader gamble? Better to go out in fire than be torn apart by one's own people. But now, between the nanotech and the handful of automated weapons platforms deployed to a position over North Korea, any major offensive across the DMZ would become a squib.

And countless North Koreans will die because of their leader's madness, he thought. It would be simple, almost *too* simple, to remove the Dearest Leader too. But it would almost certainly result in outright civil war and hundreds of thousands of refugees fleeing into the south. It could not be risked until war actually broke out. At that point, the Dearest Leader's lifespan would be numbered in seconds.

He smiled, then led Steve through the network of corridors into the small factory complex. Building it up had required the dedicated use of four shuttles – and he was *so* glad they'd been able to obtain more shuttles on Ying – but it had been completely worthwhile. Now, they could start putting together a handful of nasty surprises for the next Hordesmen to come calling at Earth.

The nuclear techs looked up from their work, then nodded. Most of them had worked for the American government in one role or another, before being invited to come to the moon as part of the joint weapons research program. Not all of them were lunar citizens – they were still loyal to the United States – but as long as they worked on joint defence, no one actually minded. Besides, the more people involved in the theoretical part of the program, the greatest the chance of a significant development.

"These were backpack nukes," Doctor Quinn said. He was younger than Kevin had expected a nuclear scientist to be, with a face that was surprisingly handsome. Some of his female research assistants were absolutely stunning. "Thanks to our modifications, they're now bomb-pumped lasers."

"Excellent work," Steve said. "How do you propose we use them?"

"At the moment, I was going to suggest using them in minefields," Quinn explained. "Our missiles are nowhere near as capable as Galactic-level weapons…and even Galactic missiles are slow, compared to point defence systems. We would need to lure the enemy towards the mines, rather than anything else."

He paused. "The good news is that we can start mass-producing these weapons very soon," he added. "And, with a little reprogramming, the fabricators can actually turn out the nukes."

"Pity about the missiles," Steve commented. "But I see your point."

Kevin nodded in agreement. The fastest spacecraft built using purely human technology crawled, compared to Galactic missiles. But even they couldn't outrace the warning of their arrival, allowing point defence systems to engage them before they entered engagement range. Keith Glass and his partners had several ideas for adapting humanity's concepts to give the aliens a nasty surprise, but most of them were completely untested. The Galactics, it seemed, had the concept of *Superiority*, even if they had never read the book. They didn't dare throw too much of their resources into scientific development out of fear of being overwhelmed by their opponents.

But you'd think they wouldn't have a choice, he thought, as Quinn kept talking, explaining the number of minor improvements they'd made. *Their enemies are slowly gaining on them in any case.*

He waited for Quinn to finish, then led Steve into the next section, where Carolyn was waiting for them. Kevin smiled at her and allowed himself a moment of relief when she smiled back, rather than the odd expressions she'd given him on the ship. He introduced Steve quickly, then looked expectant. Carolyn didn't disappoint.

"We have successfully unlocked the secret of basic antigravity," she said. "I could give you the technobabble" – both Steve and Kevin shook their heads – "but the important part is that we can produce a limited antigravity field on command. We don't have the sheer proficiency of alien technology, at least not yet, but we do have a way to get large amounts of cargo off Earth and into orbit without messing around with booster rockets. The downside" – she paused, significantly – "is that the system isn't particularly stable and requires careful monitoring."

She smiled at their expressions. "But, overall, it's one hell of a step forward," she added. "And we are working on unlocking more of their older secrets. For example, antimatter is actually quite simple to make, once we fabricate the right equipment."

Kevin had to smile. The Galactics had never realised just how many clues their tech manuals, particularly those for technology they considered primitive, could give to the younger races. Maybe they couldn't instantly duplicate Galactic technology, not now, but they *could* start understanding the underpinnings of the more advanced technology and inch towards mastering the best of Galactic science. And if they got some help, perhaps they could advance further forward than anyone dared to dream.

They'd programmed the fabricators not to produce antimatter-production systems. But the unlocked fabricators had no such restrictions. Given time, the human race would be able to produce vast amounts of antimatter too, which could be used as a weapon or converted into another power source. But it wasn't something that could ever be used on a planet's surface. The risk of disaster was too great.

"We could find quite a few uses for antimatter," Kevin mused. "And it would create some interesting problems for anyone who wanted to attack us."

"Good," Steve said, briskly. "How long until we can start mass-production of antigravity units?"

Carolyn considered it. "Give us a few months to produce a finalised design, one attached to a computer specifically designed for monitoring and adjusting the field if necessary," she said. "And then we can start churning them out on demand."

"By then," Kevin put in, "Markus thinks we will have quite a few orbital stations in place to start producing whatever we want."

He shook his head in awe. He'd never realised just how quickly the high-tech firms would move to capitalise on the promise of space-based industries, now space travel had become almost routine. American, European and Japanese firms were scrambling to win contracts and request factories on the moon, while the rest of the planetary economy was struggling to come to terms with the chances wrought in just a few months.

Given time, Kevin suspected, most of the planet's industry would be in space. That, he hoped, would please the Greens.

And once we start fitting antigravity units to cargo aircraft, he thought, *we will soar into outer space.*

They wouldn't be able to control it, he suspected, past a certain point. But they wouldn't have to.

"Very good," Steve said. "But how is it compared to Ying?"

Kevin sobered. "Very poor," he said. "But Ying has been colonised for over a thousand years."

"By a handful of rogues, criminals and refugees," Steve said. "And yet they have a much more advanced industrial base than Earth."

"I know," Kevin said, flatly. "But we have to start somewhere."

He watched Steve's back as he moved from section to section, exchanging words with the researchers and discussing the future with the more personable scientists. If Kevin hadn't known better – and he wasn't sure he *did* know better – he would have said that Steve was depressed. Why would Steve be depressed? He was on the verge of making his dream real!

But he also knows how close he came to damnation, Kevin thought, glumly. *That isn't good for anyone.*

They reached the section monitoring the alien POWs, where they were met by a handful of sociologists and psychologists. Steve listened with apparent interest as they told him how some of the POWs had started to show cracks in their mental conditioning, but Kevin knew better. Steve was only pretending to be interested; the rote responses he offered to their words only confirmed it. Kevin was rather more interested in the long-term implications if they *did* manage to humanise the Hordesmen, but Steve seemed unconcerned.

He needs a holiday, he thought, as they left the section. *But where can he go?*

"Steve," he said, finally. "You're working too hard."

Steve gave him the look he'd always given his younger brother, back when Kevin had been old enough to talk, but not old enough to tell the difference between a really good idea and a recipe for disaster.

"I think I have too much to do," he said, waving a hand around to indicate the lunar colony. "And where would I go, anyway?"

"Find an isolated desert island and go there for a few days with Mariko," Kevin advised. "I think the Maldives have places for millionaires who want to be completely away from the rest of the world. You could book one, then go there and relax."

"I could try," Steve said, "but how could I leave this untended?"

Kevin sighed, inwardly. His brother had never been good at simply abandoning his responsibilities, which was at least partly why he'd had to leave the Marines. He could be stubborn, thick-headed and generally idiotic at times, although he was genuinely devoted to his friends and the ideal of his country. But it also made him unwilling to delegate authority more than he had to.

Or, Kevin thought, *to take a holiday he desperately needs.*

"You have created a staff," he said. "Edward will handle mercenary recruitment, Charles will handle all other recruitment, I will handle intelligence, Rochester will handle the colony…"

"You've made your point," Steve snapped.

"If something happens that requires your attention, you will be called back to the ship," Kevin added. "Until then, you can just relax and take it easy for a few days."

"I don't notice you doing that," Steve muttered. It was the tone he'd used when his brothers were right and he knew it, but he was unwilling to say so out loud. "What about you too?"

"I rested on the flight," Kevin said. On the starship, he'd been completely isolated from the concerns facing Steve and Mongo. "You, on the other hand, have always been monitoring your work. This is the time to take a rest."

He said nothing else until they were in one of the offices and sitting down comfortably. "I think we're going to have to base a permanent team on Ying," he continued. "Both to hunt for starships we can buy, but also to keep track of galactic affairs. Maybe not an embassy, in the usual sense…"

"A spy mission," Steve said. "But do you think the Galactics will notice?"

"I don't think they care," Kevin said. He shrugged. "Would we be really worried if the Maldives set up an operation in New York?"

Steve paused, clearly consulting his interface. "The Maldives are an Islamic nation," he said, after a moment. "We might be worried if they opened a consulate."

"Then use Andorra then," Kevin said. "Somewhere so minor it barely registers."

He shrugged. "We'd need a long-term presence there," he continued. "And probably one in several more nearby star systems. And probably human traders, once we have more starships to use as independent ships."

"I was daydreaming about becoming one," Steve mused. "It would be something different…and it would be something away from Sol."

Kevin nodded. Like it or not, Steve had effectively ruled as a dictator. Either he ran for election, when they finally bothered to hold elections, or he stood aside…but either way, he was going to cast a long shadow over Heinlein Colony and the planned Solar Union. It would be better, far better, if he disappeared from the solar system after the elections, leaving a clear field for the new government. A trading life wouldn't be quite a return to the ranch, but Kevin had a feeling that was no longer a possibility. Steve wouldn't be happy on the ranch after seeing the boundless immensity of space.

"It might be a good idea," he agreed. "But for the moment, you need a break."

He smiled. "I'll sic Mariko on you if you don't agree now," he threatened. "I'm sure she'll force you into it."

"I'd like to see you try," Steve countered. "I dare you to tell her she needs to take a break."

Kevin stared at him, puzzled.

"She went back to New York as soon as we got some proper security in place," Steve explained. "I couldn't talk her out of it."

"Oh," Kevin said. Mariko might be small and slight, but she could be as intimidating as hell when she wanted to be, like pretty much every woman who lived on a ranch. And she was devoted to her medical work. "But…"

Steve smirked at him. "Be brave," he said. "Don't worry about a thing. Little boy with big job to do…"

"Oh, shut up," Kevin said.

Steve sighed. "I'll convince her to come away with me this weekend, all right?"

"If you're brave enough to try," Kevin said. "But really, you need to take a week."

Steve opened his mouth to answer, but his communicator shrilled before he could say a word.

"Sir, this is Tom in Tracking," a voice said. "We're picking up twenty-five separate starships heading towards Earth at FTL speeds. Estimated ETA is five hours from now."

"Those will be the ships Friend promised," Kevin said. "The first down payment for human mercenaries."

"But not warships," Steve mused. "That could be a problem."

"It could," Kevin agreed. "But I think beggars can't be choosers."

Steve jumped to his feet, suddenly galvanised. "Sound the alert," he ordered, as he made preparations to return to the ship. "I want the entire solar system on alert."

Kevin frowned. "Why…?"

"Two reasons," Steve said. He ticked them off on his fingers as he spoke. "First, we need to know just how well the alert system actually works. And second, you might be wrong and these aliens might not be friendly after all."

He was right, Kevin knew. Twenty-five starships were more than enough to overwhelm Earth by an order of magnitude. But he knew

Friend's best interests lay in cooperating with the human race. Human slaves would be far less useful than human allies.

"Good thinking," he conceded, reluctantly. He stood, too. "I'll come with you."

— —

THE NEXT FEW hours passed very slowly. On Earth, military bases were alerted and reserves called up, but there was no formal public announcement. Kevin wasn't too surprised, no matter how much he hated the Government's willingness to defend itself while leaving the civilian population to burn. If there was a widespread panic, there would be absolute chaos and thousands of people would be hurt even if the aliens weren't hostile. Besides, what difference would it make if the aliens deployed antimatter bombs? The entire planet would be cracked open like an egg.

"They're coming out of FTL now," Mongo said. "I'm reading... twenty-three freighters of various designs, one warship and one starship of indeterminate purpose."

"They're hailing us, sir," the communications officer added.

"Then reply," Steve ordered. Left unsaid was the notion that one warship, commanded by a capable crew, might be a match for all three human ships. "Let's see who they are."

There was a brief pause, then a familiar blue-skinned face appeared in front of them. "Mr. Stuart," Friend said. Clearly, he'd been studying the data he'd been sent on humanity. "It is a pleasure to see you again."

"And you," Kevin said, swallowing. "These are my brothers, Steve and Mongo."

"It is a pleasure to meet them too," Friend said. "However, we cannot wait. We will merely give you these starships and leave."

"I understand," Kevin said. The aliens wouldn't want to draw attention to Sol if they could avoid it. "But we will meet again soon."

"Indeed we shall," Friend said. "We shall see you at Ying."

He paused. "We have loaded the freighters with goods you might find useful," he added. "We give you these freely, without obligation. You are welcome to them."

Moments later, his image vanished from the bridge.

Kevin pursed his lips. Was the free gifts a bribe...or a simple consideration...or a display of just how wealthy the aliens actually were? If they could provide so many ships so quickly, just how many did they have in total? But there was no way to know. For all he knew, the aliens had spent a few hours with a fabricator and churned out everything they thought humanity might want – or need.

"Interesting person," Steve observed. He didn't sound too impressed. "Doesn't he want to stay for tea?"

"I think he fears us being noticed," Kevin commented. On the display, flashes of energy were being detected as the freighter crews were beamed onto the unknown starship. "And if Earth became noticed, the results might be dire."

Steve didn't bother to disagree.

THIRTY-FIVE

DEEP SPACE

"**A**nd there has definitely been no sightings?"

"No, Most Supreme Lord," the messenger said, banging his head against the deck. "They went to Earth and were never seen again."

Horde Commander Yss!Yaa cursed under his breath. The messengers were of no Subhorde, something that made them absolutely trustworthy, for his successor would purge them if he managed to take over through assassination or outright coup. But they could also be publically blamed for the message, if someone needed to be a scapegoat. Being a Horde Commander was sometimes more about making sure that someone took the blame than actually leading the Horde.

Three ships, one of them a valuable Warcruiser, had gone missing. It wasn't unusual for the Horde to lose starships, but to lose three of them in the same place suggested enemy action rather than the normal incompetence of his subordinates. The reports had started that Earth's odd-looking inhabitants, the human race, had no starships of their own, but the Horde Commander knew all too well just how much nonsense, misinformation and outright lies made their way through the galactic mainstream. It was quite possible that humanity had a small fleet of starships of their own.

Or the Varnar are protecting them, he thought, morbidly. *They would worry about the source of their cyborg slaves.*

Being a Horde Commander sometimes meant admitting that there were battles that couldn't be won. It was something that would have shocked the vast majority of his followers, who would have preferred death to dishonour. But the Horde Commander understood just how much their nomadic life depended on the more civilised Galactics. If galactic society as a whole decided to eradicate the Hordes, they could do so simply by refusing to sell their wares to the nomads or exterminating them outright through military force. There were times when it was wiser to back down than risk a fight they couldn't win.

But this was something different. The humans either had support from one of the Galactics or they were becoming an interstellar power in their own right. Either way, they had to know the truth – and they had to know what had happened to the missing starships. And they had to do it before the humans found too many allies among the stars. If one or more of the major powers backed them, the Horde would have no choice, but to swallow the insult and return to their wandering ways.

It wasn't something many of his subordinates would have understood, he knew. The Horde Commander, they thought, spent half of his time enjoying the perks of his position. He had the finest cuts of food, the best-looking women and the right to have as many children as he wished. But he also had to swallow his pride, while manipulating events so someone else took the blame. He couldn't show weakness in front of his followers or they would start sharpening knives, largely unaware that the Hordes *were* weak, compared to the Galactics

They dreamed of pillaging their way across the stars, looting and ransacking whole planets. But the Horde Commander knew the truth. They were, at best, scavengers, scavengers utterly dependent on the Galactics. There was no way they could ravage the entire galaxy.

But they needed to know what had happened to their missing starships.

He looked down at the messenger, who had remained in the Posture of Ultimate Respect, extending his head for the sword, if necessary. The Horde Commander felt a pang of...pity, almost regret. He knew just how futile it was to kill the messenger, yet he also felt the same lust for adventure, reckless adventure, that his subordinates shared. Wouldn't it feel good, he knew, to throw caution to the winds and just pillage the nearest worlds? But he knew they would never escape the Galactics when they retaliated.

"Inform my slaves," he said. His subordinates *were* his slaves, as long as he remained strong. But then, slaves had to be constantly reminded of their place. "We will go to Earth."

He watched the messenger crawl out of the compartment, then turned to look at the holographic display. Thirty starships, five of them ten kilometres long, looked an impressive force, but he knew just how many starships the Galactics could deploy. And to think he ruled one of the *larger* Hordes. The Galactics could have built a fleet an order of magnitude larger than his own without raising a sweat.

Go to Earth, find out what happened and back off, if necessary, he thought. He clicked his claws in irritation. *It would be easier if I went alone.*

But that wouldn't be possible, he knew. No matter what orders he gave, the entire Horde now knew they'd lost three ships. They would demand some kind of retaliation, perhaps against a completely innocent target. And if he didn't give them their retaliation, they might well try to overthrow him and take power for themselves. The Horde could not afford a major power struggle in interstellar space. Rumour had it that one Horde had managed to destroy itself through a civil war in their starships, opening them to the vacuum of space.

And if the humans were innocent...?

He snapped his claws together, then turned and walked towards the hatch. It didn't matter, he knew. *Someone* had to pay. And why not a race that couldn't fight back?

"THIS," MARIKO SAID, "is the life."

Steve shrugged, then smiled. He had honestly never considered leaving the United States after he retired from the military, but he had to admit that Mariko was right. The unnamed island, one of thousands that made up the Maldives, was genuinely beautiful. There were shimmering white sands, patches of jungle and a couple of huts on stilts above the water, looking both primitive and modern. Inside, there were beds, a fridge and a small stockpile of microwavable food. There was no one else on the island at all.

He leaned back in his deckchair, allowing the sun to beat down on his exposed chest. It had taken weeks of nagging, from Mariko as well as Kevin, to convince him to take a holiday, but he'd definitely needed it. Relaxing, taking the time to recharge his batteries and consider the future without worrying about the present, seemed to have done him a world of good. It helped that he trusted the people he'd left in charge while he was gone, he decided. He made a mental note to insist that Kevin, Mongo and the others took holidays once he returned home.

The thought struck him, suddenly. When had the starship become *home*?

He couldn't help feeling that he'd betrayed the American Stuarts. His family had built the ranch, after all, and contributed to the town that had grown up nearby. They'd placed great stock in the ranch, relying on it to serve as a training ground for generation upon generation of Stuarts. But he'd practically walked away from the ranch, converting it into an off-world embassy and then a recruitment centre for prospective lunar settlers. He'd never even been able to consider leaving the ranch before.

But Earth felt small and oppressive compared to the boundless vastness of interstellar space.

There are cousins, he thought. Several of them had gone into hiding – or travelled to the moon – when the reporters had started sniffing around, trying to score interviews on the subject of Steve's family life prior to joining the military. The others had sniffed at the very idea of leaving Montana, certainly leaving the state permanently. One of them could take the ranch, if Steve's children – or Mongo's children – didn't want to take it for themselves. As long as it stayed in the family, Steve suspected, the ghosts of his ancestors wouldn't care.

He made a mental note to ask his children about it, then stood and looked over towards the shimmering blue waves. There was something about the gentle lapping of water against the sand that was almost relaxing, even though it also reminded him of crawling through the marshes at night, years ago. Pushing the thought out of his head, he walked towards the water and allowed the waves to wash over his feet, slipping and sliding as the sand shifted under his weight. Bracing himself, he stepped further into the water until he could swim properly, then started to swim around the entire island. It was small enough that he could circumnavigate it in less than ten minutes.

It wasn't a challenging swim, something he found mildly disappointing. But the island had been billed as a private resort, a place where someone would have to be very stupid or unlucky to get themselves killed. Compared to some of the training he'd done, it was pathetic. But it was fun to relax, just for a while. Maybe, he told himself, he'd swim out to sea later and see what happened out there, past the barrier reef. If worst came to worst, he still had the interface. He could signal for emergency teleport if necessary.

Mariko waved to him as he came back into view, after swimming around the hut and coming back into the lagoon. Steve sucked in his breath, then powered through the water towards where she was standing, at the very edge of the water. She looked timeless, somehow, utterly beautiful despite the straightness of her body. Steve didn't care about the size of her breasts, or the boyish hips, merely the essence that was *her*. He came charging out of the water and ran towards her.

Afterwards, they returned to the hut and hunted through the fridge for something tasty. Steve hadn't expected much from the microwave, but the pre-prepared foods were actually surprisingly nice, far better than any of the TV dinners he'd eaten on leave. It had puzzled him until Mariko pointed out that most people who visited the island would be wealthy enough to afford the best, as well as absolute privacy. Steve didn't want to *think* about how much they were spending, even if it was cheap compared to the constant flow of money in and out of the lunar colony. He hadn't been raised to spend money excessively.

He smiled at the thought. His grandmother would have sneered at the very idea of going on holiday. To her, fifty or sixty miles from the ranch was foreign territory. God alone knew what sort of infidels lived there. But then, she'd been the daughter of a soldier, married to another soldier and mother of yet more soldiers. Most of her opinions of the outside world would have been shaped by their stories of the less-pleasant parts of the planet. Wars, after all, seldom showed places to their best advantage.

"I read the guidebook," Mariko said. She nodded towards the plastic containers. "None of this is remotely *local*."

Steve wasn't too surprised. Some people travelled to experience, but others merely went somewhere – like him – to recharge their batteries. The latter wouldn't want strange foreign food when they could have American-style meals shipped in from the United States. Steve wasn't too sure what to make of it. He'd eaten some strange things in Iraq – and he had to admit there was comfort in the familiar – but why go halfway around the world to eat food they could have found anywhere at home?

"Maybe we should go to Mali later," he said. They *did* have a speed-boat, after all, or they could simply teleport to the city-island. "See what we can find that's more local."

Mariko shrugged as she placed the trays in the microwave and turned it on. "I don't think I'd like it," she confessed. "The whole island is one giant city."

Steve nodded in agreement. It was odd, but most of his memories of large cities were marred by war. He'd spent more time in Bagdad and Fallujah than he'd spent in Washington or New York. Why would any-one, he'd asked himself as a child, choose to live in the cities when they could live in the countryside instead? But most people, he knew now, couldn't afford to live in the country. *And*, when they did, they started trying to change it to fit some ideal they'd gleaned from watching bad movies and reading junk science.

He smiled at the thought. *That* was one thing Heinlein Colony – and the smaller Wells Colony on Mars - had already experienced, although from people on Earth rather than settlers on the moon. They whined about terraforming the planet, they whined about mining for water and HE3, they whined about setting up farms…as if they could afford to import food from Earth indefinitely. Didn't people have enough troubles of their own to keep them busy?

Mariko cleared her throat, drawing his attention back to her. "What do you want to eat?"

Steve hastily replayed her words in his mind. She'd asked if he wanted curry or microwavable burgers. "Curry," he said, quickly. Like most women in his experience, Mariko got annoyed if she thought she was being ignored. "It will make a change."

"And you make better burgers of your own anyway," Mariko teased. "Far better than anything you get in the cities, right?"

Steve nodded. Her skill at reading his face was remarkable.

He stood and walked towards the balcony as she put the food in the microwave, staring out over the endless blue sea. In the distance, he could see waves breaking over the barrier reef that shielded the island from the ocean and tiny lights where other inhabited islands were preparing for darkness. They had sometimes heard planes flying overhead, but apart from the boat that had brought them to the island they'd seen no other boats. The resort owners kept all traffic away from their islands, jealously guarding their right to ship travellers to and from the resorts.

And make sure they collect as much money as they can, Steve thought, cynically. The Maldives had been largely isolated from the Middle Eastern economic depression, but they'd once had Arab Princes coming to the islands for a holiday away from public observance of Islamic Law. Officially, the islands were Islamic, but money talked louder than the Qur'an, particularly when the area was dependent on tourists. But now, there were few Arab Princes who had the funds to spare for a holiday. The smarter ones had already fled the region for Europe. There, at least, they would be safe from their vengeful populations.

There was a *ding* from the microwave. Steve turned, just in time to see Mariko pull the containers out of the machine and pour the contents onto the plates. She picked them both up and walked over to the balcony, passing Steve his plate as she walked through the door. A cool wind was blowing over the sea now, something of a relief after the heat of the day. Steve sat on the steps leading down to the water and smiled at her. After a moment, she joined him and sat down to eat.

"This isn't too bad," Steve said. Compared to some of the curries he'd eaten in Iraq, it was downright mild. The Marines had joked that the Iraqis deliberately made the curries hot as a test of manliness. Steve, however, recalled the medic saying that the meat wasn't always the best, which explained outbreaks of the dreaded D&V. The spice often helped cover up the poor quality of meat. "It could be worse."

Mariko elbowed him. "It could be better too, couldn't it?"

Steve shrugged, placed his empty plate on the floor and put his arm around her as the stars began to come out. High overhead, the stars competed with the reflected light from humanity's vastly expanded presence in space. Two fast-moving glints of light were almost certainly inflatable space stations, while others might well be the freighters Friend had sent them or one of the captured warships. Steve smiled, unpleasantly, as he contemplated the freighters. Human ingenuity, matched with alien technology, had started preparing a few nasty surprises for anyone who wanted to invade the Sol System. He had no illusions about the outcome if the Galactics really wanted Earth, but the bastards would have to fight to take the planet. And, even then, parts of humanity would be free.

He smiled, remembering just how many men and women had gone out to the asteroids over the past month. The MSM had called them everything from dupes to suicidal fools, but Steve knew better. They understood the risks, yet they were prepared to chance everything to make a new life for themselves in the new Wild West. Many of them would die,

Steve knew, but they would make history. And hidden colonies among the asteroids would help ensure the survival of the human race.

The thought made him smile. A year or two would allow him to produce a generational starship, one that could be launched out into the galaxy at STL speeds. If something really bad happened to Earth, the starship would survive and – hopefully – set up a new colony somewhere else. And, when they had more FTL starships, one of them would convey a colony mission well beyond the edges of galactic space.

They stayed outside until the moon began to rise, then stood up and went inside. Steve kissed her on the lips, then pulled her towards the bed. Mariko smiled, then kissed him back. Steve gently reached down to her bikini and started to undo it, kissing his way down to her nipples and enjoying the taste of her in his mouth. And then the interface buzzed.

"Steve, it's Kevin," a voice said. Steve bit down the urge to swear virulently. Kevin didn't have any idea of what he'd interrupted. "We have a political problem."

"I should have known," Steve commented. He reached for his dressing gown and pulled it on. Beside him, Mariko did the same. "I relax and look what happens."

He sighed. "Two to beam up," he added. "And this had damn well better be important."

THIRTY-SIX

Kevin had been trained, long ago, in reading the subtle signs of their body language. A person pretending to be annoyed, his tutors had taught him, tended to overact as badly as a child actor and start shouting in outrage at the drop of a hat. Body language wasn't entirely universal – it hadn't been universal even before the humans had first encountered the Galactics – but there were plenty of points of similarity. And all of his training was telling him that Steve was very definitely annoyed.

He looked at Mariko. Unlike Steve, she was more composed, but there was a faint flush to her face that told Kevin *precisely* what they'd been doing when he'd interrupted them. Kevin sighed, inwardly, silently cursing their bad luck. If the whole affair had waited a few more days, Steve could have dealt with it without having to deal with sexual frustration too. Or, perhaps, nipped it in the bud before it got out of hand.

"This could become a major problem," Kevin said, once they were seated in Steve's cabin. "And it needs to be handled carefully."

"No one has ever accused me of being subtle," Steve commented, dryly. "Why didn't you handle it yourself?"

Kevin sighed, out loud. "Because this requires your personal attention," he said. "Because it could have a major long-term effect on our
relationship with Earth's various governments. Because..."

Steve held up a hand. "All right," he said. "What – precisely – has
happened?"

"We've had a request for asylum," Kevin said.

"Oh," Steve said. "*Another* one?"

Kevin scowled. The previous requests had been from men and women
fleeing political, economic, religious or sexual persecution. They'd all
been given the same chance to make it on the moon, with an added note
that they would not be permitted to interfere in the affairs of their former
home countries. Quite a few of them had accepted the warning, one or
two had tried to steer events back home from the moon before they'd
been given a sharp rebuke for breaking the terms of their citizenship. But
this was different.

"Thomas Flynn," Kevin said. "Have you ever heard of him?"

Steve shook his head. Mariko nodded.

"He was accused of rape and murder, wasn't he?" She said. "I remember reading about it a year or two ago."

"He's an American citizen who studied in Germany for some reason,"
Kevin said. "While he was there, he was accused of raping and murder-
ing a German girl. There was no certain proof, but he spent two years in
a German jail before being allowed to go home – and now the Germans
want him back. He went to us and requested asylum."

Steve leaned forward. "Is there a chance he *will* be sent back to
Germany?"

"More than I'd like to admit," Kevin said. "Right now, relations with
Europe aren't very good. They're blaming the federal government for
us, believe it or not, and there's a strong field of thought in Europe that
thinks the Americans are going to get away with it again. So it's a political and diplomatic nightmare."

"I see," Steve said. "Why do I have the feeling that he was *allowed* to
flee to us?"

"I have no doubt," Kevin said tightly, "that the Europeans will raise precisely that issue."

Steve rubbed his forehead. "I don't see this as being a major problem," he said. "Tell him that we will take him in, under the same conditions as everyone else, if he agrees to undergo a lie detector test. If he's innocent, we will inform the German Government and insist that they abandon their pursuit of him. If he's guilty, he will be judged under our law."

"If he's guilty, he would be a fool to insist on pushing us," Kevin observed. "Rape and murder...they're among the worst crimes a person can commit."

He smiled at the thought. Lunar justice, having the ability to definitely separate the guilty from the innocent, was not soft. If found guilty, Thomas Flynn would be introduced to the joys of breathing hard vacuum. But if he was innocent...Kevin shook his head, remembering just how much trouble the DHS had proved over the years. Wasn't anyone smart enough, these days, to realise that admitting failure wasn't the same as suicide? But he wasn't too surprised, sadly. Success often went unrewarded, but failure always drew fire from politicians out for a few soundbites. The German police probably had the same problem.

"Yes, he would be," Steve said. "But this isn't the only person who came to us with a criminal record."

Kevin nodded. In the long run, he suspected, perfect lie detectors would change society as much as anything else. Why bother with an expensive trial when a suspect could be interrogated, then either jailed or released? But it would cause problems too, he knew. What was to stop someone from being interrogated on just about any subject? Like so much else they'd pulled from the alien databases, lie detectors were very much a double-edged sword.

He scowled, inwardly. There were several people on the moon talking about forming a canton of their own, a canton where everyone would wear personal lie detectors at all times. If anyone lied, it would sound an alarm and the speaker would be gravely embarrassed. There were some advantages, Kevin had thought, to such an arrangement, but they would also cause very real problems. What would happen if someone lied without knowing they were lying? The lie detectors could only pick up deliberate lies.

Maybe it would prove that the liar didn't intend to lie, Kevin thought. *Or maybe it would create another set of headaches because they misunderstood the difference between a lie and a mistake.*

"I'll take your message to him," Kevin said. "And do we want to do the same in future?"

"If people are being persecuted by governments, then yes," Steve said. "But we must always reserve the right to issue punishment if they are guilty."

"Which leads to another problem," Kevin pointed out. "What do we do if the person is guilty by their laws, but not by ours?"

It was easy to imagine quite a few possibilities. There were no laws restricting gun ownership on the moon, although there were dire punishments for anyone stupid enough to threaten the integrity of the lunar settlement. Nor were there any laws on self-defence, drug abuse or quite a few other issues that were criminal matters on Earth. Kevin could imagine several problems if drug abusers sought out the right to live on the moon. He didn't give a damn if someone wanted to drug themselves into a stupor every day, but if they posed a threat to anyone else...

Mariko smiled. "We can offer to take them in, while their home country can cancel their citizenship if they wish," she said. "And we can warn them that what laws we *do* have are not to be trifled with, not lightly."

"True," Kevin agreed. One problem with letting juries decide everything – including the simple question of if the criminal act was actually a *crime* – was that the results could be somewhat variable. But, as they built up much more case law, he had a feeling that problem would slowly resolve itself. "Steve?"

"Make it so," Steve said.

Kevin rolled his eyes. The discovery that Gene Roddenberry hadn't been too far wrong about the development of technology had given the *Star Trek* franchise a new lease on life. There were even suggestions that humanity's first starships should be modelled after the *USS Enterprise* or even *Voyager*. But, apart from the *Defiant*, there were few *Star Trek* starships that were actually practical as warships.

Still, we could build an Enterprise-D and call it a long-range exploration ship, he thought, dryly. *But may God help her if she runs into someone smarter than the Horde.*

"I'll see to it," he said. "And I'm sorry for interrupting your vacation."

"I bet you are," Steve growled. "Just you wait until *you* take a vacation."

Kevin swallowed. Steve was far from cruel, but he did have a nasty sense of humour, despite their mother's stern lectures. But then, he did have good reason to be annoyed. If Kevin had known just what they'd been doing, he would have let them finish before calling and requesting that they join him on the ship. Maybe that would have made them both feel better.

"I'll rest on the ship," he said. The first group of mercenaries were midway through their basic training, according to Romford. They'd be ready to leave Earth within two weeks; Kevin knew he'd be going with them. They needed to gather more intelligence and set up a permanent base on Ying, after all. And then they needed to set up other bases on other inhabitable worlds. "No rest for the wicked."

"And to think we always thought you intelligence officers spent the days making up shit and the nights trying to get into someone's pants, so you could betray her to the MSM," Steve teased. "You actually did serious work?"

Kevin nodded, expressively.

"Oh," Steve said. He smiled. "Seeing we're here, what's the current status with Mars and the other colonies?"

"The new ships have helped us move several thousand volunteers to the Red Planet," Kevin said, "now we have the bare bones of a colony to hold them. So far, there's been no major trouble, apart from a handful of rainstorms. General reports suggest that the engineered plants are taking root, but it's far too early to be sure. We may need to insert more water from Titan or a few more asteroids in the near future.

"Titan Base is slower, but coming along now that we're training up hundreds of new workers to start laying the foundations of a colony," he continued. "The plan to establish the mass driver first seems to be working, which will allow us to use Titan as a base for water collection and distribution. But it will be several months before we're ready to proceed. Until then, Mars is going to be dependent on asteroids."

He shrugged. "And the plans for terraforming Venus are being finalised," he concluded. "But it will be a harder chore than terraforming Mars."

"Well begun is half done," Steve said. "And there will be plenty of room for humanity when it is finished."

Kevin smiled. Despite the very best of human and alien medical science, it was unlikely that any of them would live long enough to walk on Mars or Venus without protective gear. But Steve hadn't let that stop him start the terraforming process. Their children would thank them, even if the current generation was more interested in the asteroids than the uninhabitable worlds. Besides, the Mars Society was already trying to create its own canton.

"Politically, Mars wants to move ahead to internal self-government," he added. "I think it's a little early, but they're determined."

Steve hesitated, then smiled. "They're still going to be dependent on us for a long time, aren't they?"

"Yes," Kevin said, flatly. "It will be years before Mars develops an industry of its own."

He shook his head. Neither he nor Steve had really grasped just how much effort the Mars Society had put into planning the settlement of Mars. Their ten-year plans might not have been tested, but at least they had a framework to use for settlement. Heinlein, on the other hand, had been pretty much an *ad hoc* affair. In the long run, it would be interesting to see which vision of the future prevailed.

"Then tell them that as long as they abide by the terms of the Solar Union Treaty, they can have their political independence," Steve said. "We don't want to rule them indefinitely in any case."

Kevin nodded. There were only two real rules for the Solar Union, the planned association of cantons that would make up humanity's interplanetary government. They had to allow free access to the datanet and free emigration, if their settlers wanted to leave. In the long run, decently-run cantons would do much better than cantons that were run by oppressive governments or outright tyrants. The tyrants would, eventually, find themselves ruling over empty asteroids.

Or planets, he thought, morbidly.

He had his doubts about the wisdom of allowing the Mars Society completely free rein, but if people could leave at will it probably didn't matter. Planning was important, yet he knew from bitter experience that plans rarely lasted when confronted with reality. If the Mars Society insisted on sticking to its plans, the results were unlikely to be good. But it was their task now, if they wanted it. And if their people didn't like it, they could always leave.

And that is one right we will enforce, he thought, bitterly. *Nothing else, but that.*

"Very good," he said. "Do you want to return to your holiday?"

Steve glared at him, then sobered. "I think we'll come back to the ship in a day or two anyway," he said. "I've relaxed for far too long."

"Mongo can take the island in your place," Kevin said. "I think Jayne and he probably need a break too."

"Good thinking," Steve said. "And how is Carolyn?"

Kevin flushed. "She's fine," he said. "And working on the first anti-gravity system."

"That wasn't what I meant," Steve said. "Have you and her...?"

Mariko elbowed Steve, hard. Kevin concealed his amusement behind a blank face. He'd taken Carolyn out to dinner every time he'd visited the moon, but their relationship hadn't gone much further. It was both frustrating and tantalising; the more he thought about her, the more he realised that she was almost an ideal partner for him. But did she feel the same way?

"Not yet," he said, tightly. "But we shall see."

"What a shame," Steve commented archly, "that you don't get to walk around with a suit, a gun and girls on each arm."

Kevin snorted. "When I get my hands on the man who invented James Bond," he said, "I'm going to strangle him."

"You'll have to hold a séance," Steve countered. "He's been dead for years."

"*Men*," Mariko said. "Kevin, if you're genuinely interested in her, give it time. And if you're not, stop messing around and get back to work."

Kevin nodded, then watched as Steve and Mariko made their way out of the cabin. He shook his head, ruefully, then accessed the interface and called Komura. There was political work to do.

— —

"I'VE SPOKEN TO Mr. Flynn," Komura said, an hour later. "He's willing to undergo the lie detector test if we swear we'll take him."

Kevin resisted the temptation to snort, rudely. *Teenagers.* Didn't they have any idea just how many people gave their solemn word in one breath and broke it in the next? Actually, they probably did…but if Flynn was innocent, he probably wasn't feeling much trust in adults and any sort of government official at the moment. And if he was guilty…

"Good," he said. "Make it clear that he will suffer *our* punishment if we discover he's guilty."

He couldn't help wondering if that would cause more of a diplomatic incident than anything else. The Germans presumably wanted to punish him themselves, even though they wouldn't kill him or do anything more than lock him up for a number of years. They might not even insist he served his full sentence, too. Liberal justice systems, in Kevin's mind, often ensured that the punishment did not fit the crime. But then, they also often had skewed ideas of what *was* a crime.

It was nearly another hour before Komura got back in touch with him. "He's innocent," he said, shortly. "He didn't kill the girl, he doesn't know who did and he hates the German government."

"Not our problem," Kevin said. "Have him moved to Heinlein – he can go into one of the basic introductory courses until we know where he will fit in. And make sure that full copies of the interrogation record are placed online. Let the Germans download it and see that they nearly jailed an innocent man."

He sighed, inwardly. In the long run, the Germans had badly damaged their cause. How many others, threatened with extradition, would use this as an excuse to delay or cancel their departures from American soil? And, for that matter, what would happen when a real criminal requested extradition?

What a fucking headache, he thought.

Shaking his head, he walked over to the console and started to tap in orders. The bloggers on the moon could start the ball rolling, ensuring that they got as much good publicity as possible. He had a feeling they were going to need it. Given time, the Germans might use the whole affair as an excuse to meddle with the new world order.

Or perhaps they will learn something from the whole affair, he thought, instead. *If nothing else, the real killer is still unidentified. He must be laughing his ass off at the Germans – but not at us. Now the mistake is known, it can be fixed.*

He sighed, again. The technology they had could be used to prevent all crime. A few billion nanotech surveillance drones, a handful of powerful computers to monitor their take…and crime would become a thing of the past. But the price would be a total loss of privacy and freedom. No one would be able to do anything without being observed. It would become a nightmare even if there was no Big Brother watching everyone. The entire human race would become neurotic.

But isn't that the promise and threat of the future, he asked himself. *The eternal balance between good and ill, between freedom and slavery, between the ideals of the future and the curse of the past?*

In truth, he conceded, he had no answer. All he could do was wait and see.

THIRTY-SEVEN

MONTANA, USA

"**E**arth's 1st Interstellar Regiment," Romford said. "Reporting for duty, sir!"

Steve had to smile. Seven thousand men, most of them former American military officers and personnel, had passed through the training camp; five thousand, six hundred had graduated. Romford's reports made interesting reading – there had been soldiers who had been unable to face the aliens, officers who thought they should automatically be given command positions – but in the end the really bad ones had been weeded out. Future officers, he'd quietly promised himself, would follow the Marine concept of rising from the ranks, having served as riflemen first. It helped ensure they knew what they were doing.

"Good," he said. He stepped forward and up onto the podium. He'd never reviewed troops before, but he'd taken time to cut the ceremony down to the bare minimum. It was always irritating to have to stand for hours while some politician pontificated on a subject dear to their hearts. Most of the time, it consisted of meaningless words and phrases. Bracing himself, Steve keyed the mike. "I won't waste your time."

A thin ripple of amusement ran through the assembled ranks of soldiers. Steve concealed his own amusement and continued.

"Many have said that you are mercenaries," he said. "Many have accused you of going off to shed alien blood in alien wars. Many have accused you of being nothing more than guns-for-hire, men and women who are paid to fight whoever the paymaster wants you to fight. But those people do not understand the true situation. You are going to fight beside aliens we desperately need as allies. And you are going to fight for Earth.

"Make no mistake. Barely a year ago, we knew nothing of affairs out beyond the edge of Earth's atmosphere. Now, we know that great interstellar powers wage war constantly, with human slaves serving in their armies. Now, we know we need to prepare for the coming struggle for a place in the universe, for independence, for survival itself. You are the ones who will learn about the universe and bring your lessons back to us, to help us prepare for the oncoming storm.

"I wish I could promise that it would be easy. I wish I could promise that each and every one of you will return, one day, to Earth. I can make no such promises. But what I can promise is that Earth will never forget you. History will enshrine your names for the rest of time – and Earth's survival will be your legacy."

He paused. "I'm not very good at making speeches, am I?

"I want you to know that you have my gratitude for volunteering and that, one day, you will have the eternal gratitude of Earth. And that's enough speechifying from me. See you at the spaceport in a week."

There was a brief cheer, then the soldiers started to scatter. Most of them, Steve knew, would head for the nearest town for food, drink and women, the last they would see of anything remotely human for several months at the very least. A handful would head home, if they were willing to use the teleporter, or stay on the base and write their wills. Some of them simply didn't have anywhere to go.

"No," Romford agreed, breaking into his thoughts. "You're not a very good speechwriter."

Steve flushed, then shook his head. "At least it wasn't faked," he said. "Not like a political verbal orgasm."

"True," Romford agreed. "I assume you have a shipping plan?"

"Yes," Steve said. "Two of the freighters will carry you and your men to Ying, where you will meet up with our allies. At that point, you should receive the supplies they promised; if you don't, or there are problems with the supplies, work with them to fix it."

He sighed. The aliens had promised everything from cybernetic enhancement to suits of powered combat armour. Given the sheer productive might of their fabricators, they could afford to fabricate literally millions upon millions of battlesuits – or anything else the human race might need to arm its soldiers. And, if there were problems with the first batch, they could easily put together another set of equipment within the first few days.

"And if they turn out to be a real problem," he added. "Use your own best judgement."

"I will," Romford said. "These men, Steve, will not be wasted."

Steve nodded. The soldiers were a diverse lot; soldiers, sailors and airmen from America, joined by a relative handful of retired soldiers from other English-speaking countries. Some of them had been old, on the verge of death, or badly crippled like Romford before they'd been recruited. Most of the ancient veterans would have signed away their souls for a chance to return to the battlefield one last time. Retraining them on Galactic-standard equipment had been one hell of a mission. But it had been done.

"Good," Steve said. "Have there been any major problems?"

"Had a few thousand protestors at the fence for a week or two," Romford said, "and caught a number trying to sneak into the base. They stopped doing that after we put them to hard labour for a few days before releasing them. Oh, and we're being sued by their families."

Steve snorted. The agreement between Heinlein Colony and the United States agreed that the training camp wasn't – legally – part of the United States, just like an embassy. Anyone who crossed the fence was entering a territory where the laws were different – and, if they crossed the fence in any case, they were breaking and entering. There were no legal grounds to sue Steve and his people for arresting intruders, or for giving them a small punishment before they were released.

"Not much of a problem," he said. "And the men themselves?"

"We weeded out most of the idiots and glory-seekers within the first week," Romford assured him. "Most of our discipline problems were handled at the same time. Right now, I have faith in both the selected officers and NCOs. If there's one advantage of giving our allies more soldiers than they asked for, it's that we can rotate officers and NCOs back to Earth to give lessons to newer recruits."

Steve smiled. "And are there newer recruits?"

"A surprising number," Romford said. He shrugged, expressively. "It could be the lust for adventure or the extremely generous benefits, but we have more volunteers than we have space to train. So far, we're giving priority to men and women with genuine military experience from the Western countries, although we have quite a number of qualified candidates from Russia too. The Chinese, on the other hand, seem quite reluctant to allow any of their personnel to sign up with us.

"Given time, I suspect we will have thousands of potential recruits from poorer parts of the world too," he added. "But that will cause other problems."

Steve nodded. Americans and other Westerners were generally well-educated – and they could all speak English. Working with soldiers from other parts of the world had convinced him that the foreigners had their own way of doing things, not all of them remotely compatible with the American Way of War. But there would be no need to humour or tolerate the locals, not now. Those who failed to make it through the training program would have no opportunity to embarrass the human race in front of the Galactics.

"Just make sure you exclude the ones who can't make it," Steve said. "What about expanding the camp?"

"I think we will have to lease somewhere else," Romford said. "Right now, the American Government is cooperating, but that might change. We are, after all, training mercenaries here."

Steve rolled his eyes. The American Government had been training mercenaries, rebel armies and foreign soldiers for years, although not all of the students had gone home brimming with love for America. There was little point in the political objections, he knew, save for a desire to look good in front of the voters. But politicians rarely changed their spots when confronted with reality.

"Start looking for somewhere else, then," he said. "It will be years before Mars or Venus is ready to serve as a training camp."

"I've been making enquires," Romford said. "Panama is a possibility – quite a few of my team have great memories from Panama – but we'd have to pay out a shitload in bribes. I don't see anywhere in Europe accepting us, at least not without a fairly hefty *quid pro quo* – maybe additional fusion reactors. Right now, if we are restricting ourselves to democracies, we may be restricted to Australia. They're quite interested in hosting one of our camps."

Steve gave him an odd look, so Romford explained.

"They're nervous about troubles spreading over from Indonesia," Romford explained. "If we want to put a camp there, they will be quite happy with it in exchange for assistance if they need it. There will be a few basic rules, but no real difference from what we have here."

"I'll speak to Komura," Steve said. "He can open discussions."

He shrugged. "Have we had any problems that might give them pause?"

"A couple of bar fights," Romford said. "One of our guys was called a baby-killer, so he hauled off and punched the bastard…and everything went down from there. Another guy was set upon by a group of thugs and defended himself admirably. Other than that, no major problems. I have made it clear that American law runs outside the fence and if anyone gets into trouble with the law we won't get off our asses to do anything about it if they're guilty."

"Good thinking," Steve said. "We don't want another rape case."

His father, he recalled, had ranted about a rape case in Okinawa, where an American serviceman had raped a local girl. The bastard should have been strung up by his testicles, Steve's father had thundered, or handled over to the locals as soon as his guilt had been established. No matter the outcome, it had discouraged the locals from wanting to keep the American military presence.

And if one of my men do something like that, Steve thought, coldly. *He'd damn well pray that the local government gets to him before me.*

"Quite," Romford agreed. "Not that *that* will be a problem, Steve. There are four new brothels in town."

Steve snorted. "Why am I not surprised?"

"The men have their new immune boosters," Romford said. "They can fuck an AIDS-infested whore from Tijuana and they won't be in any danger of actually catching anything. Or pregnancy, for that matter. We've given just about everyone – particularly the women – contraceptive implants, just to make sure there's no risk of pregnancy. But we may want to set up a brothel on Ying or another alien world."

"Maybe," Steve said. "What do the aliens think of it?"

"I went through their contracts," Romford said. "I don't believe they would have any objections, as long as it didn't interfere with military matters. We have quite a lot of freedom to determine how best to handle our affairs."

Steve nodded. If two different human cultures could have different requirements, how much harder would it be for two alien races to live by the same rules? There were races where one sex was unintelligent, races that had more than two sexes, races that laid eggs and didn't have sex as humans understood it, races that had sex anywhere and everywhere they could…and that was only one tiny aspect of the whole. What would happen when there were different religious requirements? Or food and drink? At least food professors could produce something edible to humanity, even if it didn't always taste nice. But that was just a matter of programming.

"Make sure you don't compromise our combat effectiveness," he said. "Other than that, make whatever arrangements you like."

He accepted an invitation to walk through the combat simulator and marvel at just how perfect a simulator it actually was. A combination of holographic images, force fields and gravity wave generators allowed the system to reproduce almost any combat environment, from urban-style warfare to operations in outer space. And the simulator computers tracked the whole system so perfectly that there was no need for proper umpires.

"We actually programmed the teleporter to yank anyone out if they're recorded as dead," Romford explained. "In high-intensity operations, anything tough enough to burn through a suit will very definitely kill the person inside. Low-intensity operations are probably not going to be part of our work, but we train for them anyway. One major problem is that we have little room to deploy medics. And even if we did..."

Steve winced. Humans were humans under the skin, but aliens could be very alien. Perhaps that explained why the aliens had produced autodoc systems and other automated forms of medical care; there weren't any doctors who were capable of moving from a patient of one race to a patient from another. The movie where an alien had been dissected by a vet might have been quite realistic after all.

"We should try to avoid such operations," he said, although – not being a politician – he had no illusions about the prospect of switching from high-intensity combat to low-intensity in a heartbeat. "If we do, try to keep civilians out of the fighting as much as possible."

Romford gave him a sharp glance, then nodded.

Steve reviewed the rest of the base, then teleported back to the starship to catch up on his briefings. Heinlein had expanded rapidly, to the point where two hotels had been constructed and regular tours were running from the colony to the various tourist attractions on the moon, while other tourists were being lined up for trips to Mars. Each of them was paying a substantial price for their tickets, which was going right back into the economy.

"We may well have solved the economic crisis," Wilhelm said, after he'd finished talking about the new technology he'd introduced on Earth. "Right now, literally trillions of dollars worth of currency is moving around the world, thanks to us."

"Good," Steve said. International finance had always been a closed book to him, but he was prepared to accept Wilhelm's word that more money moving around was a good thing. "Are there any problems? Or are we *causing* any problems?"

"It depends," Wilhelm realised. "You know there's a shortage of plumbers?"

Steve shook his head, not seeing the point.

"Space habitation involves a lot of plumbing," Wilhelm said. "So we've been hiring plumbers – and other outfitters – at a terrifying rate. The net result is that we have driven down the number of plumbers available elsewhere."

"Oh," Steve said.

Wilhelm shrugged. "We've got several training camps up and running for newcomers, so I think this problem will eventually restore itself," he said. "We may also have solved the education bubble."

He snorted. "We don't care about professional qualifications," he explained, when Steve looked puzzled. "So we've been taking college-age students, exposing them to some proper training, then selecting the best. Our wages are high, so they can start paying off their debts in good order. Given time, maybe we can defuse that particular problem before it actually explodes. On the other hand, we have quite a few idiots who majored in Women's Studies trying to learn which end of a screwdriver is the one they shouldn't stick in an electrical socket."

Steve frowned. "And are they actually learning something useful?"

"Oh, yes," Wilhelm said. "We came up with some pretty graphic training videos to make it clear to them that mistakes would be harshly punished by the universe. And we made them all read *The Cold Equations* and write essays explaining how a series of minor bureaucratic oversights led to tragedy. Quite a few of them quit after reading the story.

"Overall, there will be quite a few bumps, but I think that most Western governments will quietly abandon any opposition to us within the next ten years," he concluded. "We're just too damn useful. And we're taking potential troublemakers away from them. The rest of the world... not so much."

Steve nodded. "Russia still irked at us?"

"I'm afraid so, even though we're buying a lot of crude technology from them," Wilhelm said, dryly. "I think they might well have real problems in the non-too-distant future, between the dongles and the introduction of fusion technology. Their public might start asking too many questions. China, on the other hand, might just adapt once again to the change in the world."

"We shall see," Steve said. He had no love for Red China, but he had to admire how the Chinese had adapted and just kept adapting as the world changed around them. And, somehow, the Communist Party had remained in control. Would that change, he asked himself, when their people had total freedom of communication? No matter what the government did, dongles were still slipping into China. "We shall see."

The communicator buzzed. "Steve," Mongo said, "we're picking up a number of starships approaching the solar system. They're completely unscheduled. Estimated time of arrival is five hours from now."

Steve shared a long look with Wilhelm. There was no such thing as a schedule, but they weren't expecting any visitors. It was possible that Friend could be returning to Earth, yet the alien had agreed to meet the human troops at Ying. No, he realised. It was far more likely that the newcomers were unfriendly.

"Deploy the automated defences," he ordered. It was time to use a precaution he'd hoped never to have to use, at least for quite some time. Even now, if they lost Earth, something of humanity would survive. "And then order the *Mayflower* to leave orbit."

"Aye, sir," Mongo said.

"I'm on my way," Steve said, straightening up. "And you'd better warn the governments below. The shit is about to hit the fan."

THIRTY-EIGHT

SOL SYSTEM

"Earth's governments have been alerted," Kevin said, quietly. "They're standing by."

Steve gave him a sidelong look. "For *what?*"

"For what little they can do," Kevin replied, evenly. "And for civil defence, if necessary."

"True," Steve said. He looked back at the display. Thirty incoming starships, some of them clearly very large. If they wanted to take Earth, Earth would be taken. "And maybe they can swear blind that they have nothing to do with us too."

He thought, briefly, of Mariko. She'd flatly refused to go down to Earth or board the *Mayflower*, even though the latter would have given her an excellent chance of survival. Instead, she'd insisted on staying on the Warcruiser, despite the certain knowledge that the giant starship would be badly outmatched. Steve cursed himself, mentally, for not marrying her when he had the chance, even though he had no intention of leaving her at some later date. It would have shown just how much he cared.

Angrily, he pushed the thought aside. Earth's time might be about to run out. He shouldn't be thinking of anything but fighting to defend his homeworld, the world he loved. And he did love it. In the end, Earth was worth fighting for. But did he have enough tricks up his sleeve to save the planet?

"The ghost squadron and the Q-ships are in position," Mongo called. "They're ready to deploy."

"Hold them in place," Steve ordered. They'd run through countless simulations, trying to think of all possible contingencies, but the universe had presented them with overwhelming force. They could do everything right and still lose Earth to the enemy. "And inform everyone that Earth expects them to do their duty."

Kevin snorted. "Couldn't you think of a better quote to steal?"

Steve shrugged. "The old ways are still the best," he said. "Besides, I couldn't think of anything from *Doctor Who* that fitted the bill."

Mongo chuckled, then glanced at his console as the enemy ships dropped out of FTL quite some distance from the planet. "Steve," he said, quietly. "They're here."

— —

HORDE COMMANDER YSS!YAA kept his body absolutely still, betraying no emotion at all, as the fleet brought its journey to an end. His subordinates were intent on rushing forward to stake their claims to scoring victory, but he'd issued strict orders for them to stay in formation and wait for him to evaluate the situation. It was yet another problem with the Horde, he knew, as the display started to fill with data. He couldn't supervise his commanders from another ship, which allowed them to contemplate independent action – and get away with it, if they succeeded. A lucky warrior enjoyed the protection of the gods.

There was nothing particularly interesting about the human star system, but the sheer level of development in less than a local year was staggering. The humans, according to the information they'd been slipped, hadn't even had a serious space program. Now, they had a large base on their moon and there were radio sources scattered across the star system...and traces of terraforming operations on the fourth planet from their star. Earth itself was surrounded by space stations, free-floating industrial nodes and a small fleet of starships, most of them clearly passed down from the Galactics. Had the Varnar actually come to terms with their human allies?

"Scan the system," he ordered. "Are there any major warships in the sector?"

He waited as his staff ran the scan, silently cursing their incompetence under his breath as they worked. Once, having the strongest warriors move up the command chain had seemed a good idea; now, as their commander, he had other thoughts. The ones who were capable of operating a scanner were often not the ones who won fights, either in duels for command positions or outright challenges of honour. But it wasn't something he could change, he knew. If he told mighty warriors with more brawn than brains that they were being held back in favour of wimps who preferred brain to brawn, he would be overthrown. And then the brainy ones would be purged on suspicion of being dishonourable bastards who plotted to overturn the natural order of things.

"Three warships," his officer said, finally. The Horde Commander was uncomfortably aware that any of the major Galactics would have the answer almost at once. "One of them is definitely a Class-VIII Warcruiser."

Just like the one that went missing, Yss!Yaa thought. The humans had clearly taken it, presumably killing the crew in the process. He wondered, absently, just how long it would take his officers to draw the correct conclusion, if he gave them time to think. But there was no time. He had to win the battle before one of the major Galactic powers intervened. It was quite possible that the whole system was a trap.

If he could, he would have withdrawn. But his subordinates would never have tolerated it in the absence of a major threat.

"The homeships are to hold back," he ordered. Bringing the entire Horde had been a risk, but it looked like it had paid off. Earth could support them for generations to come, once they'd taken the high orbitals and poured fire on any resistance from the ground. "The remaining ships are to fall into attack pattern and prepare to advance."

He ignored the grumbling from the homeships as the fleet shook itself into formation. It still bemused him how someone could have lasted long enough to be rewarded with command of a homeship and yet refuse to accept the simple fact that their starships were not designed for interstellar warfare. No, *their* task was to carry the women and children from star to star, just incidentally making it easier for the Horde Commander to reward the officers and crew he wanted to reward. They had absolutely no place in a dedicated line of battle. But he'd had to bring them with him just to ensure he maintained control.

The human fleet didn't *look* that dangerous, he told himself, firmly. Natural warriors or not – and even he wasn't prepared to concede that there was anyone more dangerous than the Horde out there – they simply didn't have the numbers to hold him back. They could stand and fight – and die. Or they could run for their lives, leaving the planet exposed. Either one, he knew, would suit him.

But it wouldn't suit his people. They *wanted* the fight.

"Take us forward," he ordered, quietly. "And remind everyone to stay in formation."

⸺

STEVE WATCHED, EXPRESSIONLESSLY, as the enemy fleet slowly shook itself down. And it was slow, he noted, compared to what the Galactics showed in the data records. It looked as though each Hordesman regarded his ship as an individual weapon, rather than part of a greater whole. Steve couldn't help thinking of some of the fighter jocks he'd met, but even the most obsessive fast-jet pilot had never been as undisciplined as the Horde. Given some luck, his plan to defend Earth might actually work.

And they were definitely Horde ships, he knew. If the ragtag nature of the fleet – and clear signs of poor maintenance – hadn't proved it, the images the drones reported stencilled on their hulls would have made it clear. The Horde seemed to like naming their ships openly – *Tongue Ripper,*

Lie Killer, Savage Guardian – and practically daring the Galactics to take offense. Perhaps he would have been scared, if he had time. Instead, he had to concentrate on the coming battle.

"Five of the ships are staying back," Mongo reported. "The remainder are coming towards us at a slow steady pace."

Steve nodded, accessing the torrent of data through the interface. The five colossal starships had once been bulk freighters, according to the files, something that staggered him. What sort of trading community needed a starship that was over ten kilometres long? But they were now homeships, home to the Horde's women and children. He couldn't imagine why anyone would bring them into the combat zone, not when a stray missile might easily find the wrong target and slaughter helpless civilians. Wouldn't it make more sense to leave their homeships at the edge of the star system? If the battle went badly, they could simply retreat.

Maybe it's a pride thing, he thought. *Or maybe they're just stupid.*

He dismissed that thought, angrily. Assuming his enemy was stupid was the greatest mistake a commander could make. Instead, he looked down at the display, silently contemplating the alien formation. It looked crude as well as inelegant, he realised, without even a hint of showmanship. In many ways, it suggested, very strongly, that he'd been right. The Horde was simply unused to any form of coordinated action.

"We will proceed with defence pattern alpha," he said. "The ghost squadron is to remain in place. On my mark, the rest of the fleet is to begin falling back."

"Understood," Mongo said.

Steve winced. He was about to send fifty men, volunteers all, to certain death. He'd told them, back when they'd started planning the operation, that it would almost certainly be suicidal. But they'd accepted the mission, regardless. Their courage put him to shame.

"And prepare to transmit the planned signal," he ordered. "I want to make them mad."

"COWARDS," SOMEONE HISSED, as the humans started to fall back.

Yss!Yaa had his doubts. The humans knew they couldn't face the massed might of the Horde in open battle, so they were falling back on the defences orbiting Earth…if there *were* many defences orbiting the green-blue orb. Some automated weapons platforms had been spotted, but there were hundreds of other stations in orbit around the planet, most of which were completely unrecognisable. A Galactic scanner crew might have been able to identify them, he knew, yet his crew could only mark them as unknown. All *he* could do was take them out from a safe distance.

And the humans had left five freighters behind. It was…suspicious.

"The humans are to be engaged as soon as we enter range," he ordered. If it was a trap, his best bet was to spring it before his fleet was fully committed. Even the most zealous Hordesman would accept that retreat was the best option if they ran into something they couldn't handle. "And then…"

"Incoming signal," one of his officers snapped. "Sir, it's a challenge!"

Yss!Yaa listened to the tidal wave of invective and knew he'd lost control. The humans had *definitely* been studying…and they'd probably had the help of one or more Hordesmen when they'd crafted the message. If even *he* felt the outraged desire to forget caution and simply *charge* the enemy, his lesser subordinates would lose complete control of themselves. One by one, the Horde starships picked up speed and arrowed directly towards the enemy formation. The formation Yss!Yaa had carefully outlined came apart within seconds.

"Take us after them," he ordered, clicking his claws in anger. Not at the humans, but at his fellow Hordesmen. If they had been something different, they wouldn't have had to worry about the results of the challenge. But any show of weakness could be disastrous. "And prepare to engage the enemy."

"I THINK WE made them mad," Mongo commented.

Steve nodded. In Iraq and Afghanistan, they'd sometimes lured the insurgents into a suicidal charge by screaming out challenges and insults. The insurgents, largely made up of young and therefore foolish men, had taken the bait more often than they should, much to the irritation of the older and wiser terrorist leaders who wanted their deaths to actually serve the cause. In that sense, at least, the Horde was no different, with the added problem of a system that rewarded promotion by assassination. The strong survived, the Horde believed, while the weak perished. But it sometimes meant that the new holder of any given position was nowhere near ready for it.

"Very mad," he said. "Tell the ghost squadron to engage on my command."

— —

DANIEL FEATHERSTONE HAD once had cancer, a particularly vile form of the disease that had been on the verge of killing him when he'd been recruited to the lunar colony. As a former seaman on a United States Navy submarine, he'd adapted well to Heinlein…and then to the alien freighter, when he'd been offered a chance at command. Swearing loyalty to Heinlein instead of the United States hadn't been hard; he'd given the United States one life, after all. He could give his second life to someone else…

But now it looked as though his second life was about to come to an end.

John Paul Jones was no warship, certainly not by galactic standards. She was an interstellar freighter, so primitive that she didn't even have a teleport bay of her very own. The whole idea of putting her in the line of battle was absurd. But human ingenuity had gone to work and outfitted the freighter with plenty of weapons, provided her crew didn't mind the risk of near-certain death. When he'd heard about the mission, Daniel had volunteered at once. He *owed* the lunar colony.

"They're coming into range now," Christian Lawson said. She was a thin hatchet-faced woman, her face twisted into a permanent scowl. And yet she was also a good technician, good enough that Daniel had tried to talk her out of going on the mission. But she'd refused to budge. "I have weapons lock on five targets."

"It seems as good as we are about to get," Daniel said. Their weapons were impressive, by human standards, but they were all one-shot wonders. "Link into the other ships, then prepare to fire."

The Hordesmen came closer, their weapons charging as their sensors locked onto the freighters. Daniel wondered, coldly, why they weren't firing already, then he realised they were being macho idiots. Just like a particularly idiotic biker gang, he decided, they wanted to play chicken. Accidental collisions in interstellar space were rare, according to the data-files, but deliberate collisions quite easy. The incoming ship had to be vaporised completely to prevent it doing real damage.

"We have permission to fire," Christian said.

Daniel sucked in a breath. Life on a submarine hadn't prepared him for deep space warfare, not really. And it hadn't convinced him that he might have to make a last stand...

"Fire," he ordered.

— —

FOR A LONG moment, Yss!Yaa simply refused to accept what he was seeing. The freighters had fired...and nine Horde starships had simply been blown out of space. Their weapons had burned right through the defence shields and chewed right into their hulls, ripping them open effortlessly. It was *impossible*. And yet it had happened.

He watched, helplessly, as the advancing starships opened fire, their directed energy weapons slicing through minimal shields and then cutting deep into the freighter hulls. And then there was another colossal series of explosions. The entire command network crashed under the tidal wave of radiation. He swore out loud, then demanded answers from his staff as they worked frantically to reboot the system. The entire fleet was vulnerable until they managed to get the command network back up and running...

It was impossible, part of his mind insisted. But it had happened, somehow. And a number of his ships had been destroyed by a far inferior foe. How?

"Antimatter," the sensor officer said. "They crammed the ship full of antimatter and just waited for us to destroy it."

Yss!Yaa silently gave him points for brains. Yes, it was obvious now. The humans had mass-produced antimatter and turned it into a weapon. It was one hell of a risk, but it had paid off for them. The Horde had lost nine starships, at least. Piece by piece, the command network shuddered back into existence. Two more starships, it seemed, had vanished in the blasts.

But they're resorting to trickery, he thought. The Galactics rarely bothered to be subtle when they were pruning the Hordesmen down a little. *They can't be very strong.*

"Keep us heading towards their world," he ordered. He would need to do something to make it clear to his subordinates that he was still in command. They couldn't be allowed to think of him as weak, not now. He knew, all too well, that none of his subordinate commanders would be able to handle the battle. "And prepare for long-range bombardment."

STEVE HEARD HIS crew cheer as the enemy ships were struck, then the antimatter explosions slapped the Hordesmen back. The idea had been simple enough; they'd mounted dozens of bomb-pumped lasers on the freighter hulls, giving them an unexpected advantage over their opponents. As overconfident as they were, the Horde had clearly never expected the freighters to be turned into traps – and then bombs. The whole tactic had clearly caught them by surprise.

He watched the remaining Horde starships, trying to get a handle on what his opponent was thinking. In their place, Steve knew he would have backed off, particularly if his women and children were also on the line. But the Hordes seemed to be composed of prideful asses. If their leader thought better of the attack, it was quite possible that his subordinates would overthrow him and then continue the charge. The volley of insults Steve had fired at them probably didn't make it easier for the aliens to be coldly rational.

"Prepare the fallback position," he ordered, softly. On the display, the Hordesmen were finally overcoming their shock and advancing once again. "And warn the *Mayflower* to run."

"Aye, sir," Mongo said. "The Q-ships are in position, as are the mines."

All right, Steve thought, as he looked at the display. Oddly, he found himself wishing he knew who he faced. Maybe the knowledge would have provided an insight into the Horde's plans. *If you want Earth, you bastards, we'll claw you good and proper as we go down.*

THIRTY-NINE

SOL SYSTEM

"They're approaching the minefield," Mongo said. "But they're also sweeping space very carefully."

Steve gritted his teeth. The Hordesmen had been fooled once – and it was clear that they didn't want to be fooled again. Their advance was odd – it seemed to be a cross between a reckless charge and a careful approach to the enemy – but there was a strong possibility they'd pick up the minefield before they entered attack range and the mines went active.

"Contact the fleet," he ordered. "We will prepare to advance and engage the enemy."

He ran through the odds quickly in his head. Eleven Horde starships were gone and four more were significantly damaged, but that still left ten warships in reasonably good condition. He had three warships and a handful of modified freighters. The odds were not good. He could delay the Horde, perhaps distract them from going after the mines, but he couldn't stop them. Only the minefield could do that, he knew.

We should have asked Friend for a war fleet, he thought. *But that would have compromised our independence too badly.*

"We will advance on my command," he said, grimly. If they could keep the enemy from looking for threats, they might just be able to pull off a victory. "I say again, we will advance on my command."

— —

"Stay in formation, damn you," Yss!Yaa roared at one of his subordinate commanders. "We need to stay in formation!"

He cursed again as it became clear that it was a futile effort. His subordinates wanted blood, human blood, and they all wanted the honour of landing the first blows against Earth. His formation was a formation in name only, now that several of his officers had recovered from their shock and were advancing rapidly towards Earth. And, despite the best he could do, he couldn't keep them focused on the possibility of another trap.

"The human world is coming into range," his weapons officer reported. "Human defences might be insufficient to stop our missiles."

"Good," Yss!Yaa said. "Open fire."

— —

"They've started to launch missiles," Mongo reported. He sounded puzzled. "Missiles?"

Steve shared his puzzlement. The Galactics rarely used missiles, knowing that any halfway capable point defence network could simply swat them out of space. Even antimatter warheads wouldn't cause much damage unless they impacted directly against a target's shields. It was unusually stupid, even for the Horde. They didn't gain anything by giving the human ships free targets...

His blood ran cold as the truth sank in. "They're firing on Earth," he whispered. Unlike a starship, a planet couldn't dodge...and Earth's defences were puny compared to any Galactic world. The best he'd been able to set up was a handful of point defence weapons and sensor networks, enough to take down any human missile launch, but nowhere near enough to tackle a swarm of Galactic-level missiles. "They want to kill us all!"

Kevin swore out loud. "We have to stop them!"

Steve gritted his teeth. The missiles would pass through the outer edge of the fleet's engagement envelope, but only for a few seconds. In hindsight, the missile trajectories were obvious clues as to their targets. It was vaguely possible, he knew, that the Horde might be shooting at the planet's orbital industries, but a miss would be absolutely disastrous in any case. The missile would fly onwards and strike the planet...

But if they altered course to engage the missiles, they'd run the risk of being unable to cover the minefield. And they'd lose their best chance to stop the enemy dead in their tracks.

"Continue on our current course," he ordered, harshly.

Mongo looked up, sharply. "Steve..."

"We don't have a choice," Steve snapped. He hated himself for saying the words, but he didn't have a choice. The entire world would hate him...yet they'd be alive to hate him. It was better than a dead or enslaved world. "If we don't stop them, here and now, we lose everything."

— —

YSS!YAA WATCHED, DISPASSIONATELY, as the missiles passed through the human engagement envelope – five of them being picked off before they made it out again – and roared towards the human world. Whatever the odder structures in orbit actually were, he noted, relatively few of them had any kind of point defence. Seven more missiles were picked off; three more were redirected by their smart warheads to take out the automated orbital weapons platforms and clear the way for the second salvo. The remaining missiles plunged into the planetary atmosphere and sought targets. Seconds later, nuclear detonations flashed into existence for long seconds before fading away, leaving devastation in their wake.

"Twelve human cities have been destroyed," the weapons officer reported. "Should I fire a second salvo?"

"No," Yss!Yaa said. They were getting far too close to infringing the convention against genocide as it was. The Galactics might cheerfully ignore any law that couldn't be enforced effectively, but almost every power would assist in hunting down the Horde, if they were publically charged with genocide. "Concentrate on the human warships."

He smiled. On the display, the human ships were growing closer. He wouldn't underestimate them again, he vowed, but he couldn't see how they could hope to match his firepower, no matter what they stuffed into a freighter hull. This time, he told himself, it would be different.

— —

"NEW YORK IS gone," Kevin said, flatly. "Manchester, England; Paris, France; Warsaw, Poland; Moscow, Russia…"

Steve barely heard him. The devastation was simply impossible to imagine, the death rate even more so. New York alone had over eight million people. Between all eleven targets – one missile seemed to have plunged into the water, triggering tidal waves across East Asia – there might well be a hundred million dead. But it was beyond his ability to grasp. The aliens had slaughtered so many humans that they might as well be nothing more than statistics.

No wonder we rarely react when we are told so many thousands have died, the morbid part of his mind whispered. *We simply can't grasp it.*

"Enemy ships coming into range," Mongo reported. "They're locking weapons on us."

"Fire at will," Steve ordered.

The Hordesmen kept coming towards the small human fleet, firing as they came. Steve watched, dispassionately, as bursts of energy flared through the void, some slamming into his shields while others pulsed onwards and faded into the darkness. The Horde, it seemed, was showing off, while the human ships were more careful with their fire. One Horde ship exploded as she was caught in a crossfire, another rolled over and came to a halt as she took major damage. But the remainder of the Horde ships were closing in.

"Slip into evasive pattern delta," Steve ordered. Most of the Horde ships were smaller than *Shadow Warrior*, but that didn't make them ineffective. Instead, they were firing savagely and weakening his defences. "And inch us back towards the minefields..."

The display bleeped, a low mournful sound. "*Vincent Hastings* is gone, sir," Kevin reported. His voice was very calm, too calm. They'd named the Q-ship after their dead friend, but they'd known she wasn't a real warship. The only advantage she had was sheer mass and it wasn't enough to keep the Horde from killing her. "I don't see any lifepods."

"If there were, the Horde would get them," Steve muttered. "Continue firing!"

The Horde pressed closer, as if each of them were eager to put an end to the human fleet personally. They were, Steve realised grimly; they all wanted the glory that came from taking out the human ships. And it was working in his favour; from time to time, one of the ships would deliberately block another's path, just to try to prevent them from scoring a decisive blow. He smirked as he imagined the enemy commander's feelings, then concentrated on the battle. They needed to keep inching backwards...

"The minefield is active," Kevin reported. "A few more minutes and we will be ready to give them such a blow..."

"Let us hope so," Steve muttered.

———

Yss!Yaa watched, powerless to affect events, as his ships danced around the human vessels, firing madly into their shields. It was insane! They should have been able to overwhelm the humans with ease, but they simply weren't cooperating! At least one starship had been lost through another starship nudging it away...right into human sights. It was absolute madness...and yet he knew he wouldn't be able to call a halt. His people were angry; they wanted blood. Worst of all, he knew, he wouldn't even be able to penalise the idiots after the battle, because they would look like victors!

I wonder if the humans have these problems, he thought, savagely. He clacked a claw against the side of his throne as a human starship slammed several pulses of energy into his ship's shields. Unlike his people, the humans seemed to have mastered rotating their shield generators to provide additional protection, damn them. *And if they don't, why not?*

But he knew the answer, even if it wasn't something he could admit outside his own head. Everyone who might push for change had a strong incentive to keep matters precisely as they were…and everyone who didn't had no real power to force change, not even him. He might be their leader, but there were limits to his power.

"The enemy is retreating," the weapons officer said. "They're trying to pull back."

Yss!Yaa sighed. "Then take us after them," he ordered. "Let us put an end to this."

— —

STEVE WATCHED GRIMLY as the alien ships gave chase, pushing forward recklessly to try to claim the kills for themselves. They'd stealthed the minefield as best as they could, using a mixture of human and alien technology, but he had few illusions about just how long the cover would work if the aliens started to *really* hunt for them.

"The mines are active," Kevin reported. "I'm supplying them with targeting data directly."

"Good," Steve said. If the mines had started to use active sensors of their own, the Horde would have known they were there at once. But by broadcasting targeting data from the starships, the mines could remain passive. "Do they have total lock?"

"Yes," Kevin said, after a moment. "They're locked on all remaining Horde starships."

Steve sucked in a breath. "Fire," he ordered.

— —

"ENERGY SPIKE," THE sensor officer snapped. "All around us!"

Yss!Yaa opened his mouth to shout orders, but it was already too late.

— —

THE MINES WERE simple enough. Nuclear bombs had been taken from Earth and converted into bomb-pumped lasers, each one capable of stabbing out one single blast of ravenous energy. Unlike a conventional nuclear blast, which would have largely been deflected by a starship's shields, the needle-like laser struck the force fields and burned right through them.

"Mines detonated," Mongo said. "Steve, I think we got them."

Steve nodded. Only two Horde warships were left, both heavily damaged. One of them seemed to have enough motive power to start crawling towards the planet, the other seemed to be completely stranded. Given that it was leaking atmosphere from a dozen hull breaches, it was quite possible that the crew was already dead.

Because they don't bother with spacesuits or even light protective gear, he thought, shaking his head at the sheer unfairness of the universe. How had a bunch of primitives barely entering their Iron Age been allowed to obtain interstellar starships? But then, they'd never understood the ships they operated or how to actually produce more technology to replace what they'd bought, begged or stolen from the Galactics.

"Start deploying combat teams," he ordered. "I want those ships secured as quickly as possible."

"Aye, sir," Mongo said.

Steve nodded, then looked over at Kevin. "Contact Edward," he added. By now, the soldiers who should have gone to Ying would have assembled at their training base. "I want him to send five companies of space-trained soldiers to serve as reinforcements, just in case."

"Understood," Kevin said. "Sir...what about the homeships?"

"I would have expected them to run," Steve commented. But all five homeships were still there, sitting in interplanetary space and waiting. "But we can secure them too."

He looked down at his display as his subordinates got to work, silently counting the cost. *Shadow Warrior* hadn't taken any major damage, but two of her shield generators were gone and three more probably needed urgent replacement. *Enterprise* had been badly damaged; looking at the reports, it was a minor miracle that the Hordesmen hadn't managed to finish the job before they were defeated. Only *Captain Perry* had escaped almost completely. Steve wondered if the starship led a charmed life…or if the Hordesmen had wanted to recapture her rather than simply blow her out of space.

The other ships hadn't done any better. Five q-ships had been destroyed, three more were completely beyond easy repair. And the older ships they'd turned into the ghost squadron had been destroyed, of course. But they'd taken more than their fair share of enemy spacers with them. All things considered, Steve told himself, they'd been very lucky.

But it wasn't true for the civilians on Earth, he reminded himself, sharply. Eleven cities wiped out by long-range missiles, several coastlines pounded by tidal waves caused by the final missile. The death toll would be in the millions and rising fast as people died through lack of health care and other provisions. Handling such a global catastrophe would push even the most competent government to the limit.

"Deploy as many of the shuttles, surveillance gear and fabricators as can be spared to assist with the rescue operations," Steve ordered. Mariko would kill him if he didn't try to help – and besides, he certainly *wanted* to help. "Clear it with the local governments, then spread our assistance as far as possible."

"There'll be bitching if we don't put New York first," Kevin commented. He sounded calmer now, but there was still an undercurrent of rage in his voice. "Lots of us have emotional connections to the city."

"But we have a global responsibility," Steve said.

"Picking up a message from the boarding parties," Mongo said, suddenly. "They need someone who can talk to the Horde women in their own tongue."

Steve frowned. "Call Heinlein," he said, finally. "Tell them to send our alien friend."

— —

CN!LSS HAD NEVER really expected to set eyes on a woman of his kind, not after he'd effectively joined the human race. Even if he'd stayed with the Horde, it was unlikely that he would ever have been able to breed. The stupidest warrior was still strong enough to take any woman from him, no matter what he said or did. And besides, the women themselves were reluctant to breed with someone who wasn't considered a hero.

But he held up his claws in greeting as the teleport dropped him onto the homeship bridge, where the bodies of the male crew lay where they'd fallen. Instead of running, the honour-bound idiots had killed themselves. In their place, a handful of women stood there, waiting for him. Their eyes never left his body as soon as he appeared. It was no expression of lust, he knew, but caution. They wanted to know what would happen to themselves and their children.

"The humans have agreed to take us all in and build a better way," he said, once he'd introduced himself as the senior surviving Hordesman. Those who had been broken down by human psychologists had abandoned their former ranks, those who hadn't had been isolated from their fellows and left to work their own way towards salvation. "You are more than welcome to join us."

He took a breath, then went on. "Imagine an end to our wanderings," he said. His words tumbled over one another as he struggled to get them out before they could do something stupid. "Imagine, instead, that we develop a world of our own. The humans are prepared to ally with us and work towards the future. This is not the end, but a beginning."

There were other changes coming, he knew, if the women agreed to join the other outcasts in building a new world. The warrior culture would be eradicated. Instead, the Horde would start using its brains and become true members of galactic society. Some of the humans even talked about a grand alliance between different races, with all of them standing as equals before the universe. Long history said it was a pipe dream, but Cn!lss had hope. And besides, if the women joined as equals, the new society would be far more stable than anything else the Hordes had ever built.

He watched the women talk in low voices. They were in an odd position, according to the human sociologists who had attempted to understand the Hordes, both chattel and independent agents at the same time. Looking in from the outside, the women didn't have much choice about who fathered their children, but they had absolute authority over their own affairs. There were no human-style families, save for the greatest of warriors. And even they lasted only a few years before breaking up.

The women had nowhere else to go. He hoped they understood that, because they would never be allowed to leave. And even if they did leave, where would they go? The other Hordes would only return them to their familiar status, without giving them any room to grow.

"We will join you," the leader said, finally. "As long as our children are safe, we will join you."

"Welcome," Cn!lss said. He clacked his claws in the Pattern of Greeting Between Equals, then bowed his head. Few Hordesmen would offer such honour to their fellow warriors, let alone mere females. "And your children will be safe from both internal and external threats."

FORTY

New York, USA

"Dear God," Steve said. "What a fucking mess."

New York was gone. The alien warhead might have left little or no radioactivity behind, but it had utterly flattened Manhattan. Piles of rubble that had once been mighty skyscrapers lay everywhere, while – in the distance – he could see damaged towers that had been struck by the dissipating blast. Millions of people had died in the first few seconds, caught in the open by the fireball, while others had died as the shockwave toppled buildings and crushed them below the rubble.

The President nodded in agreement. "But it could easily have been worse," he said. "Your people served well."

Steve shrugged. He would always wonder, he knew, if he'd made the right decision. If they'd intercepted the missiles instead…but there would never be any way to know the truth. All that mattered was that Earth was safe again, for the moment. And that, with the destruction or capture of an entire Horde, the remainder wouldn't be inclined to attack Earth in future.

"And the population has gone mad with rage," the President added. "You'll have all the support you could possibly wish."

"I know," Steve said. "But will it be enough?"

It was victory, of a sort, but it tasted like ashes on his mouth. The world's population had been shocked, horrified and outraged by the slaughter. There would be no quibbling about the lunar colony now, or the desperate need to establish human colonies on countless other worlds. Humanity had been given a sharp lesson in the true danger of ignoring the universe.

Now, there would be no objections to placing weapons in space. But, compared to what the Galactics could produce, Earth's weapons were almost laughable. And yet, used properly, they'd given the Horde a very hard time.

He sighed. The first batch of soldiers were on their way to Ying, accompanied by Kevin, who had orders to purchase as many additional starships as he could. In the meantime, the Horde homeships were being converted for human use; they'd take a large human population out of the Sol System and somewhere well beyond the reach of the Galactics. Given time – and the information they'd obtained from Friend – they'd be able to set up a whole new civilisation. The human race would survive.

But at one hell of a cost.

"Let us hope so," the President said. He paused. "What do you intend to do with the captured Hordesmen?"

"They'll live on Mars, for the moment," Steve said. The sociologists might swear that the captured Hordesmen and women posed no real threat, but Steve wasn't inclined to take chances. Besides, if they were placed on Earth or Heinlein Colony there was a very strong possibility of revenge attacks. "And, if they grow into something we can respect, we can welcome them into our new union."

"We shall see," the President said. "Alien citizens of Earth?"

Steve smiled, humourlessly. "A century or two ago, the idea that the black man or the Native American could be an equal citizen would have sounded dangerously absurd," he pointed out, dryly. "It wasn't that long ago that Japanese-Americans like my partner were regarded as potential spies or people who would commit acts of sabotage. Why not aliens joining the United States as citizens?"

He paused. "Or the Solar Union," he added. "We will accept aliens, if they wish to join."

"Good luck," the President said. "After the battle, it may be a long time before humanity is prepared to accept aliens as equals."

"That might be a bad idea," Steve said. "There are races out there far more powerful and dangerous than the Hordes."

It was a bitter thought. The Hordesmen had been dangerously incompetent and prone to acting like single warriors rather than fighting as part of a team, but they'd bombarded Earth and come alarmingly close to outright victory. If Steve hadn't cheated and manipulated the aliens, the battle would have ended very differently. A smarter alien race, one that had actually developed its own technology or successfully copied technology from another race, would be a very different problem. Steve had no illusions. A battle squadron from any of the major Galactic powers could overwhelm Earth within hours, if that.

"We will need allies," he added. "And friends. And we must never forget where we came from when we get our hands on more Galactic technology."

"True," the President agreed. He held out a hand. "It's time to bury the dead."

Steve nodded. The ceremony was private, even though there were hundreds of thousands of people who had wanted to attend. Only the President, a handful of selected guests and Steve himself. New York had been sealed off, after the troops had searched the wreckage for survivors, in the hopes of preventing looting. The complete absence of people lent a surreal atmosphere to the remains of one of humanity's greatest cities.

He caught sight of Gunter Dawlish and winced, inwardly. The Mainstream Media had promptly blasted Steve and his men for failing to defend New York, triggering off a series of flame wars online as bloggers took sides, some agreeing with the MSM and others pointing out that Steve had had no choice. Steve found it hard to argue; cold logic told him he'd done the right thing, emotion told him he'd fucked up badly. The cynical side of his mind asked, nastily, if he would have been so upset if New York had been spared. No other missiles had fallen in North America.

At least Gunter thought before passing judgement, Steve thought, sardonically. *Some of the bloggers forgot to engage their brains before putting mouths in gear.*

The sense of being among ghosts suddenly grew stronger. Steve staggered, wondering absurdly if the dead of New York wanted revenge. Or if they wanted to tell him to stop feeling sorry for himself and get back to work. There was no way to tell. It was quite possible, he knew, that he was imagining it. And yet the devastated island seemed full of ghosts.

"I'm sorry," he found himself whispering. He'd sworn an oath to defend the United States against all enemies, foreign and domestic. By any standards, he'd failed. The vast power he'd acuminated only made it worse. "I'm sorry I failed to protect you. But it won't happen again."

＊　＊

KEVIN LAY IN his bed on *Captain Perry*, staring up at the ceiling and listening to Carolyn's deep breathing as she slept beside him. The sudden change in their relationship had come as a shock; he'd gone to her, intending to share dinner as usual, and she'd practically dragged him into bed. But quite a few new relationships had sprung up in the wake of the battle, he'd heard, either through people wanting to celebrate being alive or merely waking up to the fact that they might well end up dead, soon enough.

He was worried, more worried than he cared to admit, about the future. One attack on Earth had been barely staved off, another might be far more successful. And there were powers that wouldn't want humans to enter the galactic mainstream. And then there was Steve...

Kevin shook his head, tiredly. He worried about his brother too. Part of him had just...folded in the wake of New York's destruction, even though it was a victorious battle and humanity had survived. No man should acquire so much power so quickly without restraints, Kevin considered, even if Steve had had good advisors in Mongo and Kevin himself. And Mariko, Kevin added. In the wake of the battle, Steve had finally proposed. Kevin just hoped they'd get back to Earth in time for the wedding.

He sighed, then closed his eyes. Steve could leave, if he wanted, and become an interstellar trader. It would solve a great many problems if he did. And it wasn't as if he hadn't left a legacy behind. Given five years of uninterrupted development, the Solar Union would become more than just a name. There would be the start of a human-built space fleet, a growing network of defences around Earth, and both mercenaries and traders out in space, learning more about the universe.

And there would always be Stuarts, ready to defend their home-world; Steve and Mongo had already had children, while there was plenty of time for Kevin to have children of his own. If he had them with Carolyn, he considered, they would definitely be smart. And the family had a long history of defending their rights and their homes. Earth would be in good hands.

The future would take care of itself. It always did.

EPILOGUE

"**W**elcome home, Steve."

Steve smiled as he saw Kevin, a little older, waiting for him in the teleport chamber.

"It's good to see you again," he said, as he wrapped Kevin up in a hug. "It's been...what? Four years since I saw you and the kids?"

"I'm just glad you got here in time for the memorial service," Kevin said. "In the five years since the Battle of Earth, you only ever attended the first ceremony."

"You know the dangers of dwelling on the past," Steve said, irked. He'd left the Sol System as soon as the elections had been held, naming Rochester as the first President of the Solar Union. Steve had felt it would be better for his successor if Steve himself was no longer around. "How far would we have come as a family if we'd kept blaming the English for kicking us out of Scotland?"

Kevin smiled. "I think it was the charge of being drunk and disorderly that really got to our ancestors," he countered. "But we also have to remember the past."

Steve shrugged. "Mariko and I went quite a bit further this time," he said. "I sent back a handful of reports, but I've got a complete one here. So far, the war seems to have remained firmly stalemated. That may change though, soon."

"Because of us," Kevin said. He took the chip Steve passed him and dropped it into his pocket. "We could do with another few decades before the galaxy as a whole realises we exist."

"We may not have that time," Steve admitted. "It all depends on which way the lizards choose to jump."

He shook his head. "But enough of that," he said. "You're the Director of Solar Intelligence, so give me some intelligence."

"That would require brain surgery," Kevin pointed out.

Steve snorted, rudely. "How are things in Heinlein these days? I heard the announcement about us having the millionth citizen on the way in."

"Oddly bureaucratic, despite the best intentions of our laws," Kevin conceded. "It seems natural that we develop government, then the government starts growing out of control."

"I'm not surprised," Steve said. He took the beer Kevin offered him, then sat down. "But you know what? There's a whole universe out there. Anyone who doesn't fit in here will be able to go outwards, if they wish. And the problem will take care of itself."

"As long as the Galactics don't take care of us," Kevin said. "One day, one day soon, they will notice. And then the shit will really hit the fan."

"Give us time," Steve said. "By the time they notice, we will be ready."

The End

As always, if you want a sequel, let me know.

AFTERWORD

My writing process is fairly simple. I write three chapters a day, post them on various forums and then read the comments, insert corrections, etc. (God bless everyone who sends in a typo-note, as there's no such thing as a minor correction in the writing world.) Sometimes, I get genuinely interesting responses from people who disagree with me – or, rather, with the characters.

I had reached about twelve/thirteen chapters into *A Learning Experience* when I noted an interesting trend on a couple of discussion forums. People were commenting on what they saw as foolish and/or unrealistic actions by the main characters, the US Government and just about everyone else. A couple of those comments verged into 'mistake the author for his characters' territory and were duly ignored. The remainder struck me as interesting – and, in some respects, the inevitable result of commenting on an unfinished book.

As both Kevin and Mongo pointed out in the text, not all of Steve's actions and thoughts are wise ones. He could have avoided the 'skirmish' with the DHS, he could have found less dramatic ways to make his point and he came alarmingly close to committing outright genocide. But such is character development. Characters who are perfect are not only boring, they are unrealistic. A character who grows and develops, on the other hand, is a representative of the whole human condition.

Steve starts out heavily political; he's alienated from his country's government, he doesn't trust those schmucks in Washington and he has more or less withdrawn from society. He chooses to spend a large amount of his time dwelling on a government betrayal and grumbling about the sad state of near-future America. And then effectively limitless power (at least on Earth) is simply dropped into his hands. Steve, as several characters point out, could attack Washington and take power for himself. Instead, he chooses to set up a new Wild West and invite anyone who feels like him to reach for the stars.

Over the course of the story, Steve grows to realise – truly realise – that vast power doesn't solve everything. Nor can he hope to handle everything on his own. Very rapidly, his plans for a libertarian state are challenged by the need for a staff to handle things, for an effective system of government and a plan to defend Earth and all of humanity against an alien threat. Steve, who is armed with technology that makes wiping out large chunks of the Taliban and various global terrorist networks an easy task, comes to realise that it isn't as easy as it looks to rule a state. It sure as hell isn't easy to set the course of the future.

This is a common problem, in and out of both fiction and real life. Every election campaign, politicians make vast promises that, when they are forced to come face to face with reality, they find impossible to actually fulfil. One promise might be impossible to keep through lack of funds, another might be impossible to keep because there are international treaties underpinning the promise and removing them may open up other cans of worms, still more promises may be made when the politician was unaware of certain factors that mandated that the promise had to be broken. It isn't as simple as you might think to become a global leader – or to act as one, once you reach such a position.

These are not the only problems, of course. A single issue might be easy to handle if the President (or Prime Minister, or whatever) concentrated on it to the exclusion of all else. However, very few issues can receive that degree of scrutiny from the Head of Government. It is far more likely that smaller issues will be handled by the head's subordinates, who may butcher the job or simply decide it isn't politically important. And, naturally, when (if) this blows up in the Head of Government's face, it's *always* his fault.

This represents a serious problem with our governments that, as Steve says in elaborate detail, is a major headache for the future. As politicians become more and more interested in looking good, rather than actually looking to the future, we find it much harder to respond to problems caused by the lack of accountability. In their place, colossal government bureaucracies set out to *regulate* society – with almost no accountability at all. Worse, the departments become more interested in preserving their own positions than doing their jobs.

Does this sound insane? Imagine you work in the Department of Homeland Security. If Congress were to become convinced that your organisation wasn't doing its job, you might lose *your* job. Your incentives would lead you to find work for your department even if there wasn't anything. You wouldn't say there was no terror threat. Instead, you would ask for more resources to track down the terror threat you need to justify your existence.

I do not believe there is a single government department that is free of the taint of bureaucracies struggling to secure and expand their paper empires. Consider, for example, Britain's UKBA (United Kingdom Border Agency). The forms prospective immigrants are meant to fill in are outrageously complex (applying to join the army is considerably easier), the requirements are often absurd (how many people really bother to make exact notes of when they moved from country to country a decade or so ago?) and the screening process frankly insulting to one's intelligence. (How many terrorists would admit to it when filling in their forms?) Or various defence departments around the globe, concentrating more on defending their bureaucracies than defending the soldiers who fight and die in constant wars?

And if you were given a way to establish a society away from all that, what would you do?

Reasonable readers may disagree with Steve's actions. I would quite agree that some of them were stupid and dangerous. But I don't think they're unrealistic.

Your mileage may vary, of course.

My intentions with this series are to follow the next generation of Steve's family by skipping forward fifty years, then another fifty. If you want a sequel, of course, please don't hesitate to contact me and let me know.

And if you liked the book, please leave a review on Amazon.

Christopher G. Nuttall
Manchester, 2014

ABOUT THE AUTHOR

Christopher Nuttall is the author of 30 books on kindle and 9 books through small presses. He currently moves between Britain and Malaysia with his wife Aisha and a colossal collection of books.

Website: http://www.chrishanger.net/
Blog: http://chrishanger.wordpress.com/
Facebook Fan Page: https://www.facebook.com/ChristopherGNuttall

Made in the USA
Middletown, DE
22 June 2019